Whispering Wind
The Tomes

C. J. Medley

Published by: C. J. Medley
Copyright © 2015 C. J. Medley
All Rights Reserved
ISBN-13: 978-0-9861178-5-5
ISBN-10: 0986117854
Cover Artwork and Photography Copyright ©
Bambi J. Novinska of Novinska Prints

For McKenna
My Loua
You will always be my Princess
I love you always
Nana

My Beautiful Britt, without knowing you and learning from you, I would have never known the patience I needed to write this story. I love you.

James William, sometimes in life it is alright to think outside the box. No matter where life takes you I will always love you.

For the man of my dreams David, thank you for always encouraging me to go with it, your hand is in this story more than you know. I love you.

My beautiful friend Jenny (Lady Saphires) thank you for being a pony girl with me and for inspiring Rebecca's personality. Without knowing you this story would not have so much girl power. Autobots transform and let's roll out!!

My friend and co-editor Veronica (Roni) Colvin, thank you for reading all the pages, taking my phone calls at all hours of the day and night and for your insights. Incredible has finally seen the light of day!!!

And to all the rest who have read this story, given me your thoughts and critiques. I am thankful that you loved it so much and helped me decide to go through with it. You know who you are!

For my fallen Guardians...You will forever be in our hearts!!

Edited by Kendra Gaither. Thank you so much for your insight. I am honored to call you my friend.

For Bambi my pretend daughter. Without your keen eye and beautiful mind my covers would never have come to life. You are a remarkable woman and I am proud to call you my daughter.

We are not now that strength
which in old days
Moved earth and heaven
That which we are, we are
One equal temper of heroic hearts
Made weak by time and fate
But strong in will
To strive, to seek, to find and not to yield

Alfred Lord Tennyson
Ulysses

Prologue

The death of my family who were brutally murdered. The King who comforted me knowing he was the one who had my Father's kingdom slaughtered. The plot to save my own life, finding out who I really was and why I was born. They turned me into a killing machine. Searching and killing to find my beautiful niece Juliana. Finding and losing my love Jared. The death of my love, my sister, my counterpart Rebecca.

The lies and the deceit were too much for me to handle. The years of fighting and killing were too much. The passing of four seasons while I lay in darkness because my body could not handle all that had taken place. Awakening to discover that I would never find the peace that was promised, the happiness that was promised.

Day after day of nothing but fighting, the emotional toll was too much for me to deal with. I wanted to be happy. I wanted our family to grow and to live a happy life, like when I was a child. Only my childhood, I discovered, had been nothing but a training ground for my future.

I had been trained in mind, heart, body and soul to be a warrior, and all I wanted to be was a normal girl who fought with her parents, rebelled when it suited me, wore pretty gowns and just lived. I wanted a great adventure, but instead, I bore the blood of thousands upon thousands of men on my hands.

Ending my life was the easy way out. Staying and fighting for what was right, for what we believed in, was the hard way. I suppose years of fighting were too much for me. Four seasons of darkness were not enough. My mind broke when he deceived me and put our family in grave danger. Juliana had her unborn baby to worry over, and no one cared that she would have lost it. No one cared that death had been brought to our village, to our home, where Westin's children played in the grass and young girls were thrilled to earn wages for their service. Where I found a friend and a mother figure to help me through it all. They did not care even when I put my own sword to my throat and sliced it wide open. What they cared about, was how they were going to live without me. How, now everyone would die.

Chapter One

As Rebecca and Julian rode across time, with me laid across Rebecca's lap and Juliana weighted down with the tomes, the world that I knew was changing.

My Guardians sat in the barracks common room consoling Blake. He was the most affected by what I had done. He watched as I slid my sword across my own throat. I looked into his eyes when I did it. He deserved to see what I was capable of, how far I had been pushed. Now, though, he was unable to speak or to think. Charles walked back and forth, trying to figure out what had happened, why it had happened. He knew it was because of the lies and the deceit. Joseph, the levelheaded one, wanted nothing more than to hold Rebecca. James was crying because Juliana wanted nothing to do with him. What did they expect? I am pretty sure Charles told them I would get over it. Huh, I guess he was wrong, but then again, he was also right; I was over it.

Westin was the worst. He just sat in the chair by the fire, not seeing nor hearing. I think he died right there in that hallway. I cannot do anything about that now. Camille would help him.

Word had not gotten out yet to the people that I was no longer living. I assume Charles will keep quiet on the matter for a while. Word in the village's travels fast, and then there would be much trouble coming to Whispering Wind. There really will be no place for anyone to go. Do I feel bad? Yes, I do, but no one felt bad for me. No one cared. Once my heart stopped beating, they all just left me there. Blake walked away and left me. It is a shame, actually, because he did not see the warm glow that came after.

It took my Guardians two solid days to come back into the house. Two days they left me lying in my study, or thought that they had. It was Aiden who came, not Blake, not Charles, not Joseph or James, but Aiden. I am in awe that Blake did not come. Well, I suppose he is in shock, as he has not moved or spoken since they pulled him away and sat him down in the barracks common room. The guards did their best to keep this news silent. Charles threatened them all with death if they spoke of it. All of the house people, with the exception of Francis, were dismissed for no reason.

There were some in the village who heard Blake and Juliana's screams, but Charles told them we were playing a game inside, and that everything was fine. The villagers wandered around, wondering why no one had come out of the castle. People started asking Clare and Boland if they had seen anyone. No one had.

The life of Whispering Wind had died, and the people noticed. People I did not even know noticed we were not there, but did my Guardians? No, they did not. Charles was doing damage control; he always had to be in control. Now would be the time for him to disgrace me, now that I really was gone. I had to be a bit proud of the way he was handling the situation. Sad still that it took two days for someone to come and get me.

We rode to our destination, which took a bit longer than it would have usually, because Spirit carried two and Raiden was carrying a load himself. We climbed the mountain to the secret passageway and then down into the valley. Getting me off of Rebecca's horse was a bit tricky, but they did not drop me. As they carried me with great care and gentleness to the base of the great tree in the middle of the valley. Juliana took the cloth she had brought from the castle and laid it out as instructed by Rebecca, so they could carefully lay me on it. Then methodically she wrapped the blanket around me, like a shroud or something. They stood there waiting like something was going to happen. Juliana ran to Raiden to retrieve my sword from its sheath and placed it on top of me, just as one would do for a King.

They left me there and went about gathering what they needed to survive. They left Whispering Wind. They left their home to bring me to the one place that I was free, the one place that I would be safe from them, from everything and everyone. No one would ever find me here.

Rebecca and Juliana would live the rest of their lives here, never leaving. Juliana would give birth here. Her child would never experience pain, betrayal, deceit, or war. The child would know only love.

When they unloaded Raiden and took off his saddle, he wandered over to the tree; he had never crossed the canopy before. Rebecca watched him as he neared it. She thought he was coming to say goodbye to me. When he was completely under the tree, he changed from a horse to a man. Rebecca touched Juliana on the arm, and she turned around. He walked

5

up and bent down to kiss my head before he picked me up and turned around to nod to Rebecca and Juliana. They smiled at him, and then the glow engulfed us both and we were gone. My horse had come to take me home, to a home I wished for, to a home I wanted, one filled with warmth and love. I was at peace.

Chapter Two

Aiden had discovered that Rebecca and Juliana had left with me; Charles figured they took me to the secret valley. He remembered that I had said it was the only place that I felt free. Joseph figured out that it was because I was magic and someone somewhere would want to find my body to see if they could harness the power that I once had.

Blake had not eaten or moved in days. His brothers tried to get him to eat, but he just sat there staring off into space. They tried to change his clothes, but he refused to move. Sometimes, they would find him with his eyes closed and his face wet with tears. The only woman he would ever love was gone, and it had more to do with him than he could admit.

Westin had his wife and his children to help him. Camille had asked if Joseph could take them back to valley. They should be able to live out their days there. He had agreed, and so they left Whispering Wind behind. Joseph returned hoping to find Rebecca, but there was nothing.

Weeks went by. Clare had asked about me and wanted to know what to do with all the gowns she had made. Charles paid her for them and then took them and put them in the secret room in my study. He went there every day after they discovered that I was gone. He went to look at the blood, my blood, to remind him of what he had done, what they had all done. Boland brought the rug he had made for the great hall, and he would continue to make rugs for the whole castle, just like I had wanted. He looked for signs of me whenever he was there.

The dust started to build up on the furniture. The dishes were not used. The house was empty. No one came in it through the great doors anymore. The men ate their meals that Francis prepared for them, for she was the only one left to ramble around that huge castle.

The people started to leave because there was no life left in this Kingdom. The crops would not grow, and the orchards stopped producing fruit. The land of Whispering Wind died the day I had. It was a slow process, but before long, it would wither to nothing but dead ground. One by one, the villagers left to find other Kingdoms to live in. It took months for them all to go. Boland stayed, however, as he wanted to give me one last thing. He wanted to fill my home with warmth and color.

No one knew where I had gone or why. People talked, they suspected, but no one knew for sure. Only those who remained knew what had happened and why. Boland completed his last rug, and then he closed his shop and went in search of his son.

Francis was given a king's ransom for her allegiance to me, and then she moved on, as well. James went off in search of our hidden valley, to find Juliana, but he never did find it. He returned to Whispering Wind a broken man.

Blake eventually started to move about, but he still did not speak. He has not said a word since he left me. He was living, but he was dead inside… a broken man indeed.

Juliana had her baby, a little girl, whom she wanted to name Sabine but Rebecca would not let her. She named her Isabel, instead, and together, the three of them would stay in the valley.

Time was moving forward for everyone. They were healing and they would now be able to grow old and die. Instead of just growing old, I think Charles was the most relieved by this revelation; he finally got to leave this place and leave his regret behind.

Six seasons had passed, and still Blake had not spoken. He had no expressions, but every now and again, they would find him sitting in the corner crying silently. The pain was too much for him to bear, but he needed to feel it. He knew it was his punishment for deceiving me and for lying to me yet again. He had broken my trust, and he blamed himself for what I had done.

The seventh season had begun, and word had travelled the lands that Whispering Wind was dead. The life had drained out of it, the magic gone. The Queen had gone away and had not been seen. No one knew I was dead or really cared.

Well, that is not truth; there were those who cared, men like King Louis. When word reached his land, he sent scouts to scope the land and see if these stories were truth. He told everyone that he had scared me into hiding. When his scouts returned, he gathered his army and set out to take Whispering Wind. He had heard the stories of the wealth of the land, and if there was no one to rule it, then why should he not claim it.

In the beginning of the eighth season, Rebecca was walking from the lake with some clothes she had been washing when the tree began to glow. She stopped and watched, unable to see through the bright light, but as the glow faded she saw him. Raiden had returned, and he was carrying something. He was carrying me.

As he laid me down where he had picked me up, he kissed me on the head and turned to face Rebecca, nodded to her, and then proceeded to walk out from under the canopy of the tree, changing back into a horse. He continued to the plain and joined Spirit. Rebecca stood there, waiting and waiting, but nothing happened. She felt the tear hit her cheek when she realized it was over. Juliana saw her standing there and followed her gaze. She laid Isabel down and walked toward the tree. As she passed under the canopy, she saw me lying on the ground. Spinning around to look at Rebecca, who stood frozen, she knew that it was over.

Rebecca sat the clothes on the grass and slowly walked to the canopy. She hesitated when she reached the edge. Juliana put her hand out for her to take, and though Rebecca refused it, Juliana did not move her hand. She held it there waiting. Finally, Rebecca gathered the courage and reached for her, and together they walked up to me and sat on the ground.

Rebecca knew what she had to do. With shaking hands, she reached up and began to unwrap the cloth from my body. When she removed the cloth from my head, she gasped and looked at Juliana, who now had tears streaming down her cheeks.

My hair had been restored, and the gash in my throat was gone. Rebecca put her hand on my heart and waited. Without any warning, there was a flash of light, and then she felt it. Th-thump, th-thump, th-thump... She took Juliana's hand and placed it under hers so she could feel it, as well. Th-thump, th-thump, th-thump... They both took in deep breaths and exhaled on me. They did this three times, never removing their hands. When they finished, together they said three times, *'In this time, in this place, seek the refuge that brings you peace.'* Reluctantly, they removed their hands and sat there watching me.

As I opened my eyes, I heard them gasp. I just laid there not moving. *How did I get here? How is this possible? I was with my family, my mother and father, Jenna. I want to go back.* I did not want to be back here. I felt the tear slip down the side of my face then slowly turned my head to see Rebecca and Juliana crying. *How is any of this possible?*

Rebecca reached out and took my hand. "Well, it took you long enough," she said and smiled.

"Hi," I said back to her. "How am I here?"

"It is a long story. What do you remember?"

I tried to gather my thoughts. "I remember riding out to King... what was his name?"

"Louis."

"Yes, him. I remember riding back and waiting for Charles to return." I could not stop the tears. "They lied to me again. Blake lied to me again. I remember going into my study and telling him I was done, that I wanted him to leave. I wanted them all to leave. He kept telling me he would not leave me. I remember telling him I was going to send my family here and then end my life. He told me I would get over it, but I could not take it anymore. After everything we had done, all that I had lost, there was no peace. There was no happiness, only mistrust, lies, and deceit. I did not want it anymore. How was I supposed to live like that? The man I loved could not even be honest with me. He just told me what I wanted to hear. He told me what would keep me calm while they continued to..."

Rebecca grabbed my hand. "I know, my love."

"I remember telling him to leave or I would end it right then. He refused, so I drew my sword and…" My hand went to my throat. "I cut my throat." Looking at Rebecca, I said, "I killed myself right in front of him. I remember seeing his face, hearing him scream."

"Then what do you remember?"

"I remember hearing your voice and thinking how sorry I was, and then there was nothing. Well, not nothing but nothing. I remember feeling warmth and love. I remember feeling my mother, her arms around me, holding me."

"After they all left, your mother came to us. She told us what to do, to bring you here, to get this cloth from the secret room, and how to wrap you in it. Then Raiden came and changed into a man, and he took you away somewhere. You have been gone from here for seven seasons, my love. He brought you back today. We did not know how long you would be gone. We just knew we could never leave here without you."

Pulling myself up into a sitting position, I got a better look at Juliana. "Your baby… Did you have your baby?"

Beaming, she nodded her head. "A little girl. Her name is Isabel."

"Where is she?"

"Sleeping right now."

When I leaned forward, my hair fell down into my face. "All right, this is strange. My hair is long again?" Shaking my head, I told them, "I remember cutting it off. I liked it short."

Giggling, Rebecca said, "It was a statement. That is for sure."

"So now what do we do?" I asked.

"I am not sure. We could go back to Whispering Wind," Rebecca suggested.

"Westin… What happened to Westin?"

"We do not know, Sabine. We left shortly after you died."

12

"We need to find them." I searched for him in my mind.

'Are you here?'

'I am.'

'Hi, old friend. Thank you.'

'It is not your time, Sabine. You are to live a long and healthy life.'

'Is Westin alive?'

'Yes, they live in the valley. They are safe. The powers that be have kept them shielded.'

"Westin is safe. They live in the valley. I should go and see him."

"Juliana, where is James?"

"I do not know, nor do I care. He put me on a horse and took me into what could have been a battle. He did just as Blake did to you he betrayed me. It did not matter to him what happened to me."

"Oh, my love." I wrapped my arms around her. "I am sorry. So here we are three spectacular women out in the middle of nowhere with no one to love us but each other." Looking at one another, we started to laugh.

Chapter Three

$\mathfrak{W}$e stayed in the valley for a little while longer, having no knowledge of what was happening outside our little world. I am not so sure any of us cared.

*****

King Louis was moving closer and closer to Whispering Wind. He had heard the stories that filtered through the lands, and he knew that we were gone. Rumors had spread, telling him that the waif of a child had left her home, and that the people left with me. He heard of the jewels and the wealth that was once Whispering Wind, and as all arrogant men, he believed that it should be his.

The brothers, my Guardians, stayed there, but they dismissed the majority of the remaining Guard. Blake still wandered around, not speaking. Charles was the only one who would go into the castle. He went every day to look at the place I drew my last breath. His remorse was more than anyone could have imagined. He silently cried while he was alone in my study, saying how sorry he was. But no one heard him. No one cared.

*****

We decided that it was time for us to leave and to go find Westin and Camille. It was time for me to go back out into the world and go home. Even if my home was in shambles, it was still my home. Juliana and Isabel rode with me, and Rebecca carried the tomes, though she did not read them. They had been under the canopy so that nothing would happen to them. We did not ride like we usually did because we had young Isabel with us.

When we climbed the hills to the valley, my heart started beating faster. I knew Westin would have a hard time dealing with seeing me, but I had to see my brother. We rode into the valley, and the closer we got to the cottage the more frantic I felt. As we approached, he came out. I did not know what to expect when I saw him, but the tears just came. He stood there screaming out in disbelief. Camille came running out to see what was wrong with him. I could not get off Raiden fast enough before Westin was in my arms, knocking us both to the ground.

"I saw you. You were dead. How are you here, Sabine? I saw you die."

"Mother saved me. Rebecca, Mother, Juliana, and Raiden saved me."

"Where have you been all this time?" he questioned.

"I have been with Mother."

"Does Blake know you are alive?"

"No, my love," I tell him solemnly.

"He will be so happy to see you."

We got up, and I hugged Camille, who was now holding Isabel. "You have a new niece, Westin. Her name is Isabel."

He was hugging Juliana and then Rebecca. "I am the happiest man alive, Sabine. Our Mother is a wonderful mother. She gave you back to me."

"I know, my love, but as usual, we cannot stay. I want you to stay here. We will come back, and then this will be our home, here or in the secret valley. I need to leave these here with you." I pointed to the tomes. "I need for you to keep them safe for me. I have to go get the rest of them. Would you do that for me?"

"Yes, Sabine, I will."

"Westin, you cannot read them. You must hide them. Raiden told me that you are protected here. No one can enter the valley except for us."

"Did you do your magic, Sabine?"

"No, Westin, Mother did. She is protecting you as she protected me."

"Camille, you are the only mother I have ever known," Juliana said. "I must go with them, but I cannot take Isabel with me. Will you please look after her?"

"You do not need to ask. Of course we will."

We all hugged, and Juliana kissed her daughter goodbye before we left with our eyes full of tears. Once we were on the plain, Raiden and Spirit took off and we were flying through time. Out of nowhere, they stopped.

'There is much danger coming to Whispering Wind,' he said in my head.

'Who?'

'Louis. He comes for the wealth of the Kingdom.'

'How close?'

'He has set up camp and will move at the dark of the night.'

'The people... Will we get there in time?'

'Whispering Wind is dead. There is no one left but the Guardians.'

I could not help but think they deserved what Louis had for them. They did not know I was alive, but I could not be as cruel to them as they were to me. "Juliana, can you build a wall of fire around the village and castle, and hold it while we ride?"

"Sabine, I have not used my gift for a very long time. I do not know if I can still do it."

I could not help but giggle. "Oh, my love, you can still do it. Do not do it yet, though. I will tell when to try. Louis has made camp outside of Whispering Wind, and he will move in at the dark of night. We will not make it back there by then. Whispering Wind is dead. There is no one left there but the Guardians. Louis is after the wealth of the kingdom. He will tear the place down brick by brick. I cannot let that happen."

"Well, I know seven men who are going to lose their minds when they see us coming," Rebecca said with a giggle."

"You may be right, Rebecca."

We continued on our way. This was going to get very interesting very quickly. We rode fast, for the dark of the night was upon us.

'He is moving.'

"Juliana, concentrate and do your thing."

I could feel her body warm against mine as she grew hotter and hotter. "I got it," she said.

Charles noticed the glow in the sky, and he ran to the stables to get his horse, everyone except for Blake followed him. They went the back way and out past the hill. That is where Charles saw Louis' army. "They have set fire to the land. He is trying to burn us out. We must take shelter." Turning their horses around, they rode back. Blake was on his horse with his sword drawn.

"I have waited for this moment for a long time. Now I can die with honor," he said, speaking the first words he had spoken in nearly eight seasons.

We were nearly there. Juliana opened the wall so we could pass into the village, and Raiden and Spirit skidded to a stop just short of the stables. No one moved.

They all stood there looking at us. Blake was in shock and was immediately drawn into the darkness, quickly falling off his horse. James fell to his knees, as did Charles. Joseph was the only one who smiled; he was happy to see Rebecca.

I searched for something witty to say, but I could not think of anything to say, so I just sat there.

As Joseph took a step toward Rebecca, she put her hand up. "Do not even consider it." He stopped, but his smile did not waiver.

Juliana jumped off Raiden. I looked at her and noticed those eyes of hers were blood red. She looked magnificent. Charles had not looked up yet. I jumped down, walked up to him, and knelt on the ground in front of him. "I am real. You are not seeing things."

He picked his head up. "How is this possible?"

"It was not my time to die. Apparently, I have things to do. I am not sure what they are, but here I am."

He nearly broke my back when he threw himself on top of me hugging me. We lay on the ground laughing. "There are no

18

words to describe how I feel right now, how I have felt for the last two years."

"Well, you have let my Kingdom go to hell. That is for sure."

"When you died, Whispering Wind died."

We moved to sit and then stood up. James got to his feet and was looking at Juliana. "Our child?" he asked her. She did not answer him. He lowered his head and did not look at her again. I think she wanted him to believe that there was no child. I was not getting in the middle of that.

Blake was coming out of the darkness, shaking his head. He sat up and picked up his head before looking straight at me. I watched as his eyes came into focus, and then I watched as his mind processed what he was seeing. Life sprung into his eyes, and he quickly stood up. "How is this possible? I watched you..."

"What you did to me is an unforgivable act. I will never forgive you. I told you I was done." I turned to Charles. "I have a King to fry. You ready for this?"

He smiled. "I am at your service, Your Majesty," he said as he bowed.

We got back on our horses, this time with Juliana able to ride her own horse as we rode out to the hilltop. "Juliana, drop the wall of fire. Let Louis see us." Once she did, I realized they were closer than I thought they would be. Louis' face said it all.

"Well, the stories of your demise are not truth. I heard you ran away."

"Why are you here, Louis?"

"No one was claiming this land, so I thought it should be mine."

"This land belongs to me. I told you to leave and never return."

"You do not address me so, child."

"Well, the way I see it, I am the Queen of this land and you are here as an unwelcomed guest, so I am afraid to say this, but I outrank you."

"You are but a woman. Women are nothing to men."

I looked at Rebecca, who was smiling, and it was never a good thing when she smiled like that. "Louis," she said.

"You will address me with respect and refer to me as Your Majesty."

She laughed so hard I thought she was going to fall off Spirit. "I will do no such thing. You are nothing but an arrogant fool to think you deserve this land or its wealth."

"You are a disrespectful child, and after we are finished here today, you will heel at my feet."

I could feel Raiden twitch, so I patted his neck as I stated, "Louis, you will not finish anything this day. This will be your last day in this world. Your energy is dark, and I have banished the darkness from this land. You will join your comrades and be incased in stone. You will never see your Kingdom again, nor will you ever hurt another woman. I am done talking to you, and I am done being kind."

"You cannot win against my army."

"Watch me," was all I said before Raiden was in the air. Louis sat there on his horse and watched his line of men burn. When we dropped down, he stood alone on the hilltop.

Laughing, he said, "Do you think you frighten me? Do you think that this is the size of my army?" He raised his hand, and another bigger line of troops came up the hill.

"You will not learn, will you? What we do holds no boundaries. I can sit here and do this all night long, but you know what? I just woke from death, and I really am tired and bored with you."

He raised his arm, but before he could move it, Raiden was in the air. Those men died before he could wave them forward. Juliana built a wall of fire as the next round moved forward, burning them where they stood.

"You will not win, Louis," Charles said. "I told you to be careful and not anger her."

"She is nothing but a witch, and witches fry." He threw a fire spell at me. It was the weirdest thing to watch as the fire surrounded me but did not touch me. It was if I was in a bubble. I giggled as the flames disappeared. "You see, the problem with men like you is that you just do not get it. I was born this way. I was born with this power. You were taught yours. You cannot touch me."

Raiden was in the air again, and his army fried where they stood. The horses were up for a long time. When they landed, there was nothing but Louis. "Now, you stand here alone and have delivered these men to death. I told you before not to return here or you would die."

"Get off that horse, witch, and fight me."

I jumped off Raiden. "Sabine," Charles said.

"It is all right, Charles. I will handle this."

Louis climbed off his horse wearing his full royal war armor. I giggled. "Perhaps you should shed that armor of yours. It might just give you a fighting chance."

"I will take my chances with it on. You will not defeat me, child, not without your magic horse."

I just stood there looking at him before raising my sword, ready for him.

"I see you can hold the sword, child, but I am willing to wager you cannot wield it."

"If you win, Whispering Wind is yours."

"And if you win, Princess, what will you get, my Kingdom?"

"No, I will have the pleasure of never having to see your face or hear your arrogant voice again."

He swung at me, so I caught his sword and pushed him back. I could feel Blake's energy growing; he was not happy. Louis was easily larger than Blake. It did not matter to me. I wanted this man gone. He swung again and again, each time weakening. His armor, I am sure, was heavy, so he was using much more energy than I was. He swung again, knocking me back, and I nearly fell. I heard Raiden neigh. This guy was tough. He did not just talk tough he was tough.

I got my footing, and he swung again. This time, I was swinging up, and when our swords connected, mine glowed, distracting him. I felt his energy depleting and I pushed him hard.

He stepped back, saying, "Well, the little girl has some power. I will bet she does not have enough." He came at me full force. When I raised my sword to stop his, he stabbed a dagger into the right side of my stomach.

"No!" I heard Blake yell. Charles got off his horse. I did not fall down, though instead, swung at him with all that I had, and he went down. I held him there, sucking the energy out of him. When I stepped back, I reached down, pulled the dagger out, and threw it to the side. He was getting up slowly. I charged him and swung hard, my sword making contact with his helmet. I put my foot on his chest and pushed him backwards. He fell in a heap, and as I walked up to put my foot on his throat, he swung his sword and connected with my left arm, slicing it wide open. I stood there, looking at him and seeing nothing but fear in his eyes. He knew he was going to die.

"My father taught me to never take a man while he was down. Stand, King Louis, so I can end you."

I backed up so he could gain his footing. When he turned, he swung, and I met his sword with mine in a full swing, snapping his sword in half. I spun around then and cut his head off.

Blake was at my side instantly. "You are bleeding."

I just looked at him and hobbled back to my horse. "I am so done with arrogant men."

Rebecca nodded. "Come on. Let's go fix you up."

I turned to Charles. "I am Queen of this Kingdom, and you have a choice to make. Either live by my rule or you will leave. You do as I tell you to do, or I will end you all. You choose. Right now, I am going to go and bleed for a bit." I pulled on Raiden's reigns, turned him around, and went back to the castle.

"Well, that was pretty brutal," Rebecca said.

"What? Louis started it. He was the one who insisted I kill him."

Rebecca laughed. "Not that. What you said to the brothers."

"I am so tired of their dishonesty and their lies. Either they do as I say or they leave. If they will not leave, they will pay the price. Juliana, I think I might need some water. Would you be a dear and get me some supplies to deal with this blood?"

"Already on it," she said as she blew past me.

Charles and his brothers stood on the hilltop, speechless. Blake sat there looking at them. "She is back," he said with a huge smile on his face.

"Yes, brother, it would seem she is. The query here is how and why. She could have stayed away, and we would have never known. There is a reason she came back here."

"Do not start with your secrets, Charles. I lost her once. I will not lose her again," Blake said. They rode back to the castle.

Rebecca helped me to the couch in the sitting room. "I cannot believe he stabbed you," she said as she pulled up my shirt. "Did it hurt?"

"Not really, but it is starting to now."

Juliana came back with a bowl of water and some cloth. "I have a salve that Charlotte gave to me to put on James' wounds. Perhaps it will work on yours. I also have something for you to drink for the pain."

"Thank you. Do you know what to do?"

"Yes, here, lie down. Rebecca, get her shirt off."

I lie there, trying not to scream out in pain, while these two forces of nature worked on me. I winced a few times as it was becoming unbearable. "If I fall into the darkness, do not let Blake near me. Stand guard over me."

"Do not worry, Sabine. You will fall asleep soon. We will take care of you. We managed to get you out of here without anyone helping us before, so I think we can manage to get you upstairs on our own."

That was all I needed to hear. I closed my eyes and let the darkness come.

Charles came in to the sitting room, and they threw him out; I was, after all, lying on the couch with my upper body exposed. He stood in the grand hall against the wall. "Will she be all right?"

"We do not know. She has gone into the darkness from the pain."

"Do you need my help?"

"No, Charles, we do not. Thank you. I will come and tell you what is happening when we finish. She was very clear that she does not want to see Blake, so please keep him away from here," Juliana snapped.

"He is just outside the door."

"Keep him out, or I will level him," Juliana said. "All of you have done enough damage to her. She wants nothing to do with him."

"Yes, I know what I did."

Juliana got up and walked into the great hall. "Do you, Charles? Do you really? She cut her own throat because of your lies and your deceit. The only thing she ever wanted was for him to be honest with her, and because of you and this amazing form of arrogance you possess, you ordered them to lie to us. My own husband put our unborn child in the gravest danger, and he did not even think about it. You have no idea what any of you have done to us. She lay on that floor dead, and you all walked out of the room and left her there. No one looked back, Charles. No one came to help us. You all just went off and cowered someplace else. How long did it take for someone to come and check on us? Never mind… I can only imagine. You men are the most selfish, arrogant, deceitful people I have ever known. I will fill you in on her recovery. Do not come back into this house again, or I will level you." She turned from him then and walked back into the sitting room.

"I could not have said that better myself. Thank you." Rebecca said.

"I had to really work on not setting him on fire," she said, giggling.

"Here, hold this," Rebecca told her. She was trying to wrap my stomach with a cloth. "Her arm does not look as bad as I thought it would, but this wound has me worried."

"I do not believe that we have done all that we did to get her back just so some arrogant man could take her life again," Juliana stated.

"I think you might be right. Here help me get her upstairs."

They carried me slowly up the grand staircase and to my room, where they took turns sleeping in bed with me and getting food and water. I was never left alone, and the brothers never came into the castle.

Juliana went out there daily to let them know that I was still in the darkness, and that they were feeding me broth. The wounds were healing rather quickly, so they expected me to wake soon, and I did. I was only in the darkness for three days.

"Oh, Juliana, what did you give me?"

She chuckled, saying. "That tea stuff that Charlotte gave me. It is good that you slept. Otherwise, you would be out there trying to be the Queen."

I giggled. "Oh, do not make me laugh. I am hungry and thirsty. Is there anything to eat?"

"Well, Charles was nice enough to share part of their portions, so we have some. Here." She handed me some meat and stale bread.

"I miss Francis. You know what?"

"What?"

"Will you go get Charles for me? I have an idea."

"You sure about this," Rebecca asked.

"Oh, I am sure. My father raised me to be cunning. If I can outwit Wellington, I can surely outwit Charles. He may think he can manipulate me, but I think we will be able to figure things out for ourselves."

"All right, then, I will go get him," Juliana said as she squeezed my hand and smiled at me before she left.

I looked at Rebecca. "Were you scared when I got stabbed?"

She smiled. "For about a half of a moment, but then I saw your face. You were so mad."

"More than you know." I heard Charles coming. "Are you all right with being in here with him?" She nodded.

"Sabine, I am so glad you are all right."

"Thank you, Charles. I have some things I would like you to take care of... that is, if you are going to stay. If not, that is fine. I am sure Raiden and Juliana can take care of it."

"Sabine, I am your Guardian. I will not leave on my own accord, and neither will my brothers."

"I would like you to send someone to find Francis. I would like for her to come home if she wants to. You are not to tell her I am alive, though. You will tell her that Westin has returned to the castle. I would also like for someone to track down Clare and Boland. They had a good life here, so if they wish to return, you tell them they are welcome."

"I will get right on that, and Clare had brought all the clothes she made for you. I put them with your gown."

"Thank you. Also, since I live, Whispering Wind lives, so while the men are searching for them, make sure they have gold with them to purchase animals. It is time we get this place back on its feet."

He nodded and then left.

"Do you think they are going to be truthful," Rebecca said.

"I do not know, but I can hope. I am tired, but I just want to say thank you to you both for taking care of me."

"I like being this bossy," Juliana divulged happily. "They are afraid I will start them on fire."

"Are you going to tell James about Isabel?" I whispered.

"Eventually, but I like knowing he is suffering. What they did to us was horrible, and I am not going to live my life like that. If he wants to be a part of it, he is going to have to decide which is more important his loyalty to his brothers or his loyalty to his wife."

I nodded and smiled at her. "Sleep," I said and closed my eyes.

Juliana said to Rebecca, "I am going to go for a walk. Will you be all right?"

"I think I am going to take a sleep with Sabine. I will bolt the door, so just knock when you come back."

She left, and Rebecca crawled into bed with me. "I love you," she whispered.

"I love you, too." And then I slept.

Juliana walked to my study door and stood there. With her hand shaking, she reached for the door latch. Pushing it opened, she took a step forward, letting that night play in her mind as if it had happened only the day before. She could hear and see everything, and she was angry. Angry at them for their deceit, angry that I would do this to myself, and angry at Blake for not being truthful with me. Angry at James for just not caring enough to protect her. She shook her head, pulled the door closed, and walked outside.

James was sitting by the fountain when she walked out. He stood up and started to walk toward her. "Juliana, will you please talk to me?"

"I have said all that I need to say to you, James."

"You have said nothing."

"I said it all the night Sabine cut her throat. You put me on that horse. You did not care if our child died. The only thing you cared about was covering up yet another of Charles' deceptions."

"You left me. How was I supposed to tell you how sorry I am?"

"I left you? You, all of you, walked out of that room, leaving Rebecca and I to clean up yet another one of your messes. You walked out and left Sabine lying on the floor. No one came, James. No one came to see if we were all right. You did not come back for me. You left me there." Her eyes started to glow,

28

and James became a bit uncomfortable, starting to feel very warm. Juliana turned her head from him and shot her fire at the wall. She took a deep breath to calm herself. "Do not think that because eight seasons have passed, I have forgotten any of it or that I will forgive you. I am your wife, and yet you did NOTHING to protect our child or me. Now, please, do not approach me again. Do not think I am going to accept any apology you can give, because there is nothing you can say to undo what you have done." She walked away then, heading toward the back courtyard.

James sat down and cried. He knew... He had known all along that what he had done to his wife was the worst kind of betrayal. It was worse than telling her lies. He had so callously put his unborn child in grave danger. There would be no forgiveness for him anytime soon. For eight seasons he wandered around the known lands looking for her, asking anyone if they had seen a girl like her. He did not find any trace of her, nor did Joseph. Blake, well, he knew exactly where his future wife was. She was dead because of him. The brothers had a great deal to answer for, not only to us but to themselves. They had dishonored their father, and that was what had brought them to their knees.

I slept for a few more days before pulling myself up and out. Walking around the upstairs of the castle, I was not prepared to face any of them just yet. Rebecca and Juliana were doing a great job keeping them in line. Juliana just kept telling them not to push her or she would burn them. Considering none of them could die, it would be rather painful to burn and then heal.

I was sitting by the fire one day when there was a knock on my door. "Yes, come in."

Charles walked in. "Sabine," he said as he actually nodded. *Was this his way of bowing to me?* I almost laughed. "I have succeeded in finding both Boland and Francis. They are both here, down in the kitchen."

"Do they know that I am alive?"

"No, I did not tell them. I just said what you told me to say, that if they wanted to live here, they were welcome to come back."

"Thank you, Charles. Have they seen Rebecca and Juliana yet?"

"Yes, would you like me to help you down stairs?"

"No, I am fine. I have been walking on my own for the last few days. I will make my way down. Again, thank you, Charles."

"Is there anything else I can do?"

"There is, actually. I would like for you to go and get Westin and Camille. He is taking care of some books for me, and I would like for him to bring those along."

"Westin knows you are alive?"

"It was the first place I went when I woke."

He nodded again and then left. *I could get used to this,* I thought, chuckling to myself. I made my way to the secret staircase and then down to the kitchens, where I waited and listened to the chatter from Rebecca and Juliana. Pushing the door open, I stood there watching them.

Boland was laughing, but he looked up and then stood up. "Sabine?"

I smiled at him and nodded.

Francis stood and turned to face me. "How could this be?" She looked at Rebecca, and Rebecca smiled at her. "I saw you in your study. I saw you lying there, covered in blood. How is this possible?"

"It is a long story. I am glad that you came back."

"Come, child. Sit and tell me everything. I knew that you girls had some magic in you, but I would never have guessed you could do this," she said, talking to Rebecca and Juliana.

They laughed. "We did not do this. Sabine did it," Juliana told her.

We sat around the table in the kitchen and talked. They had all gone to live in Wellington and Blackmore where there were no rulers. Francis did nothing, for there was no one to cook for, but Charles had given her enough money to survive. Boland went in search of his son but never found him, and was weaving tapestries for some King he did not know.

"So will you stay with us?" I asked.

Francis was excited. I told her that Westin and Camille were coming back, and she smiled. Boland agreed to live here. He said he loved Whispering Wind that the Wind spoke to him. I laughed a little at that. *If only he knew.*

Life moved on, and the brothers stayed away from us. The only one I had dealings with was Charles. Slowly, people started to come back. Word had traveled that I was home and that the land had come alive again. People would come and ask permission to live here. It was finally becoming a peaceful place.

My wounds had healed, and I wanted… no, I needed to ride. I put on my pale blue gown that Clare had made me, took my sword, and walked out of my room. As I was walking, my sword had knocked something off the table by the door. I went back in my room to see what it was. Bending over, I picked it up, Mother's crown. *How did this get in here?* The last I remembered, I had left it in my study. It was not a huge crown, not by any means. It was just a thin band of gold with an equal number of red and blue stones, which were just big enough to catch the light.

My hands were moving to my head. I did not want to wear a crown; I thought it silly, but I could not stop myself. Placing it on my head, it fit perfectly. I chuckled and continued down the hall.

Walking into the kitchen, I said, "Hello, Francis. Have you seen Juliana?"

She turned and smiled at me. "Well, it is about time, child. You deserve to wear that crown, and let me just say, you wear it well."

I giggled, saying, "Thank you. I do not know why I put it on." Just then, Juliana came in the door from the courtyard. "Juliana, would you be a dear and get Raiden for me? I wanted to go for a ride."

She just smiled. "Yes, Your Majesty."

"I will take it off if you do not stop."

She giggled all the way out of the house and soon returned with Raiden.

"Francis," I started. "If anyone comes looking for me, please tell them that I am riding and I have my sword." I held it up to show her.

She turned to me and stepped in my path. "There is one who looks for you every day."

I knew she was referring to Blake, and whispered, "I cannot forgive him for what he has done. Please do not speak of him again." I squeezed her hand so she knew I was not angry with her, and then I left.

It had been a long time since I had ridden Raiden. "Hello," I said to him. "I think I would like to be free today." I went to climb on him, and he bowed. "Oh, not you, too." I swear he smiled at me. I climbed on him, and we rode out into the courtyard and through the gates. We went past Boland's and continued to the hilltop.

The Wind was blowing as I sat there on my horse and looked at the scorch marks on the land where an army had burned. I had decided that this was where my heart belonged. This was my home, and I would do all that was necessary to keep it. This was my happiness.

Blake had seen me leaving and had followed me to the edge of the orchards, silently watching me from atop his horse. I could feel his energy, but I did not care. I leaned in to Raiden and whispered, "Take me away from here," and we were gone. He came to rest in the same spot he did the day I met Cam. "This is a lovely spot. Thank you."

I sat and looked out on the plain. It was a beautiful day, the blossoms in full bloom and the ground becoming new again. Westin and Camille would be arriving in a few days. I tried to remember what it was like while I was gone but could not remember anything, just the feel of warmth and love. I could feel my mother and Jenna. I just did not understand why I was given my life back this life I did not really want anymore. But I suppose it was my station to look after these people, to look after Westin. He had been through so much in his life. So many odd things had happened, me coming back from death being the oddest.

Reaching up, I touched my neck. I was so angry at him. I had, had enough. It was clear he pined for me, and if I were admitting things, I would have to say that I missed him. But he had deceived me, and I could not forgive that. He touched me in places only a husband should touch a wife. I was going to be his wife, and he had done this to me.

I closed my eyes and lay back, feeling the breeze blowing across the new grass. The clouds in the sky were moving gently with the breeze. What more could a girl ask for, but the peaceful happiness of nothing? This was my happiness, knowing that beauty was out here.

I sat up then stood and went to get on Raiden. "Take me home please." He complied, and it was wonderful to feel so free. I had nothing in my mind, just the feel of the warmth from the light of the day on my face and the wind blowing through my hair. Today was a good day indeed.

We climbed the hilltop, and I sat there on my horse and looked out over my Kingdom. *I am the Queen. I wear the crown.* It was about time I started acting like one. I would run this Kingdom the way I wanted. My Guardians were bound to me for life, but they could not and would not run me any longer. I would fight to keep the evil away, and I would just do what I wanted. I did not need a man to make my happiness complete. I would leave the crown to one of Westin's children. That was my wish.

Raiden slowly walked through the orchards. I stopped him as we neared Boland's new shop. I climbed down and knocked on the door. He opened it, a smile forming on his face when he saw me. "Sabine, please come in."

"Hi, Boland," I said as I hugged him.

"You look like a Queen today, Sabine. It is very becoming. You should wear it every day."

"I thought it was about time I put it on. So how is your new place? I did not get to see it before I left."

"Where did you go, Sabine?"

"Do you want the truth or the story I planned on telling everyone?"

"You can tell whatever you want. I am your friend, though, so your secret will be safe with me."

"I was dead," I tell him matter of fact.

Boland looked at me. "What? How?" He looked very confused.

"I know you heard the screams the night we rode out to the orchards. Well, I had discovered that Charles and Blake had lied to me and deceived me yet again, and I had had enough. They lied to my face, and it was just too much, so I went to my study to have a good cry, you know to let it all out. I was so tired of them treating me like a child. It just felt to me at the time that Blake was there to sidetrack me so I was busy all the time, in love and not paying attention to what was really going on.

"Blake came in, and I told him I wanted them to leave Whispering Wind and that I was done with the lies. They put Juliana on a horse and took her to a potential battle while she was with child. They had no regard for her safety or the life of her unborn child. They deceived me and brought a battle to my home, the place where my brother and his children live.

"Well, Blake kept telling me he would not leave me, so I told him that I would just send Westin and Camille away and that I would end my life. He grabbed me and told me I was just upset and that I would get over it, I guess like I always did.

"I always forgave them because they are my Guardians. They are supposed to protect me, not do things behind my back and then expect me to save them all the time. I told Blake that I would not get over it and that I would end my life right there. He said that I would not, so I told him to watch me, and I dragged my sword across my throat. I died in his arms."

Boland sat there in shock. "How do you live again?"

"I really do not know. Rebecca and Juliana took me to a special place, and seven seasons later, I came back to them."

"Do you remember anything?"

"I just remember feeling warmth and love. That is all."

He bumped my shoulder. "Well, I am glad that you live again. You are a remarkable woman, Sabine of Whispering Wind. I have heard the legend my whole life, and I hoped as a young boy that I would be alive to see it. I think the fact that you are a woman was or is a bit much for men to handle, but not me." He smiled.

"Thank you. I am glad that you came back. I would have missed you. Charles is out looking for Clare now."

"Well, I was surprised to see him."

"What did he say to get you to come back?"

"He told me that Whispering Wind was alive again, that my shop was still here, and if I wanted it then it was mine. So I packed what I could carry and got a horse, and here I am. The people will return, Sabine. You watch and see."

I smiled at him. "Well, I just wanted to stop and say hello. I should get back. I have been gone all day."

"You will be all right. Things will work themselves out. You will make a great Queen, Sabine, and thank you for sharing your story with me. I will not tell another soul. Can I just leave you with one thought, and then I will not say another word about it?"

"Of course. You can say anything to me."

"That night, I heard his screams. A man who does not truly love would not have that much pain."

"Thank you, Boland."

He walked me to the door, and I hugged him good bye. I did not ride Raiden back, choosing to walk instead. It felt good to feel the way that I felt, decided and sure. I had decided that I would not avoid him any longer. I would have to face him sooner or later, so it might as well be sooner. He must know that it will never be for us. He is not my match in this life; he is not my happiness. If he was, I would have never ended my life.

36

I looked up and saw him sitting on the fountain in the courtyard. I walked past him and took Raiden to the stables. As I was walking out, a guard was standing by the barracks door.

"Your Majesty," he said and bowed. "Welcome home."

I smiled at him. "Thank you, and good night."

He nodded to me. As I walked through the courtyard, Blake was still sitting on the fountain. I walked behind him to the doors. He did not attempt to talk to me, but I knew he was watching me. I went in and closed the door, leaning my head against it for a moment. When I turned around, I was shocked. I had not been in here yet because I had been using the kitchen door. The rug in the great hall was finished. It was more beautiful than the one in my study. I ran up a few steps and turned to look at it. "WOW," I said out loud. It made this day even better than it already had been. I ran into the kitchen. "Did you see that rug?"

Juliana and Rebecca laughed. "Yes, we did. Did you have a nice ride?" Rebecca asked.

"I did. I stopped to visit Boland. It was a very lovely day, but I am hungry. Is there anything to eat?"

Chapter Four

I lay in bed alone, while Rebecca and Juliana were in the rooms on either side of me. It felt strange to be here alone. I could not sleep, so I got up and went to the window to look out at the village. The wind was still blowing gently, but the sky was clear and all the lights above were bright. I remembered what Blake had said, that everything was brighter now that the evil was gone. I had never noticed before, probably because I was busy trying to keep everyone safe from the lies and manipulations of my Guardians.

I remembered the last time I was in this room alone with him, convinced that he would be honest with me. I was convinced that he loved me and that we were each other's happiness. In that moment I sliced my throat open, I hated him and wanted nothing more than for him to suffer. It did not matter now. I could not care anymore. The moment I felt the tear fall on my cheek, I wiped it away and looked at it on my fingers. I did not want to cry for him. Looking up, I saw him sitting there still, looking at me. I turned and went to bed, where I cried silently for the things he did to me. I cried for the way he tore my heart out. I cried until sleep came.

When I woke, Juliana was sitting in the chair by the fireplace. "Is everything all right, my love?"

"Well, yes and no. I need for you to ask Charles to send James somewhere. Westin and Camille will be here in a few days, and I am not ready for him to know that Isabel is alive. He needs to suffer some more. In fact, send them all away."

"My love, Joseph has seen her. He will tell him. You have to make a choice either you forgive him or you do not. But if you would like, I will send them away and make Joseph swear to keep this secret."

She smiled. "Thank you. I saw Blake today. He asked me if you were all right. He said that he saw you crying last night. Not that I will tell him anything other than he was imagining it, but are you all right? Were you crying?"

"I am fine. I have been sorting through things in my mind, remembering, and well, yes, he did see me, though I was not crying then. It was only one tear."

"Do you want me or Rebecca to stay with you?"

"Oh, no, I am fine. I will be fine. I am like you, my love. I am just working through things."

"Do you think you will forgive him?"

"I do not believe so. He is not my happiness, Juliana. My happiness is just being me, and I have decided that is exactly what I am going to do. The problem I am having, however, is figuring out who that is."

She laughed. "Good luck with that one. I have been trying to figure that out since I left the valley to come here to live. I did not know where I fit in, or how I would be able to live with all of this. It was really hard to adjust, but now, I know that I had to live the way I did and then live through all that we have in order to become a mother."

"You are so much like your mother. She was my greatest friend. I miss her."

"I know, and I am sorry that you lost her."

"Me too."

"I am going to go down and eat. Are you coming?"

"Yes, but do not wait for me. I will be down in a bit."

I laid back down in bed. Why would he care if I was crying? He would make me cry all the time. I knew he would approach me, so I just had to be strong. I got up and put on one of my other new gowns, a light yellow one. On my way out the door, I saw my crown sitting on the table. I smiled as I picked it up and put it on.

We ate in the kitchen with Francis, and I thought it funny how this, my room, and the hallways were the only places I had been since I got back. I liked eating in here; it felt more like home. After eating, I went to get Raiden. As I approached the stables, I saw Charles and Blake talking. "Excuse me, Charles. Could I speak with you, please" Blake looked at me, well, he was staring at me.

"Of course, Sabine. What can I do for you?"

"Well, first, is there any news on Clare and Charlotte?"

"I was not aware you wanted me to find them."

"Oh, I thought I had asked you. I would like very much if you could find them. Perhaps all of you should go in different directions and spread out to find them. I would like some more gowns to wear."

"I put the ones she brought before she left with your other one."

"Yes, but… yes, I remember. I would like for you to find them, please, the sooner the better actually."

"We will leave straight away."

"Thank you," I told him and continued walking. Blake's eyes followed me, but he made no attempt to talk to me.

I saddled Raiden and walked him out into the sunshine, climbed up, and away we went. I enjoyed riding and not having to answer to anyone. It was nice to know that when I came back, I would not have to hear them yell at me for being gone all day. Perhaps Charles got the clue when I took down Louis. I could take care of myself against any man. We rode to the place Raiden seemed to keep bringing me to. This time when I got off him to sit in the grass, I actually took notice of where I was. Is there something here I am missing?

"Why do you keep bringing me here? I know it is beautiful and peaceful, but it is also one of the last places I was before I ended my life," I said to Raiden. He did not nod, or neigh. In fact, he did not even look at me. I laughed. "Oh, how obvious could you be?" I sat down in the grass and looked around. Before me was a river, though it was not large. Straight after that was nothing but plains for as far as I could see. It was beautiful how the tall grass swayed in the breeze, almost hypnotic. To my right as I faced the river was the forest, and to my left were hills. I wondered what was over those hills. *Is this Whispering Wind? Is this part of the Kingdom?* I stood, searching for him in my mind.

'Is this still the land of Whispering Wind?'

'As far as the eye can see.'

'Those hills?'

'Yes.'

'The forest?'

'Yes.'

'Do you know how big this Kingdom is?'

'Yes.'

I knew it was big, but I had no idea how big. I climbed back onto Raiden. "Will you take me back, please?" As we rode into the courtyard, Charles and his brothers were getting ready to ride. I rode up to Charles. "Do you know the boundaries of this Kingdom?"

"I am not sure what you mean?"

"Where it begins and where it ends."

"I do not think anyone does, Sabine. Why?"

"Raiden knows. Do you know of anyone who would be able to map out the boundaries?"

"I do not know anyone."

"While you are out searching for Clare and Charlotte, would you make an effort to find an honest man who is not arrogant to come to Whispering Wind and to take on the job of mapping out this Kingdom?"

They sat there looking at me as if I was crazy. "Why would you want to do that?" Charles asked.

"I am not sure, but it needs to be done." I then started to move away from them, not willing to share anything with them. They would do as I asked, and not question me, or they would leave.

They would not manipulate me again. I turned in my saddle and said, "Thank you again, Charles."

He nodded his head, and they were off. I put Raiden in the stables and went back to the house. I went in the back way to find Rebecca sitting at the table. "Are you all right?" I asked.

"Yes and no," she replied, and I giggled.

"Juliana said the same thing to me this morning. What is the matter?"

She looked at me as I sat next to her. "I think I am going to give in to Joseph. I have missed him so much these past eight seasons, and then seeing him again, and now he is gone again. I really miss him."

"I will tell you the same thing I told Juliana." I took her hands and continued, "My love, you have to make the decision to either forgive him or not. That is something only you can do."

"Do you think you will ever forgive Blake?"

"Please tell me you are not conspiring with Blake to get me to let him back in."

"No, I would never do that. I was just thinking that if Juliana and I are considering letting them back in, perhaps you should as well."

"Listen to me… you have no idea what he did to me with his lies and deceit, after the promises he made to me about not keeping anything from me. The last straw was when Louis came here and they put Juliana on that horse. You said it yourself, that they lie and bring the battles to us and expect us to fix it all. I cannot and will not forgive him for what he did to me. Rebecca, he tore my heart out and made a mockery of what I felt for him. I trusted him. I let him touch me in a way no man should or would without facing death."

She pulled me into a hug. "I know, and I am sorry, my love. I will not bring it up again."

"Thank you, but you and Juliana should always do what you think is best for you. I am doing that as well. I am doing what I feel is best for me. I am tired of running. This is our home, and I will stand and defend it against any arrogant man who believes he should own it."

"I think I might like the new you." We giggled.

"Westin and Camille should be here soon, by the end of the light of the day tomorrow. It will be good to see them. We need to get the other two tomes from the place where time stands still. Do you want to go with me?"

"Sure. We should change though."

I looked at her and then at my dress. "I do think you might be right." We laughed. She went and changed, as did I, and then we found Juliana and explained to her where we going and that we would be back. "Do not worry. We will return."

Then we left, but it did not take as long as we thought. We were back at the castle before midday. "Where should we put these?" Rebecca asked.

"The most logical place would be the secret room, but..."

"But what?"

"Would you do it, please?"

She looked at me, and I saw the tear in her eye. She whispered, "You have not been in there yet?" I shook my head. "It is all right. I will take them."

I nodded at her and went to my room. I was tired, and I did not want to face her, not yet. I lay in my bed and closed my eyes, and sleep came easily.

*****

Rebecca walked to my study door and stood there holding a tome. She reached for the latch, then stopped. Juliana walked past the end of the hallway and stopped. She considered saying something, but instead just stood there watching Rebecca. Again, Rebecca put her hand on the latch, and again she pulled it away. Juliana felt the tears well in her eyes as she watched her friend struggle with her memories of what had taken place in there.

Rebecca took a deep breath and reached for the latch once more. This time, she lifted it up and pushed the door open. The rush of emotions came flooding into her, the images of what took place that night so long ago playing out in her mind. Her knees gave way, and she slammed into the stone floor, dropping the tome. When the tears overpowered her, Juliana's hands came to her mouth to stop from screaming. She was frozen there in her spot, unable to run to Rebecca to hold her.

In Rebecca's mind, she saw me lying in Blake's arms covered in my own blood. She saw him as he felt the last beat of my heart, and then as he left me. She knew I could never forgive him. How could she forgive Joseph? They all had left us there. No one came; no one came to see if they were all right, to help them with my body.

This caused Rebecca to cry harder. She realized then that they did not care what they did. "You were right. There can be no forgiveness," Rebecca whispered through her tears. Juliana heard her, and she knew in her heart that the words she heard were truth. How could they do this and think eight seasons would erase it. She ran to Rebecca and held her. Together they sat on the floor just outside my study and cried for what we had all lost.

"I am all right," Rebecca said to her as they stood. "Thank you for holding me."

"What they did to us was unforgiveable. How will we ever get past this?"

"I do not know, but it is Sabine who suffered the most. What Thomas did to me is nothing in comparison to what Blake did to her. She is so trusting and pure, and he shattered her enough for her to take her own life. My friend, my sister laid there on that floor, and no one cared enough to come back. No one came to this room for two days, Juliana, and it was Aiden who came not Charles, not Blake, not Joseph, and not James. It was Aiden. They left us here. How could we ever forgive that?"

"You are right. I was thinking of giving him another chance, but you are right. There is no forgiveness."

Juliana walked away with tears flowing down her cheeks. She came into my room and sat in the chair, watching me sleep.

Rebecca found the courage to go into my study and pop the latch for the secret room, where she placed the tome on the floor. She noticed the gowns, and then she saw my gown that I should have worn to marry Blake. "They do not deserve us," she muttered, shaking her head, then went to get the other tome and placed it next to the one on the floor. Leaving the memories where they needed to stay, Rebecca closed the door to my study and came to sit in my room with Juliana.

*****

As I began to wake, I sensed someone in the room with me. I opened my eyes and sat up, and they were both there looking at me. "Are you two all right?"

"You are right, Sabine. There is no forgiveness for what they did to us," Juliana said. "He will know he has a child, but he will not be allowed to get close to her. I do not want that influence for her. She should be allowed a happy childhood, just like the one you gave me."

Rebecca spoke next. "I talked to Aiden. He was the only one who came back to check on us, but it was after two days had passed. They left us there, Sabine. No one came. No one came to see if we were all right. Aiden only came to take your body and bury it."

They were both crying, so I got up and went to them. We all hugged while standing by the fireplace. "I am sorry. I did not know how to explain it, how I felt, to either of you when you asked about me forgiving Blake. I cannot."

We bonded closer in that moment, if that was possible. While we stood there, I heard horses. "I believe they are here."

Juliana lit up. "Isabel!" she said, wiping the tears from her face.

"Come on. Let us go and welcome them home."

We all ran out of my room, down the hall, and the three of us took the stairs together, laughing at how silly we must look. Running out into the courtyard to see them ride through the gates, it was a spectacular homecoming indeed. Isabel's face lit up when she saw Juliana. "Momma," she said to Camille as she pointed to Juliana. Camille smiled and nodded. Juliana ran to her, pulling her from Camille's arms and twirling her around, hugging her.

Westin was off his horse and running toward me. "Oh, Sabine, it is so good to see you," he said and hugged me.

Camille came walking up and hugged me. "I have missed you, sister."

"As I have you. Your rooms are ready, and Francis is cooking a feast for us. Come on. You can all get cleaned up and have a rest before we eat."

They filed into the castle, and Joseph carried the tomes in. "Please set those by my study door," I told him. He nodded. I stood there and watched him carry each one, and when he was finished, I asked him to walk with me.

"Joseph, I know you have a bit of knowledge that is really not yours to share."

"Isabel?"

"Yes, Isabel. That is between Juliana and James. She will tell him in her own time."

"Forgive me, Sabine, but James has a right to know he has a child. He believes that Juliana lost the baby."

"It is not our concern, Joseph. That is between them. Do not make me order you to keep this secret. I am asking you not to say anything." This would be his test. This would be where he proved to me whether or not I could possibly trust him.

"I will do as you ask."

"Thank you. Was it not Charles who said that some things are just best kept to yourself?"

He chuckled, responding, "Yes, it was, Sabine, and all that happened was because we listened to him."

"If no one but us knows she is here, then no secrets are being kept. He will see her, but let that be between Juliana and James. It is their marriage and their child. It is not our concern."

"You are right, Sabine. I understand how what Charles did, destroyed you and Blake."

I put my hand up. "Blake is not up for conversation. Please do not speak of him to me."

He nodded and walked away.

Chapter Five

I headed back to the castle, knowing I had no other choice but to go into my study. It was time. I walked in the door and took a deep breath then made my way to the hallway, where I could see the tomes lying on the floor outside my study door. Forcing my feet to move, I stood in front of the door, not knowing how I felt about this. So much had taken place on the other side. People just did not normally get to see the place of their death. As I reached for the latch with shaking hand, I flipped it up, and though I did not want to push it open, I did. I could not see the spot where I had died from the position I was standing. Closing my eyes, I took a step forward and walked into the room before reaching for the door and closing it behind me.

Taking another deep breath, I turned and opened my eyes. It was as if my mind was playing the scene over. I heard myself crying and watched Blake come in. I could see the fear in his eyes. Then I heard the words I said to him, that I wanted him gone, that if he did not leave I would end it now. He told me I was upset and I would get past it. I watched as I stood up and walked to my desk. I watched as I cut my throat, and my own hand instinctively came up to cover my throat. I felt the wetness on my neck from my tears, and watched as I slid down the door and sat there with my knees to my chin crying. I watched as Blake tried to save me. I heard his screams with each one I shuddered. I was shaking uncontrollably.

"NOOOOO!" I heard. "NOOOOO!" I heard again. I watched him cry and beg me not to leave him. "NOOOOO!" I heard again. Rebecca coming to sit beside me... I saw it all. I saw all their faces. I felt their fear, their panic. "NOOOOO!" I heard again. I closed my eyes to stop it, but it continued. I watched them try to pull Blake away, and I saw him fight with them because he did not want to leave me. They made him. Juliana was screaming at them. Westin... Oh, my Westin, Camille, Francis... "NOOOOO!" The screaming would not stop. Charles was crying. James wanted to help Juliana. "NOOOOO!" I watched as Rebecca tried to put my blood back, trying to stop the bleeding. "NOOOOO!" I watched as they all slowly walked out of the room. I watched as Blake tried time and time again to get free of them. "NOOOOO!" he screamed. It would not stop. I could not take it anymore. The screaming was continuous. I felt hands on me, trying to grip me, and I could not move. Then I felt myself being lifted. *Am I seeing or feeling what happened to me after?* I heard a voice, a whisper, "I have you, my love." I felt hands on me. I could hear people crying and yelling. *What is happening?* It was too much. The darkness took over.

I woke in my bed with Juliana on one side and Rebecca on the other. They had both been crying. "What is the matter?" I asked.

Rebecca chuckled in between sobs. "What is the matter? Why did you go in there alone?"

"It was time to face what happened," I said as I sat up.

"Sabine, when I went in there to put the tomes in the room, I could not handle it. Juliana had to come and hold me. Why would you think you could do it alone?"

"Because I had to."

"You scared me almost to death with all the screaming."

"What do you mean? I was not screaming, was I?"

"Yes," said Juliana. "You kept screaming, 'No, no, no!'"

"I remember hearing it, but I thought it was what I was seeing. I watched the whole thing play out, all of it. I saw them trying to get Blake from me." They both looked at one another. "I saw you trying to put my blood back, trying to hold my throat together. I saw everything."

"Yes, I saw it, as well, when I went in. What else do you remember?"

"Well, when they finally got Blake out of the room, I felt the warmth and the love. I felt myself being lifted up, just like I did when I died. Why?"

"Sabine, Blake found you in there. They were coming back, and he heard you screaming. He kicked in the great doors to get to you. He picked you up and brought you here."

I looked at her as if she had gone mad, though I did not say a word. *Why did I feel the way I did? Why was the warmth and the love so prominent?*

"I need to get out of here," I said as I pushed my way past them.

'Meet me in the courtyard.'

I reached out to Raiden in my mind. Getting up from the bed, I picked up my sword and ran out of the room. I flew down the stairs and out into the courtyard, and Raiden was there already. As I jumped on him, I caught a glimpse of Blake out of the corner of my eye. He was walking toward the castle as I kicked Raiden in the sides. I leaned into him and hung on, for he did not have a saddle on. "Take me away," I said to him. Moments later, we were at the little river. I slid off of him and ran to the river, splashing water on my face to try to stop the tears.

"How is this possible? Why did this happen? He was supposed to be gone with Charles. I cannot believe this." I looked at Raiden. "Tell me how that was possible. Tell me."

'You needed to see what your actions did to everyone around you. You need to know how important you are to everyone. This has never been just about you, Sabine. This is about all that love you, all that you love.'

"I DO NOT LOVE HIM!" I screamed at him.

'Search your heart, Sabine. He is your match. Together you are stronger than if you are apart. The children you will have are important to what will come.'

I felt the tears coming. "What is coming, Raiden? More evil, viler disgusting men who believe they can take what does not belong to them? Tell me what is to come."

'The evil is gone from this land. Your quest has been completed, but there is more for you to do.'

52

"What more could I possibly do? I am tired of killing, Raiden. I am tired of being afraid. I am just tired."

'You will find your way.'

"I do not want to find my way. I want to just be me. That is why I ended my life, because I do not know who I am. Everyone wants something from me. I just cannot do this, Raiden. I cannot." The tears fell, and I sat down in the grass and cried. He walked up behind me and nudged me with his big head. I reached up to push him away, but he did it again. "Stop it," I said as I pushed him again. Then he rested his head on mine. I laughed. "Fine. You win. I will stop acting like a child and be the Queen, and do what I am supposed to do. Not that I have any idea what that is. I need to go into my study. Am I going to see that again in my head?"

He shook his head.

"Then let us go back." He stood there looking at me. "What?" I asked.

'You need to settle this with Blake. No matter what you think, Sabine, it is what it is, and there is nothing you can do. He has changed. Your death changed him.'

"Impossible. You are impossible."

He neighed and nodded his head, and I laughed.

We made it back to the castle in no time at all, and I walked in and went right to the kitchen. I was so hungry, and it was nice to see that everyone was in there Westin, Camille, their children, Rebecca, Juliana, and Isabel.

"Hello," I told them. They all turned and said hello back. "Is this the new dining hall?" They all laughed.

I took my seat at the table, and Francis served me food. It was fun sitting around and visiting with everyone. Isabel was starting to walk, well, run actually. This was what a happy home was supposed to feel like. We sat there for what seemed like all night, talking and laughing. Then Westin and Camille took their children up for bed, as did Juliana. It was just me and Rebecca left. "You all right?" she asked.

"Yes and no. I will be."

"You feel like talking about it?"

"Yes and no. I do, but if it could wait until the light of day, that would be wonderful."

She got up and kissed me on the head. "I love you," she said.

"I love you, too." And she was gone. I saw a bowl of fruit on the table, so I picked up an apple and walked out into the back courtyard. The dark of the night sky was sparkling. As I stood there looking up, I felt him. He was standing at a distance, watching me. I did not turn around, just took a deep breath and closed my eyes. *Why was it so important to forgive him?* He had ripped my heart out. He deceived me and lied to me, yet I could not get the look on his face out of my mind. He was terrified when I cut my throat. The pain he felt when my heart stopped beating was devastating. I felt him move closer, so I opened my eyes. I needed to turn and face him; Raiden said it was time to forgive, but I was not sure I could do it. I heard him in my head then...

'Sabine, turn and face him. It will be all right. He has changed. Your death changed him. Trust.'

'I do not know if I can.'

'You can.'

I felt him come closer still, so I took a deep breath and slowly turned to face him. He had tears in his eyes, as he stopped walking toward me and just stood there. He stepped forward,

54

but I did not move. Another step, and then another. I knew he thought I would run, and that was why he moved so slowly. I did not move, just watched him. Each and every step for him was more painful than the one before. He was close to me when he stopped. "Sabine," he whispered.

I did not say a word. Standing before me was a broken man, and I had broken him. I broke him when I cut my throat and died in his arms. The only thing I could see in his eyes was pain. I wondered what he saw in mine. Anger, fury, hate? Those are the feelings I had raging through me.

"How could you?" I asked very softly.

His tears fell to his cheeks. "I am so sorry."

"Why would you do that to me? You promised."

"I was afraid, afraid of what it would cost us, knowing who Cam was and what was going to happen because of it."

"All of you put Juliana and her baby in grave danger. You just did not care. I cannot forgive that. I will not ever forget the callous disregard you all felt toward us. You did not care enough. You did not love enough."

"You are right, Sabine. We did not love enough. We were selfish, careless, and deceptive. The price we paid was losing you."

"It was not payment enough for what you did to me. Not them, Blake, but you... You ripped my heart out of my chest, and you cast it aside. I did not mean anything to you."

"How can you say that?"

"You laid in my bed, loving me, making a promise I believed that you would never keep anything from me again, and in the next instance, it began all over again."

He hung his head. "You are right," was all he said.

I stood there, holding my apple and looking at him. When the tears started to fall, I closed my eyes.

'How am I supposed to do this? I cannot.'

'Yes, you can. You are pure at heart. You can forgive him.'

'No, I cannot not.'

'Look deep in your heart. You love him truly. He is your match, Sabine. Go to him. Feel him. You will know.'

I opened my eyes to see his. I took one step forward, and then another. We were at arm's length from one another. His hand slowly rose, and when he touched my face, I felt him lose his breath. I did not move. I wanted to run, but I did not. Raiden was right. My heart exploded; I knew then that I did love him deeply. I needed his touch. I needed him. His thumb slid across my cheek to wipe a tear, then across my lips.

"I love you," he whispered.

I closed my eyes, shaking my head. "I love you," I whispered.

Before I knew what happened, his mouth covered mine. I let him kiss me. I wanted him to kiss me. I missed him so much. He pulled away. I looked at him, then turned and walked away. I left him standing there in the back courtyard, went to my room, bolted the door, and I cried myself to sleep.

When the light of day came, I went back to my study door. I needed to do this. I had to get the tomes in there. I looked down at them, knowing we needed to read them. I reached for the latch, this time flipping it up and pushing the door open. As I stepped through, there was nothing. I continued into the room, shaking, and forced myself to look at the spot where I had ended my life. The blood was gone, but the memory was still so very fresh in my mind. I closed my eyes, trying to remember what I was thinking when I put my sword to my throat. The only thing I could see was Blake, his eyes, the pain in them. *Does he know what he did that caused me to do that?* I needed to trust.

Raiden said to trust. This would be the hardest thing I had ever done.

I walked around to my desk and triggered the latch, then went out into the hallway and brought each tome in, closing the door behind me and bolting it. As I carried the first tome into the secret room, I saw all the gowns that Clare had brought; there had to be at least twenty of them. I grabbed a few and brought them out, laying them across a chair, then grabbed another tome and brought more gowns out. I did this until the last tome was resting on the floor of the secret room. When I picked up the last of the gowns, I saw the one that had been intended for my marriage to Blake. It was covered, so I sat the gowns down and pulled the covering off of it. Still as beautiful as the day I put it on. I ran my fingers along the lace. Shaking my head, I covered the gown, picked up the ones I had set down, and left the secret room.

I could not be in there anymore. I needed to leave. I had to ride. I searched for him in my mind.

'Please take me away.'

I went out into the courtyard, where he was waiting for me. Climbing up using the fountain, I leaned into him. I did not have my sword or any food; I just needed to be free. Turning my head, I saw Blake walking toward me, and as I stared at him, the tears began to fall. He stopped and looked at me, seeing the tears. I shook my head, and Raiden was gone. "Do not stop. Just ride, please."

When I returned, he was waiting for me at the fountain, though I did not want to see him. I could not do this. I could not forgive him. I slid off of Raiden and tried to walk away from him.

"Sabine," he whispered.

57

"I am not sure I can do this, Blake."

"We can start by talking."

"I am afraid that I want to yell at you more than I want to talk to you."

"Well, yelling is a start. If you need to yell, then yell."

I sat down on the opposite side of the fountain, not wanting to be near him. He moved slightly closer. "Please stay there," I said. He sat back down. "Why did you rip my heart out like that?"

"To be honest, Sabine, at the time, I did not realize that was what I was doing. I thought I was protecting you."

"And now?"

"Now, now I know that I cannot protect you like I want to. I cannot shield you from anything. When I saw you that night, I realized you were serious. I wish I could have done something different to stop you."

"You could not have stopped me."

"When I saw you do that to yourself, everything was gone for me."

"It is always about you and your brothers. The bond you have is greater than the love any of you have for us. It is more important to follow the leader than it is to love your women."

"I am sorry that you think that way. Loving you, Sabine, is what I live for. When I believed you to be dead, I could not go on. I waited for someone to come and fight us. I waited to die. I cannot live in a world where you are not."

"You should have thought of that before you betrayed me, before you put Juliana and her baby in danger. You should have thought of that when you laid in my bed, touching me and promising me that you would always be honest with me." My voice was getting louder and harder. "You should have thought about that, the moment Charles told you to keep it from me. I should have been the only thing that mattered to you, Blake, but I was a second thought. How do you think I felt when Louis said he was looking for his son? I knew right then that you had lied. You knew I knew, and you tried so hard to justify it."

"Sabine," he said.

"No, it will not work this time. Your sweet, loving voice will not work. You hurt me as much as it hurt when he plunged that dagger into me. You took everything I had to give you, and you gave me nothing in return. You used me for your own self-gratification, not caring that you had the power to end me, and you did, Blake. I loved you so much, and you took that and discarded it as if it was waste. You do not get to use your voice or your sad eyes to persuade me to forgive you."

He did not say a word in response, but I felt him get up and come to me. He knelt down in front of me, and I closed my eyes so I could not see his. He took my hands in his. "There are not enough days in this life for me to say how sorry I am that I hurt you so badly and so deeply that you felt the only way to get away from me was to end your own life, to take you away from me forever. You will never know how deeply that cut into me. I had seven, nearly eight, seasons to think about it, yet each day was the same, I would wake to see you slide that sword across your throat. Each day I heard your words in my mind. I will never know how you felt, but I do know how I felt. Please open your eyes and look at me." I shook my head. I knew if I did I was going to give in. "When I felt your heart beat for the last time, I knew it was broken and I was the one who broke it. I made the choices I made, and you are right... You paid the price for them. You paid each and every time, and you are right. I did not think about how it would make you feel. I just figured I could always fix it. Sabine, watching you do that just to be rid

59

of me ended me. It changed me. I could never hurt you like that again. I do not ever want to hurt you like that. The fact that you came back to save us… You are incredible gift, and I am beyond the luckiest man who has ever lived to know that you loved me once."

I could not do this. I pulled my hands from him and ran. I ran to the stables, got Raiden, and ran. "Do not stop," I yelled at him. He ran and ran. I cried while I lay on him. I cried because I knew in my heart that I could not forgive him. Raiden ran and ran, and I had no idea where he ran to. For all I knew, he could have run in a circle. I just needed to be free. I needed to be away from him. I must have fallen asleep because I felt someone lift me and carry me. I woke up in my bed alone. I sat up and looked around.

'How did I get here?'

'Blake.'

Great. He was back to carrying me around. I really needed to get off the emotional ride he had me on. There was too much to do. I wondered when Charles would be back.

I was hungry, so I changed into a gown the color of Blake's eyes. On my way out the door, I put on my crown. It protected me, I believe. I giggled as I opened the door, but instantly, my mood was ruined. There he was.

"May we finish our talk?"

"No, I have other things to do that are more important, and what are you doing in here? All of you are banned from the house. You need to go. I promised Westin that there would be no more fighting, yet another thing you put into jeopardy when you all chose to do what you did. I am not in a forgiving state of mind, Blake. Please leave and do not return here."

60

"Sabine, we need to talk."

"I cannot."

"Sabine, too much time has passed. We need to get this all out. Come. You can eat, and we will go for a ride, and then Westin will not hear you yell at me."

"I have already told you, I have things to do today."

He smiled at me. "You cannot avoid this forever, you know. Eventually, you will talk to me."

I walked away from him and went to the kitchen, starving, for I had not eaten in a while. "Hello, Francis. Do we have any eggs? I am so hungry."

"Of course, child. Sit down. I will get you some. I see Master Blake carried you in last night. Did he stay with you?"

"No, he was outside my door this morning, though. He wants me to forgive him."

"Are you going to?"

"No, I cannot forgive what he did, Francis, and I am sorry, but I really do not want to talk about this. I want him the furthest from my mind."

"As you wish. Here you go," she said as she sat a plate of eggs in front of me.

They were so good. I was still hungry, though, so I took a few apples with me when I left to go to my study. I had so much to do, and I want to start reading the tomes. I wondered where Charles was, and when he would be back. Just then, there was a knock on the door. "Come in," I said. The door opened. "Well, I was just wondering when you would arrive back, and here you are."

He nodded his head. "I have located Clare and Charlotte, and they will return soon. Also, I have found a man who is a mapper." He turned and held his arm out. When the man stepped into my doorway, I nearly lost my breath. He was beautiful. His eyes were the color of the sky on a clear day, his hair dark and curly, and he had hair on his face, as well. "This is Christopher. I discovered him in a small village a few days' ride south from here. Christopher, this is Queen Sabine of Whispering Wind."

He bowed. "Your Majesty, I was told by Charles that you have a map you would like drawn."

I walked up to him and shook his hand. He turned our hands, kissing the back of mine, and then stood up. He was very tall and very beautiful.

"Yes, I do not know how big this Kingdom is, and I would like for you to ride with me and map it out."

"I would be honored."

"I will pay you for your services, no matter how long it takes. What would you charge me?"

"Excuse me, Your Majesty, but when a King asks me to draw maps, I am not expecting a payment, just a room and a meal will be enough."

"Well, the room and the meal I can provide, as well as payment. So let us see how well you can map my Kingdom, and we shall settle on a price so that you can move on to another place."

"I do not have much. Is there someone who can help me to my room?"

I crinkled my nose. "I am sorry. Did you believe you would be sleeping here?"

"I am sorry for assuming, Your Majesty, but it would be the custom."

I did not mean to do it, but it happened I giggled. "Oh, sir, you are mistaken, indeed. You can camp in the barracks with the men. There is but family who live within these walls, and it would not be proper to have a stranger come into our home.

Charles will give you your own room, and I will send someone to get you when I need you. Either that, or I will come. The stables are across from the barracks."

He nodded and they left.

Wow, wait until Rebecca sees him. I laughed.

*****

On their way to the barracks, Christopher asked Charles about me. "Now, that is one beautiful woman, and she is the Queen."

"Yes, she is, on both accounts."

"Would it be wrong to inquire as to why she is not married? She seems very young."

"I am afraid that if you wish to know things about her that you are going to have to ask her yourself. If it is one thing I have learned over the years, it is not to assume anything where she is concerned. She is a very smart woman. I do have one suggestion for you."

He chuckled. "What would that be?"

"Do not touch her."

"It would not be an honorable thing to touch a Queen, but I am a curious man, so I have to ask why?"

Charles laughed. "Because she belongs to another and she does not like when people touch her without her permission."

"Oh, so there is a man in her life."

"I have said more than I should."

They walked into the barracks, where Charles introduced him to his brothers and then showed him to his room. "So I should wait here for her?"

"Oh, no, please feel free to explore and do as you wish, just do not enter the castle." Charles chuckled.

Christopher unpacked what things he had, his quills, ink, and journal and went for a walk. He checked on the stables to make sure his horse was being taken care of. He spotted Raiden and Spirit. "Well, now, you are just a beautiful boy, and your friend here is just as lovely," he said to them. He was standing there admiring them when a guard walked up.

"Charles sent me to introduce myself. I am Ben."

"Glad to make your acquaintance. I am Christopher. Tell me about these two boys. They are lovely horses."

"The brown one is Raiden, the Queen's horse, and the tan one is Spirit, Princess Rebecca's."

"I would have not chosen any other horse for a Queen."

Ben chuckled. "She did not choose him. He chose her. He was her father's horse."

"Well, thank you Ben. It was nice to meet you. I think I will go for a walk and get myself acquainted with my surroundings."

"If you need anything, sir, just find me."

He nodded and went for a walk. Once in the village, he stopped by a few shops and talked to the people. Everyone was kind to him and welcoming. He liked it there. On his way back to the barracks, he saw Juliana walking through the back garden and stopped. "Wow," he said out loud. She was laughing, and then he saw her pick up Isabel and twirl her around on their way into the kitchen. Ben was walking up. "Pardon me, Ben, who was that maiden?"

"I am sorry, sir. I did not see. If you could tell me what she looked like, I might be able to help you."

"She was a young girl, playing with a child. She went into the kitchen there. Is she one of the kitchen maids?"

Ben laughed. "Oh, no, sir, that was Princess Juliana, and the child was her daughter, Princess Isabel."

"Well, there are a great many Princesses here."

"Yes, sir, there are."

*****

Rebecca came to my study to see if I wanted to go for a ride.

"Yes, I would love to, actually. I have some things I want to talk to you about. Oh, and there is new man in the barracks. Charles found a man to help me with the boundaries of this Kingdom. His name is Christopher. Tomorrow, at the light of day, we are going to start mapping the kingdom. Hey, do you think Spirit would let him ride him?"

"I am sure it will be all right. Are you going to wear that gown, or are you going to change?"

"I think I will change. Oh, those are the gowns that Clare brought after... well, you know. Should I grab your sword?"

"I suppose. You know they go nuts when we are without them."

I ran upstairs and changed into my new boy clothes, then grabbed my sword and Rebecca's. She was waiting for me in the great hall, and we walked out together, laughing at something she told me about Isabel. Christopher was there talking to Ben.

"Hello, Ben," I said.

"Your Majesty," he said and bowed. Christopher bowed as well.

We continued walking. "Wow, he is beautiful," Rebecca said.

"I know," I told her, and we both giggled.

Christopher said to Ben, "Now, who is that?"

"That would be Princess Rebecca."

He watched us go to the stables. "Why do they wear men's clothes?"

"You would not believe me if I told you."

"Try me," he stated.

"It is not my place to talk about the Queen. Perhaps you should speak to Charles, or even the Queen."

"Charles is less than informative. He told me the same thing, that I should ask her. He also said she belonged to another. Would you know anything about that?"

Ben chuckled, telling him, "More than I should, to be truthful. But again, I would have to say, if you want to know about her, just ask her. She is a very nice person."

He watched as we walked our horses out of the stables. "There was no one in the stables when I was in there. Who saddled those horses?" Christopher asked.

"They did, of course. It is very rare that Her Majesty lets anyone saddle him. She rides him bare back a great deal."

"Remarkable," he said.

As we trotted past them, I nodded to Christopher, and we headed into the village. Once we got past the orchards, we climbed the hilltop, and then we were gone. Raiden slowed down when we got to the little river.

"This is where you were the day you gave me your hair."

"Yes, it is. It is a very lovely place."

"Are we still in Whispering Wind?"

"I asked that same question. Raiden said yes, as far as the eye could see, among other things." I looked at him, and he put his head down and walked away.

"You seem a bit irritated this morning. Is everything all right?"

"Well, it would seem that my horse," I paused and looked at him again before continuing, "likes to give advice. I am not sure what any of it means, but I am not happy with it, either."

"Okay, I am lost. Raiden is giving you advice, and there is a very lovely new man in town who is going to draw maps of Whispering Wind. What?" She giggled.

"I have been coming here nearly every day to sit. Apparently, this is not even close to the boundary of Whispering Wind. Well, I realized I have no idea how big this Kingdom is, hence Christopher. Raiden told me that I needed to forgive Blake, that he is my match, and that our children are important. I cannot bring myself to forgive him, Rebecca. I do not trust him any longer."

"Well, no matter what your horse says..." She turned and looked at Raiden. "I do not believe that you should do what does not make you happy. Do you love him?"

"With every part of me, I do. Yes."

She did not say anything.

"He kissed me the other night in the back courtyard. I let him. I even kissed him back."

"Wow, so then you forgave him?"

"No, I cannot get past what they did to us. After what he did to me, the wound is too deep to heal, Rebecca."

"Do you want to forgive him?"

"No, I do not, and that is the problem."

"Well, I can see what the problem is then. You love him still, but you cannot forgive him. Listen to me. You were gone for seven seasons, Sabine. He was not. Again, like when you were in the darkness, we all lived. For you, the memories were still new. Blake has lived with what he did for nearly two years. Perhaps he has changed. Perhaps it is time to forgive him."

"If that is the case, then it will be nearly two years before I can make that happen. I just need to face the truth of what took place. None of us has really talked about it yet. Charles is like a little servant man, agreeing with me, not yelling at me or questioning me. So perhaps we all need to sit down and have a chat. Would you come with me?"

"Oh, I would not miss that for anything, and Juliana must be there as well. She has been giving James so much grief. He is not allowed near Isabel. If she sees him looking at her, she just takes her in the house," Rebecca told me.

"I am not getting involved in that. I feel the same way she does. He did not think twice about her losing that baby that night, so I do not believe he should be a part of the joy she brings. Not yet anyway."

Changing the topic, she stood and twirled around. "So this is all Whispering Wind?"

I stood and joined her. "Apparently."

We stayed by the river, just lying in the grass doing nothing and not talking. It felt good. I knew that Rebecca had a great deal to figure out, as we all did. I had faith that we would.

"We should get back."

"I can see why you come here all the time."

I laughed. "I do not come here. Raiden brings me here. I think there is something important here, and I just have not figured it out. Perhaps the story lies in the tomes. I am going to get Christopher started on his mapping, and then I think it is time you and I started to read."

"Sounds good to me."

We rode back into the village, and as we rode past Clare's, I noticed a glow coming from her window.

"There is your Christopher," Rebecca whispered.

I looked up and saw him walking toward us. "He is not my Christopher," I whispered back as I got off Raiden.

I ran up to Clare's and knocked on the door. When she opened it, she threw her arms around me. "Oh, Sabine, welcome home."

I laughed. "No, welcome home to you. Thank you so much, Clare, for coming back."

"The stories we heard about you were not truth. I am so glad. I left all the gowns at the castle with Charles, and I see you got them." She stepped back to admire her handy work with my boy clothes.

"I did, and they are lovely. I will come by tomorrow in the afternoon, and we can have a chat. Did your mother make it back?"

"Not yet, but she should be here in a few days."

I smiled. "I will see you tomorrow."

We hugged again, and I left. Rebecca was sitting on Spirit, gazing at Christopher. I touched her hand. "He is very beautiful, yes, but he is off limits until I get my map." We giggled.

As we made our way to the great gates, we passed him.

He bowed and said, "Your Majesty."

I smiled at him. "Christopher, I would like to take a ride tomorrow. Would you be available after the morning meal?"

"I am at your service."

"Thank you. Good night, Christopher."

He nodded. "Your Majesty."

Rebecca leaned over and whispered, "Are you going to make him call you that all the time?"

I giggled. "No, I just do not want him to think I am an easy mark. If he respects me, he will call me that, no matter what I say. Besides, I am getting used to it."

I got off Raiden at the fountain, and Rebecca took the horses to the stables. I was walking into the castle when I felt him, so I stopped and closed my eyes. He was getting closer, and stopped right behind me.

"Sabine," he whispered.

I swallowed. "I cannot do this right now," I whispered.

"It has been long enough that we have been apart. We need to talk."

I did not say anything. I just stood there, trying not to be angry, trying not to scream, and then burst into tears. I took a deep breath and turned to face him.

"I am not sure that I can forgive you."

He bent his head down to touch my forehead. "I love you."

"I am not sure that it is enough," I whispered. When I turned away, he touched my arm.

"Sabine," he pleaded.

"Please, Blake, I just cannot do this." He let go then, and I went inside. I took a deep breath and cleared my head. Hearing chatter in the kitchen, I headed that way. When I walked in, it was Juliana, Camille, Julia, Rebecca, and Francis. I sat in my usual seat and joined in.

We talked about everything, mostly about the newest thing Isabel was doing. We had pie and laughed, and chatted and laughed some more. I excused myself and went to my room. A little bit later, Camille knocked on the door. "Would you like to take a bath, Sabine?"

I smiled at her and sighed. "How do you always know? Please, Camille, I am sure there is someone else who can do this for me."

"As I have said before, it is my pleasure to take care of you, Sabine."

"Well, thank you, and yes, a bath would be lovely."

She went and gathered up the two girls that worked in the kitchen, and before I knew it, the tub was full. I smiled at them as they all left. "Would you like me to wash your hair?"

"That would be nice. Thank you. When you are done, though, I think I can comb it out."

"It is not a problem to do it," she reassured me.

"It is fine. Really, I can do it. Thank you, Camille."

She washed my hair and left. I washed and then leaned back in the water to relax. I felt myself falling asleep, so I got out, wrapped a blanket around me, and climbed into bed. I did not want to think, so I just slept.

The light of the day came too fast for me. I wanted to stay in bed, but I knew I had to take Christopher out this morning. I got up, put on my boy clothes, and went down to the kitchen to eat. No one was up yet, so it must have been early. Francis was in a good mood. I ate and went to the barracks. The guards standing outside bowed to me, and I noticed they were new recruits.

I smiled at them. "Would you be so kind as to gather up Christopher?"

"Yes, Your Majesty," the one replied quickly.

"I will be in the stables saddling the horses."

"I can do that for you, My Lady."

"Thank you, but it is not necessary," I said and headed in to see Raiden.

"Good morning, you two." Raiden neighed at me. "Spirit, I need for you to allow Christopher to ride you today. Would that be all right?"

He looked at Raiden, and I was sure they were talking. After a moment, he looked back at me and nodded.

"Thank you. We are going to ride to the end of the Kingdom to the west. I think that would be a good starting point." I looked at Raiden and asked him, "You are sure you know the boundaries?" He nodded.

"Excuse me, Your Majesty, but are you talking to that horse?" Christopher asked.

I chuckled. "Yes, I am. He is a very special horse."

"I have heard that. I will get mine saddled."

"It is not necessary. I have saddled Spirit for you. Today, you will ride him, if that is all right."

"I was under the impression that no one rides these two boys except for you and Princess Rebecca."

I turned and looked at him. "And how do you know of Rebecca?"

"Well, I saw you the day before, and I asked Ben who she was."

"And what did Ben tell you?"

"Just who she was."

"Hmmm... I will have to have a talk with him."

"Oh, please, he did not do anything wrong. He told me if I wanted to know anything that I was to ask you."

I walked toward the doors to open them, and Raiden and Spirit followed me. I opened the doors, they went out, and then I closed them again. As I was getting ready to climb up on Raiden, I felt him. I climbed on and looked at him. His eyes were full of pain, and when he saw Christopher climb on Spirit, I saw panic. We walked out through the village and turned west.

"I do not know what kind of knowledge you have obtained from those around me concerning me and my horse or Rebecca and Spirit, but what is about to happen may frighten you."

"I am about to take a ride in the countryside with a beautiful woman."

"Christopher, you should mind yourself and the manner in which you speak to me."

"I apologize, Your Majesty. I am only speaking the truth."

"Well, thank you, but it is not necessary for you to comment on the way I look. It has nothing to do with what I have asked you here for. Now, as I was saying, being on Spirit is a privilege.

72

The only reason you are sitting there is because I have asked him to allow you. I need for you to hold on, and do not let go."

He smiled. "Excuse me, Your Majesty, but I do know how to ride a horse."

"Not this one. He is special." I smiled. "You ready?"

He nodded.

I leaned into Raiden," Will you take us to the boundary in the west?" He nodded. I sat up, and we were gone. I looked over at Christopher, and his face said it all. He was terrified at what was happening. In moments, we were at the boundary, skidding to a stop.

He jumped off Spirit and backed up. "What sort of trickery was that?"

I could not help but laugh. "That was not trickery," I said between giggles.

"Well, it was not normal."

"There is much you will learn and much you will see that is not believable. But it is truth."

He stood there looking at Spirit then me. "Amazing."

"Yes, it is. Well, according to Raiden, this is the boundary."

"How far are we from the castle?"

"I do not know. That is what your job is. But seeing as how Raiden and Spirit are the only ones who know the boundaries of this Kingdom, I thought we could begin here. I can only believe that this Kingdom is massive in size. I do not have the time to travel it with you on a regular horse, so today we can mark out spots for you to travel back here on your horse. Mine does not travel in regular time as yours does."

"Yes, I can see that."

"For you, what is days, are just moments for me."

"All right, well, are we going to do the whole Kingdom today?"

Raiden shook his head. "Apparently not, so we should get started. The sooner we begin the sooner we are done."

Christopher took down the satchel he had brought with him, pulled out a piece of wood and that strange thing Ben gave me to hang my decree on the great gates. He walked over and slammed the wood into the ground, and then tied a piece of red cloth to it.

We continued to do this all day along the Western boundary. When we turned, the light of the day was leaving. I was amazed at how big just the west boundary was. "I think we should get back," I said. "The dark of the night is coming, and I have not eaten all day."

"I think you might be right. I only have one more piece left. I will have to make some more."

"I will have someone help you. Thank you, Christopher, for doing this for me."

"It is going to be a huge job. Once we get all the wood in, I will ride it all with my own horse and start mapping it out."

I smiled. "You ready?"

He chuckled. "Not really."

I giggled, and we were off. We slowed as we came to the village and took our time walking back. Rebecca was waiting for us at the fountain when we walked up.

"So was he a nice ride?" she asked.

"Oh, he is magnificent," Christopher said.

She smiled. "I was talking to Spirit, but I am glad that he was kind to you."

Christopher chuckled and shook his head as he climbed down.

"Rebecca, this is Christopher. Christopher, this is my sister, Princess Rebecca of Whispering Wind."

She gave me a look and smiled. He took her hand and kissed the back of it.

"Princess, it is my pleasure to make your acquaintance. I appreciate you allowing me to ride your horse," he said as he bowed to her.

"You are welcome, but all I did was ask him. He was the one who decided to allow it."

I climbed down. "I need to go again in the morning, and probably for a few days after that. Would you make sure it is all right with Spirit if he would come with us?"

"I am sure he would not mind, right boy?" she said as she reached up to rub his nose. He nodded at her. "He is good with that."

We walked back to the stables with Christopher. "If you would excuse me, Your Majesty and Your Highness, I am one hungry man. Good Evening, and I will see you in the morning," he said to me as he bowed.

"Good night, Christopher," we said together as we walked into the stables.

"He is beautiful, Sabine. How was your day?"

"He is, and it was good. We marked out the entire Western edge of the Kingdom. It took us all day on these two, so I can only imagine how big it really is. It is amazing really."

"Well, Francis kept some food warm for you. Come on, and I will sit with you while you eat. We have much to talk about."

"We do?"

She laughed. "Oh, yes, we do." We walked out of the stables, arm in arm, and made our way to the kitchen doors. As we approached, I felt him coming up behind me.

"I will be right in," I whispered to her. She turned and saw him coming.

"I will be right in here if you need me."

"I will be fine," I said as she went in. I closed my eyes and took a deep breath. He stopped just behind me, so I turned to face him.

"Would it matter to you if I told you that I cannot bear this separation?" he said.

I did not speak, just looked into his eyes. I think I was trying to see his remorse, his sorrow for his actions. Not so sure that I saw what I needed, I said to him, "I told you that I cannot do this, Blake. I am sorry, but I do not feel that I can trust you again. We have been over this already."

"It is not in me to just stop these feelings, Sabine."

I walked past him, moving further away from the door, as I did not think it would be right for Rebecca to hear us.

"I have the same feelings, Blake, but what you did to me overrides those feelings. If this is causing you pain, then I am sorry, but just because you feel the way you do, does not mean my feelings have had a chance to catch up to yours. Yours are nothing compared to what I feel at this moment. Do you even understand what you did to me?"

He stood there looking at me, not saying a word.

"I did what I did to escape you," I continued. "I could not look at you another minute. That is how badly you hurt me, and it was not just the one time, Blake. It was time and time again. What we shared... the love, the tenderness, everything... it meant nothing to you."

"How can you say that?"

"How? You took all that I was, and you thought nothing of deceiving me, of lying to me. It had become second nature to you. Make Sabine feel like she is the only thing that matters one moment, and then in the next, you were conspiring with Charles to lie to me. How can I say that? Are you serious? I am not a child, Blake. I do have a mind of my own. I do have emotions. But you are right I am pure, and I am innocent, and it did blind me, this obsession I had in wanting to know what this huge mystery was. But you know what? I do not care anymore!" I yelled. "You stand here wanting what you want and not caring one bit about what I want or what I need. You have not changed. None of you have. Well, you know what, Blake? I HAVE! None of you are privileged enough to know what is in my mind any longer. You all blew the trust I had for you. I gave you EVERYTHING I had to give, and what did I get in return? Dead, that is what I got."

I went to walk away, and he grabbed my arm, his first mistake. I turned and twisted his arm behind him and pushed him away. "Do not presume you can touch me without my permission!" I screamed and turned to walk away.

I felt him coming. "You will not walk away from me, Sabine," he said. I saw Rebecca and Francis come out of the door, and turned to see the men at the barracks. He grabbed my arms like he had that night in my study. "You need to deal with this," he screamed at me.

I kneed him in his private parts, and when he bent over, I brought my knee up again and slammed his face into my knee. "You forget your place, Blake. Do not make the mistake of touching me again," I said.

I turned, but he grabbed me around the waist. He whispered, "I love you," in my ear just before I slammed my head into his face.

When I turned, I saw Christopher running up. "Your Majesty, are you all right?"

"This is none of your concern. Please, leave us alone."

He backed up.

"I told you before," I stated as I drew my sword on him. "Do not presume you can touch me without my permission."

"So you are willing to run me through to prove your point?"

"I believe my point was proven two years ago." I pointed my sword at him, and he stepped forward. "Blake," I said. Again, he moved forward. I swallowed and slammed my sword into his chest, all the way to the hilt, feeling the heat from the flame. I was right in front of him. "I will not take my life again. You are not worth it!" I shouted and pushed him away. Charles had come running up. "Keep him away from me, or I will banish him."

Charles nodded, and I walked toward the kitchen. I looked up at Rebecca, and she had that smile on her face. When I reached her, she whispered as I walked by, "Good for you." I went in and threw my sword on the table, sat down, and cried.

"What gives him the right to assume I am over this?"

She came over and hugged me, trying to offer comfort. Needing to be alone, I got up and went to my room, laid on my bed, and cried.

When the light of the day broke the sky, I was awake. I think I was awake before that, but that was when I got up and made my way to the kitchen. Francis was there making bread. "Hi," I greeted her, noticing my sword on the table.

"I was going to move it, but I remembered what happened to that child and I did not want that."

I smiled, saying, "I am sorry." After picking up my sword, I put it in its sheath. "Francis, could you put some food, maybe some bread and some fruit in my satchel? I will be gone all day again with Christopher, and yesterday I did not eat."

"I know. I made you some food. Rebecca said you would be leaving early. Can I say that was quite spectacular last night? I am glad you two are working this out. It is good that he knows how much he hurt you."

"I might have gotten a bit carried away, running him through. He was not going to give up, though, and I was tired."

"Well, he deserved that and much more," she affirmed.

"Thank you for that, Francis." I ate, took my satchel, and went to the stables. Once there, I asked the guard at the barracks to get Christopher, and then I went in to saddle the horses.

'You did not need to run him through.'

"You stay out of this. It is all your fault. If I had just dismissed him in the first place, it would have never happened. I do not wish to discuss this with you."

'He is your match, Sabine.'

"Stop saying that. I will not discuss this."

"Were we discussing something, Your Majesty?" Christopher was standing behind me.

"No, we were not. I was talking to Raiden."

He smiled. "All right, are you ready to go?"

I nodded and we walked out of the stables. As I was getting up, Blake walked out of the barracks. I turned my head from him, kicked Raiden in the sides, and in a moment, we were at the Northwest corner of Whispering Wind. "I do not think I will ever get used to that."

I said, chuckling, "I suppose not."

He did not say much for most of the morning. When we stopped to eat our midday meal, he sat there looking at me.

"What?" I asked.

"I was just wondering something, and please, Your Majesty, if I am out of line, please tell me."

"Well, first of all, my name is Sabine. You may call me Sabine."

"A beautiful name for a beautiful woman. Thank you. But I was wondering if you were all right. Last night you were pretty upset."

"Thank you for being concerned, but I am fine."

"That Guard, Blake, I believe his name is... you killed him last night, and yet I saw him standing in the door when we left."

"Yes."

"How can that be?"

"I would not know where to begin."

"I know it is none of my business."

"No, it is not," I said a bit curter than I had intended. "I am sorry, Christopher. I should not be so short with you. I have had a rough couple of years. That is all."

"My apologies, Sabine. It is not my place to pry. We should get back to our task at hand."

I picked up what was left of our lunch, and we continued on. The dark of the night was soon upon us, and we still had not reached the end. "I think we should call it a day," I suggested.

"Whatever you wish." He smiled warmly at me.

We made it back to the castle in no time at all, though it was actually in the middle of the dark of night by the time we returned. Ben was standing guard at the great gates. "Ben, would you be a dear and put Raiden and Spirit up for me?"

"Yes, Your Majesty," he said as he bowed.

"Good night, Christopher. I think perhaps we should take the day off tomorrow. I would like to get some well needed sleep."

"That is fine. Perhaps I will see you in the light of the day." He bowed and I walked away.

I was too tired to even go into the kitchen to see if there was anything to eat. I went straight to my room, undressing as I walked to the bed, and climbed in without anything on. I was asleep before my head hit the pillow. I do not know how long I

80

was asleep before I woke. The room was glowing from the fire, but I did not remember there being a fire. I sat up and saw him sitting in his chair.

"Why are you here, Blake?" I asked, not realizing the blanket had fallen away.

"You know why I am here, Sabine."

"I am tired, and I do not want to do this with you." I laid back down, but I did not pull the blanket up. I was still warm and did not remember that I did not have my sleeping gown on. Rolling over on my side, I snuggled the pillow.

"There was a time when you would hold me like that."

"That time is gone."

"Why are you being so cruel?" he asked me, sounding confused.

"Why were you so cruel to me?"

"Because I was a fool and did not realize that I was hurting you," he claimed.

"So the fact that I repeatedly told you that you were hurting me was not enough?"

"You always forgave me, Sabine. Why can you not forgive me now?"

"You are not hearing what I am saying to you, Blake. You tore my heart out. I have nothing left. I have nothing to give you, and I do not trust you. I do not understand how you can say one thing and do another. I do not want that in my life. You are not my happiness, Blake. My happiness is my responsibility. It is not you."

"I cannot mend what we have if you do not let me in."

"I do not want it mended."

"How can you say that, Sabine? You love me. You said so."

"It is how I feel, and I cannot stop that, but I can stop you from hurting me again and so that is what I am doing."

"So this pain I am feeling over this is not within you?"

"No, what is in me is anger and disappointment. You were supposed to love me, but your idea of love is not the same as mine." I felt him stand. "Please, Blake, I need for you to leave."

He moved closer to the bed. "Why, because you can feel it, too?"

I felt the tears. "Yes," I whispered.

He was on the bed, and I was in his arms before I could object. "You belong with me, Sabine. Search your heart. You know it to be truth."

I shook my head. "No, it cannot be as you wish. It does not matter what I feel. Anger overrides it. Distrust overrides it."

He pulled me closer, and I knew I was going to give in. I could not stand to be this close to him and not kiss him. I could not do this. I tried to get away, but he would not let me go. "I need for you to feel my love, Sabine. I need you just as you need me."

"No, I do not," I denied through my tears.

"Do not cry, my love. I will not fail you again."

"Yes, you will. You always do, and I cannot live like that."

He slowly turned me. I tried to stop him, but I was so tired. I wanted to kiss him. When we were face to face, he put his hand on my face. "I want nothing more than to love you. I can breathe again now that you are alive. I was slowly suffocating without you."

I shook my head. "No, Blake, I cannot trust you with my love, with my heart. You have proven to me time and time again that I cannot trust you."

"Let me prove to you that you can now," he whispered so close to my mouth I could feel his breath. Before I could respond, he kissed me. I wanted to pull away, but my body would not move. He opened his mouth just enough to cause me to open mine, and I was gone. My body won over; my arms

82

instinctively wrapped around his neck, and I pulled myself up his body. His hands were moving slowly up my back. I realized then that I had nothing on, but he did not stop. His hand trailed down my back, and he still did not stop. He went to my thigh, lifted it over his hip, and continued down to my knee. Our lips only parted to breathe. He trailed his hand back to my head where he entwined his fingers in my hair. As he held me tight and close, I arched my body, and he moved with me, slipping his hand under my back and lifting me so I was pressed against him. His breath caught, but he did not stop. He did not run away. He did not pause not for a moment.

Our kiss deepened, and it felt so good to feel his touch again. He knew I would not run from him; he knew this as much as I did. I loved him so deeply, and he had been careless with that love before. My hands worked his shirt off his shoulders, so I pulled out of our kiss and started kissing his neck and his shoulders. I could hear his moans, and they made me want more of him.

I pulled up, wanting more of him. I wanted all of him. He did not stop me when I started to untie his pants. His eyes were closed when I finished, so I kissed him just as sweetly as he kissed me. "I want to see you. I want to feel you just as you feel me," I whispered into his mouth. He closed his eyes and swallowed. I moved and he stood up. Gingerly, I put my hands on the waist of his pants and slowly pulled them down. I let him take a step back and finish for me. He was magnificent to look at. I pulled him on to the bed and declared shyly, "You are so beautiful."

His mouth covered mine, and we lay there side by side kissing. His muscles were so firm, and his arms were as big as my head. I kissed him deeply, and he pulled me close. I felt his body against mine. Curious, I trailed my hand down his side to his hip. His eyes never left mine, and I finally saw what I needed to see. I saw the remorse and the sorrow as my touch brought him to tears. At that moment, I knew he would not betray me again. He truly loved me. I had no idea what I was doing; it just felt right to touch him like this. After everything we had been through before and the limits to our touching, for him, this was beyond anything else. He was doing this to show me how much I meant to him. I closed my eyes as he kissed me and turned me on my back. My legs moved up around his waist, and he lowered himself on top of me, placing himself carefully on my stomach. His hands on my face, he pulled away. "You are everything to me, Sabine. I love you. I cannot dishonor my Queen. Will you please be my wife?" I felt the tear that fell from his eye on my cheek.

"Yes," I whispered as he kissed me.

Chapter Six

$\mathfrak{I}$ woke wrapped in his arms, our bodies tangled in one another's. I had forgiven him. I knew that if he touched me I would. It was time to put all this anger away. He loved me. I knew he did. I lay listening to his heart beating as the light of the day was just arriving. It was a brand new day for us. I smiled thinking about what he had done for me the night before. Everything that he stood for, he had stripped away to allow this beautiful moment to happen. He showed me, in no uncertain terms, that he would not deceive me again.

I felt his heart beat change; he was waking, as well. His breathing changed, and I wondered if he would jump out of bed and leave me like he used to when we got ourselves into compromising positions like this. I guess I would find out. I tilted my head to meet his beautiful green eyes.

He did not speak, just covered my mouth with his. I pulled myself up his body so we were face to face as we kissed.

He pulled away. "Am I imagining this?"

I shook my head and kissed him.

"I have imagined this moment for so long, waking in your arms like this. You sure this is real?"

I bit him on the shoulder, and he laughed.

"You agreed to marry me last night," he said with a smile. I nodded, and he kissed me again. "No waiting. I want to do it today. Will you marry me today?"

"I have to finish with Christopher," I said. "But I think Raiden can take him. In fact, I am sure he would not mind."

"Then today? You will marry me today?"

I smiled at him. "Yes, I will marry you today."

He kissed me and kissed me, and then kissed me even more. We giggled and talked and kissed one another. Eventually, I pulled away from him. "Do not tell anyone. I want it to be a surprise. I will have Charles get everyone to meet in the back courtyard, and I will just show up in my gown."

"Oh, I like that," he said with a smile.

"But you must go before anyone finds you in here."

He nodded, kissed me, and got up. I was watching him dress. "I love you," he said as he kissed me. I hoped no one would see him leave.

I laid in bed and waited to get dressed. On my way out the door, I picked up my crown and put it on my head. I went to the kitchen, but Francis was not there, so I grabbed some fruit and went out the back door, where I stood and watched the light of the day come.

"Is everything all right, child?" I heard Francis say. I turned to see her walking up.

"Yes, it is. Good morning, Francis."

She chuckled and made her way into the kitchen. I searched for him in my mind.

'You win.'

'It was not a contest. You have forgiven him?'

'I have. We are to be married today. Happy?'

'I am, indeed. What changed your mind?'

'He proved to me last night that he was remorseful. He did something he would never have done before.'

'I am glad. He will not betray you again.'

'Well, I have trusted you from the beginning, and you have not let me down. I need you to take Christopher the rest of the way. Will you do that?'

'I will.'

I giggled and went into the kitchen. "Francis, I have something I need to tell you, but you must not repeat it to anyone. Can I trust you?"

"You do not even need to ask me that, child."

"Blake and I are getting married today, but no one is to know it. We are going to have a meeting in the back courtyard. I am just going to appear in my gown, and we are going to marry then. I need you to make some food, just whatever you have do not go overboard. I do not want to give it away."

She grabbed me and hugged me so tight. "I am so happy for you. It is about time you forgave him." When she pulled away, she had tears in her eyes.

"Oh, Francis, I have not forgiven him yet, but I love him and I cannot be without him. He makes me feel whole. The forgiveness will come later."

She laughed. "Come, let me feed you, child. You are wasting away. You are going to need your strength." She laughed again.

I ate and then went out into the world. It was a new day, and the sky was bluer than the bluest blue. I wandered into the village, eventually finding myself at Clare's.

"Hello, Sabine," she greeted me.

"Hello, Clare. Listen, I just stopped to see if you were busy today."

"No, just doing some sewing."

"Good. I was wondering if you could meet us all in the back courtyard just as the dark of the night is getting ready to come."

"Of course. What is going on?"

"Well, we are having a meeting of sorts, and seeing as how you are a part of my life, I thought perhaps you should be involved. Besides, I think of you as my friend, and well, I want you there."

She crinkled her eyes. "All right, is everything all right?"

I smiled at her. "I hope so." I left soon after and went down to Boland's, where I told him the same thing I told Clare. So now that was taken care of. I could not get the smile off my face. Everyone was going to be shocked.

I saw Blake as I walked through the great gates, and he stopped and looked at me. It was hard not to show him I was happy. I looked away and continued to the barracks. "Is Charles in his quarters?" I asked the guard.

He bowed. "Your Majesty, no, he is out in the orchards."

"Thank you. Would you mind getting Raiden ready?"

"My pleasure," he said.

While I waited for him, Christopher came out. "Well, good morning, Your Majesty."

I smiled at him. "Good Morning, Christopher, and it is Sabine."

He nodded. "Sabine. It has a nice ring to it."

The guard came out, saying, "Your horse, Your Majesty."

"Thank you," I said and turned to Christopher. "Will you please excuse me? I need to find Charles."

He nodded, and I rode off to the orchards. I saw Charles up in a tree pulling fruit from the branches, and I could not contain my laughter. "Well, that is something you do not see every day, my Man at Arms up a tree."

"Well, if what my brother tells me is truth, then I suppose we are going to need this fruit so I must do my part to help out."

"It would seem that we are then, and did your brother tell you to keep this secret?"

"Are secrets not what got us all here in the first place?"

"Yes, they have, but this secret shall reveal itself in a good way, not lead to a battle in our home." I turned and rode off then, leaving Raiden by the doors to the castle. "You can go back if you would like." He did. I went in and listened to see if I could hear anyone up. I heard nothing, so I went into my study and shut the door. Leaning my forehead against it, visions of the night before played out in my mind. My breath caught when I remembered how it felt when his hands touched me.

I felt him before he touched me. He embraced me, pulling me to him and sliding his hand up my body. His hand moved over my chest, grabbing my head and turning it to kiss me. His other hand was on my stomach, his fingers spread so they were just touching the lower part of my stomach, pressing me into him. I felt him moan deep in his chest.

"You are so beautiful," he whispered into my neck as we parted.

"You should not be here. Everyone will be waking up soon."

"I know. I thought, what a better way to throw everyone off if we fight in front of them."

I giggled, telling him, "That would work," before I turned in his arms. "Blake, what you did last night…"

"I had to show you that you meant everything to me. I love you, and I will always love you."

"You will explain things to me tonight, will you not?"

He smiled, reassuring me. "Oh, you can count on it. The mystery that began all of this will be over, and we can have our happiness."

I kissed him. "I like when you touch me."

"You have no idea how much I love when you touch me. It was very difficult, but I knew you would understand how sorry I am and how much you mean to me."

"I was looking for it in your eyes, and I just could not see it that is what made me so angry all the time. But last night, I finally saw it. I finally knew."

His mouth covered mine, and as he lifted me off the floor, my legs automatically wrapped around him. He leaned against the door, pressing himself into me. I felt myself explode inside, and with that came a groan. I had no idea what was happening to me, so I started to panic. Blake felt my body change and pulled away from me.

"It is all right, my love. We only have a little bit of time left, and I will explain everything to you."

"What is happening to me, Blake?"

"Your body is reacting to mine, as mine is to yours."

"I am scared."

"Me too, but we will do this together," he alleged, looking into my eyes.

What I saw calmed me. He was so in love with me; he was all I ever wanted. I could not deny that. Trust is what Raiden said, so I would trust him again. I nodded. He set me on my feet. "I should go. Will you do something for me today?"

"What is that?"

"Stop looking at me or everyone will know how we feel."

I giggled, promising, "I will try."

He kissed me and left, hopefully before anyone saw him.

I was sitting at my desk, looking at the secret room and thinking about putting on the gown later that night, when Juliana came in. "Was that Blake I saw leaving?"

"Yes, he came in here to tell me how much I hurt him when I slammed my sword into his chest."

Her eyes got huge. "I heard about that. I wish I would have been there to see it."

I laughed. "It was not pretty, that is for sure."

"So what did you say to him?"

"I told him to stay away from me or I would do it again." She laughed. "So what is going on with James?"

"He has agreed to stay away from Isabel as long as I let him watch her from a distance. I told him it was going to take a long time for me to forgive the fact that he put her in danger to begin with."

"Sounds reasonable. How is it going in the forgiveness department?"

"Oh, Sabine," she said, plopping down in the chair with a huff. "I love him so much, yet I cannot get over what he did. Do you think I will be able to?"

I got up and went to her. "My love, if you love him and he loves you, that love will come through. Time will heal you." I hugged her.

"Thank you. Come on. You want to eat?" She smiled.

"I do. I am starved." We walked arm in arm to the kitchen, finding everyone else was already there. It was good to sit with my family again. It felt like home. I could not get the smile off my face.

"Sabine, why are you smiling so much?"

"Well, Westin, I am happy, I think. My family is here, I am not dead anymore, and I get to watch all who I love for the rest of my days. I think that is enough to make anyone smile."

He nodded. We were all done, and I felt a little tired. "Sabine, what time is this meeting in the courtyard today?" Westin asked.

"Just as the light of the day gets ready to leave. Will you all please excuse me? I did not sleep well last night. I think I might go have a sleep."

I made my way to my room and laid on my bed. I was tired, very tired. Sleep came easily for me. I do not know how long I slept, but when I woke, I realized that most of the day was gone. I jumped up and ran to the window. The light of the day was leaving.

I grabbed my comb and my crown and ran out of the room, taking the stairs two at a time, which is not easy in a gown. "Francis," I yelled as I turned to run toward the kitchen.

She met me in the hall. "Yes, child."

"I overslept. Where is everyone?"

"It is fine, child. No one is out there yet."

"I will need some help getting into my gown. Will you help me, please?"

"Of course, I will."

"When they start going out, come to my study, all right?"

She laughed. "It is fine. I will be there shortly."

I ran to my study and bolted the door, then popped the latch for the secret room and went in and got my gown. After laying it on the chair, I was running the comb through my hair and could not help but think about how white it was after the cave.

92

'Thank you for giving me my hair back,' I said in my mind. The sky was getting darker, so I started to undo my gown. I stepped out of it and then took the cover off the new gown I was to be married in. Stepping into it was not as easy as I thought it would be, for there were so many layers of cloth, but once it was on and I had pulled it up over my shoulders, I felt relaxed. I looked down at it, thinking Clare had done a fantastic job, just as Francis knocked on the door.

"It is me, child."

I opened the door, and she gasped when she saw me.

"What? Does it look all right? Is it ugly? What?"

"Oh, no, Sabine, it is beautiful. You look so beautiful."

I let out my breath and smiled. "Oh, thank goodness. Here, can you lace me up?"

She did, taking her time to pull each lace to make sure they were even and perfect. When she finished, she patted me on the back. "I will go make sure they are all outside, and then I will be right back."

I nodded and she left. A few moments later, she knocked on the door, and said, "Sabine, it is time." I opened the door, letting her in.

"Now, when we get to the kitchen, I need for you to go get Westin. Tell him I need to speak to him. Tell him I am in the hallway by the great hall."

She nodded, and we went to walk out, but she stopped. "Wait, you are forgetting something." I turned around, and she placed my crown on my head. "A Queen cannot marry without her crown." I hugged her.

"Thank you so much for everything."

"It is my pleasure. Now let us go. He is waiting for you."

I smiled, and she left me in the hallway by the kitchens. A few moments later, Westin came in, calling my name. He walked through the door from the kitchen and stopped.

"What are you doing in here?" he asked.

"I need for you to give me away to Blake, Westin. We are getting married."

"Right now?"

"Yes, it is a surprise."

The tears fell from his eyes. "I am so happy for you, Sabine. No one knows?"

Shaking my head to answer, I told him, "I know, so will you?"

"Yes, of course!" he replied, ecstatic.

I put my arm in his, and we walked to the door and out into the soft fading light of the end of the light of the day. We waited until everyone saw me, and a lot of questions and ohhhs were muttered. I did not see Blake until I started walking to Charles and everyone parted. His eyes said every word he could ever think to say to me, and he smiled. The tears welled up in his eyes as I got closer. My heart was beating so fast. Charles was crying, and Rebecca was crying. Westin was smiling; he was so happy. He walked me right up to Blake.

"This is my sister, the Queen of Whispering Wind. I give her to you to take as your wife. I hope that you will honor her and cherish her until the end of your days. Do you accept this?"

"I accept her with all of my heart. Thank you, Westin, for trusting me with our Queen."

Westin kissed me on the cheek and hugged me, then went to stand by Camille, who was crying.

Blake did not turn his head when Charles started to speak.

"Today, I must say, has been a long time coming. We have all been through so much over the years, and together, we managed to come out the other end of this wonderful life together. It brings me the greatest joy and happiness to bring my brother Blake and Sabine together today. Blake, do you promise to honor Sabine for all of your days?"

Blake spoke in a whisper, "I so do."

"Sabine, do you promise to honor Blake for all of your days?"

"I so do," I whispered.

"It is by the power of God and this Kingdom that I marry you and make you husband and wife, a bond that shall never be broken. Blake and Sabine, you may kiss. You are now married."

Blake lifted his hands to my face. "You are so beautiful, wife," he said sweetly before he kissed me. He kissed me deeply, to where everyone was coughing and clearing their throats. We started to laugh, and then as we turned, everyone cheered.

Rebecca was first in my arms, whispering in my ear, "Why did you not tell me?"

I whispered back, "Because I wanted no fuss."

"I love you. I am so happy for you."

"I love you, too."

There were congratulations all around, and we stood around for quite some time and chatted with everyone. They were all so surprised and happy for us. Westin cried and pulled Blake aside, telling him, "You hurt my sister again, and you will answer to me."

Blake said, "Do not worry, brother. It will never happen again."

Westin nodded and slapped him on the back, and they laughed. I think he scared Blake a little, but that was all right with me; he needed to be scared.

We all made our way into the castle, where we ate food and had a bit of wine, and then Blake announced, "Excuse me. I would like to make a toast to my beautiful wife." Everyone got very quiet. "Sabine, I have loved you from the first time I saw you. It has been a journey through time that brought us here today, in front of our family and our friends, that I say this. I am honored that you share your love, your kindness, and your heart with me. I will never dishonor you or deceive you for as long as I live. I love you, wife."

I smiled. "I love you, husband."

"Now, with that said, I am going to take my wife and spend some time alone with her."

Everyone cheered at that.

"Can you wait a minute?" I whispered to him. He nodded.

I went to Charles. "In the morning, can you make sure Raiden is ready for Christopher? He is going to take him out to do his mapping."

"Do not worry. Go and enjoy each other."

I hugged him and said, "Thank you."

I walked past Christopher and touched him on the arm. "Raiden will take you tomorrow."

"Thank you, Your Majesty," he responded and bowed.

I smiled and looked at Blake, who was waiting for me. We walked out of the dining hall and slowly walked up the stairs together, just looking at one another. I do not know who was more scared, me or him. We made it to my room, which would now be our room. Before he opened the door, he kissed me. He lifted the latch, scooped me up in his arms, and carried me in, kicking the door shut behind us. I reached behind him and bolted it, and he carried me to the edge of the bed and set me on my feet.

"You are now my wife, and all that you desire to know I will gladly tell you. If you give me your permission, I shall show you just how much I love you."

"I am your wife, and you are my husband. You will always have my permission to touch me, to love me. You have always had it. I love you."

He kissed me, but this time it was different. He was so gentle. His hands stayed on my face for a minute before he pulled away and slowly turned me around. "I have never seen you look as beautiful as you do today. You take my breath away." He whispered as he kissed my neck. I felt him pull on the ties on the back of my gown until it was completely unlaced, and then he slowly turned me to face him.

My hands came up and untied his shirt, and I slipped it down his arms, letting it fall to the floor. I stepped into his chest and kissed it gently. I could feel his heart beating rapidly. Placing my hands on his chest, I pressed my fingers into his skin. Lifting my head, he kissed me, and then slid my gown off my shoulders. I put my arms down so it would fall to my waist. I reached up and put my arms around his neck, pressing myself against him, and he lifted me up. My gown slipped down my waist and off my legs, falling to the floor in a heap. He stepped forward and laid me on the bed. I watched him take his clothes off, and he stood before me, completely unclothed.

I looked him up and down, thinking he was beautiful. I could not help but smile. I had no idea what to do next, and my stomach felt as if it has butterflies in it. He climbed on the bed to rest above me. "I see confusion in your eyes, my love. How can I help?" he asked.

"I do not understand why your body changes like that. I remember seeing you in your quarters. You did not look like this then, but last night you were like you are now. I do not understand."

He kissed me. "You do this to me," he explained, "being with you, loving you, makes this happen." He laid on his side, still kissing me, then pulled away. "If at any time you want me to stop, you say so."

I knew he must have felt the same as me. "What are you going to do?"

He kissed me again. "I am going to love you."

I smiled, as he ran his fingertips along the bone just below my neck. My body was on fire. He trailed his fingers down my chest to my breasts. He did not touch me, just looked at me, and as he looked into my eyes, I could see his fear. I could feel his hand shake, and I nodded to him, giving him my permission. It felt like fire when he touched me. My body was changing. I was feeling things like never before. I thought I would go mad when he touched me.

"Ohhhh," I moaned.

He stopped. "Am I hurting you?"

"No, my love, it feels incredible," I managed to whisper. "It feels warm and wonderful."

He continued to touch me, and I felt the groan deep within him vibrate his entire body. His hand moved down my body as he kissed me, until he reached the area right above my thighs. He stopped kissing me to see if was all right. I had my eyes closed. I wanted to watch, but the feelings were too much and I could not keep my eyes open. He slid his hand down my body and wrapped it around my thigh, his fingers barely touching me. Whispering, he said, "My love..." He kissed me again before he moved his mouth down my body. "I have no guide, my love. I just know that I want to touch you."

"I feels so wonderful. I do not want you to stop."

He shifted his body so that he was right above me. I opened my eyes to look at him when he stopped touching me.

"I love you, Sabine," he whispered.

"I love you," I managed to say.

His hands started at my shoulders, as he trailed his fingers along my jaw and across my lips. I put my tongue on them as they slid past. He slowly moved them down my body, down my stomach to my hips. With his hand opened, it covered me from hip to hip. He brushed his thumb across the hairline, sending shivers throughout my entire body. He paused, whispering, "Are you all right?" I nodded.

He slid his hands down my thighs, to my knees, then sat himself up to look at me. "You are so beautiful, my love."

I looked at him, and he watched my face as he moved his hands up my thighs, stopping at the tops of them. I was so scared, and I think he could sense that. "My love," he whispered. "Are you all right?"

"I am scared," I said, trying not to cry.

He stopped instantly and pulled me to him, holding me. "Shhh…" he said as he felt my tears. "I am scared, too. I do not want to hurt you."

"I feel no pain, but the feelings are not anything I know."

"Nor do I. We do not have to do these things. I told you before that I will not take what you are not willing to give me."

"What does that mean? Will you tell me now?"

He chuckled. "You, my love. I want you, all of you, each piece of you. I want to touch you. I want to love you."

"The way that I feel scares me. It is so intense."

"Will you tell me how you feel?"

I pulled away from him. "I feel like I am on fire. Every touch sends shivers through me. I am shaking from them. I am afraid I am going to explode."

"I feel the same way. I think it is because I love you so much and you are now my wife. I belong only to you. I can love you now, freely and without hesitation."

"Are you scared?"

He smiled and covered my mouth with his, and when we separated, he whispered in my mouth, "Terrified."

I touched his face and looked into his eyes, and I could see that he truly was scared. He did not know these feelings either. I lay back, pulling him down with me, kissing him. "I love you so much it hurts," I said into his mouth.

"Oh, Sabine, you will never know the depth of my love for you." Our kiss lasted a long time. My body was shaking from the pleasure I was feeling.

He pushed up and I nodded to him. He moved down my body touching me everywhere, kissing me everywhere. I cried out; the feeling was so powerful. It was then that my body lost control. It felt like I had exploded. It felt as if my insides were bursting through my stomach. I cried out, and the tears came without any notice. I did not know what was happening to me.

I scared him. Not a moment passed before he had me in his arms, murmuring, "I am sorry, my love. Have I hurt you?" I climbed up him. I could not let go. My body was shaking. I found myself rocking into him, but he held me tight. I cried because I did not know. I thought I was dying again. He held me tight, and when my body started to settle down, I started to calm down and my breathing returned to normal.

I pulled away from him and covered his mouth with mine. I do not think he knew what to do with me, so he just kissed me back. When I was calm, I pulled away.

He wiped the tears from my cheeks and asked, "What happened?"

I just shook my head. "I felt like I was exploding, like my insides were going to burst through me. I could not stop shaking."

"Did I hurt you?" His eyes were so full of fear.

"No, not at all."

He smiled and wrapped his arms around me. "Well, that is good thing." We giggled then lay back down on the bed and turned to our sides.

My hands touched his face, outlining his eyes, his lips, his nose.

"You are so beautiful," I whispered.

He smiled. "I am terrified. I thought I hurt you."

I giggled again. "Now that it is over, I have to say, it was incredible. I have never felt anything like that before. How did you do that?"

"To be truthful, I did not know that would happen. I have wanted to touch you for as long as I can remember. It hurt me when I did the little that we did. I have always known that I wanted to touch all of you, every part of this beautiful body."

"I think I would like that very much."

"Good because we are just getting started."

"Blake?"

"Hmmm," he said as he lay there with his eyes closed.

"Now that you are my husband, the same goes for me. I can touch you like you just touched me?"

He rolled over to look at me. "Sabine, you do not have to. I am happy just touching you."

"But I can, right?"

"Yes, you can, but you do not have to."

I whispered, unsure that I should say this, "But I want to."

He lifted my head up. "I belong to you. I give you my permission to touch me. There will never come a time when I would not want you to. All right?"

I nodded and then smiled. "I do not know anything about this. I am just going to do the things you did to me."

"Sabine, it is not necessary."

I stuck my lip out. "But I want to. I want you to feel the way I feel. It is incredible. How does it feel when I touch you?"

"I feel whole. I feel love. My legs get shaky, and my hands get wet."

I slipped my body on top of him and leaned down to kiss him. He was responding to me as well. "Tell me what that feels like."

"It feels like soft puffs of clouds touching me."

I pressed down. "And this?"

"Heaven." He smiled.

I did what he did to me, moving my mouth and my hands down his body, and he moaned loud. "Am I hurting you?"

"No, my love, it feels wonderful."

I was gentle as I explored his body just as he had done mine. Taking my time, I watched his body change under my fingers. His muscles tightened, and his breathing began coming faster and harder. He was so beautiful. Out of nowhere, he yelled out, scaring me. He reached for me, grabbing me and pulling me up his body.

"I am so sorry. Did I hurt you? I did not mean to hurt you. I was just..." And his mouth was on mine. He was kissing me, his tongue so deep in my mouth. When he pulled away, he was crying. "I did hurt you. Oh, Blake, I am so sorry." He was shaking his head.

"You did not hurt me, my love. I do not know what happened, but it felt wonderful. I have never known this feeling."

I smiled at him. "So these are the things that married people know?"

He laughed out loud. "I was married once, and I never knew these feelings. I believe these are feelings people who are in love feel." He pulled me to him and just held me. I felt his body shaking like mine had, and as he calmed down, his grip on me lessened. His heart was calm again. We laid there in our moment of pure bliss.

His hand ran the length of my body, and I noticed that he was not like he was before. He sensed me looking at him. "What is the matter?"

"I am not sure…" I paused. "You look different now."

"I cannot explain that, and I would not know who to ask." We laughed.

"So this is what married people do? How come, when I walked in on Westin and Camille, he was on top of her, and when I walked in on Juliana and James, she was on top of him? Are we missing something?"

He laughed. "No, my love, we are not."

"Well, I do not understand."

He kissed me. In between our kisses, he whispered, "We are not done yet."

I smiled. "Good because I really liked that feeling when you touched me."

He rolled on top of me. All serious, he said, "I would like your permission to touch you elsewhere."

I smiled and nodded. He pushed himself up, and my legs wrapped around him. "I know you do not like when I do this, and I do not want you to run away from me."

He chuckled. "You were not my wife when you did this before."

I smiled and he kissed me. He lowered himself onto me, and I felt him again. He was big. I pulled myself to him. He pressed down, and I felt him push into me. It hurt, but not enough for me to make him stop. "Is this the right thing to do?"

"This is the union between a husband and wife," he said, sounding so sweet and raspy.

He kissed me and pressed down harder, and I cried out. He stopped instantly. "I am hurting you," he said and he pulled away."

I nodded. "Yes, it hurts."

He laid next to me, keeping his thigh between my legs. "This is going to hurt, but we do not have to do this."

"Why is it going to hurt? Do you want to hurt me?" I felt the panic rising in my chest. I was getting scared.

"No, my love, I do not ever want to hurt you. It is going to hurt because you are pure."

"Did it hurt your wife?"

"My love, it hurts every woman, but it only hurts once, and then you are not pure anymore."

I was not sure I liked that thought. I shook my head. "I do not think I like that thought."

He wrapped his arms around me. "I told you I would not ever take what you do not give me. We do not have to do this. I will not dishonor you by taking you."

The tears just came. "I am sorry. I am sorry that I disappointed you. I am scared, and I do not want to do this."

"Sabine, you do not have to do this. I have told you always, that if you say no then it is no. I am not a monster. I love you. You are my everything. The last thing I want to do is hurt you."

I cried into his chest. I do not remember much after that, for I cried myself to sleep in his arms.

I woke just before the light of the day was to come, and I felt horrible. I looked at him. He was my husband, but not in the way he should be. I had disappointed him. I felt the panic rise in my chest again, thinking he would look at me differently. *Would I still see the love in his eyes? How could he want me if I could not make this union he kept talking about? If I loved him as his wife must have, I would be able to do it. What if I did not love him like she*

104

did? I felt the tears coming again, so I slipped out of bed and got dressed. I could not face him, not like this, not crying. That seemed to be all I did lately get angry and cry.

I took my sword and quietly left our room, then stood by the door, wishing I could be different, but I was not. I ran down the hall, down the grand staircase, and out into the dark of the night. When I ran to the stables, Raiden was shocked to see me. I did not even put on his saddle; I just climbed on him, leaned into his neck, and told him to take me away. He ran out of the stables, and we were gone. As we rode, the light of the day was peeking in the sky, and the colors were so brilliant. He came to a stop at the little river, and I got down, walked over, and sat on the river's edge to continue my cry.

The only thing I could see in my mind was Blake's disappointment in me. He would regret marrying me when he woke, if he did not already, but he was too honorable to say otherwise. This is what happens when I do not think things through. No wonder they always treat me like a child. I have no idea what I am doing.

Blake woke to find me missing, so he got up and looked around the room. My sword was gone, which meant I was gone. "Oh, sweet girl, what have you done?" He got dressed and ran out to the stables. The moment he entered, he saw that Raiden was gone. "No, my love," he said under his breath. He looked at Spirit. "Sorry, boy, but I am going to have to ride you. I hope you do not mind." He put Spirit's saddle on him and walked him out into the courtyard. "Please do not kill me," he said to him. Spirit did not move when Blake climbed on him. "Will you take me to Sabine?" Spirit paused and then took off.

I sat with my knees to my chin, wondering how I was going to explain to everyone that we had made a mistake, that he did not want me. He did not dishonor me, so I remained the pure

Queen. I cried harder. I loved him, but we kept disappointing one another. He would be waking soon, and I was sure he would be glad that I was not there. He would not have to look at his disappointing wife.

I was sobbing and did not hear Spirit when he stopped. Blake was off him, and I was in his arms before I knew what was happening. Spirit and Raiden walked off.

"My love, what is going on?" I tried to catch my breath, but the only thing I could do was sob. He held me and rocked me back and forth. "Shhh..." he said. "Sabine, there is nothing to cry about."

"I am a disappointment," I stuttered out between sobs.

"No, no, no, my love, I would never think that. Why would you think that?"

"I cannot make a union," I sobbed.

He chuckled. *Why would he laugh? Now he is laughing at me.*

"My love, it is all right. You do not need to make a union with me if you do not want to."

I pushed away from him. He was just being honorable. He must believe I am a fool. I did not want him to hold me. He was always holding me, making me feel better. This always happens when there are bad things coming. He calms me, and then I get slammed with the big stuff. I scooted away from him. "Do not hold me and comfort me. Each time you do, there are bad things that follow. Each time we end up in a compromising position, bad things happen. If you do not want me, then tell me now while I am this way. Do not calm me and then tell me."

He reached for me with tears in his eyes. "Why would you believe I do not want you? I have wanted nothing more my whole life."

I moved away when he reached for me, "You told me you wanted nothing more than to touch me and to make a union

106

with me, and I cannot do it. Why would you still want me? There are plenty of women out there who can and will make a union with you."

He tilted his head and crinkled his eyebrows. "What are you saying? You think I would rather have someone else?" I nodded. "That is outrageous to believe that. I have fought for you my whole life. Why would you believe I would want anyone else?"

"Because I cannot give you what you want," I shouted at him. Why did he not understand me?

The tears fell from his eyes as he whispered, "Do you not want me?"

"It is you who does not want me." I stood and started to walk away, my stomach turning.

"Who told you such an untruth?" he whispered through his tears.

My stomach was going to come up. "I saw it in your eyes. I saw the disappointment." And then it happened; I retched. I felt his hands on my hips, and I tried to move but could not. I retched again, falling to my knees. There was nothing left in my stomach, but it would not stop. I do not know how long I was there trying to stop it, but he did not leave me. Finally, it ended, and he pulled me into his arms.

"Oh, my love," he whispered. "You are so far from the truth. The depth of my love for you does not allow for disappointment. You did not see that in my eyes. You bring me so much happiness that I am the one who is not deserving of you, not the other way around. This union is not something that matters to me. Just being with you, holding you, loving you is enough for me."

I felt my arms go around him. I needed him so much. I was so scared of what lay ahead for us. It was foolish of me to believe that I can go through this life without him.

Blake sat there in the tall grass and held me until my sobs stopped. He cried silently, unable to process why I would feel this way. He went over in his mind everything that happened the night before, and it was perfect. It was beautiful. He knew it would be difficult for us. He had more knowledge than I did, and he knew it would hurt, for he had done that part before.

"I love you," was all he could think to say.

I pressed into his chest, and we held each other. He slid his hand between us. Putting his fingers on my chin, he lifted my face. "You are so beautiful that it scares me that you could love me like this." He kissed me sweetly. "There is nothing you could do to disappoint me. Nothing. There will not be a day that goes by that I will not want you."

I wanted to hear those words, but he had said them to me so many times before and then bad things happened. "Will you leave me now that I am done crying?"

"I will never leave you. I am not whole without you. Losing you to death has taught me that. I will not make the mistakes I made before. Trust that I have learned from them."

I did not know what to say. I needed to prepare for what was to come next. His arms did not falter in holding me, but they never did. He always held true to his word that he loved me, but he also hurt me, time and time again. "What if it is not enough for you?"

"What if what is not enough for me?"

I felt the concern in his voice. "What if not having this union is not enough for you?"

He pulled me away from him, forcing me to look into his eyes. "Do not ever think that, Sabine. This right here, holding you…

this is enough for me. You are my wife. That is enough for me. Being bonded to you for the rest of my life is enough for me. You, my love, are enough for me. Trust me, please, to love you for the rest of our lives. Trust that I am not leaving you."

Every part of who I am wanted to believe him. My heart hurt because I loved him so much. But was it enough? Would it be enough?

"What is running through that beautiful mind of yours?"

"I want to believe you, but I do not know if it will be enough, me loving you, you loving me. I did not make a union with you."

"Hey, stop. That is not what matters to me."

"Yes, is does. It matters to all men. That is why they take what is not theirs to take. You told me that."

"I am not all men. I am your man. Not all men think that way, Sabine. You are my wife. I promised to honor you, and if honoring you means there is no union between us, then that is what I shall do. To take what is not mine to take because I feel it is mine makes me a monster like Thomas and Louis, and I am not that. If and when you want to try it again, we can try it again. If you cannot do it, then that is fine. If we never do it, that is fine by me. I want you, all of you, not the union. This was and never has been about the union. This is about me loving you and us spending our lives together, sharing moments like we shared last night, touching and holding with no boundaries."

I smiled at him. "I love you so much that it scares me to need you the way I do."

"I could not agree with you more. You are everything to me, and without you, I am nothing." He kissed me. "Now, I would like to take you home and show you just how much you mean to me. Our life is going to be a happy life, an everyday life of tender moments, kissing and touching with no boundaries. You are my wife, and if we choose to spend the day lying unclothed in our bed, then so be it. I would love nothing more. I love looking at you and touching you." He leaned in and whispered, "There is so much more of you to touch, and when I am finished, I will just start all over again."

I giggled and kissed him.

We rode Raiden home together with me in his lap. As we rode into the courtyard, midday had arrived. Rebecca was walking up from the stables. "I thought perhaps Spirit had run off, but then he told me you two were at the river. Is everything all right?"

"We just wanted to go for a ride. That is all," Blake said. I just smiled at her. "Now if you would excuse us, we have some married things to take care of." Rebecca laughed, and I felt my face get hot.

He helped me down, and we walked hand and hand into the castle and straight to our room. He bolted the door and smiled at me. I did not move as he took my clothes off and then carried me to bed.

Chapter Seven

I woke when I felt the pressure on the bed. As I slowly opened my eyes, I saw his beautiful face. "Hi," he said smiling. He had with him a tray of food.

"How did you know I was hungry?"

He laughed. "Well, we have been in this room for a whole day and night, and now it is nearly time for the evening meal. I am hungry."

"Really? I did not realize that so much time had passed," I said as I sat up and kissed him. He sat the tray on the floor and climbed into bed with me. "You have far too many clothes on." I stuck my lip out. He laughed and proceeded to undress. I loved to look at him and to touch him. "You are so beautiful," I whispered as I reached for him. He climbed on top of me and kissed me. From there, everything was blurry. The way he made me feel was like no other feeling, and he said that he felt the same way. We had not stopped other than to sleep and to eat for days on end. I was in pure bliss.

One morning I woke before him and wrapped the blanket around me. As I walked to the window, I felt my lips; they were swollen from our kissing. I ran my finger along them then turned back to look at him and giggled. He was so beautiful. I turned and watched as the light of the day came into the sky. How long had we been up here? I saw Christopher head out on Raiden, and I wondered how far he had gotten with staking the land? I wondered how Rebecca and Juliana were doing with James and Joseph.

I turned when Blake started to stir. He reached for me, but I was not there. His eyes opened, and he looked around, and when he saw me standing by the window he smiled. I watched him get up and walk to me, completely unclothed. His body was magnificent.

"I love you," I said before his mouth covered mine.

"My wife, I will never grow tired of looking at you in the light of the day." He raised his eyebrows. "Or in the glow of the night," he added, and I laughed. "That is the best sound."

We stood there kissing for a bit. "We should go back out into the world. I should find out how Christopher is doing with his staking. I have so much to do."

"I do not want to let you go." He picked me up and took me back to bed. Touching him was all I wanted to do. Having his hands and his mouth on me was like nothing I had ever known. When we were both smiling and giggling, we sat up in bed.

"I need to leave you and go run a Kingdom. We have been in this room for..." I thought about it for a moment. "I do not know how long." He laughed, and I slapped him. "I can only imagine what everyone must think."

112

"It does not matter, and they will think that we are in love, doing all those wonderful things married people do."

"Mmmm, and wonderful things they are."

He kissed me again, and then I pulled away and scampered out of bed. "We must leave this room." He followed me with his lip sticking out. I laughed as he grabbed me up in his arms and kissed me.

"Only if you promise not to forget me," he said teasingly.

"I believe, Sire, that I will not."

He smacked me on my bottom and let me go, and we dressed watching one another. I hated to watch him cover his body. He hated it when he watched me. We walked out the door together. He grabbed my crown on the way out and placed it on my head, and we went to the kitchen for food. Sitting at the table, I am sure we looked like fools staring at each other, watching the other eat, and smiling like we were the only ones alive. We finished and we kissed at the door, and then walked together to the barracks. Rebecca was coming out of the stables with Joseph.

"Well, if it was not for the trays of food outside your door, I would have thought the two of you had died in there."

I smiled at her. "You just hush." We laughed. "Rebecca, I am going to take Spirit for a ride, if that is all right. I want to go and see how far Christopher has gotten."

"Sure, go ahead. When you get back, come and find me." She raised her eyebrows at me. I smiled.

I turned to Blake and told him, "I will return later."

He kissed me and said, "Be safe."

I went into the stables and got Spirit, then climbed up on him. "Will you take me to Raiden please?" And we were off. We did not go the way I thought. We went the way to the river. It was not long, and I could see them ahead. Spirit pulled to a stop. "Hello," I said.

Christopher turned and smiled. "Hello, yourself. Good morning, Your Majesty."

I laughed. "I would like for you to call me Sabine," I said as I climbed down."

"Sabine, how is married life?"

"Oh, it is different, but lovely. Thank you for asking. How is the staking going?"

"Well, I have mapped a great many lands, but I must say that this land is the greatest by far. You have no idea how big this place is, do you?"

"No, that is why you are here. How long do you think it will take you?"

"Well, once I realized how big it was, I started taking notes. It is hard to judge the distance on your horse, because he moves faster than any horse I have ever ridden."

I smiled and patted Raiden's neck. "He is magic. They both are."

"He is faster than the wind. But as soon as I get the markers in, I can start to measure the distance and get a more accurate feel."

"And how are your accommodations?"

"They are accommodating."

I laughed. "So in other words, everything is good?"

"Yes, Sabine. May I inquire about a young woman I have met? She will not tell me much about who she is, but we have been spending some time together, walking the gardens and sharing a piece of fruit, things of this nature."

"Well, if I can. What is her name?"

He stood and looked at me. "She told me her name was Julia, but that is all she told me."

114

"Well, it is Princess Julia, to be exact. She is my niece, my brother's only daughter." A bit of concern welled in me. "Perhaps you should be careful where she is concerned. I would imagine she is much younger than yourself. My brother is a very cautious father. She was very sheltered and protected while she grew up. She is by no means worldly."

"Oh, Sabine, I am an honorable man. I would never assume anything concerning her. She is a lovely girl, and our age difference is not as huge as you would think. I believe it is only three years in difference."

I nodded. "Well, just be careful. The best thing for you to do would be to talk to Westin. He would appreciate that more than if he were to see the two of you together."

"I will do just that. Thank you."

I turned to walk to the river while he finished doing whatever it was he was doing out here. I sat in the grass and thought about that morning when Blake came to find me, all those beautiful things he had said to me, and then Spirit took off. I turned as I heard Raiden in my head.

'Danger.'

He was next to me, so I climbed up.

'Who?'

'They are coming from the East.'

He turned so we would be facing them.

Spirit ran into the courtyard. Rebecca came flying out of the castle with her sword in one hand and mine in the other screaming, "BLAKE!" She looked toward the barracks. Charles was running to the stables. He looked at her and nodded. Blake came running. "Sabine is in trouble. Charles knows where," she told him, and Spirit was gone.

I sat waiting, though I could not hear them yet.

'How far?'

'Just there.' His head nodded.

I could see the cloud then, so I turned to Christopher. "You should hide. This could get bad fast, and you have no weapon." He nodded and made his way into the high grass.

"You cannot take them all on," he said.

I smiled. "I will not be alone." Just then, Spirit skidded to a halt next to me. "I told you."

"No disrespect, Your Majesty, but you are women."

Rebecca laughed, and it was never a good thing when she laughed. "I believe you will be needing this," she said, handing me my sword, and I strapped it around me just as they came into view. There were a hundred or so men, and they were riding hard. They slowed and then stopped. About ten of them rode to the other side of the little river.

"Well, as I live and breathe, Princess Rebecca of Blackmore."

"Who are you, and what brings you to Whispering Wind? How do you know who I am?"

"I am Gerard of Collingwood."

I looked at Rebecca, but she shrugged her shoulder.

"My brother brings me here. My Father told me that he ran off with a beautiful Princess with hair like the golden sun, and well, here you are."

"Your brother is no longer among us."

"That is what I hear. My father is on his deathbed and wishes for his eldest son to take his crown, so I was sent on a journey to find him. Imagine how I felt when I heard you cut his head off."

"Well, Gerard, the last time I heard about you, you were still trying to figure out how to walk. What concern would you have with a man you did not know?"

"Do not be coy with me, Princess. I have heard the stories of your power. I have also heard the legend, and I also know that she," he pointed his sword at me, "is not pure any longer and that your magic is gone."

That man could have stabbed me and I would have been less shocked. I searched for him.

'Is this truth?'

'I do not know.'

"What you have heard is an untruth," I said.

"Well, the word passing through the Kingdoms is that you wed a commoner, and when you did that, your crown was abolished."

I laughed. "Where is it you get your information?"

"You wear that crown under false pretenses. You are beneath me. I do not answer to you, infidel."

I giggled. "Why are you on my land?"

He drew his sword. "Your magic will not work, being you are not pure. I came to avenge my brother's death."

Rebecca laughed as she drew hers. "You care to see if it still works with or without her purity? And you will mind your tongue, Gerard, or I will let her take it from you."

"Oh, no, please, you can have the honor, my love," I said.

He tilted his head. "My love? What, are you two whores with one another? No wonder you murdered my brother. You are not worthy to stand before me."

I could not help it; I laughed so loud Rebecca jumped. "I am tiring of you. Who do you think you are, talking to me like that?" I saw his energy blow out from him. This man was dark. I felt Raiden twitched. "Shall we see if the magic works?" I drew my sword and watched him swallow. "You know this sword, do you?" I mocked him.

"It could not be real. How do you wield it?"

Raiden jumped, and the light was brighter than the light of day. When we landed, only the ten were left standing. I looked him right in the eyes. "I think that blew your theory all to hell."

Blake saw the light in the sky, so he kicked his horse harder and flew past his brothers. He was coming fast. I could feel him.

"Witches," he yelled and started across the river. When he reached our side, he saw Blake and the brother's ride up. He paused at the edge.

I tilted my head. "Have you met my husband?"

He bowed his head. "Master," he said.

I turned and looked at Blake, who shrugged his shoulders at me. I climbed off Raiden. "Sabine," he said.

"It is all right, my love. This man called me a whore and claimed that my not so pure body did not hold any magic, that the legend was null. I just thought I should show him otherwise."

Blake looked at him. "You called my wife a whore?"

"They murdered my brother."

"If I remember correctly, your brother not only tried to murder my wife but my friend as well. Better he died than them. Why do you call me Master? Why do you bow your head to me?"

"I have heard of the Guardians. You are Protectors of the Bringers of Peace."

"Yes, but Charles is Sabine's Guardian."

Gerard looked down at me. "You are the Bringer of Peace?"

I smiled at him. "In the flesh."

"IMPOSSIBLE!" he screamed as he charged me.

Rebecca took off on Spirit and swung her sword, taking off his head in a brilliant flash of light. His body fell to the ground right in front of me. The rest of his men took off. She rode around and said, "Well, that felt good."

"What was that all about?" Charles said.

"I would assume it was concerning Edward. His father is dying and sent Gerard to find him to take the crown."

"Was it necessary to cut his head off?" Charles asked Rebecca.

"He called Sabine a whore. It made me mad," she said with a giggle. I turned to see Christopher standing in the tall grass.

I ran up to him. "Are you all right?"

"So you are the Legend?" he asked as he dropped to his knees. "Your Majesty, it is an honor to meet you."

I laughed. "Get up." Grabbing his arm, I told him, "Do not be so silly."

"I had no idea. I had heard the stories, but I would never have guessed." He looked at Blake and smiled. We walked back to the horses.

"You should be fine out here now. I will leave Raiden with you, and I will ride back with Blake."

He nodded, Blake reached down and lifted me onto his horse. "I cannot let you out of my sight without you getting into trouble." I laughed as he kissed me.

On our way back, I thought about what Gerard had said. If I was not pure, would I still be able to be the Bringer of Peace? I was sure if he had heard that, then the others would have as well. Christopher had said that this Kingdom was the greatest he had ever mapped. It had taken him eight days so far and he was only to the river. That was why they wanted it, because it was so big.

Blake sensed the change in my body as it tensed up. "What is it, my love?"

"A few things, actually, but I am not sure what they mean. I did not realize that Whispering Wind was so big. Christopher has been out here for eight days on Raiden and has not a clue how much more there is to go. Where we were today was very far from where you found me by the river. I think those who come here, come because there is so much land."

"That could very well be. I did not realize he has been out here for eight days."

"I was sitting by the river one day in the spot where you found me, and when I asked Raiden how big it was, he told me as far as the eye can see. Well, you have been there. The eye can see a great distance."

"I never really thought about it like that. I guess we only really think of Whispering Wind as the village, fields, orchard, and the castle. Now you have me wondering." He smiled.

"I am going to be spending a great deal of time in my study. I think I need to read the tomes, so if you need me, you will find me there."

"I always need you, my love, always."

I decided that I would not tell him the rest. *It was not a lie, or was it?* If I expected him to be honest with me, I needed to be honest with him. We came to the hilltop, and I stopped Blake from going any further.

He looked at me. "Is something the matter?" I nodded.

Charles turned in his saddle. "You coming?"

"We will be along shortly," Blake said. Charles chuckled and continued on. I slid off of Blake's horse and waited until they started to go in the village.

120

"Come and sit with me," I said to him. He got down and walked with me.

"What is going on?"

I sat in the grass, and he sat in front of me so our knees were touching. "I was always mad at you because you would keep things from me, because you were being deceitful." He nodded. "Well, I am doing the same thing, and I cannot do that. I have to trust you, so I am going to ask you to keep this to yourself."

"Sabine, you can tell me anything."

"I know, but I need your word that what I am about to say to you will not leave you, or find its way to Charles."

He crinkled his eyebrows. "I give you my word. When you agreed to marry me, Sabine, I was truthful in my words. I will never betray you."

"When Gerard was spewing his filth toward us, he said that word had gotten around that I was married, therefore not pure, and that my magic no longer works. I challenged him, and asked him if he wanted to test his theory. Rebecca does not know that we have not made a union. No one knows but us, right?"

"I would not speak of the things we do together like that, so no one knows."

"I asked Raiden if it was truth, but he said he did not know. What if it is truth?"

He looked at me, and I saw fear in his eyes. "I do not know."

"Well, the legend said that I had to remain pure in order to fulfill the quest. I was. But if I am not pure and the magic stops, then I cannot protect Whispering Wind."

"I would not know how we could find this out."

"I think the answer may be in the tomes."

"Well, we will just have to make sure you remain pure until we can figure this out."

"I want to have babies with you. I want to make a union with you."

"Oh, my love, I would love nothing more, but we are doing just fine with the way things are now. You are not ready yet, so we will be fine."

"Maybe I am not ready because deep down inside I know that if I do, then I can be killed."

"Maybe, but please trust in us."

"I am trusting you. Please, Blake, stay true to your word. We will end up in a web of lies and deceit again, and I do not want that. I want to be happy and love you and share our life together. I do not want to be angry with you. I like when you touch me and when I touch you."

He pulled me into his lap. "You must not worry. I will not betray you, and I will certainly never stop touching you or do anything to stop you from touching me." He kissed me like crazy. We ended up lying in the grass, kissing for the longest time. When we had our fill, we went back to the castle. "I have to finish my work," he said.

"I will be in my study." He swatted me on my backside and walked off.

I went into the secret room and checked over the tomes. They were not numbered, and I did not know which one was the first one, so I picked up one and opened it. The words were scattered like before, so I sat it down and picked up another, and then another. When I opened the fourth book, the page glowed and the words appeared. This one must be the first. I took it out into my study and closed the secret door, then placed the book on my desk and opened the cover.

The words appeared, and I began to read. As I read one, the next appeared, and then the one I read disappeared.

Whispering Wind

These writings are the Legend of this land, where time began.

This is where evil escaped and has dwelled with you.

When time began, the Creator started here.

The river that runs through this land is where life began.

The grass grew, the trees came, the animals were made, and this is where they lived.

Man came to dwell in this land.

It is not the garden. It is the beginning.

Man came to be, and with man came desire.

It would have been easy for creation to stop it, but with desire came greed.

With greed came power. With power came destruction.

This land was given to Samum.

He is the only pure heart to have ever come from this place.

He lived here and protected the land before he passed it on to his children and then to their children.

Time passed for many generations.

Many sons have cared for and protected these lands.

The riches were bountiful, the soil rich, the life span was tremendous.

Many people came to dwell in these lands and lived long, prosperous lives.

Each page had only one line on it. It was very difficult to read, also. I had never seen script like this was written in before and knew it must be very old. It went on to tell about the lineage of the keepers of this land. Samum was the first and only pure heart to come from here. I read the whole tome; I did not want to miss anything. I was supposed to have this knowledge, and I could not help but wonder if Rebecca should be here with me. Curious if she could read them, I decided to go and get her. I put the tome back in the secret room on the opposite side so I would not get them mixed up. When I finished reading them, I was going to have to put them back in the cave, and they would need to be in order.

I went looking for Rebecca by way of the kitchen. "Hello Francis," I said as I walked in.

She smiled at me. "Hello, child. Would you like something to eat?"

"I would, but I am looking for Rebecca. Have you seen her?" I asked as I grabbed an apple.

"No, my dear, I have not seen her since the morning meal."

"Thank you. I will be back in a bit to eat," I said and headed out the door. As I walked through the back courtyard, I saw Blake riding up. His smile said it all for me, and I smiled back. I was nearly to the barracks when Rebecca came out of them, laughing, and sure enough, Joseph came with her. I was happy for her that she was working on things, and I wondered how James and Juliana are doing.

Blake walked up behind me and grabbed me around the waist, kissing my neck. "Rebecca," I said as I turned in his arms. "I have some things I need to take care of," I said to him.

"I have a few things to take care of myself. Will you meet me after the midday meal?" He turned on his sad puppy eyes.

I giggled. "You are so bad. We will see. Come find me in my study when you are done."

He kissed me and then let me go. I turned as Rebecca came walking up with a huge smile on her face. "Are you busy right now?"

"No, why?"

"I need you to come with me."

"What is with all the mystery?" she asked as she giggled.

We started walking back to the castle, but I did not say anything until we were in my study. "Come on. I need you to see something," I said as I popped the latch for the secret room. We went in, and she lit a candle, so I started opening the tomes until the next one glowed. I took it and placed it on the desk. "Open it." She looked at me and then opened it. "What do you see?"

"Nothing, just a few letters. Why? What is going on?"

"Close it. Now, tell me what you see when I open it." I placed my hand on the cover and opened it. The page glowed, and the first word appeared. I shut the tome. "What did you see?"

"The same as before. Why? What is going on?"

I shook my head. *Should I tell her? No, I cannot tell her I am still pure.* "Nothing. I cannot seem to get them to read properly, and I just do not know what we are going to do."

"Maybe they need to be in the cave in order for us to read them."

"We cannot go into the cave to read these. Everyone will be dead by the time we get out," I said.

"Hmmm, I do not know then. Put that back and come eat. We will figure this out another time."

I let her have this one. I put the tome back and went to have our midday meal. Blake wanted to spend some time together, but I could not focus.

We were walking to our room when I touched him on the arm. "My love," I whispered. "I need to talk to you, and it is not here that we can do it. Will you take a ride with me to the hilltop?"

He smiled. "I will follow you anywhere."

We went out to get his horse and went to the hilltop. I slid off Raiden, and he followed. "What is the matter? You are very distracted."

"I am, and I am sorry. I know you wanted to spend some time together, but I am a bit out of sorts. Only I can read the tomes. Rebecca cannot see the words."

"What do you mean, she cannot see the words? Only you can?"

"It would seem so. When I open the book, the words glow, but only one word at a time. When I read it, it disappears, and then the next one appears. And there is only one line on each page. It is the strangest thing."

"Well, they have to be magic or something. Did you read it?"

"Yes, the first one was about the lineage of the keepers of Whispering Wind and what this place is. Only the purest hearts are given the privilege of being a keeper. That is all I have so far."

He put his arms around me. "You are the purest heart."

"I am the purest. What if what is being said is truth? I am sorry that I cannot spend time with you today, but I think I need to read the tomes. I need to know if this is truth. Raiden told me that I had to forgive you, and that our children are important to what is to come."

I felt him tense. "You forgave me because Raiden told you to?"

"No, my love, I forgave you because I love you. I fought it, and I fought you. I did not, could not forgive you, but when

126

you showed me how much you loved me, I knew you had changed. I love you so much, Blake, that it hurts."

He kissed me. "I love you."

"I am also worried about Collingwood."

"Why?"

"Gerard was Edward's little brother. He was the youngest, and he was sent to find Edward because there are six in front of him for the throne. Edward is the rightful heir, and they will try to avenge his death. Gerard did not go back to Collingwood when he discovered Edward's death. He came here to end Rebecca. They will return for her, and I am scared. She can die, Blake."

"They will not get close to her, Sabine."

"Thomas did," I said. He sat down in the grass in a huff.

"You are right. I had forgotten that, with you killing yourself and all. I was a little self-involved."

"How far is Collingwood from here? I am not sure, Wellington is two days' ride, and Blackmore is a half a day after that, so I would think Collingwood would be maybe three days. And we let those men go, so they will go back and tell what happened here."

"Well, we have Juliana. She can bring up a wall of fire if they get close enough without us being able to defend properly."

"What if they grab her like Thomas did?"

"Yes, I see your point. Should we tell Charles of this news?"

"I believe Charles knows. He is not a stupid man. He knows a great deal more than he lets on. If I were guessing, I would say he has knowledge of my purity as well, but we are not going to ask him. I would like to keep that with us."

"It will not come from my mouth. I gave you my word. I could talk to him about Collingwood, though."

"Would you? Will you be truthful with me if he concocts a plan and wants to leave me out?"

"I have already told my brother that there will be no more plans, information, or anything that is kept from you. He agreed, so hopefully he does not ask me, because I will have to betray my brother."

"We should get back. You talk to Charles. I will be in my study. Oh, and Blake?"

"Yes," he said with a smile as he was standing up.

I threw myself into his arms so we were face to face. "I love you," I said, and I kissed him. We parted laughing.

I was in my study reading the second and third tomes, which seemed to read more like the lineage of the keepers of Whispering Wind. I was nearly at the end when Charles and Blake knocked on the door. I put a piece of paper in the tome and closed it as I said, "Come in."

"Blake spoke with me about Collingwood, and I believe you might be right. I have sent men to stand guard in stages, so that word can get back to us quickly. I will not allow them to hurt her, Sabine, not after what Thomas did to her, nor after what I did to her. She deserves to be happy, and I believe she has found that with Joseph. I have informed him of the possibility of Collingwood."

"Thank you, Charles. I think we need to inform Rebecca, as well. She needs to be aware that she may very well be in danger."

"I will take care of that," he said. "If you will excuse me I have some things I need to do." He nodded and left.

He nodded to me all the time now. My hand went to my head, realizing it was the crown. I was not sure why I wore it.

"What is the matter, my love?" he asked as he came to sit on the edge of my desk.

"I feel very uneasy."

"How so?"

"I am just finding it strange that Collingwood is coming now to look for Edward. More than twenty years have passed, and Rebecca still looks the same. How would Gerard know who she was? He was just a child when Edward left, and he called you Master. Why would he do that?"

"I do not know what that was about. He said that he had heard that we were the Guardians to the Bringer of Peace, but only those who have met us know this. How would Gerard know this and know my face?"

"Something is not right here, Blake. Something is wrong, very wrong. You know everyone calls you Master. What are we missing?"

He stood up and started walking back and forth. I got up and went to the door and opened it. I stepped out into the hall, and I was going to yell for Francis, but one of her helper girls walked by. "Excuse me," I said to her.

She bowed. "Yes, Your Majesty."

"Would you please ask Francis to come in here right away?"

"Yes, Your Majesty," she replied and ran off toward the kitchen.

"Why do you want Francis?

"Well, when I woke from the darkness, she was the first one who referred to all of you as Master. Perhaps she could give us a clue."

"I did not ever take notice, but people do say that. I guess during that time I was preoccupied with worrying about you."

I went to him and held him. "I am sorry about all of that."

"You had no control over falling into the darkness for so long." He pulled me closer and kissed me. We were interrupted when Francis came in.

"Oh, excuse me," she stammered.

"No, it is all right, Francis. Come in." I went to greet her and close the door, then walked her to the chairs. "I have something I need to inquire about."

"I will tell you anything I know."

"Thank you for that. What we would like to know is why do you call Blake and his brothers Master?"

She sat there looking at us like she had done something wrong. "Well, when I came here to live, the story was that Charles was the Master at Arms."

"Well, why do you call Blake Master?"

"Before I came to live here, there were stories of seven brothers who were chosen or destined, which ever version of the story you heard."

"There is a story?" Blake asked.

I looked at him, and he smiled and shrugged his shoulders. I giggled.

"Yes, there is a story. So these brothers were chosen before their birth to be Guardians over the chosen one. No one knew who they were, only that they all bore the same Mark."

Blake sat up. "What Mark?"

"The one on your left hand," she said, pointing to his hand.

I looked at him, and he looked at his hand. "This indent here?" He touched the Mark on his hand.

"Yes, it is called a Fleur-de-lis. It is a symbol of royalty."

"This Mark? This here?" He showed her the Mark again.

"Yes, that Mark," she said. "It is said that those who bear the Mark shall not perish."

We sat there looking at her, not knowing what to say. "So why do you call him Master?" I needed to know.

"Because we serve them. They have the key to immortality. They cannot die, not until their service to the chosen one has ended."

"I have an odd question," Blake said. "How long have you known this story?"

"Oh, my whole life. I was sure you knew it, as well. When the Mark appeared on your eldest brother, your father must have known that he needed to have seven sons, and he knew that the chosen one would come in your time. Only the generation who bears the Mark would hold the chosen one."

"That would explain a great deal. Is there anything else, Francis?"

"No, child."

"Thank you."

She left then, and I turned to Blake. "This is why Edward and his father thought him to be the chosen one. Samuel knew this, and so did Gerald. I wonder if Charles knows."

Blake sat there looking at his hand. "Why did I not know this?"

"If he knows, he has deceived you, as well," I said cautiously.

"He knows a great deal more than he is telling, that is for sure, but we were told by our father that we were not to interfere, that we were to protect you."

"So you are of royal blood. See, I knew you were special," I said, giggling.

He grabbed me and kissed me. "Only to you, my love. Only to you."

We kissed for a little while. "I need to get back to reading."

"Yes, and I am going to have a chat with my brother."

He left, and I went back to the tome.

I opened the book and continued to read. This must have been where the witch entered, where Raiden was turned into a horse. I remembered the story he told me.

Raiden, son of Loren, is where the line is interrupted.

A great evil was drawn from this land and will be used to take control.

Another was to come Tristan, who was also pure of heart.

Henry son of Tristan

Huge son of Henry

Phillip son of Henry

Reginald son of Phillip

Alexander son of Reginald

Stephan son of Alexander

Twenty-five generations in all, the land suffers.

The Bringer of Peace shall reign in the twenty-fifth generation.

The Mark of the Guardian shall appear in the twenty-fifth generation.

The tome ended there. If this book had been written so long ago, then how did all of these names get in them? I shook my head and went to put the tome back. I had read enough for now and decided to continue the next day. I had just sat down at my desk to think about all of this when Rebecca came storming into the room.

"Can you believe the nerve of that man? How dare he tell me what I can and cannot do? What do I look like, a child? I mean, really! 'Do not wander off alone.' Who is he?"

I laughed. "What are you talking about?"

"Charles! He thinks he can tell me what to do."

I sat there looking at her. She was beyond angry.

"Why would he think I would listen to anything he had to say to me? I mean, he was barking orders at me as if I was one of his men or something. I am not going to listen to him. I will do what I want. He does not control what I do."

"Rebecca."

"I should just go get on Spirit right now and ride off alone, see how he feels about that."

"REBECCA!" I shouted.

"What?" She spun around.

"You still love him."

"What? Do not be a child, Sabine. I do not love him."

"Yes, you do."

"What is with you people today? No, I do not!"

"Yes. You. Do. I acted and reacted the same way to Blake. You are so angry with him for hurting you. You still love him."

She sat down, her eyes never leaving mine. I saw them change as she realized that it was truth. "No," she said as she shook her head. "How can I still love him?"

"Because, my love, he is your match. You can fight it all you want, just like I did, but he is your match."

"But I love Joseph now."

"Yes, but you are in love with Charles. You do need to listen to what he says. It is my request that he delivered."

"You want me to stay close?"

"Yes, we let those men go, and they will go back to Collingwood. Edward still has six more brothers who are alive, and I cannot shake this feeling that now you have killed yet another brother and they will be coming for you. I lost you once, nearly twice, and I do not want to chance a third time. I cannot live in this world without you."

She smiled. "Well, if he had said it like that, I would not have gotten so angry."

"Just stay close and do not go anyplace alone, please."

"I will do as you ask. So how is it going with the books?"

"No luck yet. I am not too worried about them right now. I just wish Christopher would hurry and finish mapping the kingdom."

"Why is that so important to you?"

"I am not sure. It is just a feeling I have, that there is something important out there and I just do not know what it is."

"Hmm, well, when you figure it out, let me know. I am going to sulk some place. How is it possible that, after everything he has done to me, I could still love him?"

"Because I believe he is your match. Hey, you want to ride out to see Christopher tomorrow? We could have our midday meal out by that little river."

"Yes, that would be great. Hey, why are you and Blake not in bed? I mean, I would be. Juliana and James were in bed for days and days."

I giggled. "Well, I do have other things to do, as does Blake."

"Hold on." She stopped walking and turned. "Are you two all right? Is everything working properly?"

"What does that even mean?"

She laughed. "I will see you later." And she left.

I went to find Blake, who was at the barracks. "I need you," I whispered in his ear.

"What is it, my love?"

I smiled at him, took his hand, and led him across the courtyard, up the grand staircase, and to our room. I pushed the door shut and bolted it. His smile was more than I needed to know that he knew exactly what I needed. He wrapped his arms around me and held me.

Chapter Eight

As we lay in one another's arms, while circling my fingertip around the Mark on his hand, I asked him, "So did you talk to Charles about this Mark?"

"Yes."

I smiled, realizing he had been sworn to keep it from me. At least I knew now how he sounded when he was told to lie to me. "Let me guess, you were told not to say anything to me about it?"

"Yes."

"Hmmm, well, I suppose then that I should go ask him myself. I would not want you to betray your brother. It is better for your brother to betray me," I stated and I started to get up.

He put his hands on my waist to hold me into place. "I told you that I would never lie to you, betray you, or keep anything from you."

Smiling, I turned to face him. "Why does he not want me to know these things?"

"Because he does not want to sway your confidence."

I crinkled my eyes. "What do you mean?"

"Well, Charles believes that if you have certain knowledge, then you may not be as confident as you are. That is all."

"So if you had not promised me, would you think it wise to tell me what you know?"

"No, I would not, but I did promise you. You are my wife, and you are the most important thing to me. I do not want to argue with you, nor do I want to hurt you."

I sat there and thought about what he had said. "If you believed that I would be better off knowing something, would you tell me?"

"Yes, and I have many times."

I thought some more, and realized there were many times he had told me things Charles thought he should not. "If I asked you to tell me this, would you?"

"Yes, but I do not want to."

"Will it make me mad if you do?"

"No, it will not. It may shift your confidence, though, and we do not want that."

"Who is we?"

"All of us, you, me, all of us," he said, waving his arm in a circle, meaning everyone here.

"So perhaps if I know that all I have to do is ask you to tell me, I think I can deal with that, knowing that you will tell me. And you still promise to tell me the things you believe I should know?"

"Yes and yes. Sabine, if you want to know anything, I will tell you. I promised you that. If you want to know this, I will tell you, but as your husband and the man who loves you more than life itself, I would like to be able to decide if you should know something important. Is that acceptable to you? But no matter what, if you want to know, you just need to ask and I will tell you."

"All right, I will not make you betray your brother, as long as I do not get betrayed as well."

"It will never happen, my love, not again. Besides, I am pretty sure that if I do, I will not be able to do this again." He grabbed me and kissed me before he continued, "And I am sorry, but I prefer this."

I giggled. We kissed for a bit, but then I pulled away. "Rebecca is still in love with Charles."

"As he is with her. A love like that does not die, just like ours."

"I also discovered at the end of the last tome that was written however long ago that my father was named, and it said that in the twenty-fifth generation the Bringer of Peace would reign and the Mark of the Guardian shall appear."

"So it was foretold, just as Charles said."

"Are you all right?"

"I am. Thank you for telling me this. Would it be all right if I mentioned it to Charles?" he asked.

"What, that the Mark was mentioned in a book that was hundreds of years old? Of course. I am, however, going to go and start to read the third one." I swung my legs over the side of the bed and started putting my gown back on. He laced me up, and then I kissed him and left him lying in our bed with nothing on. When I reached the door, I turned back to gaze upon him. "You are so beautiful," I whispered. He smiled and I left.

I went to my study and got the third tome. I actually had to prepare myself for what it could say, so I sat it on my desk and lit the candles to give me even more light, not that it made a difference because each of the words glowed as I read them. Then I closed my eyes, took a deep breath, and opened the tome.

Twenty-five generations will pass from Tristan to Stephan

The Heir will bear a Mark the same as Tristan.

The Heir shall come to light with the Coming of Death.

The fourth element to seal the land will come in the twenty-sixth generation.

Death will ride across the land, taking everything in its path.

Only two will survive -- the Heir and the Keeper

"The Keeper?" I whispered. "What does that mean?" I closed the book and started to walk the room. The only two who survived were Westin and I. *Was Westin the Keeper? How could that be? Would he even know it?* I looked at the door. *Maybe I should go ask him... No, I should read some more. Perhaps it would tell me who the Keeper was.*

I looked out my window, and the dark of the night had come while I was reading. As I looked at the book on my desk, I took a deep breath and went to sit in the chair. Reaching forward, I picked it up and opened it.

The Keeper is pure at heart and must stay hidden until the Coming.

The evil that has escaped the land must be calmed.

The knowledge is coupled within the swords of the forefathers.

When the Heir forges the swords of the forefathers, the knowledge will be coupled within them both.

The Keeper shall possess it all but shall not reveal until the Coming.

The knowledge has been passed along and will leave those who possess it when death comes.

The Heir will inherit.

I closed the book, leaned back in my chair, and said out loud, "The Coming?" *What is the Coming? Who is the Keeper?* I looked at the door. I needed to figure this out, so I took the tome back to the secret room and went to the kitchen. Everyone was sitting around the table talking.

"Hello, Sabine," Westin said.

I smiled at him. *Who was this man I believed to be my brother? Was he really my brother?* "How was your day, my love?" I asked him as I got a plate.

He laughed. "Blake helped me trick Francis. She was so mad at me."

I looked at Francis, who stated, "He nearly sent me to my death."

"Yes, he is known for his tricks." I turned to Westin. "I am happy to see you happy. It is good that we are living like we should." I looked at him probably longer than I should have.

"Are you all right, Sabine?" he asked me.

"Oh, I am fine, my love, just tired."

"Yes, doing all those marriage things made me tired at first." He looked at Camille, and said, "Now I do not get so tired."

Camille turned a bit pink. "No, you do not," she whispered.

I had to giggle. "Hopefully, I will not tire so much either."

We all laughed. I sat there in my own thoughts concerning this keeper and my brother. *What does he know?* I listened to everyone talking and chatting. I did not even notice when Blake came in. I really needed to talk to Westin. *Should I talk to him? Would he even tell me anything? Does he know?* I looked at him, and noticed he was staring at me. His eyes were different. I smiled at him, and he smiled back. *Does he know I know?* I could not tell Blake what I had learned. I needed to keep this to myself. I wondered if I were to take Westin to the valley, if he would talk to me there. *How do I tell him I know?* Blake said

143

something to me, and I did not hear him, for I was too involved in my thoughts.

"Sabine," he said.

I just smiled. I looked at Westin again, and he was looking at me again, as well. There was definitely something different with his eyes. He nodded. *What does that mean? Does he know I know?* I think I need to sleep.

"Sabine," Blake said.

I got up and gave Francis my plate. "I am going to go to bed. Good night, everyone," I said and walked out of the room.

Blake sat there watching me. He had said my name two times, and I did not hear him. He got up and came after me. "Sabine," he said, but I did not hear him and kept walking. He touched my arm.

I looked at him and smiled. "Hello," I said, distracted.

"Are you all right, my love?"

"Yes… well, no." I crinkled my eyebrows. "I am not sure."

"Do you want to talk about it?"

"No, I do not think I can at least, not right now. I am going to our room. Will you be up later?"

"Yes, I could come now if you would like."

"No, that is fine. You finish your work. If I am not there, I will be in my study," I told him and walked away.

He stood there watching me, worried about my behavior, and then went back to the kitchen.

I thought if I slept for a bit that I might be able to get a better hold on this. I laid in bed and closed my eyes, but sleep did not come. I could not get the look on Westin's face out of my mind. "He knows I know," I whispered. I sat up and looked around my room. I needed to know what exactly was the Keeper and the Coming. I ran down stairs and into my study, got the fourth tome from the secret room, and sat it on my desk. I was not sure

144

I really wanted to know what was in this book, but I needed to know. I leaned forward and opened the tome.

When the evil is given back to the ground in which it escaped

With the incantation of calming

Then it is time to prepare for the Coming.

The Heir will seal the fate of those who are left.

The Keeper keeps the final secret safe within him, then it is his duty to keep this land.

To achieve the final Coming, the Heir must map the land,

Finding all the boundaries and the Markers of Time.

To achieve the Coming, the Heir must incorporate the Unknown Heir.

All the elements of this land will go forth with the Markers of Time

To the place in the center of the land.

The Coming will be the end.

Only those pure of heart may enter this land.

The Bringer of Peace will have brought peace throughout to no known end

I closed the tome and sat there. I was not the Keeper of this land; it had to be Westin. I knew I was the Bringer of Peace and that only I could do this. *What does it mean to incorporate the Unknown Heir?* All the elements... that one is easy that would be all of us. Markers of Time... I had no idea what those are or where I would find them.

Blake had been there for some time, standing in the doorway watching me, but I did not see him. I got up and walked to the window. *How was I to find out if Westin was this Keeper?* I needed to ask him; that was the only way. *But do I really want to know? Would he even know?* I cannot shake his eyes and the way he looked at me. I searched my memories but could not recall him ever looking like that. *He knows I know.* I shook my head. Perhaps he knew what the Markers of Time were, for I surely did not. "Father's journal," I whispered and turned to look at the tapestry. "No, I would have read it." I turned back to the window and then to the desk. Next, *'the drawings'* popped in my head. I went to my desk, and as I turned to bend down, I saw him standing there. I looked at him, seeing his eyes full of concern.

"Hi," I said very softly, like a child who had been in trouble.

He tilted his head. "I am worried about you."

"I am worried about me, too." I smiled.

"Sabine, it is nearly the light of the day. I have been in here three times."

I crinkled my eyes. "What?" I looked at the window, and the sky was no longer dark.

He walked up to me and took me in his arms. I was shaking. "What is wrong, my love?"

"I do not know. Something bad is going to happen, Blake. I do not know what it is, but it is bad."

"It will be all right," he tried to comfort me.

I pulled away from him. "I need to go to the place where time stands still. I need to retrieve some drawings that we left there. Do you want to come with me, or should I take Rebecca?"

"I will come, but, Sabine, you need to sleep first."

"I cannot sleep, Blake. I have five more tomes to read, and I need to get those drawings."

"Then you go change, and I will get the horses. I am sure Rebecca will not mind."

I hugged him. "Thank you." I quickly kissed him and ran out of the room.

He opened the book, but there was nothing on the pages for him to see. He shook his head and went to the stables. Before I met him out front, I put the tome back in secret room.

He put on his sash, which looked rather silly, and then we were to the river in no time. As I was crossing it, I could not help but wonder if this was the same river as the one Raiden always took me to. I would have to ask him.

I ran into the cave and grabbed all the drawings, and when I came out, it was the light of day again. I made my way back to Blake, who was lying on the ground sleeping. I kissed him, and he smiled. "I am sorry, my love. I did not think it would take that long."

"I should have let Rebecca come with you. I am hungry."

I giggled. "Come on. We can go home now."

I guided him to Spirit, and then we went back to the castle. He went and got us some food and then came back to my study. We sat on the floor, eating and looking at the drawings. "What are you looking for?"

"Markers of some kind."

"Markers?"

"Yes, something I read about finding the Markers of Time."

He sat there, looking at me, then reached up and moved my hair out of the way, tucking it behind my ear. "You are so beautiful."

I turned my head and smiled at him. "You are the beautiful one, my love."

He kissed me. "I am one lucky man to have you love me." I could not stop myself as I leaned in and kissed him deep. One thing led to another, and when we were finished, I found myself lying in his arms with nothing on. "I could get used to this," he said.

There was a knock on the door. The latch lifted up, and before I knew what was happening, he was on top of me, shielding me from whoever it was. "Oh my," I heard. "Please, Your Majesty, excuse me." And the door slammed shut.

I was laughing. "Who was that?"

"I do not know, but that will not happen again."

I could not stop laughing as I said, "You jumped on me like, I do not know what."

"I did not want anyone to see my wife with no clothes on. What if that was Charles or one of my brothers? No one sees you like this except for me."

I could not contain myself. The laughing would not stop. It was so bad that he started to laugh, so we laid there in the middle of the day on the floor of my study laughing.

We made our way to the kitchen for our midday meal, and it was obvious who had walked in on us. The poor little maid was shaking and dropping things. Blake and I just giggled. When we were finished, he went his way and I went back to my study. Shortly after I shut the door, there was a knock. I was sitting on the floor, so I said, "Come in," not paying attention to who walked in the door.

"Your Majesty, I came here to get my punishment."

I turned my head with crinkled eyes. "What are you talking about?"

"For walking in on you and Master Blake, I am here to get my punishment."

"Why would you think I would punish you?"

She looked at me. "For seeing you the way you were, for walking in on your private moment."

"I am sorry?" I asked.

"Well, Kings would have either had their way with me or put me to death."

"For walking in on them?"

"Yes, Your Majesty." She was bowed to the floor, obviously shaking.

"What is your name, child?"

"My name is Rachael."

"Rachael, there is nothing to punish you for. You may stand. What happened was not your fault but mine for not bolting the door. There was no harm done."

"But, Your Majesty," she started.

"My name is Sabine. Please call me Sabine."

"But, My Lady, I saw Master Blake."

I giggled and said, "I suppose you did." I giggled again. She was looking at the drawings. "Do you know this place?"

She took a step forward. "I know that place," she said, pointing to the drawing next to me.

I picked it up. "This place?"

"Yes, My Lady, that is on the other side of the forest, on your way to Wellington. We passed it on our way here. I remember that line along the trees."

"If I were to take you there, would you be able to show me?"

"Yes, My Lady, but my brother knows it, as well."

"Your brother?"

"Yes, My Lady, he is a guard for Master Charles."

"What is your brother's name?"

"His name is Raphael."

I picked up the drawings and rolled them together. "Would you come with me and help me find your brother?"

"Of course, My Lady, and then are you going to punish me?"

"Rachael, I am not going to punish you. It was not your fault."

We walked to the barracks, and she asked the guard if he was there, but we were informed that he was out on guard with another man.

"Would you please have him come to the house to my study when he comes back?" I asked.

"Of course, Your Majesty. I will send someone to get him."

"Thank you. Do you know where Blake is?"

"He is in the village, Your Majesty."

"Thank you," I told him, and we started back to the castle. "Thank you, Rachael. Next time, I would appreciate it if you would wait for an answer when you knock on the door."

"Yes, Your... I mean, Sabine."

I smiled at her, and she ran off. I went back to my study and thought about reading a tome, but I was not in the mood, so I just sat there in my chair. I wondered what Father did in here. He probably came in here to get some quiet because it was really quiet in here.

Blake came in a few moments later. "One of the men said you were looking for me. Is everything all right?"

I giggled. "Yes, but the little maid who walked in on us saw you without clothes."

"Oh, she did?" He raised his eyebrows as he got closer to me. "How do you know this?"

"She came here, ready for her punishment for walking in on us."

"Did she now?" he said as he took me in his arms. "And what punishment did you give her?"

"Death, of course." And I laughed. "I did not punish her at all. It was not her fault."

He picked me up and kissed me. "Did she mention whether or not she thought I was beautiful?"

I laughed so hard. "No, not at all." We were still laughing when someone knocked on the door. We both yelled come in and laughed.

A young man that looked just like Rachael walked in. "Excuse me, Your Majesty," he said as he backed out.

"No, come in please," I said. "You must be Raphael."

"Yes, Your Majesty. Joseph said you were looking for me."

"I was, and you can call me Sabine. Your sister told me that you would be able to take me to this place," I explained as I unrolled the drawings and showed him the spot.

"Yes, it is on the other side of the forest, on your way to Wellington."

"Wonderful. Would you please go saddle the horses, and we will be right there? We can go now."

He bowed and left.

"We are going on a ride?" Blake asked.

"Well, I am going. Are you going with me?"

He smiled. "I will not have my wife riding around the countryside with another man."

I laughed. "I am going to change. Meet me in the courtyard?" I ran up to change and grab my sword. Then I met them in the courtyard, and we rode out to the spot.

As we headed out onto the plain, I turned to look at the forest line. After finding the spot that matched the one in the drawing, I turned to Raphael. "Thank you for bringing me here," I said, nodding to him. He rode off then, and I whispered to Blake, "Will you go make sure he has left?"

He gave me a funny look and rode off. I followed my line of sight and walked right up to the spot Father had marked on his drawing. I climbed off Raiden and looked around but could not see anything. Stepping into the trees, I searched farther for whatever it was I was looking for but still saw nothing.

Blake rode up. "He went back to the castle. What are you doing?"

"Looking like a fool," I said and started back to Raiden. I was nearly to him when I stepped forward and froze. I could feel the vibration under the ground. I looked at Blake. "Or not. Come here." I motioned to him. He got down off his horse and walked over to me. "Step here and tell me what you feel."
He put his foot where mine was. "Nothing. Why?"

I placed my foot next to his and felt the vibration. "You do not feel that?"

"No," he said, and he put his arm around me. "Wait, now I feel something. It feels like you are shaking."

I smiled. "Then you can feel it through me?"

"Yes, what is that?"

"It is a Marker. Come on. We need to get out of here."

I climbed on Raiden. "Follow me," I said, and we rode to the hilltop.

"I do not think I am supposed to tell you the things I read in the tomes, so I can only tell you this. There are Markers out there, apparently buried in the ground of Whispering Wind. I do not know what they are for or why they are there, or why I am supposed to find them, but I am. I need to have them all for something, so I think we are to dig them up. I am not sure yet. Blake, I am scared. Something big is going to happen, and I am afraid that I do not know what to do about it."

He wrapped his arms around me. "As long as you stay pure, your magic lives. You and Rebecca, along with Juliana, will be able to handle just about anything. We will be all right."

I let him hold me. I let him make me feel safe. Although I wanted to believe him, something inside of me said different. This was not over. We went back to the castle.

"I need to read some more," I said to Blake.

"My love, you have been in that room for days now. How about you wait a day and have some rest. You are not going to be any good to anyone if you do not sleep. Come on. I will hold you so you can rest." He took my hand and led me to our room.

He slowly began to undress me, kissing my neck and shoulders as he did. It felt good to feel his touch, so I closed my eyes to enjoy the fire his lips brought to my flesh. "If you continue this way, we will not be resting."

He chuckled and said, "Perhaps, but at least you will relax enough to fall asleep," and he continued on until I stood before him unclothed. He lifted me in his arms and carried me to the bed, laying me down gently. He stood in front of me and undressed before climbing into to bed with me, and my troubles seemed to disappear as he kissed his way down and around my body. I fell asleep listening to his heart beat with a smile on my face.

When I woke, it was still the light of day. I reached for him, but he was not here, so I sat up and looked around the empty room. Stretching, I could not help but smile; Blake made me happy. I heard the latch on the door and quickly laid back down to pretend I was sleeping, but it did not fool him. He always knew. He came to the side of the bed he had vacated and sat a tray on it, then came around to my side. It took him a minute to get in the bed, but when he did, I knew why. He had undressed again. Sliding in behind me, he wrapped his arms around me.

"I know you are awake," he whispered in my ear as he kissed it. I giggled.

"How do you know?"

"How do I know what," he whispered as his hand trailed down my body to my thigh.

"How do you know I am not sleeping?" I asked as I turned my head to kiss him.

"Because of your breathing." His hand came around to the front of me and pulled me up his body. "I want to try something."

"Mmm… Blake," I moaned as I pressed against his chest with my back. The moans came from deep within me. His hands were caressing me, while he moved his mouth from the back of my neck to my ear. When he groaned, I felt it to the core of my body. I put my hands up to grab his hair. I was going to burn from the inside out again. As I turned my head to kiss him, my body started shaking and my insides burning. I could not help but cry out as his mouth covered mine. We lay there shaking, holding one another. I turned in his arms, our kiss so deep and unnerving I wanted to crawl inside of him.

When we parted, he had a beautiful smile on his face and his eyes were sparkly. I noticed his cheeks were wet, so I reached up to wipe them dry. "I love you so much it hurts me," he whispered. I covered his mouth with mine.

I listened to his heart calm as we lay in each other's arms. He pulled away to look at me, moving my hair off my face and then holding my face in his hand. "You are the most incredible woman. You make me feel like we are the only two people alive. There has been nothing in this life that has ever made me feel like this."

I did not know what to say to him, so I just leaned my head into his and touched his face while I kissed him again.

154

Chapter Nine

We ate our food and then got dressed. As it turned out, we ended up sleeping the light of the day away. "I cannot believe we slept the day away and then the night and now half of the day again."

"Oh, my love, if you really want to count the time we slept, well, it was just one night." He smiled at me.

I walked up to him and kissed him. "Well, yes, I suppose, and thank you."

He wrapped his arms around me, laughing. "There is no need to thank me. It was my pleasure." We giggled.

It was nearly midday by the time we emerged from our room. Everyone had gathered in the kitchen. When we walked in, the giggles and the smiles were abundant.

"It is about time the two of you came down," Rebecca said with a giggle.

I swatted her as I walked by. "I was tired."

Laughter erupted around the table. We had a lovely midday meal, and then everyone scattered and went about their business. I went to my study, and Blake went to work. I wondered what it was he did all day and decided I would have to ask him.

I was sitting at my desk, looking at the drawings from the cave, when there was a knock on the door. "Come in," I said.

I looked up to see Christopher. "Your Majesty, I have completed the staking of the Kingdom."

"Thank you, and please call me Sabine," I said as I got up to sit in the chair by the window. He came in and sat in the other chair.

"This is the biggest Kingdom I have ever mapped out. Did you know that the majority of Wellington is included in this land?"

"No, I did not know that. How strange..."

"I will start the drawing of the actual map when the light of day begins. I was wondering if you could be present when I spoke to Julia's father."

"What do you mean?"

"Well, I am going to take your advice and speak to him, and I was wondering if you would be present."

"I am not sure what I can do, but I do not see why I could not. Would you like to do it now, while I have a moment?" I got up and walked to the door.

"That would be fine."

I opened the door, and walking down the hall was Rachael. "Excuse me, Rachael, would you find Westin for me and ask him to come in here, please?"

"Of course, My Lady," she said and was off and running.

A few moments later, Westin came in. "Hi, Sabine. Rachael said you wanted to see me."

"Yes, my love, I do. This is Christopher, the man who is going to draw a map of our land. Christopher, this is my brother, Westin." They shook hands.

"So what is wrong, Sabine? You are not leaving again, are you?"

"No, my love, it is not I who wishes to speak with you. It is Christopher."

Westin's eyes changed then, just like that night at the table. "What is this about?" His voice was different, more stern, more structured than usual.

Christopher stood up. "Sire, I am a good man, an honorable man."

"You would have to be for my sister to trust you," Westin said in that strange, not Westin, voice. I sat there watching him. *What is going on with him?*

Christopher continued, "Sire, Julia and..."

Westin put his hand up to stop him. "Julia is my only daughter. When you start a sentence with Julia and... I would presume you were going to say I. It does not make me happy."

"I am sorry, Sire. We have met and have spent some time together in the garden."

"You have been alone with my daughter?" Westin said rather loudly and rather mean.

"No, Sire, never alone. That would not be proper. I like her a great deal, and I think she likes me. I thought it best to come to you and to ask your permission to spend more time with her."

Westin did not say a word, he just stood there staring at him. He then looked at me before just turning and walking out of the room. I was stunned.

"I am sorry, Christopher. Please excuse me while I go speak to Westin. You can go back to your quarters. I will come and find you when I am finished."

He bowed and left with me. When I went to Westin's room, I could hear him in there screaming. I knocked on the door, and it stopped. Camille answered the door.

"May I come in?" I asked.

"I do not think that would be a good idea right now," she said, and then Westin pulled the door from her and stood there looking at me. This was a man I had known my whole life, and I had never seen this part of him. I looked back into his eyes and saw what I had seen that night at the table.

"What do you want, Sabine?" he asked very angrily.

I stood there looking at him. "Who are you?"

He did not say anything, but his eyes softened and his body became less tense. He changed right there in front of me. I did not think he knew that I noticed.

"I am your brother, Sabine. Who do you think I am?"

I was stunned and turned to walk away. I did not know what to say to him, but that man was not the sweet, kind, carefree man I had grown up with. That was a very angry man. I stopped halfway down the hallway and turned around; he had slammed the door when he went back in the room. "Oh, no you do not, big brother," I said as I made my way back to the room. I stood outside the door and listened.

"You will not see that man again!" he yelled.

"But, father," Julia was crying.

Then I heard it. I could not believe I heard what I did, but I heard him slap her and say, "No daughter of mine will be marked as a whore! Do you hear me?"

"Westin, calm down," Camille said.

"Do not presume you can tell me what to do. She will not see him again."

I opened the door just as he started to move toward Camille. I ran in, grabbed him, and threw him to the floor. "Oh, no you do not, brother." I looked at Camille, telling her, "Take her and go, now!" Camille grabbed Julia, and they ran out of the room. I turned to Westin and screamed at him, "WHO ARE YOU?" He started to get up. "Stay down, Westin."

He laughed. "Little sister, you have no idea what you are doing." He started to stand, but I put him down again.

"Stay down, Westin."

"You will not treat me this way, like I am one of your guardsmen. I am your brother."

"You are not my brother. WHO ARE YOU?" I screamed at him.

He jumped up and came at me, so I grabbed him by the throat and slammed him on the floor. "Do not make me hurt you," I said.

He laughed. "Like you could."

He got up again, and again he came at me. This time, I moved faster than him, and when he slammed into the wall, I drew my sword. He spun around and laughed. "You going to kill me, Sabine?" Then he charged me.

I ran my sword through him to the hilt, slamming him and my sword into the wall.

Then I heard Blake scream, "SABINE, NO!" But it was too late.

I leaned in to Westin and said, "The answer to your question is yes."

"You cannot kill me. I am the Keeper," he whispered.

I let go of my sword and backed away from him, looking at him. He had blood in his mouth when he smiled. Blake stood there shocked. "What the hell is going on here?"

I did not say a word, just stood there watching my brother try to move. He could not die either, like Charles. I could run him through, and run him through, and he would recover. My eyes never left Westin's. "Blake, you need to leave."

"I am not going anywhere, Sabine. Tell me what is going on."

"Go now! Please, just go."

He stood there, looking from me to Westin.

"BLAKE!" I shouted.

He left and closed the door behind me.

"Who are you?" I asked Westin. "You are not my brother."

He laughed, trying not to choke. "I am your brother."

"My brother would never strike his child, or his wife, so I will ask you again. Who are you?"

"I am your brother."

I stood there looking at him.

"I am who I have always been."

"I have no knowledge of this person you are."

"No one does. The Westin you know is a farce to protect the Keeper."

"Who is this Keeper?"

"I am the Keeper of the land, of the secrets. I am the Keeper of life."

I shook my head. "What? Why?"

"Father told me to keep myself hidden in plain sight, so no one would find me. It has worked for all these years."

"Until today... Why did you slap Julia? Do you make it a habit to hurt women?"

He choked when he laughed. "I have never struck anyone in my whole life well, with the exception of you the day the barbarians came."

"You slapped Julia, and I saw you going after Camille."

"Yes," he choked. "Could you take this sword out of me now?"

I shook my head. "No, I do not think so. You are going to talk to me and tell me what is going on."

"I cannot. I have already told you too much."

"Well, the way I see it is you really have no choice in the matter."

"Why did you slap Julia?"

"Because she made a mockery of me. She told me I had no idea what it was like to be in love. In love, Sabine... She thinks she is in love."

"Westin, she is past the age where she should already have a husband."

"Yes, a proper husband, one that can provide for her."

I laughed. "My love, you and I do not live in that time any longer. He is a good man, and is that not what you would want for your daughter? Or would you prefer to give her in marriage to someone who does not love her?"

He did not say anything. "She thinks I am simple minded."

I laughed again. "Yes, we have all been led to believe that. Why would that be again?"

"I need to not stand out. I need for people like Samuel to think I am not all there."

"But now you are not?"

"I have never been. My job is to watch over you and to keep this land."

"Then answer me this, Keeper. If I am not pure, do I lose my magic?"

He stared at me. "Yes."

"So you know then?"

"That you and Blake have not made a union? Yes, I know. I am rather impressed with him. He was a good choice."

"It is not his choice but mine. Who else knows?"

"About you and Blake? No one but Camille and me."

"I will remove the sword, but you need to reign your temper, and you will apologize to your daughter and then consider Christopher. He is a good man, Westin. In these times, she could do no better."

"I give you my word. Will you tell Blake of this?"

"I cannot tell Blake anything from the tomes. You, I discovered from the tomes."

"I knew that you had figured it out that day in the kitchen."

I pulled out the sword, and he crumpled to the floor so I helped him to the chair. "This conversation is not over," I told him and walked out of his room. Camille was in the hallway. "He is in the chair, and you and I need to have a chat soon." She nodded and moved past me. Blake was waiting at the end of the hall when I got there.

"You will never dismiss me like that again," he said.

"You, my love, will not presume to tell me what I can and cannot do." I continued walking.

"Sabine," he said. "Sabine, stop and talk to me."

I just kept on moving, making my way out the door and across the courtyard. I could feel Blake coming at me, so I spun around. "Do not make me hurt you. I am in no mood to discuss this with you." Again, I kept walking.

"I do not care what kind of mood you are in. You will tell me what I want to know. What the hell was that?"

I ignored him and made it just to the stable doors when he grabbed me and spun me around. I kneed him in his private

162

parts, and he bent over in pain, so I hurried into the stables and got Raiden. Once in the courtyard, I jumped on him and we were gone. "Do not stop, and do not tell Spirit where we are."

He did not stop moving. I was pretty sure he was just running in a circle, but I needed to feel free. I needed to think. No, I needed to run. How could I face Blake, knowing I would never be able to have a union with him? I wanted babies, lots of babies, and now I could not have any. The tears started to flow, and I could not stop them. The only thing I ever wanted was to have babies.

Raiden ran and ran, while I cried and cried. I just could not go back there. I did not want to go back there. Westin knew I could not make a union with Blake; he had known all along. Why did he not tell me? I leaned in to Raiden's neck and hung on to him. He slid to a stop, and before I knew what was happening, I was in Blake's arms, sobbing uncontrollably.

"My beautiful girl, what is wrong?"

I could not answer him. I just sobbed. He knelt down on the ground then sat down, holding me in his arms. "Sabine, my love, please tell me what is going on."

I shook my head and just cried. He did not push me; he just let me cry. *How could I tell him? How could I tell him we would not have lots of babies?* I cried harder just thinking about. I could feel the tension radiate from his body as he held me. He had no idea why I was so upset. As my sobs subsided, his hold on me loosened. "Can you talk to me?" he whispered.

I shook my head, trying to compose myself. I felt full of dread, just as I had that day when we went back to the valley. Nothing mattered to me anymore. Everything I had been through had been for nothing. I would not get my happiness, and Blake would not get his children. He would not even get to have a union with his wife. "I cannot be your wife anymore," I told him, unsure why I even said it.

He pulled me away from him. "What are you talking about?"

"I cannot be your wife anymore. You should be with a woman who can give you what you want. I cannot be that woman."

His eyes filled with tears. "Why are you saying this to me?"

"Because the longer we put it off, the harder it will be."

"You are my wife, and there is nothing anyone can do about that. I do not want anyone else. You give me all that I could ever want."

I shook my head. "I cannot give you the union you want. I cannot give you the children you want. I am nothing. Our happiness will never be."

He got serious and sat me on the grass in front of him. Taking my hands in his, he said, "Listen to me. I have no idea where this is coming from, or why, but you are the woman I choose to spend my life with. It did not matter if we were given to one another by your father. If it had not been you I was told to marry, I would not have married. The union you speak of is not something that is important to us. Having children... well, I will be truthful. I would like to have children with you, but it is not necessary for us. I love you. I love everything about you. I love that you are strong and smart. I love that you have such high emotions. I love the way you kiss me, the way you look at me, and the way you love me. You do love me?" I nodded. "Then why would you not want to be my wife?"

"The things you speak of are things that every man wants. The union is the most important."

"Sabine, we have been married for some time now, and we have been doing fine without having this union. Where do these thoughts come from?"

I sat there looking at him, and I wanted to tell him but I could not. I knew he would not understand. He saw me run Westin through. He knew Westin could not die.

"What happened with Westin?"

Again, I said nothing but just sat there. The tears welled in my eyes again, knowing I would have to keep these secrets from him. After everything I made him promise, now I was doing to him what he did to me. I could not stand this anymore. "I have become you." I stood and jumped on Raiden and went back to the castle. He was on Spirit, so he came right behind me. I ran to our room, threw myself on the bed, and sobbed. He was there immediately, holding me. *Why is he so good to me when I was not so gracious with him?*

There was a knock on the door, and then Westin came in. "I think we all need to talk," he said.

I lay in Blake's arms, crying.

"I believe you may be right, perhaps you can answer some questions for me," Blake said.

"How about I tell you a story, one that I think will answer all your questions," Westin suggested in his not-Westin voice. He pushed the door open, and Camille walked into the room. Westin shut the door, bolted it, and they sat in the chairs by the fireplace. Blake sat up and pulled me up with him.

Westin started, "When Sabine was born, I was in my eighth year. She was the sweetest thing I had ever seen. Her eyes were the brightest blue, and her hair... well, you know about her hair. My father and mother came to me one night and told me a story, the same story you have heard throughout your life. They told me that this land was special and that only a special person would be able to heal it and drive the evil from it. They said Sabine was that special person. But there was also another one who was called the Keeper of the land. The Keeper holds the secrets and keeps the land safe. I am that Keeper. I was trained, just as Sabine was. The only difference is that I cannot die. I will not die. Sabine was able to die until the swords were forged. That is where her Guardians came in, and after that, she was given the gift of life as I have. She cannot die, however she can kill herself, as we all know. But until the land is sealed, she will be like us and given back her life. When she went to the cave and cast the spell to remove the evil that once escaped this land, she accomplished only one of her tasks. But there are plenty of men out there who are dark and have dark hearts. They will come, and they will continue to come, until we seal the land. Then and only then will we be safe.

"I think I know why Sabine is in the state she is in, Blake. I know you two have not had a union like married people should. She was not supposed to marry you yet, because there is still much to do. That is why everything kept getting in your way, and I know this because her magic is still alive. Once she is not pure, her magic will leave and the land will sit in unrest, as it has for so many generations. I know you have read the tomes, Sabine. I knew it that day in the kitchen. When you looked at me, you saw it in my eyes. I was surprised, actually, when you did not confront me.

"I am sorry for what happened today, and you are right. It is just that they grew up in the valley. She has no experience in this world, and there is still so much bad here. I know you, and I know you would not let anything happen to her. I have agreed to allow them to spend time together, with company of course. I will never forgive myself for slapping her, or for going after Camille, and I deserved everything you gave me and more. I was out of control.

"There is so much more for you to achieve, Sabine, and so much we need to do. I cannot help you. I cannot tell you

166

anything. I should not even be telling you this. Blake, you must give me your word that none of this is to leave this room. I will go about playing the role of simple minded Westin, for it is the only way. There are people out there who know about the Keeper, and if I am discovered, things will turn out badly. We all have to be together when the Coming happens. You were right to hide us because they would have used me against you."

I sat there looking at him. Blake, I think, was in shock with the new Westin.

"When the barbarians came, you hit me in the head to send me to the darkness?"

"Yes, I actually hit you with a rock. I am so glad you do not remember that. Being the Keeper also meant I had to keep you safe. If you had died before the swords were forged, all would have been lost and Roman would have won."

"Why did you just stand by and let everything happen?"

"Because, as with Charles, I cannot interfere. I have a specific task to do in all of this. You need to do this on your own."

"I read in the tomes of the Unknown Heir who needs to take place in this Coming. Do you know who that is?"

"Yes, I do, but it is not my place to disclose that information to you. You will figure it all out, Sabine. You have done it all on your own so far."

"Why does everyone get to know things I do not?"

He smiled at me. "But you do know it. You know more than all of us. You just do not know you know. In the tomes, it stated that all the knowledge would be forged with you when you forged the swords and then possessed them. You know, Sabine. It will come to you."

"What is Camille's role in this?"

"Same as Blake's. She bears the Mark of the fleur-de-lis, as well. She is who I was to marry. Their bloodline is of the ancients, Sabine. They have waited for us for a very long time. Our bloodlines must become one."

"Juliana and James?"

"Yes, the children we produce are the heirs to this kingdom. That is probably why I was so upset with Julia and Christopher. I am still not sure it is a good match."

I looked at Camille. "When did you know about him?"

"The night we were married, he told me everything."

"Am I allowed to tell Blake everything I am learning in the tomes?"

"He is your husband, Sabine. If you cannot trust him, then I would say no." He smiled.

I felt a rush of relief come over me as I looked at Blake. "Part of tonight was about me keeping secrets from you. I was not sure if I could tell you all that I have learned, and I felt horrible because I was so mad at you all the time for keeping secrets from me."

He smiled. "The secrets you have kept are very different from the ones I have kept. I do not hold ill will, Sabine. But Westin," he turned to look at him, "what is this about, this voice this person who sits before me? This is not the man I know, although it would explain what you said to me when I married Sabine."

He laughed. "Yes, sorry about that. I need to keep this simple minded man facade alive. No one must ever know who I am. No one, not even Charles. His role in all of this is complete, as is for all the Guardians. It was complete when Sabine forged the swords. He should go and have a life, marry and have some children. They all should."

"Yes, good luck with that," Blake said. "As for Sabine, you can trust me with her honor. I will not cross that line."

"Well, you are a bigger man than most. I mean, my sister is beautiful. I do not know how you stop yourself."

"All right, this conversation is going where I wish for it not to, so you cannot tell me anything?" I asked.

"No, and you must keep my secret. Even my children do not know, although I think Julia might suspect otherwise." He chuckled. "So are we in an understanding then?"

"I still cannot believe you are this man, but yes, we are in an understanding. One last thing, do you know what the tomes say?" He just smiled, and then they got up and left the room.

Blake and I sat there in silence for a very long time. I did not know what to say to him. I had betrayed him. I knew how that felt, so I sort of knew what he was feeling. I got off the bed and left the room, and he did not stop me. I went to my study and sat in the chair by the window in the dark. I had betrayed my husband. I wiped the tears from my eyes. Bringing my knees to my chin, I curled up, and I must have fallen asleep.

When I woke, I was still there and the light of the day had begun. Looking around the room, there was no sign of Blake. He was very upset with me, and I did not blame him at all. I took a deep breath and went to the kitchen, but there was no one there. I found some eggs sitting on the warmer over the fire, so I ate them. I just left the plate on the table and went to our room to change. There was no sign of Blake in there either, and he had not slept there the night before. My heart started beating fast; he did not sleep in our bed. He did not come to find me and tell me everything was all right. He just left.

I changed my clothes and realized I was crying. Wiping away the tears, I grabbed my sword and went to my study. I got the drawings from the desk then went to the stables. While I was putting Raiden's saddle on, I saw that Blake's horse was gone.

Once on Raiden, I leaned in to him. "Will you take me to Blake?"

'I cannot.'

'What do you mean?'

'He asked me not to follow him.'

I sat there not knowing what to say or do. My heart sank. I felt like my stomach was turning inside out, so I got off of him and stood there.

One of the guards came up to me. "Your Majesty, is everything all right?"

"When did Blake leave?"

"I was not aware he was gone."

"His horse is gone. Please find out when he left."

The guard nodded and left. I went into the stables, found another horse, and put a saddle on him. After walking him out into the courtyard, I climbed on.

The guard came out and said, "No one seems to know, Your Majesty."

I looked at him and kicked the horse in the sides. We were off. I did not know which way to go, so I went to the hilltop and then down the other side. Riding a regular horse was different, that was for sure. I just kept riding. I had no idea where I was going, but I did not stop.

Charles had come out and asked why Raiden was standing in the courtyard, and the guard explained.

"And you just let her take a horse and ride off on her own?" he asked.

"She is the Queen. How was I supposed to stop her? She would have beaten me to a pulp."

"I suppose you are right." He walked up to Raiden. "So what did you do to make her mad?"

Raiden did not move. He just stood there.

I rode more than half the day, and I saw no sign of Blake. I had crossed the river and was farther than I had ever been on my own without Raiden, but I did not care. I had to find him. But he could have been anywhere, and my horse was starting to tire, so I had to stop and let him rest. I pulled on his reins and slowed him. He trotted to a stop, and I got off, walking in the direction we had been riding in. I would find him one way or another.

I walked until I noticed the light of the day was leaving the sky, and then I got back on the horse and rode toward the forest. I decided to sleep in a tree that night and continue on in the light of the day. I found a nice tree, tied the horse to one a bit away, in case someone came, and climbed up to sleep. The birds woke me, and when I got down, the horse was still where I tied him up, so we began again. I rode most of the day and then walked again. I did this for four days.

On the fifth day, I came to the hills that led to the valley, though I was sure I did not know the way there. I walked up the hills, pulling the horse with me to the top, where I sat down to rest and to look and see if he was here. There was no movement near the cottage, and the light of the day was nearly gone. I did not move. I waited for the dark of the night to come, to see if a fire was glowing. Nothing happened. Nothing glowed. I found the guard station and got comfortable. Where could he be? Why did he leave me? I felt the tears well up in my eyes. He had been gone for five days. If he had returned, he would have brought Raiden to find me.

I must have fallen asleep, for the light of the day woke me. After I got up, I made my way down into the valley. I was so hungry and knew there must be fruit there somewhere. Westin and Camille lived there, so there had to be something. I found the little orchard we had, picked a bunch of fruit, and filled a satchel I found in the barracks. Climbing back on the horse, I continued across the valley, up, and over the hills. I had no idea where I was going, but I needed to find Blake. I rode the horse hard across the plain well into the dark of the night. We managed to find a patch of trees to take cover in. Again, I slept in a tree. It was half way through the dark of the night when he was in my head.

'Where are you?'

I woke but did not answer him. I was mad at him because he would not take me to Blake.

'I cannot find you. You have been gone for so long. Everyone is worried.'

Good. Let them worry. I was not going to get any sleep with him in my head, so I ate some fruit and then climbed down to ride some more. I rode hard into the next day, sure the horse was going to stop for good soon. At that point, I really had no idea where I was or which way was home. I just needed to find Blake. Never had I been out there on my own; it had always been with Raiden.

He was right. I had been gone for more than six days now. If I did not make contact with Raiden, he would not find me. Good. Let him suffer.

Days went by as I rode the land, looking for Blake and punishing Raiden. I had no idea where I was, nor had I seen anyone. After coming to the conclusion that I was lost, I decided I was not going to let him know where I was; I would just wander around until I found my way home. It did not matter if it took me four seasons to do it.

I felt the tears well up again in my eyes, knowing my husband had left me because I betrayed him, just as he had betrayed me, but quickly wiped the tears away. I was strong, and I would find my way home. Realizing that I had not strayed from the line I took from the valley, I thought perhaps if I went left, I would find my way.

I pulled on the left rein, and we turned, heading West I hoped. The valley was East of Wellington, and Wellington was Southeast of Whispering Wind, so I would hope that I was going West. I continued in this direction for three more days. On the fourth day, I spied one of the stakes from Christopher, so I was now back in Whispering Wind, at least a day's ride to the castle. I could make it just after the dark of the night would come.

I did not stop. I was sleeping on his neck when we rode into Whispering Wind. He stopped in the courtyard, and I must have fallen off, because when I hit the ground, I heard some people screaming for Blake.

I tried to open my eyes. There were people screaming and shaking me, mostly male voices. I tried to push their hands off me, but then I felt him lift me and whisper, "I got you, my love. I got you." And I was gone into sleep.

It was the warmth from the light of the day that woke me. When I opened my eyes, he was not there in our bed. Had I imagined his voice when he carried me to bed? I stretched and looked around the room. Nothing. I was alone again. I sat up, wondering if I had imagined him. There was a gentle knock on the door, and then it opened.

It was Camille. "Did I wake you," she asked. I shook my head. "I will get your bath ready. You are filthy. Sabine, is everything all right? We have been going crazy looking for you."

"Nothing is right, Camille. It will never be right. Yes, I would like a bath, and then, please, I would like to be left alone."

She nodded. It took only a few minutes to fill the tub, and then she was gone. I dropped my clothes on the floor and got in the tub, where I washed my hair and then washed me. When I got out of the tub and looked at the water, it was so dirty. I had been on that horse for eleven days nearly non-stop. And I could not find my husband.

As I was getting dressed, I heard the door open and felt him come in. I did not move, though my gown was half way on. I waited for him to touch me, but he did not, so I put my gown on then my shoes. I did not turn to face him, as I picked up my sword and the drawings then turned to leave. He was standing by the door with his arms folded across his chest, but I did not look into his eyes. I walked toward him to leave, yet he did not move. I picked up my crown from the table and moved around him. His eyes never left me, but I did not look at him.

I went to the kitchen to eat and then to my study. I thought it strange that I saw no one here. I did not hear anyone, either. I wondered where everyone went. I laid the drawings out on the rug that Boland had made for me, and walked around in a circle to get different views. None of these places looked familiar to me. Perhaps Christopher had seen one of them. I did not even know how many Markers there were, or how big they were. I just knew that they vibrated when I was near them. This was going to be difficult at best to figure out.

As I made yet another circle around the drawings, I realized that, like the ones with the clues, perhaps these were like them.

I started placing them on top of one another and holding them up to the light. After the third match up, I saw it.

"Very clever," I said out loud.

I knew this place. It was by the river where Raiden kept taking me. I kept these two pieces separate. Down on my hands and knees, I was gathering up the pieces when I heard the door shut. I sat back on my feet and turned toward the door. Blake was standing there. *What, was he going to just stand and stare at me?* I was not going to play this game with him, so I finished what I was doing and rolled up the drawings, rolling the two that matched together. I put the big roll of drawings in my desk, keeping the matching ones with me, then took my sword and walked to the door. Blake just looked at me, not saying a word. I was not in the mood for this, so I was just going to leave. As I reached for the latch, his hand gently touched mine, and I paused. He did not say anything, so I continued to flip the latch and pulled the door open. I did not look back at him when I walked out the door. He did not follow me.

I went to the stables and took another horse. Raiden stood there looking at me, but I ignored him. I got on the horse and headed in the direction of the river. Once I got there, I got down to look at the drawings. Turning in a slow circle, I saw the spot I wanted and walked over with the horse. Once I reached the trees, I was just one step in when I felt the ground vibrating through my shoe. Marker two. I smiled, having accomplished something.

I got on the horse and went back to the castle. The dark of night was just upon us when we arrived, so I went in the back way, ate, then went to our room. Blake was not there, so I put on my sleeping gown and got into bed. I was still very tired, so sleep came easy.

I was awakened when he wrapped his arms around me. I was so angry with him for leaving me, and now he wanted to sleep in bed with me. Pulling away from him, I got up and went to the chair by the fire. I pulled my knees up to my chest and tried to sleep there. He would not have it; he wanted to make amends. He came over, picked me up, and carried me back to bed. I let him, hoping he would not get back in bed, but he did. I got up and left the room, and went to my study, where slept in the chair. When the light of day came, I found a tray of food on my desk, but I did not eat it. He put it there. He would not be taking care of me.

I went upstairs to get dressed in my clean boy clothes, got my sword, and left again. I ate in the kitchen alone, and went out in the back courtyard. Charles was walking up. "Good to see you have slept. Can I inquire as to why you are running all my horses to the ground and not riding Raiden?"

"You may inquire, but I believe the horses belong to me. I am not riding Raiden simply because I do not want to."

"Can we talk?"

"I thought that is what we were doing."

"You were gone for a very long time, Sabine. I still have men out there looking for you."

"You should not waste your men like that, Charles. I am perfectly capable of taking care of myself."

"Oh, I know that better than anyone. Your husband, however, is a whole other story."

"My husband is really none of your business, and I would appreciate it if you could find some way to make him not my husband anymore."

He stood there looking at me, obviously confused. "What? What happened?"

"As if you did not know, Charles. You know everything. Why would you not know this?"

"Sabine, what has happened?"

I just shook my head and made my way to the stables. I picked a horse that looked up for a run and saddled him. Raiden stood there looking at me, but I did not give him notice. As I walked out into the light of the day, I saw Charles talking to Blake. I climbed on the horse and rode out of the courtyard through the village, and instead of going to the hilltop, I went in the opposite direction.

I rode for half a day, took out the drawings, put them together, and then searched the tree line for the spot I wanted. The forest had grown, so it was difficult to locate, but after some time, I finally found it. I walked into the forest and found the third Marker. Pleased with myself, I rode back to the castle. Only, I did not go in, and instead went to the barracks where I asked one of the guards if he knew where Christopher was.

"He has been gone for three days now. He said that he would be back in five."

"When he returns, would you please tell him to find me before he leaves again?"

"Yes, Your Majesty."

"Thank you."

I walked back to the castle and went to my study to put the drawings away. As I was leaving, Blake came in and shut the door behind him. I knew Charles had said something to him. He stood there looking at me, not saying a word.

"I am tired and really do not wish to play this silent staring intrigue with you," I said as I walked toward him.

"Why did you leave?"

"I left to find my husband who had left me. Funny thing, my horse would not bring me to him because he asked him not to follow him. So do not inquire as to where I was when you are the one who left. Now, I am done. Charles was set with a task, and hopefully soon, you will not need to bother with me. Now, if you will excuse me, I am tired and would like to eat and go to bed."

"I left you food, and you did not eat it."

"It is not your concern what I do. You made that perfectly clear. Now please move so I can pass."

He stood there looking at me. "Why will you not look at me?"

"Probably the same reason why you left, because I do not wish to see you."

"That is not why I left."

"It does not matter, Blake. I told you I was done with all of this. I do not want these emotions. I am tired of crying over you. In fact, I am just tired. Now, I have asked you twice to move, and I am not asking anymore. Get out of my way or I will move you myself."

"I am afraid neither of those things are going to take place here. You and I need to talk, Sabine."

"I needed to talk to you fifteen days ago, but you left me."

"I did not leave you. I went to have some time to myself to think. A great deal of information was laid on me that night. I wanted to think."

"And I merely went in search of my husband, who made it perfectly clear he did not want to be found."

"We need to discuss this, and we need to do it sooner rather than later."

"No, Blake, the time for discussing was fifteen days ago. I am done. I have a great deal to do in order to keep everyone safe. I do not have time for this," I waved my hand, "between us."

"You do have the time, and it is now," he demanded, raising his voice.

"Do not presume you can tell me what to do. I have asked Charles to…"

"I know what you asked him, and there is no undoing this, Sabine. You are my wife, and you will remain my wife!" He yelled.

"Then it shall be a marriage void of contact and love."

He chuckled. "You do not love me anymore?"

"I do not wish to continue this farce of a marriage. I cannot give you children, and I cannot make a union with you. I am forced to keep secrets from you. It will not work, and I am done trying. I spend more time worrying and crying than I do anything. And you know what, Blake? I am done with it all. I am perfectly capable of taking care of myself. You heard Westin. I do not need you."

"But you still love me?"

I shook my head. "I will ask you one last time to please move out of the way so I can go to bed. I have things to do in the light of the day, and I need my rest. I did not get much while I was out looking for a man who did not wish to be found."

He did not move. I walked over to the window and opened it, then climbed out and went around the castle and up to my room. By the time I got there, he was already there. I walked out and went to my parents' room, bolted the door, and went to sleep.

When the light of the day came, I went to my room and changed, and then made my way to the kitchen ate the food that had been left for me before going out to the stables.

All the horses were gone except for Raiden. I looked at him and walked out. I decided I would walk today. One of the places on the drawings was about a half a day's walk, perhaps a little longer, but I did not care. They would not break me.

I wandered around on the plain for the majority of the morning, finally finding the spot I was looking for well after the midday meal. I searched for the Marker, but I could not find it. After wandering too far into the forest and getting turned around, I ended up lost. The dark of the night had come fast, so I searched for a tree. As I was climbing up, my foot slipped and I fell backwards to the ground. The darkness came fast.

Blake and Charles had made sure there were no horses for me to ride, trying to get me to take Raiden so they could find me when they wanted. Raiden could not locate me as long as I did not talk to him.

When they returned to the castle with the horses after midday, Blake went looking for me, all proud of himself thinking he had kept me there. He searched high and low for me. Rebecca looked in all the places she thought I would be, but I was nowhere to be found. They met in the courtyard to talk.

"Blake, this is ridiculous, making everyone stay away from her so she will talk to you. You left her, and now she is hurt."

"I know, but she will not yield."

Charles spoke. "All of this is not important. She is gone, and we have no way of knowing if someone took her."

Rebecca giggled. "Really? You think someone might have taken her?"

"What? Did she just walk out of here, because Raiden is right in there?" He pointed to the stables.

"She is on foot. Spirit asked Raiden, who said she looked at him and walked out, heading toward the back gates."

Blake panicked. "She is walking? She is out there walking?"

"Your idea, remember, Blake?" Rebecca snorted, and walked away.

She went in the stables and got Raiden and Spirit. "I will find her, and when I do, I suggest you back off, Blake. You did this.

You should have never left, and you most certainly should have never told Raiden to not follow you."

"I will go with you," Blake said.

"I am sure she does not wish to see you. I will go alone." And she rode off. Raiden did not know where I was, but he followed my scent. It took a while for them to find me lying on my back in the forest.

"Sabine," Rebecca said, but I did not respond. My leg was twisted, and my arm was behind my back. She turned to Raiden. "Go and get them, and hurry. Something is very wrong." Raiden neighed and stomped his hoof and took off. Rebecca rubbed my hand and called my name. "Sabine, come on. Wake up. What are you doing out here?" She looked around. The dark of the night was very dark. "What happened to you?" There was a loud crack. The branch that I was climbing on had broken, and just as Rebecca looked up, it broke away completely and fell out of the tree, slamming into Rebecca who laid across me to shield me, taking her into the darkness.

Spirit started neighing and took off toward the castle. He flew into the courtyard screaming. Everyone was getting on their horses. Raiden and Spirit took off, making it difficult for Blake and Charles to follow them. Raiden had to go back twice to get them. When they rode up and saw us lying on the ground under the giant tree branch, no one moved.

Blake was the first there, lifting the giant branch off of Rebecca. Charles lifted Rebecca off of me and lay her gently on the grass. Blake knelt on the ground next to me and began touching my face. "Beautiful girl, open your eyes," he said with tears streaming down his face.

"Rebecca, my love, wake up," Charles said. Joseph was kneeling down on the other side of her.

My eyes fluttered open. "What happened?" I asked Blake.

"I do not know. Are you all right? Can you move?"

I looked up into the tree; it was so dark out. "How did you find me?"

"Rebecca found you. Come on." He reached for me. "Try to sit up."

I took his hands and let him pull me up. "Does anything hurt?"

I turned to answer him and saw Rebecca lying on the ground. I went to move, and there was terrible pain in my hip. I cried out but kept going.

"What happened?" I asked Joseph

"Rebecca left to come and find you with Raiden and Spirit, then Raiden came back and we were getting our horses to follow him when Spirit came into the courtyard screaming, and here we are. What happened?"

"I do not know. I got lost in the forest, and I was trying to climb the tree to sleep in it, but then the branch broke and I fell. That is all I remember." I leaned into Rebecca. "Come on, my love. Wake up. Come back to me. I need you," I whispered into her ear. Laying my head on her chest, I listened for her heart, finding it was still beating. I scooted over to her and pushed Charles out of the way, so I could hold her. "Come on, my love. Wake up."

"Sabine, we should get her back to the castle," Charles said.

"No, do not touch her. We will stay here until she wakes," I said. I lay there next to her, holding her until the light of the day came. They all sat around and waited with me. I did not speak to them; I just held her as she had held me when I went into the darkness. Her heartbeat changed, becoming a bit faster. I whispered in her ear, "Come on, my love. Wake up."

"No," she whispered. "It hurts."

I felt the tears fall from my eyes. "What hurts?" I whispered.

182

"Everything."

"Can you move?"

"Yes, I think so." I felt her move her hand and draw her legs up, which let them know she was awake.

"Rebecca," Charles said. I put my hand up to silence him.

"Can you sit up?" I asked her.

"Yes, I think so, but I do not want to."

I giggled. "Well, I do. I have been laying here in this position for a very long time holding you, and I think we should do it together."

She nodded. I sat first and then helped her up. "What happened?" I asked her.

"The tree was falling on you, so I had to protect you."

I chuckled. "I do not need protecting." I got on my knees and started to stand, using her shoulders to help myself. Then I grabbed her hands and she got up. We hobbled over to Spirit, I helped her up, and then I got on behind her.

No one said anything or tried to help. They just knew not to interfere.

Spirit had us back at the castle in no time. As we were walking in, I was yelling for Camille. She appeared at the top of the stairs.

"Please get a hot bath ready for Rebecca in my room."

It took us some time to make it up the stairs, and by the time we got to my room, the tub was nearly full. "Is everything all right?" Camille asked.

"For now it is. Thank you."

I helped Rebecca get out of her clothes. She had a huge bruise on her back where the tree landed on her. "Come on, my love. Get in and have a soak. Camille, will you stay with her? I will be back in a little while."

"Go easy on them, Sabine. Blake just wants you to talk to him."

I laughed. "Trust me. There will be no talking on his part." Then I left.

I waited by the stables for them to arrive. One by one, they rode in and dismounted. I waited until they were all off their horses. "I can only imagine whose idea it was to take all the horses and leave Raiden. You will not attempt to control me again, or you will all be banished from here. Is that understood?" They nodded, and I looked at Blake. "You and I are done. Do not try to fix this. You left me, and then you made my horse deny me. He is done. There is no forgiveness here. Do you understand? I do not want to talk to you. I do not want to see you. You left our bed, and then you left me. There is no turning back from that. I spent eleven days searching for you. Never once did I run and stop you from coming after me."

I looked at Charles next. "The next time you try to manipulate me, control me, or interfere with what I have to achieve, you will be banished and you can be assured that I will not come looking for you. I do not need your protection any longer. Your service with me is complete." I looked at the rest of them. "This goes for all of you. I do not care what your relationships are with anyone in my family, but you endangered Rebecca again because," I turned to Blake, "you feel the need to manipulate and control me, you are all done." I turned and walked away. I felt him coming but I did not stop.

He grabbed my arm and spun me around, I swung but he grabbed that arm as well. "You are my wife."

"Not anymore. I do not wish to be married to you. I am tired of these intrigues with you. The last time you hurt me like this, I cut my throat. This time, you will not be so lucky. This time, you will see me and you will know that you will never have me again."

"Why would you say that? Why would you think I would not want you?"

I screamed at him, "You left me! You manipulated me! You tried to control me! Something you promised never to do again. You spout your untruths like they were truths."

"Blake, let her go." It was Westin, and he had his other voice on.

Blake released me. I turned and walked away. Westin walked up to Blake and put his arm around his shoulder. "I told you not to hurt her again."

"It was not intentional, but she will not listen to me. After everything you told us, I needed time to think. I went to think, and when I came back, she was gone. She did not take Raiden. You know all of this."

"I will talk to her, but stay away from her, Blake. She has more important things to do. You know this. Do not cloud her judgment."

Blake nodded, and Westin walked away. He found me in my study, crying. He pulled me into his arms. "You are the strongest woman I know. Your tears are tears of love. I know you love him, sister, and he loves you. It is truth." I shook my head.

"What kind of wife can I be? I cannot give him children. I cannot make a union. All I do is cry all the time."

"You cry, my love, because you love him so deeply. Do not think for a minute that I do not cry when I am with my wife. I love her that much that she brings tears to my eyes. These things will take place, Sabine. They will. You need him. He needs you. The energy the two of you produce when you are together can move mountains. He is a good man. You were not here when he returned to find you gone. He was out of his mind with worry. We all were. Raiden could not find you."

I sobbed into his chest. "I cannot forgive him."

"Sabine, there is nothing to forgive. He did nothing wrong. Your guilt is on you, for keeping secrets from him. I suppose that is my fault for not telling you sooner. He did nothing wrong. Do you think I would allow him to hurt you again?"

I looked up at him, and he wiped my tears away. "Why could you not have been this brother all along?"

"Because you would not have grown up to be this incredible woman if I had." I giggled. "Now, forgive your husband or make amends, whatever you choose, but let him back in, Sabine. You need him."

I think it was the look in his eyes that made me think he knew what he was talking about. I nodded. "Good. Now, I will go get him, and you two make it right." He let go of me and left the room.

A few moments later, Blake walked in. "Westin said you wanted to see me." I had my back turned to him.

"Apparently, I am wrong in being so angry with you, and I am sorry for thinking and for believing that you left me."

He spun me around, and his mouth covered mine before I could take a breath. "I would never leave you," he said as he kissed me again. "I was only gone for a short time. I needed time to think about everything Westin told us." He kissed me again, and I did not fight him. Westin was right. I needed him. "I have missed you so much," he said through his heavy breathing. "I have missed your touch so much it hurts me." He put his forehead on mind. "I have been so scared for you out there on your own. There are still men out looking for you."

I looked into his eyes. They were frantic, which made me cry. "I was so scared you left me."

"I would never leave you, Sabine. We may have our differences, and that is fine, but never would I leave you. Never do I want a day without you." He kissed me again, but this time it was not so frantic. It was gentle and loving. Our tongues were doing my favorite dance. One of his hands was on my face holding my head, the other on the small of my back pulling me into him. He pulled away. "I love you," he whispered.

"I love you. That is what hurts so bad. Why did you not leave me a note or tell someone where you went?"

"I did both. You must not have found the note. I left it on our bed, and I told Charles where I had gone. You did not find Charles. You spoke to a guardsman."

I threw my arms around him and pulled myself up his body. He helped lift me. "I did not know how I was going to do any of this without you. I have suffered by my own betrayal of you. I have kept huge secrets from you, and I could not deal with that. That is where my anger comes from."

"There is no blame to be made here, my love. Let us just forget it all. You do not need to tell me anything if you do not want to. As your brother pointed out, you have one last responsibility to take care of, and I should not cloud your mind. I need to help you the best that I can. The next time I need to think, I will wake you before I go."

I crinkled my eyes. "You came in here that night?"

"Of course I did. I watched you sleep, and I did some thinking, but the light of the day was breaking in the sky and I needed more time to think. I kissed you on the forehead and I left."

"There was no sign that you had been here."

He kissed me. "Let us just forget this mess we managed to make. Know, my love that I will never leave you."

I felt the tension leave me, as did he. "Now, may I have my wife again? I have missed her so very much."

I nodded, and before I knew what was happening, we were lying on the floor basking in the afterglow of our love. "Rebecca is in our bed," I whispered to him as I kissed his hands.

"Is she going to be all right?"

"Yes, I believe she is. She has a huge bruise across her back, and she is sore."

"How about you? From what I saw, you took a nasty fall as well."

"I am sure I will feel it soon enough." I giggled. "Just as soon as I stop quivering from the things you do to me."

He laughed. "Well, I have more things I would like to do to you. I would like to try this again." He turned me so my back was to him. "That is, if you would like."

"Oh, I would like, all right. It feels incredible," I said as he pressed himself against me.

We laid on the floor of my study well into the dark of the night, loving one another until neither of us had any energy left. I giggled while we lay exhausted in each other's arms. "You did miss me."

He chuckled. "I think you missed me more?"

We laughed and kissed some more before we fell asleep. The light of the day came blazing through the windows, waking us both. His hands were all over me as he kissed the sleep from my body. Waking up with him was better than going to sleep with him. How could I think he would ever leave me? When we finished, we lay sedate on the floor.

"I am going to check on Rebecca," I whispered.

"I will get us something to eat. Meet you back here?

I smiled, got dressed, and went to check on Rebecca. She was sleeping, and Camille was sitting in the chair. "Did you and Blake work everything out?"

"Yes, thanks to Westin," I said as I looked around the room for his note. I saw it under the bed. I bent down to get it. My hands were shaking as I turned it over to read it.

My Love,

I have much to think about. I will return when I am done. Do not worry.
I love you
Blake

He had left leave a note. I really needed to tell him everything, so I could stop feeling this bad.

I looked up at Camille. "I will be in my study. When she wakes, will you please have someone come and get me?"

"Of course. I am sorry about keeping things from you," she said.

I smiled at her. "The best kept secrets are the ones no one tells. There is no need to worry."

She nodded, and I went back to my study. Blake had not arrived yet with our food, so I laid the drawings out on the floor and marked the new Marker that I had found. I placed them in a different order to see if something new appeared, and was walking in a circle around them when Blake came in.

"Come and sit," he said as he looked at me. "What are you doing?"

"Well, I am looking to see if something comes to mind."

"What is all this?" he asked as he wrapped his arms around me.

"There is so much to tell you." I turned in his arms and kissed him. "Let us eat and I will tell you all that I know so far," I promised, kissing him again.

"You keep doing this," he whispered between kisses, "and the only thing you will be doing is getting unclothed so I can have my way with you again." He smiled.

We parted and sat in the chairs, where we ate while I told him everything that I had learned.

"So how many Markers are there?"

"I have no idea, but I also have four more tomes to read."

"Who is the Unknown Heir? I remember you asking Westin."

"So far, none of the tomes have said who it is. I would imagine that it would be one of Westin's children, though, seeing as how we cannot have a child yet, or perhaps it is Isabel. I am hoping that when I start to read again, I might find out."

He nodded. "So you have found only three Markers, and perhaps two more, but you could not find them?"

"Yes," I said as I looked at the drawings. "Father was very clever in hiding the whereabouts in plain sight. Raiden kept taking me to that river, but I cannot seem to find what he was trying to show me."

"Did you ask him?"

"Oh, I am not talking to him. I am very angry at him for not taking me to you. He is my horse, and he should not have kept that from me. Oh, I found your note. It was under the bed, so that is why I did not see it. Thank you for leaving it for me."

He smiled and chuckled. "It did no good."

I giggled. "No, I suppose it did not, but making up with you sure was fun." I felt my face get hot.

He pulled me onto his lap. "Yes, it was, but I do not need to be angry at you to love you like that." And he kissed me. We sat there for a bit, just kissing, until someone knocked on the door.

"Come in," we both said, giggling.

Rachael pushed the door open. "Your Majesty, Lady Camille has asked me come and get you. Princess Rebecca has awakened."

"Thank you, Rachael." I smiled at her as she left.

"I will be back. I need to check on Rebecca," I said, then kissed him and left.

I ran all the way to my room, where I found her sitting up.

"Well, it is about time," I said and we both laughed. "How are you feeling?"

"I am sore, and my back is killing me, but other than that I am fine. How are you?"

"Oh, me, I am fine."

"From the look on your face and the sparkle in your eyes, I would say you were better than fine. So you and Blake made up?"

"Yes, I was wrong, but we are good now. So what is going on with you? Are you with Joseph or Charles?" I asked, hoping to change the subject.

She smiled at me and shook her head. "Neither, actually… Joseph and I had a long talk. He has agreed to back off and let me figure things out. As for Charles, I do not think I can forgive him. You were in the darkness. You have no idea what he did to me."

"Yes, he may be my brother, but he did do some unforgivable things," Camille said. "I still have not forgiven him, and he is just my brother."

"Exactly. I will never be able to get that vision of him and that girl out of my head. I will never be able to look at him the same.

My heart may think it loves him still, but my mind will not allow me to. I think I may just let them both go and just be me."

"Sounds like a plan. When you are better and feel like it, I need your eyes for the drawings Father made of the kingdom. I will explain later, but not until you are ready. Blake and I are going for a ride. I am going borrow Spirit, if that is all right."

"You need to forgive Raiden, Sabine. He knows what is best for you, as well. He did what he did because he knew you two needed time."

"He is my horse. He is not Blake's."

"I am not going to argue with you about a horse, but he would not do anything to hurt you. So, yes, it is fine if you need to borrow Spirit. I think, in a day or two, I should be fine. I am, however, going have Camille help me to my room, so you and Blake can have yours back."

I kissed her. "I love you," I said as I went to leave.

"I love you, too. Be safe out there."

I giggled. "Always." I grabbed my sword and my crown and went back to my study.

Blake did not hear me come in. I watched him as he moved in a circle around the drawings. He moved one here and one there, then moved them again. I saw a smile come to his face, so I walked up behind him and wrapped my arms around him.

"I love you," I told him.

"I love you. I think I might have something here. I know this place." He pointed to the place he made by combining the drawings. "This is just on the other side of where Thomas was camped. Care to take a ride?"

"I have something I need to do first, and then I will meet you in the stables." I kissed him. "Roll the drawings, please," I said as I left. I walked to the stables. There were some guardsmen standing around.

192

"I would like for everyone to be removed from the stables, and to clear this area, please."

"Yes, Your Majesty," one of them said as he bowed. It did not take long for them to leave. I went into the stables and shut the doors behind me. Raiden was looking at me.

"You and I are going to have a little chat," I said. He backed up. "Oh, yes, you should be scared. You are my horse, my Guardian, my counterpart, not Blake's. You do not take orders from anyone but me. Is that understood?" He nodded. "I do not care if you think something is good for me or not. NO ONE tells you what to do but me. You caused me great grief by not doing as I asked. You do that again, and I will never ride you anywhere." He nodded at me.

'Would it matter if I said I did what I did because you needed to take that journey of discovery?'

"No, it would not. Now, we have work to do. I would like to finish this so I can have some babies."

I did not hear Blake come in. "You want babies?"

I turned to see his face light up. My voice softened as I professed, "Yes, I want lots of babies with you."

He ran to me and scooped me up, smiling, and kissed me. "That, next to hearing you tell me you love me, is the best thing I have ever heard."

I laughed. "I say that all the time."

"And it gets better every time I hear it," he claimed as he spun me around.

We took the horses, and in no time, we were at the spot Blake had discovered on the maps. I got down and walked around for a while. There was no tree line, no real reference point. I was just about to give up and walk in another direction when I felt it. I looked up at Blake and smiled.

We rode back to the castle, and after I marked the place, we continued to move the drawings in search of more spots to check. All in all, we found two more, so that made five Markers, all of which were buried in the ground.

"I am going to ride out and find Christopher. I need to know where he is with his mapping. Do you want to come?"

"No, I have some things I need to take care of. Will you be all right?"

I smiled at him. "Yes, I will be back later." I kissed him and left. It did not take long for Raiden to find Christopher.

"How is it going?" I asked.

"Your Majesty, I am glad to see you have returned. I would like to say thank you for helping me with Julia."

"You do not need to thank me. How are you doing with your mapping?'

He walked over to a little table he had set up. "I am at stake ninety out of nine hundred."

"Really? You have been out here for a very long time."

"You have a very large kingdom, My Lady," he announced with a smile. "Once I get to the river, it should be a bit faster. I have already drawn some of that. I should be done by the time of the harvest, just before the cold season."

"Well, that gives me time to finish all that I need to finish. Thank you, Christopher."

He nodded, so I climbed on Raiden and rode back to the castle. I was in my study, trying to figure out how much time I had to find all the Markers. I needed to know how many there were and what I was supposed to do with them.

I looked at the tapestry. The tomes. Popping the latch, I went into the secret room to get the fifth tome. I put it on my desk and sat down in the chair, then took a deep breath and opened the book.

The Markers are twelve in number.

Each shall be brought forth

One by each who bear the Mark of the Guardian

One by each element

Placed in a circle in the center of the land.

Time will stand still, just as when time began.

The current will light the dark of the night for a fortnight.

No sound shall pass through this enchanted time.

On the last night of light

As the new day begins

The Heir, along with the Unknown Heir, shall bring the Coming to an end.

Light the night with the knowledge of the forged

Bring forth the peace known only to this land

Where time and life once began.

I closed the book and laid my head on my hands, suddenly feeling very overwhelmed. There were twelve Markers we needed to dig up. Each Guardian, there were seven, and then Spirit, Raiden, Juliana, and I were the elements of this land, so that made eleven. Westin or Camille must be the twelfth. So again, I waited on Christopher. I did not know what the current was that would light the dark of night for a fortnight, or who was the Unknown Heir.

I shook my head and growled. "Why is this so hard? What am I missing?"

"Perhaps it is me," he said.

I picked my head up to see Blake leaning against the door. "This is so confusing."

He laughed. "It will come to you, my love. It always does."

"It speaks of this Unknown Heir, and I have no idea what it means. Now, it is talking about some kind of current that will light up the dark of night for a fortnight. I think I am tired of this."

"Did it mention how many Markers there are?"

"Yes, twelve in all."

"How many have you found?"

"Five, counting the one we found today."

"Well, we will just have to find the other seven."

I smiled at him. "I am hungry, husband, and in need of a bath."

He walked in the room and closed the door. "I am ready to serve you, Your Majesty."

I giggled. "Help me put this book back, and I will let you."

He walked over and picked it up. "Which shelf does it go on?" He moved to the center of the room.

I could not help but giggle. "I forgot you do not know." He turned to look at me, so I bent down and popped the latch to the secret room. I raised my eyebrows and said, "Follow me." I pulled back the tapestry, and he followed me to the secret room. As we went in, I lit a candle.

He stood there in shock. "I would have never…" he said.

"I know. I found it on accident. This is where Father hid everything. Here, put that down right here."

He laid it next to the ones I had read. "This is something," he said, putting his arms around me.

"Now, Sire, my food and my bath?"

He smiled kissed me, and then we went to our room. He had gotten Camille and the two kitchen girls to get my bath ready, and Francis made us some food. When he came in, I was sitting on the bed waiting for him. He placed the tray on the little table by the fireplace and then bolted the door.

Slowly, he undressed me and then picked me up and put me in the tub. He took great care in washing my hair and then my body. He made sure he got between each toe, which made me giggle. He washed my back, my bottom, my front… He washed everywhere. Then he held a blanket up so he could wrap me in it as I stepped out of the tub. He lifted me and placed me on the bed, then went and got the tray for me to eat while he bathed in my water. We sat on the bed, wrapped in blankets, eating, talking, and laughing.

I had missed him. I had really missed him.

Chapter Ten

I lay in his arms as the light of the day began its trek across the land. Looking at him while he slept, I noticed the lines on his face around his eyes were becoming greater as time passed. I wondered what mine looked like, so I reach up to touch my face.

He felt me move and encased me in his embrace, kissing me. "Good morning, my love," he said.

"Good morning. I am so sorry for doing what I did and treating you the way I did. I do not ever want to be away from you again. You are everything to me, Blake. I love you so much it hurts."

He covered my mouth with his, pulling me to lie on top of him. I brought my legs up on either side of his body. I could feel his hands in my hair, grabbing it, pulling it. I felt that beautiful sensation I got whenever he touched and kissed me. His body tensed up, and his tongue moved deeper in my mouth before I heard his muffled cry in my mouth. I pulled away as waves of pleasure released through my body. I could not breathe. I cried out my body shaking, his body shaking. He wrapped his arms around me, pulling me to him while my body quaked with emotion. It was so intense that I cried. I scooted up his body, absorbing his warmth and wanting him to feel me, when I realized he had tears as well.

"You are so beautiful," he whispered.

I smiled as I kissed his tears away gently. "I do not know what happens when we do this, but I do not ever want it to stop."

His laughter echoed through our room. "As long as I am alive, this will never end."

"Why do you cry when we touch each other?" I asked.

"Oh, my love, the emotion is more than I can bear. The way I feel about you, and when you touch me, is like nothing I have ever known. It is so beautiful that it brings me to tears."

I kissed him. "I love you so much. I have never known this kind of love, this feeling I get when we do this. My body aches to feel you next to me."

Our kiss was long, tender, and beautiful, and when it ended, I wanted more. I always want more of him.

"We have to get up and do some more hunting for Markers," he said, smiling.

"I do not want to. I want to do that again and again."

"How did you know to do that to me?"

"I just did what you do when you lay behind me. Did I do it wrong? Should I try again?"

He laughed again. "Oh, no, my love, you did nothing wrong. It was beautiful, just like you. And, yes, I would love for you to try it again and again." He kissed me, and we did try it again.

We did not emerge from our room until the midday meal, and I did not want to leave it then. We made our way to the kitchen to eat with everyone, and then went back to my study to get the drawings.

"Do you think we should dig up the ones we found?" I asked.

"What did it say in the tome?"

"It said that each shall be brought forth, one by each Guardian, one by each element, placed in a circle in the center of the land. Time will stand still as it did when time began. Then it said that the current would light the night for a fortnight, and at the break of the new day, the Unknown Heir and I will do whatever it is we are supposed to do. So I think we should leave them buried until we find them all, and then figure out who the Unknown Heir is."

"I would have to agree, but there is one problem here. There are seven Guardians and four elements. That is only eleven. We need twelve."

"I know. I do not know who the twelfth is, Westin or Camille. She bears the Mark, as well. When it comes time, we will have to ask Westin."

"So first, we need to locate the Markers, and then we need to locate the Unknown Heir."

"I have three more tomes to read, so maybe they will give me a clue as to who that is."

I heard him in my head.

'Outside now.'

I looked at Blake. "Something is wrong," I told him. Turning, I ran out of my study to the courtyard. Raiden and Spirit were there. Rebecca came out a moment later with my sword and hers. We got on our horses and headed toward the river. "What is wrong?" I asked Raiden.

'Collingwood is coming.'

I looked at Rebecca, and at the same time, we both said, "Collingwood."

I sat here in my new blue gown, with my sword and my crown. I could not stop the giggle; it just happened. Rebecca looked at me. "What is so funny?"

"Look at us. We sit here in our fancy gowns, wielding swords, and I have a crown on." I turned to look behind us. "And we are alone. There is no way Collingwood is going to take us seriously," I said and giggled again.

"Here they come." Rebecca nodded toward the horizon, where the plume of dust was rising.

I took a deep breath. "Could we try not to kill anyone today? I was having such a lovely day."

She started laughing. "You are so funny sometimes."

We sat there giggling like little girls when Collingwood rode up. They sat on their horses, looking at us. Rebecca knew David and George of Collingwood, and George remembered her.

"How could this be? How have you not aged?"

"Well, thank you for noticing, George. What brings you to Whispering Wind?"

"I think you know, Princess," George said. "And I would presume you are Princess Sabine, although the crown you wear would suggest otherwise."

I giggled again. I could not help it, thinking of how funny we must look. "Well, George, that is very observant of you. I am now the Queen of this Kingdom, and I would like to know what you are doing here?"

"Well, Your Majesty," he said, being rude. "It would seem that Princess Rebecca has laid to rest two of my brothers, and I am here to ask why."

I closed my eyes to feel his energy. It was not as dark as his brother's, but it was not good either. I opened my eyes. "Your brother tried to kill me, so Rebecca did the only thing she could do. She was defending me."

"You are not capable of defending yourself?"

I laughed now. "I am, indeed. So if you came here to find out why your brother got what he deserved, then why would you bring this army of men with you?"

"I was told that you are witches and that you hold great power. I was merely being cautious." He looked past me. "Looks as though your Guardsmen are late."

I could feel him coming, and he was not happy. Charles rode up on one side of me and Blake on the other.

George stepped his horse back a few steps. "Master," he said and bowed his head.

"You do not bow to me. You bow to my Queen," Charles said.

"You are the Guardian of the Bringer of Peace. Why are you here with these girls, when my brother was the Bringer?"

"Your brother was not who your father claimed him to be," Charles declared.

"You are telling untruths. He was paired with the Princess here, but she killed him to give the honor to Sabine. We have heard the stories."

"Sabine is the rightful heir, George, and your father knows that. He is drunk with power, as was Wellington and Blackmore," Charles said.

He laughed. "You expect me to believe that a girl is the Bringer of Peace?"

"I would be careful, George. She does not like being called a girl," Blake warned.

George turned his attention to Blake. "You are Blake, her supposed husband. Well, if that is the case, then she is not pure and her magic will no longer work."

I looked at Blake and then at Charles. Rebecca giggled. "I would not believe all that you hear, George."

"I am here to avenge my brother's death, and I would expect that being the Queen, you would do right to keep the peace of our Kingdoms by giving me Rebecca to return home and deliver the punishment she deserves for ending his life."

"Rebecca will be going nowhere," Charles said. "You see, she is my wife, and you will not touch her."

Rebecca and I looked at one another.

"I am sorry, Master, but I must insist."

I stepped in. "I will tell you what, George. If you can take her on your own, I will let you."

"Sabine," Charles said.

"It is all right, Charles. She will be fine."

George just sat there looking at me. "I cannot fight a woman."

I did it again; I giggled. "You cannot fight a woman, but you can drag a woman home to your father so she can be put to death by someone else?"

He sat there, still just looking at me. "I need some sort of justice for the death of my brothers."

"Your brothers tried every effort to kill me. Their lives were taken in my defense. Is this not an honorable way to die, trying to kill a Queen?"

"It is, but…"

"There is no but about it, George. I am Queen of this Kingdom, and I request that you go back to your father and tell him that he has lost two sons in battle, or you can send your men home to tell your father that three maybe four of his sons have been lost. I know that you are next in line for the crown, so either you leave my Kingdom peacefully or they," and I nodded to his men, "can take your headless body back to your father."

He sat there on his horse for a moment longer than I cared for. "I am afraid that I cannot do that. Rebecca will come with me on her own accord, or I shall take her."

I drew my sword. "I would really like to see you try that."

"How is it you hold that sword? That is the sword of the Bringer of Peace."

I just smiled at him.

He looked at me, then Charles, then Blake. He turned his horse and left.

"This is not over, Sabine," Charles said.

"I know, but what can we do really, kill Collingwood? Wait a minute…" I looked at Rebecca and then at Blake. "I know how to end this. Rebecca, are you up for a ride?"

"I am always up for a ride. Where are we going?"

Looking right at Blake, I suggested, "I think we should pay a visit to Collingwood and end this?"

"I am your husband, and I promised not to try and control you, but I say no. Sabine, once you are off Raiden, it will be hand to hand combat with thousands of men. You cannot defeat them alone."

"I suppose you are right, but why would I get off Raiden?"

"Collingwood is dying. He will not come out to greet you."

I looked at Charles. "Do you have a thought?"

He laughed loud. "I am with Blake. Going to Collingwood would not be a good idea."

"Hmmm," I said.

We rode back to Whispering Wind together. *Would it be the best thing to just go to Collingwood and settle this?* Blake does have a point, and I could not ride Raiden into a castle and then into the King's bed chamber. *Oh well, I suppose I will leave Collingwood alone for now.* But I knew they would return. George would not risk sitting on the throne. He would wait until his father died, and then he would come. I shook my head.

"What is it, Sabine?" Rebecca asked.

"Well, I was just thinking. George will wait until his father dies, and then he will come back as King. He may send his younger brothers in his place to ensure he stays on the throne."

"You are probably right. Their arrogance is just as Edward's was. And to think, they believed him to be the Bringer of Peace, as well. The things parents tell their children is unbelievable."

I laughed. "Yes, and what they are told as children is what they believe as mature people. I hope that I do not tell my children things that will not be truth when they grow up."

"The stories we will tell them will be truth, like how their mother was this great warrior and how she defeated evil."

We both laughed as we rode into the courtyard. "Rebecca, now that you are feeling better, would you come to my study, please? I could use your help."

She nodded, and we made our way to my study. I laid all the drawings out on the floor. "When we were trying to find the clues to calm the stones, we managed to put drawings together to find the places. I need for you to look at these and do whatever you need to do to see if any of these places look familiar to you."

"What are you looking for?"

"Markers of some kind. We have found five of them, so far, but there are twelve all together."

"Markers for what?"

"I am not sure yet," I said, chuckling.

She stood, she walked in circles, she moved a few pieces, and put a few together. For most of the day, she did this and marked three places that looked familiar to her.

"This is great. Come on. Let us go for a ride and check them out."

We made our way to the stables, running in to Blake on our way.

"We have found three more places, so we are going to go and check them out. One of them is in Blackmore."

"Really? Do you want me to come with you?"

"I am sure we will be fine." I kissed him, and we got our horses and left. When we returned, Blake was waiting for me in our room.

"Any luck?"

I smiled and jumped on the bed. "Yes, we found three more, so now we are up to eight. Four more and this part of the intrigue will be finished."

He smiled and kissed me. "Do you really want lots of babies?"

"With all that I am." I covered his mouth with mine and took control over our touching. By the time I finished with him, he was quivering, holding me so tightly while his body calmed down.

"You are the most incredible woman. Where did you learn that?"

I laughed. "I did not learn it anywhere. When I think about you throughout the day, I just think, hmmm, I wonder if I can do that."

He laughed. "Oh, yes, you can. I love you."

"I love you," I said as I kissed him. We slept in each other's arms for a while, and when we woke, it was my turn to feel and experience what he thought about during the day. After he finished, I was a quivering mess. I could not stop the tears. They just came as he held me.

"My love, what is wrong?"

"I was just thinking about not being able to make a union with you. If we feel this way without it, how are we going to feel when it does happen? Or will it ever happen? I guess I am just thinking too much."

"My love, one day we will make this union, and I have no doubt in my mind that we will feel this and so much more. I am not worried about it, and you should not either. You have things to do before we can, anyway, so when it is all over, then we will."

I cried as I fell asleep in his arms, which seemed to happen nearly every night. It made me wonder how I could be this Bringer of Peace and cry all the time. I should be tough like a man. Perhaps that was why I was a girl and not a man. Perhaps my emotions were what made it possible. They had said that I needed to feel certain emotions to accomplish things, and a man would not feel as deeply as a woman would.

When the light of day arrived, I woke alone. I sat up and looked around the room and the bed for a note. I was hanging over the side of the bed when Blake came in and laughed.

"What are you doing?"

"I was looking for a note," I said as I sat up.

"What note?"

I smiled. "I thought you had left again, and I was looking for a note in case you left me one."

"Why would it be under the bed?"

"That is where I found the last one, so I thought perhaps that is where this one would be, but you did not go anywhere."

He smiled. "I did go somewhere. I went to the kitchen to retrieve some food for my wife."

207

I fixed the blankets on the bed, so he could put the tray down. Instead, he sat it on the table and climbed into to bed with me, then began kissing me and laid me down as he did. "You will get your food, wife, but first, I need some of these luscious kisses."

I giggled and kissed him. "Please, Sire, your wife is so hungry. She worked up an appetite."

"That she did, so I suppose I should feed her."

He got the tray, and we feasted. When we were finished, I got dressed in my green gown, the one that matched Blake's eyes, while he took the tray back to the kitchens. After he got back, he tied my gown.

When I turned to face him, he was smiling. "This," he ran his finger across the top of my full breasts, "I like very much."

"I am not sure of this. There is a great deal more of me showing than in the blue one," I said.

"Yes, but this lace is very becoming," he said and kissed me.

I grabbed my sword, Blake put my crown on my head, and we walked down stairs together. "I am going to see Clare, so I will be back later. Then I am going to be in my study reading. I need to figure out what we do next."

"I have some things to do, too, so I will meet you there later." He kissed me goodbye in the courtyard, then he went his way and I went mine.

As I made my way to Clare's, I noticed that there were a great deal of people that had come back to the village. They were bowing and greeting me, and I could not help the smile on my face. I knocked on Clare's door and waited, and a gentleman answered.

"Your Majesty," he said and bowed.

"Hello, is Clare home?"

"She is, Your Majesty. Please come in."

"I am afraid that I do not know you," I said.

"My name is Gerald. I am Clare's brother."

"Hello, Gerald. I am Sabine." I put my hand out to shake his, and he kissed it. I had to giggle; being the Queen was going to take a lot to get used to. He excused himself and went to get Clare.

"Sabine, how nice to see you. How have you been?" she exclaimed when she came out.

"Really good, and how have you been doing? I am sorry that I have not come to visit, but we have been really busy."

"I know. I have come by a few times, but you were unavailable."

"Really? No one told me you came by. I will have to ask about that. You are always welcome."

"Thank you, but I did come for a reason. I have more gowns for you and everyone."

"Really? I am so excited, and I know Julia will be thrilled. She has been spending time with a gentleman."

Clare smiled. "Yes, I have seen her and Christopher out walking with a Guardsman."

I giggled. "Yes, my brother was hesitant, but I believe Christopher is a good man."

"Yes, he seems to be. Would you like some tea?" she asked and then laughed. "I forgot you do not drink tea."

We laughed as I sat down. "I am actually here to ask a huge favor of you."

"Anything you need, I will do my best to do."

I looked around. "I do not mean to be rude, but where is your brother?" I whispered.

She raised her eyebrows and whispered back, "I do not know." Then she spoke rather loudly, "Gerald, are you here?"

It sounded like he was in the other room when he answered, "Yes, I am back here."

I whispered, "Could you ask him to leave? What I want to talk to you about is rather personal."

She nodded. "Gerald, would you be a dear and go down to Boland's to ask him if he has some of the deep purple thread he gave me the other day?"

"Yes, sister, I will be back soon."

Once I heard the door close, I leaned in and whispered, just in case he had not left, "I was wondering if you could make something for me."

"Of course," she whispered back.

"This lace..." I put my hand to my chest. "You made this, right?"

"Yes, I did. Why?"

"Well, Blake likes it very much, and I was wondering if you could make me a sleeping gown out of it?" I felt my face get warm.

"Of course, I could, but it will take a while. When did you want it?"

"I do not want anything but the lace."

She smiled, and I noticed her face get pink. "Oh, I see. Of course."

"I would appreciate your discretion. It is for a very special occasion."

"I will keep it between us."

"Thank you, Clare. I would also like it to fit my body snugly."

She smiled at me. "Whatever you want."

"Great! I will pay you for your time. If you made this, I can only imagine how hard it will be to make an entire gown. Oh, and when would you like to come with the new gowns?"

"I appreciate you wanting to pay me for my services, Sabine, but again, I have to say it is not necessary. As for the dresses, when is best for you?"

"Well, how about tomorrow, after our morning meal. We can have a girl's day again."

"That would be great," she said.

"Good. I will send the kitchen girls to help you, and I will ask Francis to make us some cakes or something. We can make a day of it."

She laughed. "It will take a day to try them all on." Just then, her brother came in with the thread.

"Really? You have that many?"

"I have been busy. I have five Ladies to sew for, and I even made the little one a few gowns."

I smiled and shook my head. "You are amazing." Standing, I hugged her. "Thank you, Clare, and I will see you tomorrow."

"Thank you, Sabine, and tomorrow it is."

As I shut the door, I heard her brother say to her, "You know the Queen well enough to hug her?"

She laughed. "Yes, we are friends. I even go to her house and visit on occasion, just as she comes here."

I smiled as I walked away. As I walked through the town, I noticed the guards walking around, which made me feel good. I was looking around and not really paying attention to where I was going, when I walked right into a man standing in my path. "Oh, excuse me," I said.

He put his hands on my waist, I suppose to steady me. "It was all my fault, Your Majesty."

He did not remove his hands. I stepped back, but he did not let go. In fact, he pulled me closer. "A Queen should not be out wandering around alone."

I tilted my head as I looked up at him. "Would you please take your hands off of me?"

"You are the one who walked into me. You are out here alone without a guard, so I would assume you are looking for something."

"I will not ask you again," I said.

"I believe you heard the lady," Blake said, having seen what happened.

The man turned his head to look at Blake, but he did not release me. "Go about your business, boy. This is man's business."

I looked at Blake and slightly shook my head just as the man turned to face me. "Now, little lady, what would you be out here all alone looking for, a real man, perhaps? I have heard the rumors that your husband cannot fulfil his duties. Maybe that is what you are looking for."

I could not stop myself from giggling. By this time, there were people starting to gather, and I felt Charles and Joseph walk up.

The man tilted his head. "You think I am funny?"

"What I think is funny, first of all, is that you believe that I would want anything to do with the likes of you, and second, that you believe you can take from me something I am not willing to give."

"I do not believe that I need to take it. Why would a woman like yourself, one who is obviously dissatisfied with her choice, be away from her boy husband, out in a village looking for a real man?"

"I asked you to remove your hands from me, yet you refuse. You stand here and speak to me as if I am some whore, when I am in fact the Queen of this Kingdom. Then you assume I would want to lie down with you and engage in a union that is only reserved for my husband, who incidentally is standing

212

right there." I nodded my head toward Blake. "This is my village, and if I choose to walk around it unescorted, I will do just that. Now, I am telling you to remove your hands from me."

He smiled and turned his head to Blake. "Some husband. He will not even defend your honor."

"Oh, Sire, please do not make the mistake and assume my wife cannot defend herself."

He laughed. "She is but a waif of a child. What could she possibly do to me?"

Charles chuckled and leaned in to him. "She does not like it when people call her a child."

He turned back to me. "Your guard will not even defend you, so I am sure they would not mind if I did this." He reached up and put his hand on my breasts. Blake was on him so fast. The man had a hold of my gown and ripped the material down the front of it. Charles covered me, while Blake beat the man pretty badly. When he finished, Joseph and a few guards dragged him to our special place. Blake scooped me up in his arms and took me back to the castle.

When we got in our room, I could not stop the giggle. "I really wanted to do that."

Blake did not find anything funny about what just happened. "That man will be put to death for defiling my Queen. I beat him for touching my wife."

I did not know what to say. I had only ever seen him like this when Cam had come into our room. I tried to lighten him up, but he was shaking when he set me on my feet.

"Thank you," I whispered.

He put his finger under my chin and lifted my face so he could see it. "For what?"

"For defending my honor, and for loving me."

"I will always love you, and defending your honor was easy to do. He ruined your beautiful gown," he said as he reached to try to fix it.

"I know, and it is the one that matches your eyes. I wonder if Clare can make another."

"You had this made because it matches my eyes?"

"Yes," I said as I bit my bottom lip, which was more than enough for him. I could feel his calm as he lifted me and carried me to bed. We spent the better part of the day there, loving one another. We finally made it down to the kitchen in time for the evening meal.

The laughter and the conversation was more than I deserved. This was my family, and what a wonderful family it was. I thought it funny how we no longer ate in the dining hall. Francis had become one of us, along with the kitchen girls. They still called me 'Your Majesty' but that was all right.

"Westin, my love, would you come with me to my study? I would like to talk to you."

"All right, Sabine, but you are not leaving again, are you? Every time you want to talk to me, you tell me you are leaving. I do not want you to leave again. Our family is finally having fun."

I smiled at him. "No, my love, I am not leaving."

"Good," he said and then turned to Camille. "I am going with Sabine to her study. You can get the children in bed, right?"

"It is fine, Westin. You go with Sabine."

"I can go with you, Sabine. Do you want to go now?"

"In a little while." I smiled at him. It was so strange to see him like that now that I knew he was just putting on a show. I figured it must be hard for him to let his children think he was simple minded. I chuckled to myself, and Blake touched my arm.

"You all right?"

"I am fine, my love." I smiled at him.

We sat and chatted for a bit longer, and then I got up to leave.

"Are we going now, Sabine?"

"Yes, my love, we are."

He kissed his children goodnight and followed me to my study, where I closed the door.

"Father left me some drawings. I used them to find the calming spell to calm the jewels. I have discovered that they also have been guiding me to the Markers of Time that I need to find. We have found eight, but there are twelve in all, and I was wondering, being that you know this land better than anyone, if you would be able to help me locate the other four?"

"I cannot, my love. I am afraid that this is a journey you have to take on your own. I cannot help, nor can I interfere."

"I did not think so, but I had to ask."

"Do not worry. You will find them in the time in which you are supposed to."

"Thank you," I said as Blake came in the room.

"So I am glad to see that the two of you have worked things out," Westin said, looking at Blake.

"Yes, we have, and thank you for your help."

"You two are meant to be together, just like me and Camille. Well, I am going to help with the children. They are getting big enough now to know that they can sneak out of bed."

"Good night, my love." I smiled at him.

"Good night, Sabine, Blake."

"Westin."

"So what would you like to do?" he asked me with a sheepish grin on his face.

I giggled. "Well, I was going to read another tome, but I think I might be able to be persuaded not to. What did you have in mind?"

His laughter bellowed out of him. "Oh, my love, you do not want to know what is on my mind."

"Yes, I do," I said as he scooped me up in his arms.

"I want to take you back to our bed," he whispered.

"I was hoping you would say that," I whispered back.

When the light of the day broke through the dark of the night, I was awake. I had a great deal more to read. I slipped out of bed and went to the kitchen to get Francis to make us some food. She was already part of the way done when I got there.

"Good morning, child. How have you been?"

I smiled at her. "Better now. How have you been?"

She laughed. "All is well, my dear. Blake is usually the one down here this early. Letting him sleep in, are you?"

"Yes, but I am sure that he was awake when I left. I think he was faking it. But I could not sleep, so I thought I would surprise him for a change."

"You know that man really loves you."

"I know, and I love him, too. Just sometimes, I forget that."

"Yes, I think we all do, but you two just keep finding your way back to each other and all will be good. When are we going to have another little one running around here?"

I raised my eyebrows. "Not sure. I guess, when it is time, it will be time. Until then, I sure do like trying."

She laughed as she handed me that tray. "Go and feed your man."

"Thank you, Francis." I took the tray and went to our room.

I thought it odd that she asked me that. Is everyone wondering why I am not with child yet? So having a union was how a woman ended up with a child; that was not hard to

216

figure out. Everyone thought we were having a union, so they must have been wondering why I was not with child.

I walked into our room, and Blake was sitting up. He must have seen my face.

"Sabine, what is wrong?" He was at my side instantly, taking the tray from me.

"I think everyone is wondering why I am not with child yet. They all think we have had a union."

"Sabine, we have only been married for less than a season. It takes time to make a baby."

"To make a baby... you do that by having a union, right?"

"Yes, my love. There is no other way that I know of."

I could not help but think about that. "So how do you think that happens?"

He looked at me with sad eyes. "You do not know?"

"I do not think so. Do you?"

"Yes, would you like me to tell you, or would you rather talk to Camille?"

"Camille," I said, and I turned and left our room to go to talk to Camille.

After knocking on their door, I heard her say, "Come in."

I opened the door, finding her alone. "Can we talk?"

"Of course. Come in."

A while later, I walked out of that room with more knowledge than I cared to have, I think. I was not sure I would be able to look at Blake the same way again. I walked right past our room and went to my study. Sitting in the chair by the window, I went over everything that Camille had told me. It made sense; I just did not think I wanted that to happen to me. I mean, I knew girl stuff, and I knew what had happened to Rebecca, but I honestly had no idea that was how it was done.

I was not aware how long I had sat there before Blake came in. He touched my arm that is what got my attention. He was kneeling down in front of me.

"Are you all right?"

"Truthfully, I am not sure."

His smile was gentle. "Do you want to talk about it?"

I took a deep breath. "This making a union...."

"Yes," he whispered.

"This is how a baby is made."

"Yes."

"I am not so sure. When we tried, it hurt."

"Yes."

"Camille said it hurt more than just once, until she got used to it. She said she was so scared the first time, and even more scared the second because she knew how bad it hurt the first time." He did not say anything, but his eyes never left mine. "Blake, I am afraid."

He pulled me off the chair and onto his lap. "My love, you do not need to be afraid. I have told you many times that we do not have to do this. Right now, we cannot, and it is all right. I love you, and if we never have a union, I am all right with that. I do not love you so we can have a union. I love you because, without you, I am not whole."

"But it is the only way to have a baby with you, and I want lots of babies with you."

He hugged me. "As I do with you, but it is fine if we do not. As long as I have you, it is enough for me," he whispered at my neck.

"Will it be enough for the rest of our lives? Will not having children be enough?"

"Oh, my love, you are enough. Please, do not think about this. There is nothing we can do about it right now. You cannot cloud your mind with all of this. How about we put it away until you have done what is left to do, and then we can revisit it and worry about it all then. But, please, Sabine, having you as my wife and in my life is so much more than I ever dreamed possible. I love you, and if we do not have children, I am fine with that. There will be plenty of babies around for us to enjoy."

I nodded into his chest. "I love you," I said, sighing.

He kissed me and laid me down on the floor. "There is no one alive that is more for me than you. I love you, wife." Then he covered my mouth with his.

We rolled around on the floor for some time, and when we finished, I was feeling much better.

"I need to read the tomes so I can figure out what this Coming is, and who this Unknown Heir is."

"And I need to go see what Charles has done with our new guest."

"About that... Next time, can I hurt him?"

He chuckled. "I cannot promise you that. No man will ever touch my wife like that and get away with it."

"Oh, no! I was supposed to meet Clare here today. She has made more gowns for us, and for Isabel. Would you please stop by her cottage and let her know that tomorrow would be a better day?"

"Of course I will. Are you going to be all right?"

"Yes, I will put it all away for now." I kissed him and got up. Once he left, I went to get the sixth tome. I sat it on my desk, took a deep breath, and opened the book.

*****

Blake left and went straight to Clare's to let her know, Clare was understanding. On his way back to the barracks, there was a woman climbing up on a table to hang a sign outside of her cottage.

"Can I help you?" he asked.

She did not turn to see him. "I think I have it," she said, struggling. She managed to get the sign up, but as she was turning, she slipped and fell.

Blake caught her. "I got you," he said as he set her on her feet.

"Oh, my, thank you so much. I am so embarrassed."

"It is not a problem. I am just glad I was here to help you. You could have gotten hurt, and then..." He looked up to see what her sign said. "Where would we get bread from?"

"Oh, you are being..." She looked up at his smiling face and stopped talking.

He nodded at her.

"I am sorry. My name is Sarah. I am a," she pointed to the sign, "baker."

Blake laughed. "Yes, I see that. My name is Blake, and welcome to Whispering Wind."

"Thank you, Blake, for both the welcome and the save."

"It was my pleasure for both. You have a good day now." He nodded and started to walk away.

Sarah stood there, totally stunned at his beauty. She wanted to stop him from leaving, but she did not know what to do. "Oh, Blake, excuse me."

He turned. "Yes, Sarah," he responded, walking back to her.

"Can I pay you with a piece of cake or something, some bread? For the save, I mean."

"Well, thank you, Sarah, but that is not necessary. As I said, it was my pleasure. You have a lovely day." He nodded and walked away, leaving Sarah standing there watching him.

"Wow," she whispered. "Now that is a man, and a Guardsman at that."

He turned into the courtyard and was no longer in her sight, so she went about her business.

Blake did not give it a second thought.

Chapter Eleven

The number from the center is twelve.

The number between is twelve.

Each to stand with the Marker brought forth

With the Heir and the Unknown Heir in the center of the land

Bring forth the forged raised to the current

Brings the light the empowered knowledge has given.

All who are pure of heart remain.

All with the dark will turn to ash.

Only the pure will enter this land.

No dark is able to cross over

To bring evil to this land.

The Bringer will bring Peace.

The Keeper then speaks to seal this land.

The Unknown Heir shall be born into the peace.

I stopped breathing, feeling panic rising up. I looked around the room. It felt as if the walls were closing in on me. Struggling to breathe, I ran to the window and opened it. I leaned out, trying to get some air, but it would not work. Blake saw me and came running, but I did not see him. Feeling dizzy, I turned to walk to the door, and then there was nothing.

I felt him holding me. "My love, come on. Wake up," My eyes fluttered open. "What happened?" he asked.

I closed them again. "I cannot breathe," I whispered.

"Sabine, you are scaring me. Please, open your eyes."

I opened them and then sat up quickly, trying to get to my feet, but he would not let me go. "Let me go!" I yelled.

He released me. I ran to my desk and read the words again.

The Unknown Heir shall be born into the peace.

I looked at Blake.

"Sabine, what is going on?"

I could not get the words out of my mouth. I looked at him and then the door, then back to Blake. Working my way around the desk, I bolted for the door. I did not stop running, though I did not have my crown or sword.

I made it to the stables and got on Raiden. "Go, go, go," I said to him as I kicked him in the sides. He bolted. I saw Blake running toward the stables as Raiden took off out the back gates. "Do not stop. Run." He did not disappoint me.

'The Unknown Heir shall be born into the peace.' What? I could not handle this. The Heir, that was me, and the Unknown Heir in the center. I knew I was the Heir. That meant that the Unknown was a child within me. I searched for him in my head.

'Is the valley still protected?'

'Yes.'

'Take me there, and then I want you to go back and get Blake.'

'I will have Spirit bring him now.'

'Thank you.'

Raiden did not stop moving.

Spirit was making a spectacle in the stables as Blake came running in. "What is it, boy?" he asked.

Spirit reared up and nodded at Blake. He opened his stall, and Spirit ran out into the courtyard and just stopped.

Blake walked out. "What is it?"

He reared up, neighing at him. Hearing the commotion, Charles came out.

"What is going on out here?"

"I have no idea, but Sabine just took off, and I think Spirit wants me to go with him."

Charles just stood there. "Yes," he said. "Raiden told him to bring you to them."

"Thank you, brother," Blake said as he got on Spirit.

"Does she have her sword?"

"No, she has nothing," was all Blake got out before Spirit took off.

Raiden and I made it to the valley in no time. I was walking back and forth in front of the cottage as they started their decent from the hills into the valley. My stomach turned and turned again. I could not stop it. I bent over and emptied the contents just as he was jumping off of Spirit.

"Sabine," he yelled.

I put my hand up to stop him, retching again and again and falling to my knees. When I was finished, he lifted me up into his arms.

"My love, what is going on?"

I looked at him, pushing on his chest for him to let me go. He put me down, and I walked away. I could not get away fast enough, so I ran out onto the plain. He followed.

"Sabine, talk to me."

I was crying now. "NO!" I screamed through my sobs. "NO!"

Realizing he stopped, I stopped, as well. I dropped to my knees and screamed, while he stood there, helpless, with tears streaming down his face as I screamed again, and again. I screamed until I had nothing left in me. He took a step forward, and I shook my head at him, but he did not stop coming. I put my hands up to block him from touching me, though it did not work. He knelt down next to me and pulled me into his arms.

"My love, what is going on?"

I shook my head no and pushed on him to release me, but he refused.

"Please," I said and pushed again. He loosened his grip but did not release me.

"What did you read in the tome?"

When I looked at him again, he saw the fear in my eyes. I could not even process this; the Unknown Heir was an unborn child within me. *Whose child would it be? We could not have a union, or my magic would leave me. I needed my magic to finish this, so how was an Unknown Heir supposed to get inside of me?* I did not want a child that was not his. He would not want me then. I pushed him away. This thought brought on more tears, more sobs, and more retching. His hands and arms never failed me, holding me while I cried. He held me while I screamed and retched.

"Please, my love, talk to me," he pleaded.

I could not say the words, so I just stared at him.

"Was it something in the tome?"

I nodded very slowly.

"Was it about me?"

I shook my head slowly.

"Was it about you?"

I nodded my head slowly.

"Are you going to die?"

I shook my head slowly.

He let out his breath. "Then it is something we can work out together."

I shook my head.

"Are you going to do something to hurt me?"

I nodded my head.

"Are you going to kill me?"

I shook my head slowly.

"Are you going to betray me?"

I did not move my head then, just looked at him through the tears in my eyes. How else was I going to be with child? I could not imagine myself betraying him. If I was not going to have a union with him, why would I have one with someone else? He is the one I loved. He is the one I could not live without. But he would leave me when he learned of this betrayal. I heard myself say out loud, in the tiniest of voices, "I know who the Unknown Heir is."

He looked at me. "What did you say?"

I sat there in silence, looking at him. "I know who the Unknown Heir is," I finally said again, unable to make my voice any louder.

He did not move; I think he even stopped breathing. His eyes never left mine, but I saw something different in them, something I had never seen before, but I was not sure what it was. "Who," he asked, swallowing hard.

I wanted to look away, but the look in his eyes had gotten my attention. I could not bring myself to say it. Shaking my head, I looked away from him.

"Sabine," he whispered.

Pushing on him to let me go, I got up and made my way back to Raiden. I took several deep breaths, trying to get control of myself. It was time for me to get back. I had left the tome on my desk, and I needed to finish it, to know how this Unknown Heir would come to be. Though I knew I would not betray my husband, I stopped walking, asking myself. *Is it me? I am the Heir.* I turned to look at him. *What was that I saw in his eyes? Does this Unknown Heir come from me? Blake is of royal blood, so he would be able to produce an Heir.* I felt my stomach turn over. I had to get these thoughts out of my head. He would not betray me like that. *He loves me.*

I jumped on Raiden.

"Are we going back?" Blake asked.

I nodded to him as he jumped on Spirit. With one last look deep into his eyes to see if it was still there, I kicked Raiden in the sides and we took off. When we finally rode into the courtyard, Charles came running out.

"Is everything all right?"

"Yes, we are fine," I told him. "Please, excuse me. I have some things I need to take care of." That was my polite way of saying, 'I do not wish to talk to you right now'.

Charles looked at Blake, but Blake was watching me. I looked at him but did not smile and did not say a word to him; I just walked by and went to my study. The tome was still on my desk. Walking over to it, I read the line on the page again.

The Unknown Heir shall be born into the peace.

Slowly, I turned the page. I closed my eyes and took a deep breath, bracing myself for what was next.

The Unknown Heir shall be brought forth

By the purity of the Heir

With the Heir giving all knowledge instilled

To be given to the generations to follow

I turned the final page, having reached the end of this tome.

Sitting back in my chair, I closed my eyes. *What does this mean? I thought the Unknown Heir was in me. This could mean otherwise, so I still do not know for sure.* Well, I knew for sure that it would not be me. It could not be me. If my purity were gone, so would be the magic.

After picking up the tome, I popped the latch to put it away. I still had two more tomes left to read. *Do I want to read them now? Not really. I am tired and need to sleep.* I put the tome down then made my way out of the secret room and up to my room. Not even bothering to get undressed, I crawled into bed, shoes and all. My eyes closed and sleep came quickly. I did not even feel the weight of Blake as he slipped into bed next to me. When I woke, I was alone, but I knew he had been here, for the bed was in disarray.

I sat up and looked around, but he was not in his chair by the fireplace. I needed to find the other Markers. Looking around in case Blake had left a note, I found nothing, so I got up and changed my clothes. This day, I decided to wear my boy clothes. I was going to talk to Boland, for he had been around quite a while. I thought that maybe he could make something of Father's drawings.

Grabbing my sword, I left the crown. I did not feel like being a Queen, but just wanted to be me. I made my way to the kitchen, putting some fruit in my bag as I was on the way out the door. I walked around the castle, hoping to see Blake before I left, but he was nowhere in sight. Briefly, I wondered what it was he did all day. I walked through the front courtyard and to the great gates. I was just starting to head into the village when I heard Blake laugh. Stopping, I looked around, turning to see if he was in the courtyard, but he was not.

As I continued walking, I heard it again. Perhaps I was hearing things. I shook my head and continued on my way. I knocked on Boland's door, who answered with a huge smile.

"Well, hello, Sabine. Please, come in. What brings you here today?"

"Hello, Boland," I said as I hugged him. "I came to ask a favor."

"Anything at all," he replied with a smile.

I took out the drawings that I had tucked in my shirt and started to lay them on the floor. "I have these old drawings, and I was wondering if you could have a look at them. I have discovered that when I put a few of the pieces together, I can find certain places, however I am stuck. You have traveled a great deal, so I thought perhaps you might have a look and tell me if you see anything that looks familiar to you."

"Well, I can have a look," he offered, and he did. I sat at the table and watched him put them together. He did this for quite some time, moving the pieces around. When he finished, he had found three places that he knew, and explained to me where they were. "I hope this was helpful."

I hugged him. "Thank you, Boland. I will let you know."

I made my way out of his shop and started back to the castle to get Raiden. I was a few cottages down from Clare's when I saw Blake walk out of a cottage just past hers. In fact, it was Boland's old place. He stopped and turned then started laughing. When he started to walk away, I went to yell for him, but I froze when I saw a brown-haired woman come out yelling his name. He turned and trotted back to her, taking something out of her hand, smiling.

There I stood, frozen in place, watching him walk away and watching that woman watch him. She did not go back inside until he had turned into the courtyard. I actually shook my head and forced myself to move forward. As I walked to the cottage, I noticed the sign outside said 'Baker'. Who was this person, this woman who was singing inside?

Standing there, I wondered if I should knock or if I should go find Blake and ask him what was going on, but eventually decided I was going to do nothing. I needed to get Raiden and go find the three new places that Boland had told me about. By the time I got to the stables, I had forgotten all about Blake talking to the dark-haired woman. I saddled Raiden, and on my way out, I saw a guardsman. "Would you please tell Blake or Charles that I am going out riding and that I will be back later?"

"Yes, Your Majesty," he said and bowed.

"Thank you," I said as I got on Raiden.

I spent the better part of the day, right up until the dark of the night came, riding with Raiden, but I had found two more Markers. As I was riding into the village, I saw that woman from the Baker shop talking to Clare.

"Hello, Sabine." Clare waved.

I smiled and waved back to her. "Good evening, Clare." And I kept on going. I just left Raiden by the door and went to my study to mark the spots, then to the kitchen to eat before heading to my room. I stopped by Camille's to ask her if she could get the kitchen girls to help me get a bath ready. Of course, she would not hear of it, and in what seemed only moments, I was sitting in a very warm bath.

I was tired, so I got out and just climbed into bed. I did not feel Blake's weight on the bed when he climbed in, but I did feel him as he pulled me close to him. Again, I woke after he had gone, and again, I found no note. What is going on here? I knew he was just giving me time to figure things out, for he told me that I needed to focus. Well, today I was going to play dress up with the girls. I jumped up, put on a gown, and ran down stairs to the kitchen.

"Francis, would you please send the girls down to Clare's to help her with some gowns, and then have all the girls meet me in my study?"

"Of course, are you trying on new gowns again?"

"Yes, would it be too much trouble to have some cakes and drinks, as well?"

"No trouble at all," she said.

I hugged her. "Thank you."

She just laughed. I went to my study and waited for them to arrive. Soon, it was full; all the girls were here, and the gowns were beautiful. I asked Clare if she could make another green one for me, and she agreed. Isabel looked so cute in her new gowns. Julia, Camille, everyone... we laughed and tried on gown after gown. Clare measured and pinned, and when Francis came in, I had her stand still so Clare could make her something new, as well.

All in all, we had a wonderful day. Everyone left, and I was alone. I sat there thinking, and realized Blake had not come into my study all day. So I went looking for my husband. I went to the barracks, but he was not there. When I went to the stables, his horse was there, so I was sure Blake had not left.

Clare needed me to come by to see the lace she had made to make sure it was what I wanted, so I thought I would head over there. As I walked through the gates into the village, I heard Blake laugh. I turned to see if he was anywhere to be seen, but he was not. Thinking I might be hearing things, I kept walking. Clare promptly let me in after I knocked on her door, and the lace was beautiful. I happily approved.

"I can start making that gown you wanted in another week or so."

"Oh, Clare, that would be wonderful," I told her cheerfully. I was holding the lace in my hand. "It is so beautiful." Getting ready to leave, I hugged her. As I opened the door, though, I again heard Blake's voice...

"No, no, Sarah, I could not possibly." And then he laughed.

I pushed the door shut and peeked through the crack.

"What is it, Sabine?" Clare asked. I put my hand up to quiet her.

"Oh, come on, Blake. Do not be like that. Just one more..."

"No, I really should be going. My brother is going to start wondering where I have been all this time."

"Well, tell your brother it is none of his business."

"Oh," I heard Clare say.

I pulled away from the door and closed it. Turning to Clare, I whispered, "What do you know of this?"

"I just knew that one of the guardsmen was spending time with her, helping her build her fire thing for her baking. He's doing some repairs, stuff like that."

"You did not know it was Blake?"

"No, I never saw him, and she never told me his name."

"Would you do something for me?"

"I would do anything."

"Do not tell her who I am, and do not tell her that he is married. I am not the Queen. I am just your friend, Sabine."

"All right, but will you tell me why when it comes out?"

"Yes." I smiled. When I turned and opened the door, Blake was walking away and that woman was watching him. As he turned into the courtyard, she went inside. I closed the door and leaned against it.

"Sabine, he loves you. He would not do what you are thinking."

"I am not thinking anything right now, but now that you mention it..." Just then, there was a knock on the door. We both froze.

"Who is it?" Clare said.

"It is me, Sarah. Are you decent?"

Clare motioned for me to sit down, and I did just as she opened the door. "Of course I am. I was just visiting with my friend, Sabine. Come on in."

"Oh, you are the girl on the horse. Why do you wear boy's clothes?"

"Yes, I am. It is easier to ride in them than it is in a gown."

"I would imagine it is. So am I bothering you two, or do you want to hear about my lovely day?"

"Oh, well, I was just leaving," I said as I stood.

"Oh, no, you do not have to leave. My, you are a tiny thing. How old are you, darling? You must be, what, in your fifteenth year?"

I thought Clare was going to explode. "No, I am in my twenty-third year."

"Wow, you are a little bit of a thing, anyway." She turned to Clare.

"He came back today. He was here just as the light of day broke the sky, all ready to work. Oh, he is so good looking. We had the midday meal together. He is so funny, too. I sure could get used to looking at him all day long."

"Did he not bring anyone else with him?" Clare asked.

"No, why should he?"

"It is not proper for a gentleman to be alone with a lady."

"He is a gentleman. That is for sure. The manners on that one are something."

I sat there quietly, doing my best not to fling myself on this woman and start pulling her hair out.

"So is he coming back tomorrow?" Clare asked.

"I am not sure. He had mentioned that his brother would be wondering what he was doing there all day."

"What was he doing there?" Clare asked. She was good at this.

"Nothing, really. We just talked, mostly, getting to know one another. Like I said, he is a very lovely man."

234

"If I am not being too forward, what kinds of things did you two talk about?" I questioned bravely.

"About life, the places we have been, the things we have done, the things we want to do still while we are young. He wants many children, though I would be happy with just one or two. Stuff like that, mostly."

I could feel my anger boiling. I needed to get out of this cottage. That woman was planning her life with my husband. I stood. "Clare, I must get back. I do not want to worry anyone. It was nice to meet you," I said as I moved to the door.

"You be careful out there, little one. Too bad my new friend has already gone, or he could have walked you home."

Smiling, I nodded to Clare then left. I was so angry I could have killed someone. I walked slowly well, as slowly as I could to the barracks. I did not stop when the guard said something to me, just walked right into Blake's quarters right as he was stepping out of the tub.

"Sabine, what are you doing here?"

"Really? You are asking your wife what she is doing in her husband's quarters, which should not be your quarters at all. You should have moved all your things into our room."

He just stood there, staring at me. He reached for a blanket and covered himself up.

"Oh, do not start to be shy now, Blake. I have seen it all already."

"Sabine, what has gotten into you?"

I laughed. "Me? What has gotten into you? You do not come to our bed until well after I am asleep, and then you are gone long before I wake. Where is it you go so early in the morning, and where is it that you stay until late into the night?"

"I have work to do, Sabine, and you have been distant since that day at the valley."

I stood there looking at him, looking into his eyes, and there it was again. I did not know what it was, but it was there.

235

"Do not come to our bed again. You are obviously needing to stay here. Your clothing is here, your belongings are here, and you bathe here. This is your home. I get that now."

"You are my home."

I laughed, because if I did not, I would have cried. "I am a home when it suits you." I turned and walked out. Charles was in the hallway when I left.

"Sabine, is everything all right?"

"Charles, we have known one another for a very long time... two lifetimes, I suppose. Why is it that you try to control me in every aspect of my life, but when I obviously make a huge mistake, you say nothing? I know. Do not answer that. I need to figure things out for myself." I walked away.

As I was coming out of the barracks, I saw Sarah walking up with a basket. I did not look at her as she did not see me. She walked up to the guards and asked to speak to Blake. I turned around to watch the interaction.

He came running out the door, almost knocking her down. "Oh, Sarah." He stopped. He actually stopped.

"I have those cakes you asked me for. I thought I would bring them by again."

Blake smiled. "Well, thank you." He took the cakes, and she just stood there.

"We can eat some now if you would like. We can sit in the courtyard like we did last night."

I turned and walked into the castle, up the stairs to my room, got my sword, and walked back out. Blake and Sarah were walking to the fountain. He did not see me coming. I slammed my sword into his chest, all the way to the hilt.

Sarah screamed and screamed. Blake just stood there with a curiously confused look on his face. I was only inches from his face. "You are not worth my life."

Sarah was screaming, "What are you doing? Have you gone mad?" She tried to grab the sword, but I shoved her away. I pulled it out of him, letting him fall to his knees. Sarah was on the ground, trying to help him. "Oh my, someone help him," she was shouting. The guards from the door were already on their way. Charles came running out.

"Sabine, what is going on?"

Sarah answered him, "She just walked up and slammed that sword into him. Help him! Take her away! She has gone mad!"

"Sabine?" Charles asked.

"You heard her. I just slammed my sword into her new mate's chest. I have gone mad. Take me away."

"Her what?" He was obviously just as shocked as I was.

Sarah was yelling at Charles. "You are his brother! Help him!"

"Is what she says correct? Is he your mate?"

"We have been spending a great deal of time together, yes! Please help him."

Blake remained silent, while Charles walked around to look at his brother. "Is this truth?"

"It is not what you think?" Blake stated.

"It does not matter what I think. What matters is what I see."

Blake got his breath back, which meant he was healing. He used Sarah to help him stand, putting his arm around her shoulders and leaning on her.

By this time, we had a crowd gathering.

"Why is no one doing anything? Someone needs to restrain that girl," Sarah demanded of Charles.

"Blake, what am I seeing?" Charles asked him again.

"You are seeing, as usual, brother, what you choose to see." Blake looked at me then, and there it was in his eyes. I looked from him to Sarah and then back to him.

"You did not," I said to him.

He did not say a word. My rage took control, and before I knew what was happening, I had my sword in his chest to the hilt again. Leaning in, I whispered in his ear, "Tell me you did not, or I will cut your head off."

"I. Did. Not." he whispered back.

Just as I pulled my sword out, Sarah came after me. She actually jumped on me, and then began hitting me and pulling my hair. "You mad bitch!" she yelled.

It took me by surprise. I grabbed her by the hair, whipped her to the side of me, and then rolled on top of her, pinning her to the ground. "Get off me! You have lost your mind."

I think I was rather calm as I said, "Do not touch me again, or I will end your life." She stopped fighting me, and I got up.

"Sabine," Blake sputtered out. "Stop this."

I picked up my sword and slammed in into his chest once more, only this time, I pushed him off of it. "When I am damn good and ready." When I turned around to walk away, Westin was standing there. As I moved past him, I said, "Was this part of the master plan, as well?"

Charles helped Sarah up, telling her, "You need to go back to where ever it is you came from."

"Are you not going to do something about that girl?" She pointed to me and watched me walk into the castle. She stood there as Charles watched her put it together.

"You are very lucky to be alive," he said.

"That is..." she said.

"Yes, that is," was all Charles said before he motioned for one of the guards. "Please see that she gets home."

"But what about Blake? He is hurt."

"Oh, I would not worry about Blake. You have bigger things to worry about. He is a big boy."

He watched as they walked away then turned to Blake. "Well, brother, you have a great deal of explaining to do, not only to me but to your wife, who, if I am guessing, is pretty angry right now."

"I did nothing wrong," Blake said as he stood.

"Apparently, your wife does not think that way."

"I need to talk to her." He went to take a step but saw Westin shake his head. "I will talk to her in the morning." Westin nodded.

I walked into the great hall and threw my sword, watching as it went right through the stone to the hilt. Continuing up the stairs, I headed to my room. I was so angry, but I was not going to cry. He did not deserve my tears, not again. I laid on the bed but could not sleep, so I got up and walked the room, back and forth.

What did I see? He would not do that to me. He loves me. That woman was planning her life out with my husband, though. Will she be the one to hold the Unknown Heir? Did I lose him to her? She is rather pretty... No, Sabine, do not think this way. He loves you. It is just another misunderstanding. But why has he not made this his home? Yes, he sleeps here, but he leaves here at the light of the day and goes back to the barracks to change and to bathe. Why does he do that?

I looked around my room. This room was plenty big enough for us both. I walked and walked and walked, finally making myself tired, so I took off my clothes and climbed into bed with nothing on. I just wanted to feel nothing. After closing my eyes, eventually, sleep came.

The light of the day warmed and woke me. I stretched and just laid there. This was not going to be a good day. I had to deal with Blake and his new friend. She was lucky I did not end her life the day before.

As I sat up, I drew my legs to my chest, resting my chin on my knees. I wondered what he was doing at that moment.

*****

Blake walked up to Sarah's cottage and knocked on the door. When she answered, she was smiling. "How do you feel?" she asked, reaching for his chest to touch the spot where I had slammed my sword into him. He took a step back.

"I am afraid that I left out something while we were getting to know one another, though it was not on purpose. I am just used to everyone knowing. I am married, very happily married, to the woman who slammed her sword into my chest. She is the love of my life, and I am afraid that me being here alone with you has caused her great pain. It was not my intention to mislead you in anyway."

"She has a temper on her, but I do not understand why she lives in the castle and you live in the barracks, if she is your wife."

"I never really looked at it that way. I have always lived in the barracks. I suppose I have been waiting for her to ask me to move in with her."

"How long have you been married?"

"Nearly two seasons."

"Well, I knew you were too good to be true. May I ask how come you are not dead?"

"I am a Guardian, and as long as our Queen lives, I live."

"Yes, I have heard of this Queen, that she is kind and just. That is why I came to live here. I have never seen her, however. Does she not leave the castle? Is your wife one of her ladies in waiting?"

Blake laughed. "No, Sarah, she is not a lady in waiting."

"Oh, is she a maid or something?"

"No, Sarah, she is my Queen. Her name is Sabine of Whispering Wind."

Sarah just stood there looking at him. "You, a Guardsman, married the Queen?" She giggled. "I am sorry, but that is unheard of. Why would the Queen marry beneath her?"

Blake smiled at her. "I am of royal blood, so I am not beneath her. I just wanted to come and let you know that someone else will help you from now on. I have hurt my wife deeply, though that was not my intention. I was just being kind." He then nodded to her and walked away.

Clare had seen and heard everything he had said. Sarah saw her standing by her door and walked over to her.

"Did you know that girl was the Queen?"

"I am sorry. Yes, I did. Sabine asked me not to say anything."

"Sabine? You call her Sabine?"

"Well, yes, that is her name."

"Who calls their Queen by her name?"

"She is my friend. Why would I not call her by her name?"

"You and the Queen are friends? You mean, she comes to you for gowns?"

"No, we spend time together. She is just a woman like you and I. Her family was slaughtered when she was a child. It was just her and her brother for years. She is a remarkable person, and I am glad she is my friend."

"I hope she is not too mad at me."

Clare patted her on the arm. "She is forgiving and kind."

Sarah went back to her cottage, and Blake came to find me. He walked past my sword stuck in the wall and swallowed hard. He knew I was angry. After knocking on the door, he came in.

"We need to talk."

"I think I have said all that I needed to say."

"Well, I have not. It is hard to talk when you have a sword in your chest. I did not dishonor you. I did not make a union with that woman. I was being kind. She does not know anyone here, and I was just talking with her. After we left the valley, your silence was my cue to let you be. Obviously, you have a great deal to work out, and Westin had told me not to crowd your mind. I am guilty of staying out late and leaving early, but I was just giving you the space you needed. I have already spoken to Sarah and told her that it was my fault for not clarifying to her that I am in fact married to you. I am just used to everyone knowing that. As for me not living here, as you put it, you have never asked me to move in. I was just waiting for you to do so."

I sat there looking at him. I knew that I had to forgive him, for he had done nothing wrong. He was in fact a very kind man, and I had not asked him to move in here.

"I would have assumed when you married me that this would in fact become your home. You have told me time and time again that I am your home."

"Yes, but you forget that I have sworn not to dishonor you, and to assume that anything belongs to me would be doing just that."

I lost my breath. "I belong to you," I whispered.

"As I belong to you, but the fact remains the same. This castle is not mine, just as this kingdom is not mine. You, to me, are not a possession. All that I have is in that room I bathe in and keep my belongings."

"I give you all that I have," I whispered.

"The only thing I want... no, the only thing I need in this life is you," he promised.

"You have me. You have always had me. I am just too stupid to know that you are all I need in this life. I need nothing more."

He did not move, just stood there at the end of our bed, looking at me. "As I have told you before, my love, you will never know the depths of my love for you. It hurt me deeply, knowing you believed even for a moment that I would dishonor you. You are the most beautiful woman I have ever known. There is no one who can compare. The things we share in this bed are things I could never share with another."

I wiped the tear from my cheek. *This man is incredible.* "I think I got a bit carried away with what I read in the tomes. My imagination took me on a wild journey, and I was seeing things that were not there," I whispered.

"To anyone else, they were there. I should not have been alone with Sarah. I should not have left our bed to spend time with her, and come to it late in the night after leaving her. But you must know that I would not dishonor you or our marriage."

"I know this. I kept telling myself that you would not, that you love me. But as I said, things just got out of hand. She was planning a future with my husband, and it got the best of me. I suppose, if I had told her who I was, it would have ended. I am guilty of letting it get out of hand."

"You spoke with her? Why did you not tell me?"

"I did not really. She came to Clare's after you had left yesterday, and then when I walked into your quarters to find you stepping out of the bath, I thought... well, you do not want to know what I thought."

He put his hand on his chest. "I know what you thought. Sabine, if you were taken from me, there would never come a day when I would or could take another woman as my wife. You are the love of my life, and I have told Sarah as such. I was in fact bathing to come to you. I have missed you, wife. I was coming to see if you were ready to talk to me."

"I miss you, too, so much. Blake, will you move in here with me? Will you share my kingdom with me? Will you be my King?" The smile on his face made me crawl to the end of the bed and up him to kiss him.

"I love you. No matter what I say or do, I will love no other," I said as I covered his mouth with mine.

Our kiss was deep and desperate. I felt the groan from deep within him as his hands came around and lifted me off the bed. I wrapped my legs around him, pressing my arms on his shoulders so I could move up to meet his face. He pulled away from me to look into my eyes. "I love you, wife, now and forever. Never forget that."

I shook my head. "I will not."

He moved from his spot at the end of our bed and carried me to the edge, slowly lying me down. I let go of him only so he could undress. He reached for my hands, pulling me up, then

243

put his hands under my arms and lifted me so he could kiss me deeply. His hands got tangled in my hair as I kneeled on the bed, his tongue doing my favorite dance. He laid me back and kissed me until I could not do anything but shake in his arms. We did not stop kissing or touching.

I smiled at him. "You are so beautiful."

He smiled a gentle smile as his hands trailed up my sides, and I could not stop myself. I wanted to be nowhere else, but here with him. He was everything to me. Nothing mattered or made sense with us apart. We lay in each other's arms, basking in the aftermath of our love, him playing with my hair and me running my fingers through the hair on his chest, neither of us saying a word. We did not need to. I knew how he felt about me, and he knew that he was the only man I would ever love. We must have fallen asleep because Raiden woke me.

'Collingwood is coming.'

I jumped up and flew out of the bed. "What is going on?" Blake asked sleepily.

"Collingwood is coming. Hurry, get dressed." I was nearly done, already pulling my boots on. "I will meet you on the plain. I love you." I grabbed my crown and ran out the door.

Rebecca was standing in the great hall with her boy clothes on, looking at my sword stuck in the wall as I took the stairs two at a time. "Well, that is interesting."

I giggled. "I was angry," I explained as I pulled it from the wall. Together, we ran out the door and into the courtyard. Charles and my Guardians were walking up with the horses.

"Where is Blake?" he asked.

"He is coming." No sooner did I say it than he came running out the door.

I got on Raiden and took off. This time, Collingwood had crossed the little river. It was not George this day but one of the other brothers. As we rode up, they stopped.

244

"I am Steven of Collingwood. My brother, George the King, has sent me," he said.

"I am Sabine of Whispering Wind. I must say that I am sorry for the loss of your Father. What brings you here?"

"Thank you. I was sent to retrieve Princess Rebecca of Blackmore. She is to pay for her crimes against my family."

"As I told your brother, the King, there was no crime. It was a matter of self-defense. Your brothers tried to murder me." I felt him coming, and they were riding fast.

"I know not what you are saying to me. You are nothing but a mere woman. What would your life matter to the royal family?"

Just then, Charles rode up. "It would be wise to watch your tongue, boy. You are speaking to my Queen."

"Your Queen? This child is your Queen?" He laughed.

I raised my eyebrows at him just as Blake walked up beside me, and stated, "As well as my wife."

He laughed harder. "A Queen who marries guardsmen? How preposterous is this?"

One of the men sitting next to him reached over and touched his arm. Steven looked at him and then leaned over while the man whispered in his ear. Steven turned and looked at Blake. It was fear I saw in his eyes next.

"Well, it would seem that your brother failed to tell you who I was," I said.

"Impossible," he said. "It is a myth. After Edward died, all was lost."

"Your father was misinformed," I corrected.

"No, you are an imposter."

"I can assure you, I am not."

"But you are a woman. It would be unheard of for a mere woman to be The Bringer of Peace. It is a man's duty. What harm could you possibly do? Look at you, you are a mere child."

Charles leaned forward, offering a warning. "She does not take kindly to being called a child."

Blake laughed. "She is no child, I can attest to that." I smiled at him.

"It would seem that we are at an impasse here. I am who I am, and you refuse to believe it, so I think we have a decision to make. I can assure you that Rebecca here is going nowhere with you, and you are in my Kingdom uninvited. Go home to your brother, the King, and tell him to stop this crusade to obtain something that he has no rightful claim over, or we shall pay Collingwood a visit you will not soon forget."

"Do not threaten me. As I have said before, you are nothing to me."

Charles moved his horse in front of me. "I told you to mind yourself. She is our Queen, and you will treat her as such."

He looked at Blake, his eyes momentarily focusing on Blake's hand. "You are the true Guardians?"

"We are. You know that you will lose this battle if you choose to continue. I will not allow you to take Rebecca anywhere."

"My army will destroy you," he said.

I felt Raiden twitch, and I drew my sword.

"What trickery is this? How is it possible that you wield that sword? It was stolen from my father many years ago."

"Here, you want it back?" I asked as I handed it forward.

He waved his hand, motioning for one of his riders to come up and take it from me. He got close enough to take the hilt, when a flash of light came out of the end and he fell to the ground.

"Only the Bringer of Peace can hold that sword. If you think it is your bloodline, then you are the one who needs to take it," Charles told him. Steven did not move.

"I have had enough of this. Get off my land. Go back to your brother and tell him the fight is not worth your life, because you will most assuredly lose it here today."

"Do not threaten me, child."

I felt him and looked at Rebecca, who was smiling, and it was never a good thing when she smiled like that. We raised our swords, and Raiden and Spirit jumped. The light was intense, the screams were loud, and when we landed, the front line of Steven's army lay in ashes.

I looked him square in the eyes. "It is not a threat. Leave my land or you will be next." I turned to ride away.

I felt him before Blake yelled my name. I jumped off Raiden and turned in time to catch his sword as he swung, knocking him off his horse.

"That was your first mistake," I said.

He jumped up. "I make no mistakes," he shouted and swung his sword. I caught it with mine and slammed it to the ground. He spun and kicked me in the stomach, sending me flying and landing on my back, so I threw my legs over my head and stood up.

"That was your second," I warned. He came at me time and time again, and I felt his energy continuously depleting. I lost my footing and stumbled. He grabbed my hair and pulled me up to his face, licking my cheek. I hit him in the throat, and he released me. Blake was off his horse, but I looked at him and shook my head.

"That was your third. Do not touch me without my permission." I swung my sword. The fire exploded from it as I held our swords together. His began to glow red. He screamed and let go of it as it burned his hand. I put the tip of my sword on his throat. "It is a shame that three of Collingwood's sons will die," I said as I slammed my sword into his throat, cutting his head off.

I turned to his army, wiping my cheek on the sleeve of my top. "Tell your King that if you return here, I will end you, and then I will come to Collingwood. When I am done, there will be nothing left."

They just sat there on their horses, looking at me. The man that had whispered in Steven's ear looked at Charles. "Master," he said and nodded. They turned and left.

I looked at Blake. "I need a bath."

He laughed and hugged me. We rode back to Whispering Wind together on Raiden. As we walked through the village, I saw Sarah leaving Clare's. She turned to look at us, her face was appearing unhappy.

"Can we stop for a minute?" I said to Blake. He gave me a concerned look and pulled on Raiden's reins. I slid off him and called her name, "Sarah, could I talk to you please?"

She stopped and turned, so I began, "I must apologize for last night. I am afraid that I was out of sorts. It was wrong of me to assume that Blake would deceive me in the manner in which I thought. It was not your fault, and I understand how easy it is to enjoy him."

She bowed. "No, Your Majesty, it is I who was wrong. I should not have attacked you. I have been waiting for the punishment I deserve."

I giggled. "My name is Sabine, and you do not deserve anything. Why would you think I would punish you for wanting to be with my husband? He is a very good man, kind, gentle, and generous. It is not your fault."

"I thought because I attacked you that you would put me to death."

I laughed loud. "Do not be silly. All is forgiven Sarah. Welcome to Whispering Wind. Blake said your cakes are very delicious. If you would like, you could bring some to the castle, and I will have Francis pay you for your services. I am always in the mood for a good cake, though pie is my favorite. I have a little niece, Isabel, who loves cake, as well."

"That is very gracious of you, My Lady, but you do not need to pay me."

"Nonsense, if you work to provide a service for us, then you should be paid for it," I told her before turning and walking back to Blake. With one arm, he bent and picked me up, placing me in front of him on Raiden. "It was nice to meet you, Sarah," I said as we rode away.

"You are an incredible woman. Now, let me take you home and give you that bath you requested." He smiled.

When the kitchen girls finished pouring the last pot of water, Blake came in with a giant tray of food. He dragged the table over to the side of the tub, and then walked up to me and removed every piece of my clothing before proceeding to remove his. I tilted my head and smiled at him, thinking we were going to have some fun first, but that was not the case. He picked me up and carried me to the tub, setting me in the hot water very gently. He then got in at the other end. I giggled.

He smiled, saying, "You made a comment last night that I do not bathe with you or in our room, so I thought I would remedy that."

We laughed, we ate, we washed, and when we were done, we loved one another.

Chapter Twelve

We lay in our bed just being together, feeling one another. Hours passed as we giggled and talked, kissed, and touched. "I love you," I told him, feeling content.

"I love you."

"I found two more Markers. That is ten in all so far. I have two more to find, and two tomes left to read."

"Well, that is good. How did you find two more?"

"Boland helped me."

"Sabine, you were pretty upset about what you read in the tomes. Do you think you can tell me what was in it?" My body tensed up. "It is all right, my love, if you cannot."

"It scares me what is in that book. I do not understand it. I think it played a role in what happened between us, and I am second guessing myself, us, this whole thing."

"What do you mean 'us'?"

"Our marriage, the fact that we cannot make a union, children, how we want so many and we can have none. When I heard Sarah saying that you wanted lots, it set me off. When I ran out of my study and went to the valley, what I read in that book tore my heart out. I thought that you were going to leave me and make a union with someone else, and then I saw you with Sarah. It makes no sense."

He chuckled. "No, my love, it does not. I am completely lost."

I sat up and looked at him. In my tiny voice, I said, "The Unknown Heir shall be born into the peace. The Unknown Heir shall be brought forth by the purity of the heir."

He sat up, his eyes never leaving mine. "You thought, because we cannot have a union, that I was going to have one with someone else and bring forth an heir?" I nodded. He grabbed me and pulled me into his lap. "That will never happen, not ever. You are the only one I want a union with. It must mean something else."

"I still have two more tomes to read, so I am hoping that something else will be revealed. I am so confused by this Unknown Heir. It is a baby I am sure of it, but whose baby?"

He held me. "I have no idea, but we will figure it out."

He held me for a little while, and then we got up. "I have some things to take care of," he said as he kissed me goodbye, and then he just left. I stood there in our room, smiling and shaking my head before going to my study to get out the seventh tome.

Setting it on my desk, I took a deep breath and opened the cover. When I looked at it, though, nothing happened. The page was empty. I turned another and another, but there was nothing. I went back into the secret room to look at the last one, but the same thing happened. *Perhaps I am not ready to read these.* I closed the door to the secret room and went out into my study. Placing the drawings on the floor, I looked at all the places I had marked; there were ten in all. I walked around and around, looking at them, but I was drawing a blank. I shook my head, and figured I was not meant to learn anything that day, so I decided I would go for a walk instead.

I found myself wandering through the village, and noticed there were a lot of new people who have moved into the kingdom. I wandered over to Clare's cottage and knocked on her door. Her brother, Gerald, answered the door.

"Your Majesty, please come in."

Before I walked in, I asked him, "Is Clare home?"

"No, My Lady, she is not, but please come in."

"It would not be proper for me to come in, but thank you. Please let her know I came by."

"I will do that."

I smiled and walked away, and continued on my walk. I made it all the way to Boland's before Blake caught up with me.

"My love, what are you doing?"

I smiled at him. "I thought I would take a walk. What are you doing?"

"Following you," he said with a smile.

"Why are you following me?"

He put his arm around my waist. "There are some new people here that seem a bit unsociable, and I really do not feel comfortable with you wandering around alone or without your sword."

I giggled. "So you came to defend me?"

"Oh, I know you do not need defending, but yes. Come on. We can start back."

"But I wanted to visit Boland."

"He is not there. He has gone to another village to pick up some thread for Clare."

I looked at him and smiled. "How do you know these things?"

"Well," he said as he pulled me close to him, moving us to side of the building to kiss me, "a man touched my wife, so now, I make in my business to know everything that is going on around here. You have a job to do, and it is my job as your husband to make sure you stay safe until it is done."

"Do you not mean as my Guardian?" I kissed him.

"Remember, according to Westin, my Guardian duties were fulfilled when you forged the swords. So, as your husband, I swore to keep you safe."

We walked out from the side of the building to see Sarah standing a few feet away. *Is she watching us?* I wondered.

"Oh, I am sorry. I did not see you there. I was coming to visit Boland."

Blake smiled at her. "Boland is not home, I was just telling Sabine that he has gone in search of thread for Clare."

"Oh, such a shame. Oh well, perhaps I will go see Clare."

"I was just there, and her brother said she was not at home, but perhaps she has returned."

"Would you like to go with me, Your Majesty?"

"It is Sabine, and no thank you. Apparently, I have something that needs my attention, but please, if she is home, will you pass along that I stopped by?"

"Of course. You two have a nice day." She turned then to walk away.

Blake held on to me to hold me back while she moved ahead of us. I looked up at him. "What is the matter," I whispered.

"We need to talk," he whispered back.

"All right, hold on." I searched for him in my mind.

'Can you get out of the stables?'

'Yes.'

'Would you come to Boland's?'

"Raiden," I said as he arrived, "Can take us to the hilltop."

Blake jumped on him and then reached down to grab me. I had on a gown, so jumping on a horse was not easy. We rode to the hilltop, and I asked, "Raiden, is there anyone around to hear us?" He shook his head.

Blake sat down. "I think Sarah is here to side track me, to draw my attention away from you, to separate us. There are a few new men who have come to the village. They are with women who are not their wives, women who sell themselves."

"Sell themselves for what?"

He looked at me, his eyebrows raised. I think he was waiting for me to get it, but I did not. "For favors to men. Men pay them money to have unions with them."

"What? In my village? No way. They must leave. How do you know this?"

"One of them asked James. I think they are trying to distract us."

"Oh, do you think they are after Rebecca? Do you think it is Collingwood?"

"Well, that is what I wanted to talk to you about. Charles and I have a plan. We want to set them up to see if it is Rebecca they are after, or if it is you."

"And you think Sarah is in on it?"

"Well, it would make sense that she is, since she targeted me. She came to the barracks, inside the castle walls. She just walked right in."

"Anyone can. I like it that way."

"My love, I am going to tell you something. Please do not get angry with me, but Sarah came to my quarters the night before last. She had sweet talked her way past the guards and was sitting on my bed, waiting for me, when I walked in to bathe before I came to be with you. That is why I was so late."

"Seriously, so something is going on. I wonder if Clare has a clue."

"I am not sure, but her brother showing up out of nowhere is suspicious."

"Yes, and today he insisted that I come in while Clare was not home. When I refused, he seemed a bit agitated. Okay, I will wear boy clothes from now on, and my sword will never leave me."

"There is something more. Do not eat Sarah's cakes. I think she has put something in them. That day you saw me coming out of her cottage, well, I had eaten one of her cakes. When I tried to leave, I had a hard time. I was late that night, as well, when I went to my quarters to bathe I fell asleep. When have you known me to sleep anywhere you were not?"

"Has anyone said anything to Rebecca?"

"No, but I think we should go and do it now." I nodded in agreement, and we got up and went back to the castle. Rebecca was in the kitchen with Francis.

"Francis, has Sarah delivered any cakes here today?"

"No, not today."

"When she does, please take them from her and pay her, but do not eat them. Throw them out and, please, do not let Isabel have any. Be careful. Things are not right. Rebecca, we need to talk. Can you please come to my study?"

"Sure," she answered, appearing curious.

We walked in silence to my study, where we waited for Blake to come with Charles. I put my hand up and went to my desk to pop the latch. Rebecca pulled the huge drapes across the windows, and we went into the secret room.

"What is going on, Sabine?" Rebecca asked.

Charles started talking, filling us both in on what he had found out. "There are five new men who have moved into the village, and with them are five women who allow men to have unions with them for payment. My father called women like this, harlots. Anyway, these women have approached a few of my men, James included, for their favor. Clare's brother, although we have no real proof, would make six, though I am not even sure he is her brother. I have had numerous conversations with Clare, and not once did she mention a brother," Charles said.

"So what do you think they are doing here?" Rebecca questioned.

"Well, when all of this happened with Blake and Sarah, I could not help but wonder how she did not know you," he looked at me, "were the Queen or Blake's wife. I think she was supposed to keep him busy. I believe they are either after Sabine, which would not make sense, or they are from Collingwood and are here to take you back to pay for killing Edward."

"Are you serious? So what should we do?" It was clear that Rebecca was annoyed by this news.

"We have a plan. We are going to set them up and see who it is they want."

After discussing the plan, we decided that the sooner the better to end this mess.

"I think we should just ride to Collingwood and end it there," I stated.

"Yes, but we are not sure what they want or who they want, or if they want anything at all. It could just be that they heard that you were kind, so they feel they can get away with that kind of behavior."

"That man who tore my dress, was he one of them?"

"I think so, but he did not talk."

We left the secret room. Charles went back to the barracks, and I went to change into my boy clothes and to get my sword. If this was going to happen, I could not fight in a gown with my breasts sticking out. When I got to our room, I pushed the door open, but it would not open all the way. I stuck my head in to see it was filled with things, trunks, boots, all kinds of stuff, and I could not help but smile. I felt him behind me and I turned.

"You have more stuff than I do, and I am a girl."

His laughter filled the hallway. "I think we need a bigger room."

I worked my way through the stuff to the chairs by the fireplace. "So it is official. We live together."

"Looks that way. So which side of the bed is mine?"

We laughed. "The middle, right next to me," I answered, looking around the room. "You know, we could take out that wall and extend this room into the one next to it."

He stood there looking at the wall. "We could do that. I will have some men take care of it tomorrow. Now, come here so I can kiss you, wife."

I reached for him, but there was too much stuff in the way. "We need to make a path so we can at least get to the bed, the door, and the tub." We started moving things here and there, and once we managed to make our paths, I got my boy clothes out of the trunk. "Will you untie me, please?"

He smiled and came over. Moving my hair out of the way, he slowly untied my gown, kissing my neck as he did. As I slipped it off and put on my undershirt, his hands came around to the tops of my thighs. He slipped them up my body, pulling me into his chest. I laid my head back and let him touch me. I loved these little moments we shared. He bent down and kissed me, and everything around me went away. We were the only two people in the world, until we heard someone clear their throat.

Blake turned so his back was to the door, shielding me with his body. I giggled.

"Excuse me, sir, but Charles has sent me to look for you."

"It is customary to knock on a door before you walk into a room, especially the Queen's bed chamber. Leave now and wait for me downstairs."

"Yes, sir," he replied and was gone.

"I am sorry, my love. That will never happen again."

"It is all right. He did not see me."

"Get dressed. I will wait for you." Our little moment was over. I dressed quickly, and we went down stairs together. The guard that was waiting at the bottom of the stairs was a new guard I had not met before.

"You are never to come into this house again. Do you understand me?"

"Yes, sir, I was just following orders."

"Your orders were not to walk into my bed chamber unannounced. If you come into this house again, I will personally see to it that you do not walk anywhere for a long time. Now, get the hell out of here."

The man ran out, and we followed. Charles was walking up.

"There you are," he said to Blake.

"Do not send another guard into that house again looking for me. That man walked into our room while Sabine was half-dressed, unannounced. Why was he in the house?"

Charles turned to look at the man. "I do not know. I did not ask him to come and find you."

I looked at Blake. "Where is Rebecca?"

We all ran into the castle and up the stairs. I burst into her room to find some man trying to restrain her. I hit him in the back of the knees just as Blake and Charles came in. He turned and struck me in the jaw, sending me flying to land against the wall. I sat there in horror as I watched Blake throw him out the window. He was by my side in an instant. "Are you all right?"

"I am fine. Rebecca?" I looked over, and she was lying on the floor in a heap with Charles next to her.

He picked her up and laid her on the bed, moving her hair from her face. It was such a kind and loving gesture. I could not help but feel bad for him.

I got up and went to her. "My love, come on. Open your eyes."

She moved her head and moaned, "What the hell," she whispered.

"What happened?"

"Oh, it is Collingwood, all right," she stated furiously.

I looked at Blake. "This ends now. This is our home, and I will not have it here. There are children who live in this house." I got off the bed and went to the center of the room. Pulling my sword from its sheath, I drew a circle on the floor around me, then slamming it on the floor, I said,

"With the thread of the crimes of your own design

I bind your evil

Three times seven times.

I bind you from Behind

I bind you to the ground

That you'll hurt my people never ever more."

I felt the wind blow in the room, my hair flying in the air, and then it was silent. I opened my eyes. "Those who are here to hurt us, you will find bound to the ground just as Roman was." I told Blake, "I am going to Collingwood, and this will end."

I walked out of the room, down the hall, down the stairs, and out into the courtyard. Blake followed me, and we found three guards pinned to the ground. As I made my way to the great gates, I saw what I hoped I would not see Sarah wrapped in the roots of the ground in front of her shop.

"Why would you do this to us?" I asked her.

"Collingwood has threatened to murder my family if I did not help him."

I shook my head and proceeded to Clare's. When I opened the door, I found her brother bound by the roots as well. Clare, however, was not.

"You are a witch," he yelled.

I shut the door and looked at Blake. "Find the others. When you have them all accounted for, get guards to handle each one, and I will release them. Then take them to our special place, so we can deal with them at another time. I will wait for Rebecca and then for you and the Guardians." I walked away.

Sarah looked at him. "Are you really going to let her talk to you like that?"

He smiled. "She is my Queen, and I am but her humble servant."

I laughed as I walked back to the castle. Rebecca and Charles were coming down the stairs. "We are going to Collingwood. As soon as you discover all that are bound by the roots of the ground, let me know so that I can release them. Put them in our special place. I am done playing this intrigue."

He nodded and left, and Rebecca and I went to the stables.

"Where did that casting come from?" Rebecca asked.

"To be honest, I do not know. It just happened, but I will not have people coming into our home and into our bed chambers to cause us harm. How are you?"

"I am fine. My face hurts."

I stopped and looked at her face. Just across her cheek was a bruise forming. "I am so mad that they hurt you."

"I am not so happy about it myself." She chuckled.

When we walked into the stables, there was a guard in there bound to the ground. "What is your excuse?" I asked him.

"She killed our King," he sputtered.

"Well, it is better your King than my Queen," Rebecca said to him. "And now, your Kingdom is going to burn. Too bad your King does not listen."

"You will be slaughtered. Our Kingdom is the greatest in the land."

I could not help it as I leaned in and said, "Not anymore. Now, it will be brought to ashes."

We saddled our horses and walked out into the courtyard. I saw James running out of the barracks. "There are five in there," he said to me.

"There is one in the stables as well."

When all the commotion was done, we had discovered forty men and women who had been sent to Whispering Wind by Collingwood to lay in wait to get Rebecca and distract me. When there were men in place to take them all, I stood in the courtyard, took my sword out, and put the tip on the ground. I drew a circle then slammed my sword into the ground. The roots of the ground released them. It was quite a commotion watching our guards dragging them to our special place.

Clare had come running into the courtyard. "Sabine!" she yelled. I turned and started walking toward her. "I am so sorry for what happened. He is not my brother. Collingwood has my mother. George said that if I did not go along with them, they would kill her," she cried.

"I thought that might be the case. I wondered why she has not returned. It is not your fault, Clare. I do not blame you. We are going to Collingwood, and I will make sure your mother is safe."

She hugged me and made her way back home. As I was walking back, Charles and Blake came walking up.

"Well, they are all locked away. We can go now," Charles said.

Blake came up to me. "Are you sure you want to do this?"

"I am sure. They were in our house, in our room. I will give Collingwood a chance, but I know that George will not yield. He is Edward's brother."

He hugged me. "Then so be it. Come on. We should get going."

We rode hard. Collingwood was just on the other side of Blackmore, which was just on the other side of Wellington. We made it just as the dark of night was coming across the land on the second day. Charles thought it best we wait until the light of the day, but I thought it best we end this now.

As we rode into Collingwood and straight to the castle, guardsmen quickly surrounded us.

"I wish to see your King," I ordered.

"Our King does not see unannounced visitors, especially ones who are wanted for murder."

I leaned down to get at eye level with the one who had spoken. "Tell your King that Sabine of Whispering Wind is here to see him, or I will show you what murder is."

The guards drew their swords. "You will not win this fight. You are but ten."

Rebecca leaned over to look at him. "Good to see you can count."

I drew my sword and pointed it at him. "Either you run along and tell George that I am here, or I will tell him myself."

"I serve my King, not you."

"As you wish," I said as I raised my sword and Raiden jumped. I actually felt bad for turning them to ash. As we landed, another group of guards came running. "Now, I can do this all night. Perhaps one of you has a mind of their own and will run along to tell George that I am here to speak to him."

The guard standing closest to me motioned with his hand, and another guard ran into the castle.

"Finally, someone who can think for themselves," Rebecca said and then giggled. "Such a rare trait for a man these days."

Moments later, George came out in his armor. I could not stop the giggle, for he looked silly. "Why have you sent your people to Whispering Wind?"

"I demand justice for my brothers' deaths. She will pay for her crimes," he stated, looking at Rebecca.

"What you have done, George, is sentence these men to death." I waved my hand around.

"You ride into my Kingdom and threaten me. You are but ten, while we are thousands."

"George, there are just a few things in this life that anger me enough to level armies such as yours. Wrong doing and arrogant men who think that women are beneath them. You ride into my Kingdom and threaten me, then you send your

263

little henchmen to take refuge in my village, and now, you stand before me, thinking it is expectable to punish a woman for defending her Queen against those who wish her dead. I will not tolerate you believing you are superior to me."

"It does not matter to me what you believe, Princess. I am the King of..."

I cut him off. "You are an arrogant man, and you are nothing." I raised my sword, and when Raiden landed again, hundreds of men were but piles of ash. "I will destroy Collingwood and leave you with nothing."

I have no idea how it happened, but I heard the arrows flying through the air. My arm went in the air, only Raiden did not jump. The words just came out of my mouth.

"Protection here, night and day

The one who should not be touched,

Let them fall into flames

Let his fingers burn and twitch."

The arrows burst into flames. It was quite spectacular to see the flying flames and then hundreds of men's hands burst into flames.

I heard Rebecca giggle and then whisper to Charles, "I told you that you had no idea what she can do now."

I looked at George. "We can do this all day. Now, you have hundreds of archers who have no hands. Either you yield or I will destroy you."

"You are a witch," he said.

I screamed at him, "I am the Bringer of Peace!"

He took a step back. "I will not yield."

"I am tired of this intrigue you insist on playing with me. You are just as your brothers were, just as your father was, tainted

264

by his greed. You shall receive the same fate." I raised my sword, and Raiden jumped. The dark of the night glowed, bringing the light of the day to Collingwood. Men screamed, burning, and when we finally landed, the barracks were on fire, cottages were on fire, and the castle was on fire. Standing on the steps was George with his sword drawn. I jumped off of Raiden and walked up to him. "How foolish are you to draw on me now? If it is death you are seeking, I am more than willing to give it to you."

He stood there looking at me, and I could see his fear. I could feel his rage. He would not back down. His sword hit the stones. I turned to walk away, willing to leave Collingwood alive, but his arrogance would not allow a woman to beat him. I closed my eyes to feel his energy, which grew darker as I watched. His hand reached to his side, drawing a dagger. As he moved forward, I spun, and with one blaze of fire, his head rolled down the stairs.

I looked up to see Blake watching me. He was off his horse, and I was in his arms before I could blink. I do not know why, but the tears just came. "Why did he do that?" I asked.

"I do not know my, love," he said as he held me.

People started to come into the courtyard. I looked at Blake then at Charles. "You need to find the dungeons and free the people in them." He nodded and then rode off. I heard something behind me, and turned in Blake's arms, wiping the tears from my face. Standing in the door was a woman.

"Thank you," was all she said as she walked out with two children following her. I watched as she walked out of the courtyard and into the village.

We sat on the steps waiting for Charles to return, which did not happen until the light of the day came. "We have freed everyone." I looked past him to see Charlotte walking up. Her clothes were tattered, and she was filthy and looked as if she had been beaten. I ran to her.

"Thank you for coming to end this tyranny," she said weakly.

I hugged her. "You are coming home with us. I know Clare will be so happy to see you. How many others were taken?"

"I do not know."

"Come, you can ride Blake's horse. He will ride with me." We walked to the horses, and Blake helped her up.

"Charles, I would like to go home now. We will ride ahead of you. Please make sure Charlotte gets home to Clare," I told him.

"As you wish, Your Majesty." He nodded.

Blake climbed on Raiden and pulled me up. I sat with my head on his chest. "Raiden, take us home please." He nodded, and we walked slowly through the village. There were people cheering, some crying; it was all very overwhelming. When we hit the plain, we were gone, making it back to the castle by midday.

Blake went to get us some food, and I went to our room. I undressed and put on my sleeping gown, crawled into bed, and waited for Blake, but sleep came instead.

I did not feel his weight as he climbed into bed with me. I did not feel him draw me into his chest and wrap his arms around me. I did not feel his sweet lips on my forehead. I did not feel anything.

When I woke, he was still next to me, and the light of the day was new in the sky. I listened to his heart beating and knew he was still sleeping. As I tilted my head to look at him, his lips cracked. He had awakened. "Good morning, my beautiful girl. You have been asleep for some time now."

"Mmmmm, and I do not want to wake now."

"Perhaps I can send you back into the slumber you wish to have," he said and pulled me up his body, kissing me. And he

266

was right. He exhausted me, and again, I slept in his arms. Only this time, it was because of his love.

When I woke again, I was alone. I stretched out in the bed, smiling. Noticing a cloth lying on the bed next to me, I picked it up to look at it, then giggled when I realized what it was. It was my sleeping gown, only it was not a gown at all. He had torn it from my body. As I looked at it, he came in the room carrying a tray.

"Sorry about that," he said with a chuckle.

"Mmmmm," I mumbled. "You are the most passionate man I know."

He chuckled. "I am the only man you know." He set down the tray on a trunk and climbed into bed, covering my mouth with his and taking the gown from me as he did. "The desire and passion we feel for one another clouds all thoughts in my mind. Apparently, in yours as well, for you do not remember tearing this gown."

"I did this?" I asked.

"Well, we did it together, along with these." He leaned over and picked up his under garment. We burst into laughter. His voice softer, he told me, "You have slept for two days. Come and eat. I know you are hungry, and Francis has cooked up a storm." He climbed off the bed and got the tray. Setting it down, he removed the cover. Seeing all that food made me realize just how hungry I was.

"I think, when I use this magic in me, it depletes me."

"That could be. You slept hard. I think I benefit from it as well, because when you wake, our loving is explosive."

I felt my cheeks get warm as I giggled.

"Clare has come by a few times. I told her I would let you know. She wants to see you."

"When we finish, I will go over there and visit her. Did Charlotte get back safely?"

"Yes, Charles delivered her to Clare. He said it was quite a reunion."

"Good, and what about Sarah's family?"

"Believe it or not, George had her children in those dungeons. He put her husband to death."

I suddenly lost my appetite, so I got out of bed and put on a gown. Blake did not say a word, but just watched me. "Will you tie this for me?" He got up and tied my gown. When he finished he turned me to face him.

"You are the most compassionate woman I know, and I love you." He gently covered my mouth with his and kissed me so sweetly, I almost wanted to take him back to bed.

"I will be back later. Do I need my sword?"

"I do not think so. I am going to have them start with this wall today."

"That will be fine. I love you," I said as I put my crown on and walked out of the room.

I made my way to Sarah's, where a beautiful little girl answered the door. "Hello, is your momma here?"

She nodded. There was no joy in this child's eyes. She did not speak, just turned and walked away.

I heard Sarah. "Who is it, my love?" Then she appeared at the door. "Your Majesty," she said as she bowed.

"Sarah, I have asked you to call me Sabine."

She threw her arms around me and hugged me. I held her while she cried. "Thank you so much for bringing them home to me."

I pulled away from her, holding her hands. "I wish you would have told us what was happening. We could have avoided all this mess."

"I was so scared that they would kill them as they did my husband."

"I know. Blake told me what happened. I am just glad that you got them back. I wanted to stop by and make sure we are all right with everything. You have nothing more to fear. I want you to stay here and live your life. You are safe here."

"Blake was right about you."

"What do you mean?"

"When he came to let me out of the dungeons, he told me what you had done and that you were a kind and just woman, and I did not have to fear punishment. He loves you very much."

I smiled at her. "I know he does, and he was right. You have nothing to fear. I am going to go by Clare's and see Charlotte. I will have her make your children some new clothes. I see that you have nothing for them."

"That is not necessary. I have nothing to pay her with."

"Well, now that I know you are not trying to harm us, my offer for the cakes still stands, so I will pay her for the clothes. My gift to you and your children."

She did not know what to say. She just stood there with tears falling from her eyes. I smiled and squeezed her hand and then left. I knocked on Clare's door, and when she opened it, she nearly knocked me to the ground, throwing herself at me and hugging me. We laughed. "How is your mother?"

"Come in and see for yourself."

Charlotte was sitting on the couch, drinking tea. "Oh, my dear child, come in and sit with me," she said as she patted the couch.

"My Lady. I am sorry that I did not know, otherwise I would have come sooner."

"You sure have been through a great deal in your young life."

I smiled, feeling a tear welling in my eye. I tried to pull it back, but it fell onto my cheek. "Yes, I suppose I have."

"Life will get better for you. I know the legend, and I know that the time is coming for it to all end. We will be safe, and you will be the reason for it."

I half laughed. "I hope you are right."

We sat and visited for a while; it was nice to see her. It was good to know she would be all right.

"I must be going. They are doing some construction in the castle, and I want to check on it. Clare, would you do me a favor?"

"Of course, Sabine." She smiled.

"I was wondering if you could make some gowns for Sarah's daughter and some clothes for her son. I will pay you for your time."

"Oh, you do not need to pay me, Sabine. It would be my pleasure."

"Thank you." We hugged and I left.

As I walked through the village, I felt eyes upon me. I did not bother to look around, for I did not feel threatened at all. When I approached the fountain, I saw Juliana and James in the back courtyard, looking as if they were having a civil conversation. I smiled, hoping they were working things out.

There were men walking in and out of the castle, carrying stones from the wall in my room. When I got up stairs, it was almost completely gone.

"Hi," I said to Blake as I came in. He was covered in dirt. When he turned around, I had to giggle because he looked silly. His face was dirty.

"Hi yourself," he said as he came over. I put my hands up to stop him, but he did not stop. He wrapped his dirty self around me and rubbed his face on mine, making me laugh, and then kissed me. "I found something in the wall that you might find interesting." He pulled a scroll from his shirt.

I looked at him and took it. Unrolling it revealed words that were not readable. I thought of the words on the walls of the cave and in father's drawings, and looked around for my mother's looking glass. With all of Blake's things here, I could not see anything.

"What does it say?"

"I do not know, but I will be back later." I kissed him and went to find Camille. She was in her room.

"Hi, do you by any chance have a looking glass?"

"I do. It is small. It belonged to my mother. Charles gave it to me when we came from the valley." She went to the table and picked it up. It was very beautiful, silver, and it was carved. "You push this little lever here, and it pops open."

"Can I borrow it for a little while?"

"Of course," she said.

"Thank you." I went to my study and unrolled the scroll. Putting the looking glass up to the words, I began to read.

In this place, this circle round
I consecrate the sacred ground
With golden light this space surround
All power here contained and bound
From earth, the things that manifest
From air, the things of mind
From fire, the things that motivate
From water, the souls refined
And yet no place or time there be
Between the worlds, my word, and me
Welcome, Ancient Ones and see
This place is sealed

I sat the looking glass down my hands were shaking. What is this? I picked up the scroll and took it into the secret room. I was not sure this was something I should have just yet. After placing it in the drawer of the desk that was there, I walked past the two tomes I had left to read. I stopped and opened each one. Still nothing. I shook my head and went to sit out in the back courtyard.

There was so much that did not make sense to me. Why would that scroll be hidden in a wall? I could not help but wonder what was going to happen with this Coming. I suppose the query here should be what exactly is the Coming? That and who was this Unknown Heir to be brought forth by me? I shook my head. *The Markers of Time, what are they?* I wondered if I should dig one up.

Collingwood creeped into my mind. Why would George do the things he did? His whole family was now gone, the whole line. My whole family was gone, all of this over this land, over power and greed. *Why do men think this way? Are they jealous of what the other has?* Well, now no one has anything. They are all dead. The Kingdoms that once were are no more, nor are there Kings to rule them. Am I the only Queen left to rule a Kingdom? I giggled, saying softly to myself, "I do not even want to be Queen."

"Why not? You are a beautiful Queen."

I smiled. I had not heard Blake come up behind me, for I was so deep in thought. "How long have you been there watching me?" I did not turn around.

"Just a moment or two." He came over and sat down. "Are you all right?"

"I am not sure what comes next. The tomes will not let me read them. I have two more Markers to find, and I have no way of knowing where they are or how to find them. I do not know what I am supposed to do with them when I find them. And then you find this strange scroll buried in the wall. I am confused and lost. I murdered another Kingdom, just as mine was murdered."

"No, you did not. You gave Collingwood the chance to save himself, and he chose to draw that dagger. You did not murder those people, Sabine. You freed them. You gave them back their lives, and, my love, when this is finally over, we shall have ours." He kissed my forehead. "Do not over think this. Just let it come to you in the order in which it is supposed to. Now, I have finished taking down the wall, and the kitchen girls are up there cleaning our room. Would you like to see it?"

"Not just yet. I think I would like to go for a ride. I need to be free, or at least feel free. Is that all right with you?"

"Of course, my love, you go and ride. I will be right here when you get back." He kissed me once more, and I went to the stables.

"Hello, boy, you want to go for a ride?" He nodded. I put his saddle on and walked him out into the courtyard. As I climb on him, I saw Blake watching me. I smiled at him, but I think he knew that it was not genuine. I closed my eyes to feel his energy, and it was pure. I turned Raiden to go out the back gates. "Just run," I said, and he did. Closing my eyes, I rode, needing to feel free. I wanted to be free.

When we returned to the castle, the dark of the night had fallen on the land. I was walking up from the stables after putting Raiden up for the night, when I looked up at my window. He was there, waiting for me, the soft amber glow letting me know that he had a fire burning for us. My heart filled with love for him. I made my way up the stairs and to our room, then took a deep breath and opened the door.

I could not believe my eyes; the room was huge. He had moved the bed and set in with the head against the wall with the windows. There was a bigger tub on the new side of the room, and all of his things were put away. A magnificent rug covered the floor, nearly reaching all corners of the room, and there he sat in the chair by the fireplace, waiting for me.

I closed the door and bolted it, never taking my eyes from him. I reached up and untied my gown, then slowly slipped it off my shoulders. His eyes followed the movement as it slipped down to my waist. I dropped it on the floor and stepped out of the material, taking my shoes off as I stepped. I had not moved far before he was in front of me.

Gently, his hand trailed up my body to rest on my face, his thumb gently brushing across my bottom lip, lifting my face to see his. The love that poured from his soul was prominent in his eyes. I reached up and gently undid his shirt, then his pants. Sliding his shirt off his shoulders, I stood on the tips of my toes to kiss him. My fingers like feathers, I moved the shirt down his muscular arms, letting it fall to the floor. His mouth gently and passionately covered mine as his hands lifted me off the ground. He stepped out of his pants and carried me to our bed. The dark of the night, combined with the amber glow of the fire, was filled with so much love and tenderness that we cried together while we lay in one another's arms.

"I love you," he whispered in my ear.

"I love you," I whispered back, and we kissed our final kiss of the night in our new room.

Chapter Thirteen

$\mathfrak{I}$ felt his fingers along my cheek as he moved my hair from my face, and I smiled. He was watching me sleep. I stretched in his arms and opened my eyes to see his beautiful face. "Hello, beautiful girl," he said.

"Hello, my love." I put my hand on his face and kissed him.

He pulled me in his arms, and that was more than enough for me. "You are so beautiful, Sabine."

When we were finished with each other, we held one another. I whispered, "I need to take a bath. Would you care to join me in that giant tub over there?"

"Oh, you better believe it. I will go get some food and send the kitchen girls up here to fill it."

I giggled. "I will wait right here."

He jumped up and threw on some clothes, tossed me a shirt of his to put on, and left. I sat in bed, leaning against the headboard, looking around the room. He had done a very good job, and he did it in a day. I giggled again. A man on a mission... I looked at the tub. Where did he get that thing? There was a knock on the door. "Come in," I said. It was the kitchen girls.

They bowed as they entered. "Your Majesty, Master Blake said you wanted to take a bath."

"Yes, that would be lovely, and you can call me Sabine."

"My Lady, it would not be proper for us to do so. You are our Queen."

"Yes, but I am also a woman with a name." I smiled at her.

She nodded and started warming the pots. The other girl must have gone to another room because she came in a few moments later with a pot full of warm water. I did not count how many pots it took to fill this large tub, but it was many. I was getting out of bed when Blake walked in. I had not noticed the table next to the tub, but that is where he set the tray.

I walked over and put my arms around him. "I am a lucky woman, indeed, for it is the woman's job to take care of her man."

He laughed. "It is more than my pleasure to take care of you." He turned in my arms and kissed me. "I believe, Your Majesty, that you are wearing far too many clothes." I giggled as he untied the shirt he gave me to wear, dropping it to the floor. He held my hand while I stepped into the very large tub.

"Where did you find this?"

He laughed. "It is the one from my quarters."

"Well, it is huge."

"I am a big man. Scoot forward." He smiled as he stepped into the tub and sat behind me, pulling me to his chest.

We sat like this and ate our food, and then we washed one another. He got out first to get a blanket for me. "The cold months are coming. Soon, it will be the harvest, and I must keep you warm."

I smiled. "They are, indeed. I wonder what we will do with ourselves." I could not stop the giggle as I watched him wrap himself in a blanket.

He walked over to me and wrapped us both in his blanket. "I know quite a few things we can do." That statement sent me into a flurry of giggles.

We dried ourselves off and got dressed. Blake went about his day, and I went to my study to see if the books were going to let me read them. When I opened the first one, there was nothing, but the second one glowed, so I picked it up and took it to my desk. I sat in the chair and closed my eyes. Taking a deep breath, I leaned forward and opened the book.

The Unknown Heir is present within

The discovery of the twelve Markers of Time

Will set into motion the beginning of the Coming

To bring the Markers forth, the Heir must be in the center of the land

To say these words and bring from the land

Stones of Time

Black to White

Dark to Light

Come forth to thee

Come forth to life

Each element brings forth a Marker

Each Guardian brings forth a Marker

The season of the blossoms will come to an end

The light will fill the dark of the night

And the Coming will begin

I sat back in my chair. "So I do not bring forth a Marker? Then who? It must be Westin and Camille. It would make sense," I said out loud. 'The Unknown Heir is present within.' *What does that mean?* I closed the book, put it back, and went out for a walk. I wandered around the courtyard, walking and thinking. It has to be a baby, but whose baby? I wondered if Juliana and James were together again. I spun around, searching for James, and walked to the barracks. One of the guards standing outside bowed to me.

"Your Majesty, is everything all right?"

"Yes and no, is James in there?"

"No, My Lady, he is out in the orchards."

I turned and looked at the great gates. "Will you get my horse saddled for me please?"

"Yes, My Lady," he said, and then he was gone. A few moments later, he appeared with Raiden.

"Thank you," I said as I climbed on him. "I need to see James," I said to Raiden. He trotted off toward the orchards.

There were many people out today, and many men in trees. I could not help but smile. I asked a guard, "Excuse me. Have you seen James?"

"Oh, Your Majesty, yes, he is that way." He pointed to the farther side of the orchard.

I rode Raiden down that way, looking in the trees for him. It was not until I reached the end of the grove that I found him. "James, can I have a moment, please?"

"Of course, Sabine, just let me get down." He climbed down the tree like he had been doing it his whole life. I climbed off of Raiden and waited for him. "What can I do for you?"

"Well, I have a rather odd query for you. How is it going with you and Juliana?"

He smiled. "We are making progress. She has let me play with Isabel, and we are talking through everything that happened. Why? What is this about?"

"So you have not gotten back together then?"

"No, not in the manner in which I would like. Sabine, is everything all right?"

"I am not sure. Thank you, James." I got back on Raiden. Leaning in, I said, "Will you take me to Christopher?" He trotted out of the grove, heading toward Wellington, and took off. I loved riding through the forest; it was a blur of green. We came upon Christopher inside of Wellington.

"Oh, Sabine, how nice to see you."

"Hello, Christopher, how are things going?"

"Well, as you can see, I have made great progress. I am more than halfway done. I would think I should be done just about harvest time."

I smiled. "That is wonderful. I have been wondering how things are going between you and Julia."

"Oh, they are wonderful. When I finish this, we will be able to spend even more time together."

"So, it is getting serious?"

"Yes, it is. She is a wonderful girl."

"Well, that is great to hear. I am also very excited about seeing the map you are drawing. I will not keep you."

"As I have said before, you have a very large Kingdom."

"Yes, so it would seem," I said, a bit distracted. "Thank you again, Christopher." He nodded, and I rode off with Raiden. We got back to the castle, and I went in search of Camille. I found her in the kitchens with Francis.

"Camille, can I talk to you in my study, please?"

"Of course, Sabine, I will be right there."

"Thank you," I said, picking up an apple.

I sat in the chairs by the window, waiting for her. She came in and sat with me. "Are you all right? You look a bit pale."

"Oh, I am fine. I was wondering something, actually. Is there any way you could be with child?"

Her laughter threw me. "Sabine, I have not been unclean for many years now, so it would be impossible for me to be with child. What is this about?"

"Oh, nothing, I am just trying to figure something out."

"You can tell me, and I might be able to help you."

"Thank you, but I will be fine. It is not a huge deal, just some things rolling around in my mind. Would you do something for me? If you see Blake, could you tell him that I went for ride and I will be back later?"

"Of course, are you sure you are all right?"

I nodded and smiled at her, and then I left. Riding Raiden always made me feel better. I wished I had some help with the prophecy. I had no idea what I was doing.

Putting my hands out as he ran, I thought it always felt like I was flying like the birds in the sky. He slowed as we came to the river. I climbed down and walked the river's edge, and Raiden followed me. Soon, I came to a hill, so I climbed it. Standing at the top gave me a view I had no idea was here. Beyond the hill was a slight hilly valley with rolling green hills. It was beautiful. I wondered if this was part of Whispering Wind, also.

Sitting down, I drew my knees up to my chest. A breeze blew across the hills, brushing across my skin. I closed my eyes and just got lost in the peacefulness of the moment. The light of the day warmed my face as the breeze blew through my hair. I felt alive and free sitting here. I felt at peace. After all the years of fighting and death, a moment like this was rare, to feel no burdens, to feel happy. I smiled and put my hands in the air to feel the breeze. I do not know how long I sat on that hill, but it was turning into the dark of the night when I got up and headed back.

We rode into the courtyard just in time to see the men coming back from the orchards with all the fruits of their labor. Blake tilted his head and looked at me. I just smiled at him.

I got off of Raiden and went in the door to the kitchen, where I sat at the table and just did nothing. A calm had come over me while I sat there. Nothing seemed to matter to me.

Blake had come in, yet I had not even noticed him. He stood in the doorway, leaning up against the door, watching me.

I took a deep breath and got up, heading to my study. He followed me, not saying a word. I sat in the chair by the window and watched the dark of the night come. The sky was bright with the far away lights. It was beautiful.

Blake leaned against the door, watching me, but I did not feel him. I did not see him.

When the light of the day was completely gone, I stood to leave. When I turned, I saw him there, and I smiled. "Hello, my love," I said.

He tilted his head, smiling at me. "Is everything all right?"

I nodded, walking up to him. "Please hold me."

"There will never come a day that I will not." He wrapped his arms around me and pulled me into his chest. "Are you hungry?"

"I am not sure what I am. Perhaps, yes."

He chuckled. "Come, wife. I shall hunt you food."

I giggled, and we walked to the kitchen arm in arm. Everyone had already eaten, but there were two plates on the warmer shelf above the fire. Blake got them, and we sat down at the table, and had our evening meal together alone. I seemed to be very hungry, because I ate everything on my plate and then started picking at Blake's. He smiled at me and slid his plate over to me. I laughed and ate what was left.

We did not talk while we walked to our room. We did not talk while we undressed. We did not talk while we lay in each other's arms in the afterglow of our love. We did not talk when he kissed my head as I fell asleep lying on his chest. He held me there all night long. I woke feeling warm and comfortable lying on him this way. His arms were in the same position they were when I fell asleep, listening to his heart beating.

He sensed I was awake, and I felt his embrace tighten against me. I picked my head up and smiled at him. "Thank you," I whispered as I kissed him.

"Anytime, my love," he whispered back.

I laid my head down and let him hold me. The light of the day had just arrived, so the house was starting to come alive. The noises from the courtyard lingered up through the windows. I thought it funny how I never noticed those things before. I looked across the room, and I could see the little particles of dust floating in the air. Everything seemed so alive and bright. I reached for one, and my hand made a wave in the air, sending it spiraling around. It was beautiful to watch it dance on the air.

Blake's hands trailing up and down my back felt different somehow. It felt like tiny feathers touching me, soothing and gentle. I could have laid here all day, watching the dust fly around the room, but I knew we could not. As I pushed myself up to look at my husband lying beneath me, his brilliant green eyes sparkled, filled with so much love as he looked back at me.

"I love you," I whispered and then covered his mouth with mine. Even kissing him felt new. Our dance felt like it was something extraordinary. He rolled me over onto my back, holding my head in his hands while he deepened our kiss. I was more than willing to accommodate him. It felt incredible. Even when he moaned, it felt different against my skin, sending waves of pleasure through me. This moment was like none other we shared. When our kiss ended, I felt like I had the first time he kissed me, like nothing else mattered. I did not want this moment to end.

He laid on his side, pulling me into his arms, holding me. Nothing was said. Nothing needed to be said between us. We both knew how we felt. We both knew it was never going to be the same. I think, this was the day that our lives made sense. After all that we had been through, all that we had seen and done together, through countless years, this was the day it all made sense. I know he felt it, too.

We got up, not saying a word to one another, and got dressed, sharing a smile here and a smile there. I decided to put on my boy clothes today. On our way out the door, he stopped, drew me in his arms, and kissed me. Then he placed my crown on my head, smiled, and we walked to the kitchen.

Everyone was there, laughing and talking. I wondered if we were ever going back in the dining hall.

I watched Francis cooking and carrying on with everyone. We had become her family, and she had become ours. I watched Juliana with Isabel, and noticed Julia had a secret smile on her face; she was falling in love with Christopher, if she had not already. I looked at Westin, who was looking at me with his not Westin eyes. He half smiled, and I smiled brightly. He did not look away, just nodded to me, so I nodded back. Stephan had met a young girl in the village, and he was rambling on about her. Camille was giving him pointers on how to be the perfect gentleman. I looked at Blake, who was doing the same thing I was doing, just eating and enjoying being with everyone. Rebecca was not at the table. I secretly hoped she was with

Charles, but I was not going to worry about it. *What will be will be.*

Everyone started to get up and leave to start their days. Blake and I were the only ones left. He turned in his seat to look at me. Bringing his hand up to touch my face, he leaned in and kissed me, whispering in my mouth, "I love you."

I smiled as he got up and walked to the door. He turned to look at me before he left, and I could see it in his eyes that no words needed to be spoken. I sat there looking at all the plates with all the food left on them, and I suddenly became very hungry. I took each plate and dumped the food onto mine. Francis did not say a word as I sat and ate it all. With my belly finally full, I wandered out the door and into the back courtyard.

I saw Blake walking from the stables with his horse. He must have sensed me looking at him, because when his eyes met mine, my heart exploded with love. He smiled and nodded to me, and I watched him ride off through the great gates.

I went to my study to sit and think. Time disappeared, and I could not remember thinking of anything at all, when I realized that the dark of the night was upon us. I had not eaten since the morning meal, and I was hungry. I stood and turned, finding Blake leaning on the door. He was not smiling. In a gentle soft, whispery voice, he said, "I am worried about you, my love. You seem to be somewhere else. Do you want to talk about it?"

"Not just yet. I am still working it out, but I am fine, better than fine." His smile came back and he nodded. "I think I would like to eat in our room."

"You go up, and I will get us some food."

"Are you sure? I can help," I offered.

"Well, if you want, then let us go and raid the kitchen." We laughed.

The light of the day came as we lay awake in one another's arms. "I was able to read the seventh tome."

"I thought you might have," he said as he trailed his fingers down my arm.

"It said that the Unknown Heir was present within."

"What do you think that means?"

I giggled. "I do not know, but the other day, while I was out riding, something happened to me."

I felt his body tense. "Oh?" he asked curiously.

"I was down by the little river and walked up the little hill there. The other side is a valley of rolling hills. I sat there for most of the day, and a feeling of incredible peace filled me. I have not been the same since. Everything is so new to me our touch, the sky, everything. I have never felt this calm before. I want nothing more than to be with you. It is hard to explain how I feel."

"I know the feeling, my love. I feel it as well. Do you think this is it, the beginning of our happiness?"

"I believe it is, my love."

Chapter Fourteen

The days passed, the harvest came, and the cold season had moved in. Christopher had finished and spent most of his time in the dining hall, drawing his map. I checked on him from time to time, but he did not want me to see it until he had completed it.

A third of the way through the cold season, I got a visit from Clare. I was in my study, looking at the drawings Father had made, when she knocked on my door. "Come in," I said.

She walked in with a huge smile on her face. "Hello, Sabine," she greeted me. I noticed a cloth draped over her arm.

"Hello, Clare. What have you got there?"

She smiled at me. "I have your lace gown. It is finished."

My eyes got huge. "Really?" I whispered.

She nodded with a smile. I ran over and bolted the door then pulled the drapes. She unwrapped it from the cloth. I had never seen anything so beautiful before.

"Oh, Clare," I whispered as I reached to touch it. "This is exquisite. How do you do this?"

"It is a gift, I think. Would you like to try it on?"

I nodded, so she helped me untie my gown, and then I stepped into it and slid it up my body. It hugged me like my skin did.

She crinkled her eyebrows as she stepped back to look at me.

"What?" I asked, confused.

"Well, I know exactly how big you are, and I thought I had it perfect, but it seems to be a bit tight around your chest. Turn sideways," she said. Then I heard her take in a deep breath and whisper, "Oh."

I looked at her and noticed she was smiling. "What is it?" I looked down at my body.

She walked over and put her hand on my stomach, and with a huge smile on her face, whispered, "Sabine."

I looked at her, confused. *Why is she touching my stomach?* With a shaky hand, I put mine on top of hers, but I did not feel anything. I took the sleeping gown off. "Can you fix it?" I asked as she tied up my gown.

She was wrapping it up in the cloth she brought it in. "Sabine, I do not need to fix it right now."

"Why not? I think it might be a bit tight."

"Yes, it is." She turned to face me. "How are your other gowns fitting?"

"Just fine. Well, the yellow gown is getting tight across my chest. Why?"

"Sabine, I believe that I am going to have to make you some new gowns."

"You have made plenty of gowns for me, Clare. I could, however, use a new cape."

"Yes, I can do that, as well, but soon, the gowns you have now will no longer fit."

I thought about that; I was not as busy as I had been, so I thought I must be getting fat. "I might be getting a bit bigger now that all the excitement has calmed down. I have been eating better. In fact, I am always hungry."

She smiled. "Well, that is to be expected."

I tilted my head. "What are you talking about, Clare?"

She walked up to me and put her hand on my stomach again. "Sabine, I believe I know why your gowns do not fit well." I looked down at her hand, then at her, and she nodded.

My heart started pounding, my ears were ringing, and the room went black. Clare was screaming for help. One of the kitchen girls came in and screamed.

"Go get Blake," Clare yelled at her.

Moments later, Blake came running into the room. "What happened?"

"One minute, she was standing there, and the next, she was lying on the floor."

"Thank you, Clare." He picked me up and took me to our room. He did not leave me until I woke.

"What happened?" I asked.

He chuckled. "I do not know. Clare said, you were standing there one moment, and the next, you were lying on the floor."

"Uhh," I whispered. I looked at Blake and then at my stomach. "No, no, no, this cannot be truth. No, no, no."

"You are scaring me. What is wrong?"

I got out of bed and walked to the other side of the room. I could not stop the tears. *How can this be? I did not have a union with him. He will not understand. I do not understand.* "How can this be?" I whispered through tears. I felt him move from the bed. "No, do not," I said. He did not stop. "Please, Blake, no," I said through my sobs. He stopped.

"My love, what is happening?"

I did not say a word, just held my stomach and cried. Putting my head back, I screamed, "Nooooo!" I felt myself sink to the floor. I could not control the tears, letting them fall as I screamed again, "Nooooo!" Blake did not move.

"Sabine," I heard him say. "Please, my love, let me hold you."

I shook my head, crying. I sat there on my knees, holding my stomach, crying, and wanting this not to be truth. I leaned down and put my head on the floor. My hands in fists, I slammed them to the floor and screamed again. "Nooooo!"

Westin had come running in the room. I heard him tell Blake to leave. "She is my wife, Westin."

"I know, brother, but she needs me right now."

Blake left, but he was not happy about it. Westin came up behind me and pulled me into his arms. I cried, screaming into his chest. "Nooooo!"

"Yes, my love."

"It is not possible," I managed to get out between sobs.

He rocked me, holding me, calming me.

My sobs subsided, and I pulled away from him. As he wiped my tears, I saw the truth in his eyes. "How?"

He smiled. "You know how, my love."

"But we never," I said.

"You did not need to. Think about it, Sabine. You know what a union is. You know what happens between you two. It is truth."

I shook my head. "It is not possible. He will not believe. I do not believe." I whispered franticly.

"He will believe. Find it in your heart, Sabine. You know it is truth."

I sat there looking at him, and I knew he was speaking the truth. I looked past him to see Blake standing there.

"What is truth?" he whispered.

I did not take my eyes off of his as my hands moved to my stomach. His eyes changed from fear to wonder, then to fear as he realized what it meant. He dropped to his knees. "How is this possible?" he said so softly I barely heard him.

Westin stood and walked over to Blake. He leaned down, whispered in his ear, and then left. Blake did not take his eyes off of me. They changed again to wonder. He looked at my hands, and I saw a tear fall from his eye and run down his cheek. His eyes moved up my body, locking on my own. I saw love, devotion, and wonder as another tear fell down his cheek. Neither of us moved. We were across the room from each other, but I could hear his heart slow as he took it all in.

He slowly stood and walked over to me, picked me up, and carried me to the bed. I could not tear my eyes from his. He climbed in bed with me and wrapped his arms around me, holding me tight. Not a word was said. I fell asleep while he held me. When I woke, he was there sitting on the bed, looking at me.

"Are you all right?" he whispered.

I nodded, not sure if this was the calm before he exploded in anger. He moved his hand to place it on my stomach, looking at me for permission. I nodded, and he gently placed his hand on what was obviously a slight bump. His hand was huge, covering my stomach from hip to hip. I saw a tear form in his eye and fall to his cheek before he whispered, "The Unknown Heir."

I tilted my head. "What did you say?"

"The Unknown Heir."

I looked at his hand. "I am sorry. I did not make a union with another man, Blake. You must believe me."

"Shhh that is not what I am thinking. I know you would never do that. This child is ours, Sabine. I know this."

I moved his hand and sat up. "Well then, perhaps you can explain it to me, because I am pretty sure that I am about to lose my mind."

He smiled and sat back on the bed, getting comfortable. "Well, from what I understand, having been married before and having to have a union with my wife then to produce children, I know a bit more than you do about how things work between a man and woman."

I nodded and raised my eyebrows. "You do know that you are going to finish that statement, and you are going to tell me how this is possible."

He smiled and took my hand in his. "When I had my union with her, the same thing happened while I was within her as happens when we do what we do. We may not be joined in a union, but the seed is the same. Somehow, it has happened. I believe, and you should as well." He sat up and put his hand on my stomach. "Our child is in here, Sabine, the first of many."

"But I am still pure. How can this be possible?

"I do not know, but it is truth."

"Why is it truth, Blake, because Westin said it was truth? What did he say to you when he whispered in your ear?" I snapped.

He smiled at me. "He simply told me to go love my wife."

"I need to get out of here," I said as I got up.

"Sabine, we should talk about this."

I opened the door. "I know, but I cannot. I need to think. I will be back. I do not know when, but I will be back."

I walked out of the room and half ran down the hall. I searched for him in my mind.

'Please come and take me away.'

Blake was yelling my name as I ran down the stairs, but I did not stop. I opened the doors, and Raiden was there waiting on me, so I jumped on him, which was not an easy thing to do while wearing a gown. "Go," I said, and we were gone.

He took me back to the little hill by the little river. I got off him and walked to the top. It was not my intention to cry, but the tears came anyway. *How is any of this possible?* I put my hand on my stomach. *I have a baby in here. A baby!* I was tired and did not want to think about it anymore.

I just sat there and watched as the light of the day lowered itself in the sky, the colors were so beautiful. The dark of the night was upon me, and I knew I should get back, but it would mean I had to face him. *How can I face him?*

I stood and looked out over the valley of hills, wishing for a simpler life. I wished that my parents were here to help me through this. I did not hear Spirit when he stopped, and I did not feel Rebecca walk up behind me.

She wrapped her arms around my shoulders and said, "There are a lot of people who are worried about you."

I laid my head back on her shoulder. "I know. Did Blake tell you to come?"

"He wanted to come, but he asked me instead. Apparently, he believes you do not want to see him."

I felt the tears come. "I cannot."

"Do you want to tell me what is happening with you? I have been busy, and I am afraid I have not been around."

"There is so much you do not know, so much I have kept from you, from everyone."

293

"Well, I am here now."

I turned to face her. "I am going to have a baby."

Her face lit up, and she grabbed me. "Oh, Sabine, that is so wonderful."

"There is more."

She let me go. "Come on. Sit and we can talk."

"You know how Collingwood said that if I was not pure, my magic would not work?"

"Yes, but it does."

"That is because I am still pure. Blake and I have not had a union." She sat there staring at me. "Yes, and I am having a baby."

"You have not had a union with your husband? Sabine, you have been married for two seasons. How are you having a baby?"

"We do other things, and apparently, you can still have a baby when you do other things." She just sat there looking at me. "I have been reading the tomes. I have only one left. The seventh one would not allow me to read it, apparently, until I was with child. I have not tried the eighth one yet. But they speak of an Unknown Heir. I could not figure it out, but I have now."

"You can read the tomes? What do you mean it would not let you read it?"

"Well, the pages are blank. You saw them. When I read the others, one word would glow, and when I read it, that one disappeared and the next one glowed. Remember when I asked you if you could read it?" She nodded. "Well, that was the day it happened."

"So, Blake sent me because he is afraid?"

"Oh, no, he thinks this is the greatest thing ever. I am not as accepting of it."

"Why not? You are having a baby. That is a wonderful thing."

"I cannot explain how I feel. I do not know why he sent you, but I am glad that he did. I have been wanting to talk to you, but I have just been so involved with all of this."

"I know, and I have been busy as well."

"With Charles?"

"Yes, with Charles… He is working his way back into my life, and I am not sure that I want him to."

"He loves you deeply, Rebecca."

"I know he does, but he gave himself to that girl right in front of me, and I am not sure I can forgive that. He said he does not remember much of what he did, because he was full of drink, but that does not take away what I see in my mind."

"It will disappear, my love. You two have been through a great deal together. Your love is something that has not faded. It has just been blocked by circumstance. Just keep talking it out. You owe that to yourself."

"I know, and I have been. We will see where it goes. Are you going to be all right?"

"I am not sure, but please do not say anything about us not having a union. No one knows."

"I will never tell your secrets, but we should get back. He is worried about you."

"I know. I cannot right now, though. Please tell him I am sorry. I just need to be alone for a while."

"Are you coming back tonight?" she asked hesitantly.

"No, I cannot. I am going to go to the secret valley. I will be safe there. Tell him I will be back in a day or two. I just need to be alone with all of this." The tears started. "I just do not know what to do."

"Sabine, do you want me to go with you?"

"No, I need to be alone with this. Just tell him not to worry and that I love him." I got up and got on Raiden. "Take me to the valley."

It was the light of the day when we arrived. I was tired, cold, and hungry. As I walked under the canopy of the tree, I was instantly warm. I ate a lot of the fruit and then fell asleep.

*****

Rebecca returned to Whispering Wind to find Blake in tears in our room. She went in and held him. "She did not come home, did she?" he asked.

"No, I am so sorry, Blake. She went to the secret valley. She told me to tell you that she loves you and not to worry, but she needs to be alone with all of this. I had no idea what was happening between the two of you. She told me everything. She is terrified, Blake. I have never seen her like this."

"She does not want our child, Rebecca." He turned his face into her shoulder.

"She did not say that. She said she cannot believe it. I think she believes it is not yours, and that is what is hurting her."

He pulled away from her. "I need to go to the valley."

"Blake, she will come home, just give her some time. If she is not back in a few days, I will ask Spirit to take you there."

"I will give her three days, and then I am going. Thank you, Rebecca. I would like to be alone."

Rebecca hugged him again and then left. Blake cried himself to sleep. He did not leave our room again.

Chapter Fifteen

When I woke, I had no idea how long I had slept. It could have been days, but nothing had changed. I was having a baby, the Unknown Heir, even though I had never had a union with my husband. He was so kind about not having one, and so very understanding, and now this. Now, I had a child in me that could not be his. That day on the hill, something happened to me, something different. *Was it magical? Had this baby somehow been put inside of me?* I closed my eyes, wanting it to be over, all of it. I could just stay here for the rest of my life with this child. I could go to the cave, where time would disappear and everyone would be gone.

I pulled my knees up to my chest and rested my chin on them. Looking around the valley, I thought it could be a nice place to raise a child. Westin and Camille had done so. I got up and picked some fruit, but I needed to have some water. I started to walk down to the lake, but when I got to the edge of the canopy, I could not leave it. There was something stopping me, so I looked for Raiden, but he was out on the plain.

"Sabine..." I heard my name. Turning slowly, I saw my mother. I shook my head and closed my eyes. "Darling, open your eyes and see me."

"No, you are not real."

"Sabine, my love, there is so much I did not get to tell you as you grew up, so much you do not know about life."

"Why did you have to leave me? I am so scared."

"I know, my love. That is why I am here. There is just one thing left to do, and then your happiness is yours."

I snapped at her, "How can my happiness be mine? I am having a baby that is not my husband's. I followed all the rules, Mother. I have not had a union with him. He has been respectful of that, and now I told him I am having a baby that could not possibly be his. So tell me, how can my happiness be mine?"

"Oh, my love, it is his child. It is yours and his together."

"That is not truth. It is impossible. Camille told me what happens, and I have not done what she says. I still have my magic. It is impossible."

"No, my love, it is not impossible. Please, trust in what is happening. I promised you that you would have your happiness. A baby, Sabine, a baby with the man you love that is your happiness. It is almost over. The Legend is nearly complete. You must believe and trust."

"You stand here from beyond this life, trying to convince me that I am this chosen one, that I am the only way to save this land. Why, Mother? Why me? I just want to be the girl on the hilltop, dreaming of what life could be, not this woman standing before you who has murdered tens of thousands of men. I have been places, seen things, and done things that NO ONE should ever have to do. Now, you stand here and try to tell me untruths about a child that was not conceived in the traditional manner, and want me to believe that it is my husband's. The man I love is expected to accept this when I cannot. I find this all a farce, as Westin would say."

"Sabine, I love you. I have loved you your whole life. I did not want this for you, but I had to accept it. I fought it, believe me, I fought. I wanted a different life for you, but that day we left you, I knew there was nothing I could do but pray Westin got to you. I want nothing more than to hold you in my arms again. I wish there was some way I could show you that the child you carry is yours and Blake's. Go home, my love. Go home to him. He is in so much pain."

"Yes, because he knows deep down that this is not his child."

"You are wrong. It is because he knows it is. You are everything he has ever wanted in his life. He is your true love, just as your father is mine, just as Ardes is to Jenny, just like Rebecca is to Charles, and James to Juliana. This is truth, my love. Go home to your husband. He needs you. Finish this and have your happiness, the happiness I have wanted for you since the day you came into this world."

I stood there looking at her, the tears streaming down my cheeks. "I cannot live a lie with him. I love him too much to put this burden on him."

"Search your heart, child. You know it is truth. I love you." Then she was gone.

I stood there crying alone in the middle of nowhere, wanting nothing more than my husband. Turning, I found Raiden behind me. I climbed on him, and he flew. I did not have to tell him a thing; he knew. As I laid on his neck, I cried all the way home. I climbed off him and ran into the castle, made my way up the stairs, and slammed open the door to our room.

Blake was lying on the bed. He turned to see who had entered. When he saw me, he was off the bed and pulling me into his arms. We held one another while we cried. He carried me to our bed, where we laid in one another's arms and let our tears wash away our fears, crying ourselves to sleep.

He did not let me go when our room filled with the soft amber glow. My mother and father were standing beside our bed. I could feel the warmth radiating through the blankets as she touched me, so I opened my eyes to see her smile before she left. I started to cry again, which woke Blake, so he held me tighter. He dried my tears with his thumbs, and then he kissed me.

"I am so sorry I ran," I said through my sobs.

He pulled me close to him. "I love you, Sabine. Please, never forget that."

"I love you so much it hurts."

He kissed me and made all of my fears disappear. He touched me with such tenderness that it made my heart ache. He paused at my stomach and kissed it, laying his head on my little bump. I felt the tears when he lifted his head. "I have never known such love." As he put his hand there and gently pressed down, he said softly, "Our child lives in you." I put my hand on his.

"It is almost over. The happiness we were promised will be ours soon."

"I could not imagine feeling greater than I do in this moment."

We slept for what seemed like days. When I woke, he was there to hold me, to make me forget my name, time and time again. Once we had our fill of one another, we bathed and ate, and then loved one another all over again. I was happier than I could have ever imagined being. His kindness, his gentle hands, and his huge heart took care of me.

We finally came to terms with the truth that this child was ours. It had been created from our love. I believed it now; I think I believed it then.

We emerged from our room days later to announce our news. There were tears of joy, slaps on the back for Blake, and hugs for me. Francis even cried because she was so happy.

There was nothing left to do except find the last two Markers, but the cold months would not allow me to search for them. So I waited for the tome to allow me to read it. I waited for Christopher to finish the map. All the time I waited, my stomach got bigger and bigger. Every morning and every night, Blake would put his hand on my stomach then lay his head on it and kiss it. This baby was already loved so much.

My body was changing greatly. Blake enjoyed it a little more than I think he should have, but he told me every day how beautiful I was, even if I did not feel it.

The cold months were becoming less and less. I had just come out of the secret room checking to see if the tome was ready to be read, when Christopher knocked on the door.

"I am finished," he said.

"Really?"

He smiled and I followed him into the dining hall. The map was huge. It hung over all the sides of the table. "Wow," was all I could say. "Christopher, you did a spectacular job."

"It is the best map I have ever done, the biggest as well." He chuckled. "I think it is because this has become my home." He turned and took my hand in his, kissing the back of it. "Thank you, My Lady, for finding me and bringing me here."

I smiled at him. "Thank you for coming. Do you think it will fit on the wall of my study? We can hang it over the bookcases.

I want to see the whole thing. I will go get Blake and his brothers." I turned to walk out.

"Did I hear my name?" Blake said.

"Christopher finished the map. Do you think we could hang it in my study?"

He smiled and wrapped his arms around me. "Whatever you want my love."

It took all of them to secure it on the wall, but once it was up, it was beautiful. He had marked everything. Wellington and even parts of Blackmore were really Whispering Wind. I found the river, following it to the hilltop and beyond. The little valley of rolling hills was Whispering Wind. This kingdom was indeed huge. "Christopher, could you do one more thing for me?" I asked him after everyone left.

"Of course." He smiled.

I went to my desk, opened the drawer, and took out the drawings. "I have places marked here on these drawings. I was wondering if you could find these places and mark them on that map."

I sat in the chair by the window with Blake and watched him put a mark on each of the ten spots. It took some time for him to locate each one, but once he was finished, I saw the pattern emerge. It helped me figure out where the last two Markers might be. I looked at Blake, who was smiling and nodding at me.

"One last thing, I need to know exactly where the center of this Kingdom is. I need for you to mark it on the map and then tell me how far it is. Then, perhaps, could you take me there?"

He was on that ladder for a long time before he turned and smiled at me. "Here is the center," he said, marking it. "It is about a day's ride from here on a regular horse."

"Now, the marks that you put up there for me, how far from the center is each mark?"

"Well, the Kingdom, going in this direction," he put his arms out to his sides, "is nearly five days' ride. And from this direction," he put his arms up and down. "It is nearly six days' ride."

I looked at Blake. "This Kingdom ends just before the valley."

"I see that. I wonder if Wellington and Blackmore knew that their Kingdoms were in fact yours."

I turned to Christopher. "Thank you so much. I will have Charles pay you what is due. I also had them build you a cottage. I thought you might be staying."

"My Lady, that is more than generous. The cottage will be payment enough."

I smiled. "No, it really is not."

He thanked me again and then left. I got up and stood in the middle of the room, looking at the map. "How are we going to do this? The distance from the Markers to the center of the Kingdom is great. It will take you days to get back once I release them. I must have read it wrong. I will have to go back and read it again."

He was behind me. "The season of the blossoms is nearly upon us. This all takes place soon. You will be ripe with this baby, Sabine."

"Do not worry, my love. I had to learn to trust, and so must you." We stood looking at the enormity of this Kingdom. I could not help but wonder if Father knew how big it was. I could see the Markers now; they seem to go in a circle around the land. There was a gap near Wellington, and one near Blackmore, that I figured must be where the last two Markers were. "This must be where the other two Markers are. Will you go with me to find them?"

He chuckled as he put his hands on my stomach. "Do you believe I would not go with you?"

I turned in his arms. "I believe you would worry if you did not. This child is safe inside of me. Nothing is going to happen to it."

"Oh, I believe that, but I still worry." He kissed me.

"I would like to go soon. But first, I need to read the tome again, to make sure I have it right."

"I think it would be best to wait for the season of the blossoms to begin."

I smiled at him. He was so caring. "I love you," was all I could say to him as I kissed him. His hands held my face while he kissed me back.

"You and this child are my world, Sabine. I will not allow anything to harm you."

Our kiss deepened. Soon, we were lying on the floor, holding one another while our bodies calmed. Being with him was more intense now that I was with child. He helped me up and took great care not to tie my gown too tight. When he finished, I turned in his arms and kissed him again.

He put his forehead on mine. Smiling, he said, "This," he trailed his fingers across my very ample breasts, "is very nice." I busted out giggling.

"I am sure that it is, and just think, they will get bigger yet."

His eyes popped open. "Really?" he said with a huge smile on his face, which sent us into a fit of giggles.

There was a knock on the door. I stood in front of him, putting my hands on his thighs and pulling his unclothed body against my backside. "Come in," I said.

It was Charles. "Oh, excuse me," he said as he pulled the door closed. We laughed.

"Hold on, Charles. Give us a moment." I turned to Blake. "I have to protect you. I cannot have anyone seeing my husband."

His laughter filled the room and my heart. He dressed. "You can come in now, brother."

Charles was a bit flush in the face. "I did not mean to interrupt you."

"You did not interrupt us, brother. We were just having a moment."

"Sabine, can I talk to you?"

I looked at Blake. "Of course you can."

"Alone," he said looking at Blake.

Blake smiled and kissed me, saying, "I got it." I watched him leave as I shook my head, and then turned my attention to Charles as he closed the door.

"What is going on?"

"Well, this is on a personal matter, and I thought that, because you managed to forgive Blake, you might be able to help me."

"Rebecca?"

"Yes," he said as he lowered his head.

"Can I speak freely, Charles?"

"Of course, Sabine. Always."

I smiled. "You may not like what I say to you, but what I am going to say is truth, even though you may not want to hear it."

"I am sure you are right, but I need to hear it."

"Charles, you destroyed her. You shared a part of you that she believed belonged to her, and you did it in the vilest manner possible. Then you tortured her for your mistake. The fact that she is speaking to you at all is a huge step for her."

"I have no reasoning behind my actions, and all that I have done to not only Rebecca but you. I know I disgraced you and dishonored her, and I have to live with that for the rest of my days. I never stopped loving her. I will never stop loving her.

But because you were able to forgive Blake, I guess I am hoping that maybe there is a chance for her to forgive me."

"Charles, Blake did not have a union with another woman, and he certainly did not do it while I stood there watching. You did that to her on purpose. You knew she was there. You looked at her as that girl climbed on you and took you within her. You ripped Rebeca's heart out, and then after what Thomas did to her... She is a shell inside. She feels she has nothing to give to anyone. The things he did to her were things I could not comprehend. She is healing still, but the fact that she is letting you in bit by bit says a great deal. I know Rebecca loves you, Charles. She just needs time to learn how to forgive you. You need to not push her. Let her come back in her own time."

"I want to hold her and help her."

"I know, and she could probably use being held, but she will not allow you to get that close to her again, at least not yet. Do you even realize what damage you did to her?"

"When you brought her home after Thomas did those things to her, I knew more deeply than I cared to how much I hurt her because of the rage I felt. She was so broken to begin with." He stopped and put his head down. I watched him as his hand came up and wiped the tears from his eyes. "What I did was so unforgiveable. I love her so much, and I have never stopped. How did you get past the betrayal?"

"To be honest, Charles, I am not sure that I have. I know Blake loves me, that is one thing I do not doubt, but he played a part in putting my family in danger, just as you all did. You did it with malice. I think that is what pushed me over the edge. To me, it seemed as if the only thing you cared about were yourselves. I could not stop the pain I was feeling, and I knew it was never going to end. No matter what I said or did, it would continue, so I ended it. Rebecca is stronger than I am.

306

She may not be in some ways, but with all of this, she is. Give her time. Although I am not sure time will heal her wounds, it may give her the ability to look past them to see you as the man she loves, and she does love you deeply."

"I know she does. I can see it in her eyes. There are times when we are together that she will laugh, and then it is like she sees what I have done and she withdraws from me."

"Yes, I do the same with Blake. When I found out I was having this baby, I ran. Sometimes, Charles, we just need time to sort it all out. Neither one of us had mothers when we came of age. We have no one to talk to but each other, and we really do not know a great deal about how to handle our emotions."

"Has she ever told you about what Thomas did to her?"

"I never asked her. I am sure it is something she relives every day, but she is strong, and I am sure, one day, it will just be something that happened to her. I know this is not the answer you might have hoped for by talking to me, but, Charles, just give her time. I know she loves you. Just give her time to find her way back."

"Thank you, Sabine. I have no choice in waiting. I guess, I just wanted to make sure I felt from her what I do, and you have answered that." He stood and hugged me. "How is my niece or nephew doing?"

I giggled. "Growing, but we are good."

He nodded and left. I heard him talking in the hall, and then Blake came in. "Well, wife, I have things to do, but I wanted to do this before I left you for the day." He pulled me in his arms and kissed me. "I love you more than life itself."

"I love you more than you will ever know," I responded and kissed him.

When he left, I went in and got the tome to re-read it. I needed to make sure that I knew what to do. If the center of this

307

Kingdom was two to three days' ride, we needed to make sure we had enough time. I sat the tome on my desk and looked at the map. "Soon, it will be over," I said and opened the tome.

The Markers are twelve in number

Each shall be brought forth

One by each who bear the Mark of the Guardian

One by each element

Placed in a circle in the center of the land

Time will stand still just as when time began

The current will light the dark of the night for a fortnight

No sound shall pass through this enchanted time

On the last night of light

As the new day begins

The Heir, along with the Unknown Heir, shall bring the Coming to an end

Light the night with the knowledge of the forged

Bring forth the peace known only to this land

Where time and life once began

It does not say that they will bring them from their places, so I must do that when I bring them from the ground. This is good to know. I think I have it now. I took the tome back to the secret room, and just for fun, I opened the last tome. Nothing yet. I went back and sat at my desk, looking at the map. The chair was not comfortable, so I moved to one of the chairs by the window so I could see the map better and curled up there. It was not long before I was sleeping. I felt him lift me and carry me to our bed, opening my eyes as he laid me down.

"I am getting heavier," I said with a smile, "and I am hungry," was all I said before I fell asleep.

He went to the kitchens and brought up a tray of food. Kissing me on the forehead, he said, "My love, come on. Wake up. I have some food for you."

I stretched, but when I did, I felt something wrong in my stomach and froze.

"What is it?"

"Something happened." I put my hand on my stomach.

Instinctively, his hand was there, and it happened again. "Did you feel that?" I whispered.

"Yes, what is that?"

"I think it is the baby," I said.

"Really? I had no idea it could do that."

I giggled and it moved again.

"She is like her mother, very feisty," Blake said in amazement.

"How do you know it is a girl? Perhaps it is a boy, and he is just like his father?"

He laughed. "Well, if size is any indication, I would have to say you are right."

I slapped him. "Are you saying I am fat?"

"No, my love, you are even more beautiful, and there is so much more of you to love." I saw his eyes move to my breasts.

310

Chapter Sixteen

The cold months had passed, and it was the beginning of the season of blossoms. Blake and I went and found the last two Markers. All twelve had been located, and Christopher had marked them on the map for me. I was in my study when I heard him in my mind.

'Trouble is coming from the north.'

'Who?'

He did not answer me. I got up and tried to run up the stairs to change. When I turned to come down the stairs, Rebecca was in the great hall, laughing at me.

"You look so cute waddling around. You up for this?"

I smiled. "Oh, you had better believe it," I said as I hit the floor half-running. We made it out the door as Blake was riding up.

"I know it will not matter what I say, but I just want to go on the record by saying I do not like this."

I was climbing up on Raiden. "I know, my love, but we have no choice."

"There is always a choice, Sabine. You are putting yourself and our child at risk."

I looked at him. "Do you really believe I would put this child at risk? Or that Raiden would?"

He did not say anything. Rebecca and I took off until Raiden stopped suddenly,

'This is going to be bad,' he said.

'Is the baby safe?'

'No harm will come to you.'

I looked at Rebecca. "You ready?"

She laughed. I know that laugh, and it was never a good thing. "Oh, I am ready." We sat and waited until Charles and Blake rode up one on either side of me.

"Why are we waiting?" Blake asked.

"Well, apparently, it is going to bad. I believe Raiden wanted you here, so we wait." And wait we did.

I felt the ground vibrate just as it had that day on the hilltop. There were a great many horses coming. I looked around. "Raiden, get me to higher ground," I said. He did, but not far from everyone. I looked out over the plain, and there it was that ever so familiar cloud that looked like rain. I turned to look for Blake, who was riding up. He looked out over the plain and then at me. "It is just as it was that day my family was slaughtered."

"Sabine, should we be here?"

I turned to the sound of a horse riding up, and I smiled when I saw the all too familiar black hair flying in the wind. I nodded. "We will be fine."

Blake turned to see Juliana riding up. "I thought you might need some help," she said with a huge smile on her face.

I reached for his hand. "No matter what happens here today, our child is safe. Raiden has promised. I love you." I leaned in to kiss him.

I rode back over to Rebecca. "Well, sister, are you ready? This is about to get as real as it gets."

"I am ready, my love. No matter what happens, I love you."

"I love you," I told her, and we hugged.

We had no idea what was going to happen; I just knew it was going to be bad. I went back to the hilltop, and everyone followed me. I wanted to see them coming. The ground vibrated with a force I had not known as the cloud got closer and closer. We were noticed, and the thunder slowed. I wondered what we looked like, the ten of us sitting on a hilltop, ready to face what looked to be tens of thousands of men. *Why would someone come to Whispering Wind with such an army?*

The cloud started to settle as a group of about twenty riders separated and continued toward us. We rode down the hilltop to greet them Adian, Steven, Juliana, James, Rebecca, Blake, Charles, Joseph, Edward, and me. I could not stop myself from giggling.

Blake and Charles looked at me. I just shrugged my shoulders.

The riders we coming fast. "Here we go, two for each of us," I heard Rebecca say, and it happened again. I giggled.

As the riders stopped in front of us, Charles asked them, "What brings you to Whispering Wind?"

The lead man just sat there looking at me. I could imagine what he must be thinking, a woman with child sitting on a horse in a potential battlefield. His eyes shifted to Rebecca and then Juliana, who had no sword. She smiled at him, but he did not smile back.

"I am Kelvin, son of Kracken."

I felt Raiden tense up. I heard him in my head.

'The sorcerer who took my sister...'

I patted him on the neck. The man looked at me.

"I have been searching for years for my daughter, and my search has led me here to this Kingdom. Where is your King?"

Charles knew who he was. "Our King was murdered by your daughter and her band of barbarians."

He laughed, "Well, then I would suspect that she is ruler of this land."

"You would suspect that, yes, but she is not," Charles corrected.

"Do not play with me with your words, guardsman. Where, then, is my sister?"

I felt Raiden twitch, so I put my hand on his neck to calm him.

'Not yet, my friend,' I said to him.

"Your daughter is not here any longer," Charles told him.

"Well, all roads have led me here, so if she is not here, then where might she be?"

It just happened; I do not know why, but I giggled. The man jerked his head toward me, then rode up to me. I felt Raiden tense underneath me, so I put my hand on his neck. "Child, what do you think is so funny?" Then he saw that I was with child. "What is this?" he said. He sat there, looking at me, actually appearing confused. He turned and went back to Charles. "Do you think that bringing a child with child here will stop me?"

"She really does not like when people refer to her as a child?" Charles warned.

"I do not care what she likes. I want to know where my daughter is, and if I do not get an answer, I shall continue on after I have cut the unborn child from her dead body and have had it for a snack."

Rebecca went to open her mouth, but I put my hand up. "If I tell you where your daughter is, will you leave my Kingdom?"

"Your Kingdom?" He laughed. "Who has ever heard of a woman, let alone a child, ruling a Kingdom?"

I tilted my head and smiled at him. "Are we going to have a problem here? Why should it matter if I am a woman or a man? Your sister murdered my Father and Mother. In fact, she murdered my whole Kingdom."

He sneered, "And now all that is left are you and this little band of rabble? She was gracious, and that is not like her."

"You see, Kelvin, I do not have an army to stand before you simply because I do not need one."

He noticed my crown and smirked. "Do you think that because you wear a crown, I will not end your life? I have eaten Kings bigger than you."

"Now, now, we do not need to be going off and eating anyone," I said, leaning forward. "What exactly do we taste like? Never mind. This crown belonged to my mother, and the day my brother put it on my head and made me the Queen of this Kingdom, I became who I am today. My name, Kelvin, is Sabine of Whispering Wind, and this rabble that stands before you are my Guardians."

He did not smile, nor did he flinch. He just stared into my eyes. I could feel him trying to control me, which in turn made me giggle again. "Do not strain yourself, Kelvin. You cannot touch me."

I felt his rage jump from him, and Raiden felt it too. "We shall see about that, child."

I felt the heat blow off of Juliana, and behind Kelvin, a great wall of fire appeared. His horse jumped as he turned to look at it. "Oh, I have tricks of my own child."

"Perhaps you do, but this is not my trick." He looked at me and then at Juliana. "Yes, she is the child your daughter stole from my family. She is not just a legend. She is real."

I could see the greed on his face. "A great asset she will be to me."

"She will go nowhere with you. Frankly, I am getting tired, and you know, Kelvin, women who are with child tire easy. Leave my Kingdom."

Rebecca giggled. He snapped his head to look at her then looked at Charles and then Blake. That was when he saw the Mark on Blake's hand. I could read him, and watched as his energy went cold when he saw the Mark. His eyes fell upon mine.

"Where is my daughter?"

"Your daughter is gone. That is all you need to know. Stop looking for her. She is no more."

He drew his sword, and I did as well.

"You will die on this plain today!" he shouted.

I laughed. "Get off my land. I will not ask you again."

Rebecca drew her sword as I pointed mine at him, warning, "You really do not want to do this."

He looked at my sword. "How is it possible that you wield such a sword?"

"I am who you think I am. You will not win here today. Leave my Kingdom."

"IMPOSIBLE," he yelled. "You are but a mere child."

One of his men jumped the line and went after Rebecca. She swung her sword, and with a brilliant flash of light, his head fell to the ground. Kelvin backed his horse up.

"My daughter was to end you."

"It seems as if she missed me when she murdered the rest of my family. Now, I have asked you once, and I will not ask you again. Get off my land."

Their attack was quick. Raiden and Spirit did not have a chance to jump before they were on us. James tried to protect Juliana, but somehow, she was knocked off her horse. Her concentration broke, and the wall of fire disappeared. The thunder came again. I felt it vibrate through Raiden.

Kelvin's men started swinging. We fought as best we could after being caught off guard. Rebecca and I were the only ones who had our swords out. Kelvin's men started to fall.

Kelvin came after me. Aiden moved in front of his swinging sword, and it went right through him, nearly hitting me. I had to shift to avoid it, which had me falling off of Raiden. It was difficult to get my footing. I heard Blake yelling for me to get up. He swung his sword and killed the man he was fighting. He was off his horse and running, slicing men down as he moved toward me.

I looked up as Kelvin got off his horse. "Now, I will have your child," he sneered.

I could not get my balance to get off the ground. He swung at me, but Raiden kicked him, causing him to stumble and giving me time to get up. He swung at me again, slamming my sword to the ground. It was unreal, the power this man had. I stood there looking at him while he held my sword on the ground.

317

Charles thrust his sword through him. He jerked back, and I got a hold of my footing.

Before I could swing, he spun around and slammed his sword into Charles. I swung my sword at him, catching his, and fire blew from the impact. He had Charles' sword stuck in him, and still he just kept coming. I swung and swung, but I could not feel him weaken. I must be weaker with this baby. I felt fire behind me and heard screams, then the smell of burning flesh, but I had no time to look. Juliana was setting them on fire. I swung at him again with all that I had, and could finally feel him beginning to weaken. I swung again and again, until he went down on one knee. One of his men pulled the sword from him, which seemed to help him regain power. He hit my sword with so much force that I nearly lost grip of it. Blake came out of nowhere and jumped on him, putting his sword across Kelvin's neck. I saw a sword come through Kelvin, and then watched Blake fall to the ground when his man pulled it from him. Kelvin smiled at me and kept coming, swing after swing. I went down, hearing Rebecca scream my name as she went flying through the air to land on the ground just behind me. Kelvin raised his sword above his head to slam it in my chest. Joseph hit him in the side of the head, knocking him back.

I had enough time to slam my sword into the ground, causing a ripple and making Kelvin stumble. Pushing Joseph out of the way, I swung my hardest, taking his head off. The explosion from his power hit me hard, slamming me against Joseph, and we both went down. Pain filled my body, but I had to get up or we would all die. I saw Blake starting to get up. The pain in my body was intense, but I forced myself to get up just as Raiden came close. Joseph grabbed me and shoved me up on him.

I looked for Rebecca, finding her fighting two of them. Raiden took off toward her, and Joseph was running to her. I took the head off one, and Joseph got the other then grabbed Rebecca and threw her up onto Spirit. I turned to see the cloud coming.

Rebecca nodded and we were in the air. It took a long time to end them. When we landed, I fell off Raiden and the darkness came.

*****

When I woke, I was in his arms and he was crying. My hands went to my stomach. "The baby," I whispered. Blake pulled me to him. What was he doing? I tried to look, but he would not release me. I was feeling my stomach. There was still my bump, but I was wet. I managed to get my hand to my face. Blood. My hand was covered in blood. The last thing I remember was screaming.

Chapter Seventeen

Charles and Aiden lifted me to Blake, and Raiden took us back to the castle. Blake carried me to our room. Camille sent one of the kitchen girls to get Charlotte. She and Francis cleaned me up, looking for a wound, but there was none. I was bleeding from the place Rebecca was when Thomas hurt her.

"Blake, I am afraid that the baby is in danger," Camille told him in the hall.

He slid down the wall, crying. "Please, Camille, save her. Save our baby."

"I do not think I can, Blake. I am so sorry."

"Nooooo," he screamed. Charles sat next to him, holding his brother.

Charlotte came running down the hall and stopped when she saw Blake. She looked at Camille, who was crying as well, then pushed past them and into our room. Camille followed her, shutting the door.

They worked on me while I lay in the darkness, trying everything Charlotte could think of to stop the bleeding, to save me, to save our baby. When they exhausted all of their knowledge, they stood there looking at me and then at one another. Together, they left the room, leaving me alone. Camille shut the door. Looking at Blake, she shook her head and said softly, "I am so sorry, brother."

"Nooooo," he screamed so loud that the people in the village heard him. He drew his legs to his chest, just as I always did, and laid his head on them, rocking back and forth. He pushed Charles away. "Leave me," he said.

Everyone walked away sobbing. Blake sat there looking at the door for the longest time. He knew I was dying or dead. How was he going to go on with us both leaving him? Our baby would never know his love like I had. I will never get to feel him again. He closed his eyes, trying to stop the tears.

When he opened them, he noticed a golden glow coming from under the door. Slowly, he got up, not taking his eyes from the door. He reached for the latch and lifted it then walked into the room to see my mother, Jenna, and two other women with their hands on my stomach. He stood there in the glow and watched as they healed me, as they healed our child. It lasted for a very long time, but he felt the warmth, the love, and the energy.

When they finished, my mother turned to him. "All is well now. Love your wife, Blake."

He nodded, and then as the warmth left, as the glow faded, he walked to the bed and climbed in, drawing me into his arms and holding me, loving me. He did not leave me.

When the light of the day came again, Camille came to prepare me for burial. When she walked in, the tray she was holding fell from her hands. Blake was in the bed, holding me.

"Blake, you have to let her go," she said.

"No, she is not gone. The baby is not gone," he said.

"Blake, look at her. She is pale. Her lips are blue. She is gone."

"NO," he yelled at her. "Leave, Camille. Leave now or I will remove you."

"Blake, please do not do this."

"GO! You made me leave her once, but I will not leave her again. She is not gone."

Camille backed out of the room crying. She ran to get Charles, trying to explain to him what had happened. Charles came to our room, knocking gently on the door. Blake did not answer him, so he let himself in.

"Brother," he said.

"Charles, do not attempt to remove me. I will fight you. You made me leave her once, when I should have stayed. I will not leave her again."

"Blake, she is gone."

"No, she is not gone, and if you say that again, I will toss you out the window. She is alive. The baby is alive. Run your sword through me and take me so I can be with her if you think she is gone."

"I will not end your life, Blake."

Blake reached for his dagger on the table next to our bed. "I will do it. You will see she is alive." He then slammed the dagger into his chest, into his heart.

Charles screamed, running to him and pulling the dagger from his chest.

Blake smiled at him. "I will be with her either way," he said and closed his eyes.

322

Charles could not contain himself. He started crying and screaming, shaking his brother, begging him not to die.

Rebecca came running in the room, and saw the blood coming from Blake's chest. "Noooooo," she screamed.

Charles turned to face her. Through his sobs, he managed to say, "He wanted to be with her. He could not live without her."

Rebecca ran into his arms and held him. Together, they sank to the floor. She held him while he cried for the loss of his brother. They bonded on the floor of our bedroom, while we lay in the slumber of death on our bed. Rebecca leaned her back against our bed as Charles cried himself to sleep. She cried for him. She cried for us. She cried because the man she loved was in so much pain. She eventually cried herself to sleep.

I felt the warmth touch me. I felt the love holding me. I felt the loss they all felt. It was love that pulled me back, the love from him, the love of our child, and the love of the life I was promised for my sacrifice. It was the love of my family.

I took a breath, feeling him next to me, but I did not feel his warmth. I moved my hand up to his heart to feel his love, but it was cold. The warmth I felt was not his. My eyes fluttered open. I knew she was here. I knew she was with me. My mother, who could not be here in life to hold me, was here in death to love me and warm me. Her embrace was never ending; I realized now the magic of life was a gift. I had been given it three times, three times she has brought me into this world. She had been with me always, even when I did not know it. I tried to find her in my vision but could only feel her. My hand on his heart, filled with warmth, touched him. I felt it th-thump, th-thump. The smile came to my face. "Thank you," I whispered. Then I felt her lips touch my head before she was gone.

Rebecca heard me speak then moved, which woke Charles. She rose from her spot at the end of the bed and turned to look at me. With tears streaming down her cheeks, she laughed and cried, watching as I opened my eyes. In a whisper, she said, "Well, it took you long enough."

Charles got on his knees in time to see Blake's eyes flutter open. His hand coming up to lay on mine, our fingers entwined. He turned his head to look at me with tears in his eyes, and he kissed me. Before we could move, Charles and Rebecca were in bed with us, hugging us. I could not fight them. She kissed me and kissed me, then she kissed Blake, and Charles did the same. We were all laughing and crying, and then Charles grabbed Rebecca and kissed her, as well. She did not resist him, for it was not a huge kiss, but it was a kiss none the less.

They got off our bed. "We will be back, but I think the two of you need some time," Charles said. He took Rebecca's hand and led her out the door.

Blake reached up and moved my hair from my face. "You are here," he whispered.

"I am, but how?"

"Your mother... she told me all was right, but you did not wake."

I patted his heart. "You did this?"

"They wanted me to leave you so they could prepare your body for burial, but I would not leave you again. I did not want to live in a world without you. If we could not be together here in life, I would be with you in death. But how am I here?"

I smiled. "My mother. I am sorry."

"No, I am sorry for not being able to protect you."

"Please, do not ever let me go, not again, not ever."

He pulled me close, taking my hand from his heart, and placed it on my stomach with his, holding our baby together. "She is safe now."

"He is strong." We both smiled and fell asleep.

Everyone in the house wanted to see us, but Rebecca and Charles kept guard over our room so we were not disturbed. We slept for a day and a half. The commotion in the hall is what woke us.

"What is going on out there?" I whispered.

"Should I go see?" he asked quietly.

"No, stay with me."

He smiled and pulled me close. "We are covered in dried blood. I think we should take a bath and have something to eat."

"Yes, we should, but do you want to get up?"

"Mmmmm," he said. "Not really."

The noise in the hallway quieted down, and we fell back to sleep. When I woke again, it was the dark of the night and I was alone. I felt so tired. I did not have the energy to get up. Hearing voices in the hall, I reached for the striker to light the candle, but knocked it off the table.

Blake came in the room. When he opened the door, the light from the candles in the hall flooded the room with a little light. He looked like he had been dragged through the mud, tired and old.

"What is going on?"

"Everyone wants to see you for themselves. There is quite a gathering out there," he said as he climbed into bed.

"Mmmmm," I said as I wrapped myself around him.

"I tried to calm them down so you could sleep."

"Do not leave me. I cannot sleep if you are gone."

He chuckled. "I will never leave you."

That is all I remember before sleep came again. It was not a long sleep. The warmth from the fire and the smell of food woke me. I opened my eyes to see him looking at me. He moved my hair from my face and then kissed me. "Francis brought some food. She insists that the baby must eat."

I smiled. "Yes, he is hungry. He has an appetite like his father."

"Well, I am pretty sure she can eat like her mother. Come, sit up and I will serve you." He helped me sit.

"Why am I so weak? I really had a hard time defeating Kelvin."

"My love, I watched when you cut his head off. The power that escaped from him threw you pretty far. I am just glad it was Joseph you hit and not a rock."

"He was very strong. That is for sure. Is everyone all right? I know Rebecca is, but what about Juliana?"

"Everyone is fine. When you finish eating, they will all be in here."

He sat the tray on the bed and lifted the lid. There was so much food, yet I could not stop myself. There were little round things of bread, meat stew with vegetables, pie, and little cakes. It was all so delicious. We ate everything on the tray. I laid back and put my hands on my stomach, while Blake put the tray on the table. He came back to bed, placed his hands on mine, and then kissed the baby. When he did, he got a sweet response; the baby rolled in my stomach. When he picked his head up, I saw that he had a tear in his eye.

"I thought I had lost you both."

I reached up to touch his face. "You did."

He kissed me fiercely and deeply. "I know," he whispered into my mouth before kissing me again. We did not part until we heard someone clearing their throat.

We parted but he kept his forehead on mine, looking into my eyes. "What is it, Charles?"

"Well, there are a great many people in this hallway wanting to see Sabine," he said happily.

Blake kissed me again. "If they must," he responded with a chuckle.

They all piled in Charlotte, Clare, Juliana, Julia, James, Aiden, and Steven, all of them. It was quite the reunion. As we were all chatting, I had noticed that Charles and Rebecca were standing in the back. I looked through everyone to see their hands entwined, and I could not help but smile. She had found her way back to him. We all visited for a bit before Blake asked everyone to leave. Camille, Francis, and the two kitchen girls filled our tub, and then we were alone.

When Blake bolted the door, he turned to me. "My Lady, your bath awaits you."

I started to get up and he stopped me. "Do you trust me," he asked.

"With my life."

He smiled and reached for his dagger. I watched as he put it between my breasts and pulled toward him, cutting the front of my gown. He continued to my bump, sat the dagger down, and then ripped the rest of my gown to the floor. As I smiled at him, he slid it off my shoulders and then lifted me, carrying me to the tub and gently sitting me in it. I watched as he tore his shirt and pants off, and then climbed in to sit behind me. He took great care in washing me, as I did with him. When we were done, the water was a dark brownish color from the blood. He got one blanket, and we wrapped ourselves in it and climbed into bed. I fell asleep listening to his heart beating.

We spent our days in our room, visiting with everyone, eating, laughing, and just being together. The season of the blossoms was in full bloom when we emerged. I needed to find the last two Markers and the center of the land.

Blake and I went in search of the Markers, which took longer than either of us had expected. After days and days of searching, we finally located them. Christopher marked them on the map for me, forming a circle.

I was sitting in my study, looking at the map. Since they were already in a circle, was I supposed to move them? I went looking for Christopher, finding him and Julia in the sitting room.

"Christopher, can I talk to you in my study?"

"Of course." He kissed Julia's hand and then followed me.

"I wanted to know if you could tell me the distance between each of those marks I had you put on the map."

He stood there looking at the map. "Yes, I can, but it will take me some time."

"I will wait." I sat in the chair by the window and watched him. We were there for a while. One of the kitchen girls came in to see if I wanted something to eat, so I nodded and she left.

Francis came in with a tray of food for me. "Here you go, child. You must eat."

I smiled at her. "Did Blake ask you to make sure I eat?"

"He did indeed." We both giggled.

When she went to leave, I noticed she gave Christopher a strange look. I wondered why, and decided I would have to ask her later. I sat and ate, and as always, it was delicious and filling. Christopher climbed down off the ladder and came to sit with me.

"From what I can tell, they are all exactly the same distance from one another."

"What is the distance?"

"Half a day's ride between each mark."

"Thank you. How are things going with Julia?"

He smiled a huge smile. "They are fantastic. I really care for her."

"Well, that is great. I see my brother has removed the escort."

Christopher laughed. "Only when we are indoors, but Westin is not far away at any time. He does not trust me to be alone with his daughter. I cannot blame him or find fault in him. But he must know that I will not harm her."

"She is his only daughter."

"Yes, I know. Can I ask you something?"

"Of course,"

"I have noticed that Westin is sort of childlike in many ways."

"Yes, he is," I said raising my eyebrows. "So what is your question?"

"I suppose it is not a question so much as it is an observation, is all."

"What are you implying, Christopher?"

"Nothing. I probably should not have said anything."

"Thank you for helping me," I said as I stood, which was his cue to leave.

He nodded. "It was my pleasure."

I watched as he walked out of the room. *What was that about? Why would he question Westin? I do not like that.* I was beginning to think that perhaps Christopher was not all that wonderful.

I went looking for Blake, needing to talk to him. It felt good to be out in the warmth of the light of the day. I slowly made my way to the barracks, where the guards were sitting by the door. I wondered what they did there or why they were there. I would have to ask Charles.

"Excuse me. Have you seen Blake?"

They stood and bowed. "Yes, Your Majesty, he is out in the fields, helping with the planting."

"Hmmm, would you please go and get him, and ask him to please come home? Make sure you tell him I am fine." I smiled.

"Of course, Your Majesty," one said and ran to the stables to get a horse. I started walking back to the castle. By the time I got to my study and sat down, Blake was coming in the door.

I laughed. "From the time it took me to walk from the barracks to this room, it took that guard to get you and for you to get here. I am getting fat!"

He laughed with me. "The fatter the better, my love. It just means our child is getting bigger. What did you need?"

I stood up and walked to him. "I need this," I said as I kissed him.

He smiled when we finished. "You dragged me from my work in the fields, Your Majesty, so you could have your way with me?"

I giggled. "And what if I did?"

He pulled me as close to him as he could get. "I would feel honored to know that my wife loves me enough to want to kiss me in the middle of the day." He kissed me again.

"I really needed to show you something and to talk to you about all of this. Come and look at this." I tugged on his hand, pulling him into the center of the room.

"I had Christopher which we need to talk about but not now. I had him place the last two marks on the map. Tell me what you see."

He stood there looking at the map. "They are all in a circle."

"Exactly, and they are all buried. It said in the tome that I must find all the boundaries and the Markers of Time, which I have. Then to achieve the Coming, the Heir must incorporate the Unknown Heir, which I have within me. It says then that all the elements of this land will go forth with the Markers of Time to the place in the center of the land. I have the casting that releases the Markers from the ground. But if you look at the map, each Marker is half a day's ride from the other and then nearly three days' ride to the center."

"All right," he said.

"Well, is everyone expected to be where the Markers are and to bring the Markers back to the center, or do they stay in the circle where they are?"

"It would make sense that we would bring them to you."

I grinned at him. "That is what I thought. The season of the blossoms has been here for some time. We need to get the Markers to the center of the land. It said, the discovery of the twelve Markers of Time would set into motion the beginning of the Coming. We have found them, so it has all begun."

"Then each of us needs to be by a Marker when you do whatever it is that you do."

"Yes, and I think, considering we do not know how big they are, that we should do it sooner rather than later. I mean, what if they are giant Markers? How will we get them here?"

"Okay, I see what you are saying, so we need to talk to Westin to find out who the other person is."

"I already figured that out. Camille bears the Mark of the Guardian, so she is the eighth. Westin is the Keeper of the land, so that makes twelve. I have to be in the center."

"I will go and gather everyone, and we can meet on the hilltop. I will have one of the guards help you on Raiden. Please, be careful."

"You are so funny. He would not hurt me."

"Not funny, I love you." He left then, and while I waited, I went in search of Francis, finding her in the kitchen.

"Hello, Francis. I was wondering if we could have a talk."

"Of course, child, what is on your mind?" she said as she sat down across from me.

I leaned in and lowered my voice to just above a whisper. "I saw the way you looked at Christopher. You do not care for him, do you?"

She did not say anything for quite a while, but then she leaned in and nearly whispered, "I do not trust him. There is something about that boy that just is not right."

I sat back and crinkled my eyebrows. "Why would you say that? Is there something you know?"

She half-whispered, "It is something I feel. The way he looks at everyone, like he is studying them, and Westin, he is always watching him. I just do not feel comfortable."

"I have a meeting I need to get to. Will you talk with me later?"

"Of course, child, I will wait here for you to return." I squeezed her hand and smiled.

Walking into the stables, I asked one of the guards to help me put on Raiden's saddle. I checked all the straps then walked him out into the courtyard.

One of the guards by the door came over to me. "Your Majesty, Master Blake asked me to help you."

"Thank you," I said as I put my foot in the stirrup, pulling myself up as he helped lift me. "I am sorry to be a bother. I must be heavy for you."

"No, My Lady, light as a feather." He smiled and went back to his post.

Raiden walked me out into the village, through the fields, and to the orchards. "Are you ever going to actually ride with me?" I said and then giggled as he took off running. I sat on the hilltop looking eastward. The plain was coming alive with birds flying in the sky. It was very peaceful. I looked to the sky and said aloud, "Thank you for all you have given me."

Blake had ridden up without me hearing him. "I do that a great deal myself," he said, startling me.

"Do what?"

"Thank whatever powers may be for you, for this life we have, for this child we shall have. I am a very lucky man."

I smiled. "Blake, I am scared."

"Me too, my love, but we will get through it. We always do."

The others rode up then. Charles, Aiden, Steven, James, Joseph, Edward, and Camille, combined with Blake made the eight who bear the Mark of the Guardian. Then we had Spirit, Raiden, Juliana, and Westin, the four elements.

"I have asked you all here because the time is coming for the last task that has been set before me. Some of you know what this is about, and some of you do not. I am the Bringer of Peace. I have given the evil that escaped this land back to it. Now, it is time to seal the land, which is called the Coming. I do not know what it all means, but I know what needs to be done.

"There are Markers buried out there that I have spent the last three seasons looking for. They are called the Markers of Time. I have found them all, and according to the tomes, it is time to bring them forth. Now, I have no idea how big they are, because they are buried in the ground. According to the tomes, they must be brought forth, one by each who bears the Mark of the Guardian, and that is the eight of you, and one by each element. That is Juliana, Spirit, Raiden and Westin."

"Why me, Sabine?" Westin asked.

"I represent the earth, and you are my brother, so you represent earth as well. I have to be in the center to say the words so the Markers of Time rise. Now, I have no idea how big they are. They are two, almost three, days' ride from the center of Whispering Wind. I have all the places marked on the map in my study. We cannot all go in at once, so when we return one by one, you will come in over the next light of the day and choose which Marker you will go to. I will have Raiden and Spirit take each of you to the spot you have chosen. When everyone is in position, I will do the casting, Raiden and Spirit will come and get you all and your Markers, then they will bring you to me. You must not tell anyone what is going on.

"At the end of the season of the blossoms, for a fortnight, the dark of the night will be lit with lights that make it feel as if the light of the day is coming. On the final night, we are to gather in the center. That is when I will tell you what needs to be done next."

"Sabine?"

"Yes, my love." I turned to Westin.

"Why are we on the hilltop?"

I smiled at him. "Because, my love, this is an intrigue, and we must not tell anyone what we are doing."

"I like a good intrigue, Sabine. I will not tell anyone."

"Thank you. Now does anyone have any questions?"

Juliana spoke. "Sabine, what if these Markers are huge stones?"

"That is why we are doing this now instead of waiting. I have no idea how big they are. If they are huge stones, then we will still have time to get them to the center of the land." I looked at Westin, who looked back with his not-Westin eyes and nodded. I was not sure what that meant, but I hoped it was him saying I was doing the right thing. "Anyone else?"

Everyone shook their heads. One by one, they made their way back to the castle. "Blake, will you stay with me?"

"Of course, my love," he said.

We watched as everyone left, and Charles followed the others. "I need to talk to you about Christopher."

He tilted his head. "What is the matter?"

"Well, today, we were in my study, and Francis brought me some food. Thank you, by the way, for looking after me."

"I know you get busy and forget to eat. I am just making sure my wife and child are fed." He smiled.

"When she left, I saw her give Christopher a strange look. Then once he finished, he started asking... well, not asking me, but saying things about Westin."

"Things like what?"

"He made a comment about Westin being childlike. He said it was an observation, but it felt to me as if he wanted information about my brother. It felt wrong."

"Christopher seems like a very lovely man. He is kind and considerate, and is always helping in one way or another. Perhaps he is just wondering about the man whose daughter he is in love with."

"I am concerned about Julia, as well. She beams when he walks into a room, and she is so innocent."

"You know, come to think of it, when he first got here, he had asked Ben who Juliana was, as well. Ben told me he had made a comment as to how beautiful she was, but when Christopher heard that she had Isabel, he did not question him again about her."

"I am not so comfortable with Christopher. Will you keep an eye out and watch him when he is around you. Something does not feel right here. Francis said that she did not trust him, and for Francis, that it is saying a lot."

"Yes, it is, and yes, I will. If he is up to something, I will do my best to find out what it is."

"Thank you," I said as I walked away from him.

"Is there something more you are not telling me?"

"I have been remembering what that Kelvin had said. It was the same thing Devious had said, that she was the daughter of

Kelvin and the granddaughter of Kracken. I do not think this is over. If Devious lived as long as she did, then it would be safe to say that this Kracken is still alive somewhere."

He grabbed me and pulled me into his chest. "I will not allow anything to happen to you, not again. The season of the blossoms is coming to an end. Whatever it is you are supposed to do, we will get it done. Do you know what this Coming is?"

"We are to seal the land. Only the hearts that are pure may enter."

"So it would be right to believe that we will all be safe, and that we will be able to enjoy this life?" He held me tighter.

"That was the promise from my parents, yes."

He stood there holding me. "I love you, wife."

I smiled. "I love you, husband."

We walked back to the castle, and it felt good to walk. As we made our way through the village, we stopped at Clare's to see how things were going. Then we made our way to the castle just as the dark of the night was falling upon the village. The kitchen was full. The table was full. Everyone was there, even Charles, James, and now Christopher. He had become a part of our family, and I could only hope that the feeling I had was wrong. We found our places and sat to eat the evening meal with everyone. The chatter was grand, with everyone laughing and carrying on, and then I caught Christopher looking at Westin. I wondered if Westin was aware of him. I thought I would give Christopher a test.

"Westin, my love," I said.

"Yes, Sabine."

"I was wondering if you have played any tricks on Francis lately."

He dipped his head down in the shy manner I was used to then picked his head up with his Westin grin.

336

Francis looked at him and then at me, saying, "Oh, yes, he has. I swear, he will be the death of me yet."

Westin burst into laughter. "I did, Sabine. I hid and jumped out to scare her. She hit me with a tray." He was laughing so hard and then moved his hand to his head. "I still have a bump."

Camille shook her head. "One day you will cause her to stop breathing, and then it will not be so funny."

He laughed harder. "You are just mad because I did it to you, and you threw all the clothes all over."

I smiled at him and shook my head. "Just do not do it to me, please, at least not until after the baby comes." I was watching Christopher out of the corner of my eye. He watched intently. I think he was trying to see a flaw somewhere. Westin was good at playing his part. He had tricked everyone for his whole life.

The meal finished, and everyone was going this way and that way. I watched as Christopher said good night to Julia, kissing her hand. I happened to see Westin's face; my brother was furious, but he just smiled and trotted off with the rest of the children.

Blake got up and went to leave. I think he expected me to join him. He stopped and looked at me. "Sabine," he said.

"Oh, go ahead. I am fine. I would like to have a chat with Christopher. I will be up later."

"No, I will wait for you in the sitting room."

"Thank you, my love, but go on up. I think I would like a bath."

"You got it." He smiled and left.

Christopher sat down across the table from me. "Well, you have got him trained."

I tilted my head. "What exactly does that mean?"

"You are the Queen and he is your guardsman, so it would be within reason to say you married beneath you."

"Julia is a Princess and you are a mapper, so would it not be the same to say that about the two of you, as well, that you are beneath her?" I countered a bit more defensively than I had intended.

"I am sorry if I angered you. It was just an observation."

"My life with my husband is not something you should concern yourself with, and I would appreciate it if you kept your observations to yourself. Now, I would like to know why you are seated at my family table."

"I suppose I do not consider this to be your family table, so to speak. You are the Queen. Your family is royal. Would your family table not be in the great dining hall, where the rest of the Kings of these lands sit to eat their meals?"

"If your logic stands to be correct, would any table I sit at then be my family table?"

I saw a bit of fear in his eyes. I do not think he expected I would be able to best him in logic. "I suppose that would be the case, yes."

"Well, Christopher, it would seem to me that you tend to make great observations concerning me and my family, so let me ask you this. What exactly is it that you think you may know about me?"

"I know you are the legend, the Bringer of Peace. I know you wear men's clothing, and you wield a sword nearly your size in length as if it were a stick. I know you married a guardsman and are having his child. I know that you have run your sword through your husband, and yet he did not die." He leaned forward, continuing, "I know that you throw fits, and everyone is afraid of you so they give you what you want. Like Blake there, you mention you wanted to take a bath, and he is up there making sure the tub is full."

I tilted my head and smiled at him. "You are a very brave man, Christopher, to spout your arrogant thoughts at me."

"I am not afraid of you, which makes me different from everyone else."

"You should be afraid of her," I heard from the doorway. I leaned over to see Charles standing there.

Christopher turned in his seat. "I meant no harm, Charles. We were just talking frankly. Is that not right, Sabine?"

"Charles, would you please escort Christopher here to his quarters, and would you be so kind as to make sure he stays there until further notice?"

Christopher turned to look at me. "Are you serious?"

As I stood, I reached over and touched his arm. Leaning in, I said, "I am always serious, Christopher, but keep in mind, no one wants to see me throw a fit." I smiled and left the room. This man was dangerous. He should be kept under lock and key. I turned and went to the kitchen door. "Charles," I called out.

He turned and started back toward me with Christopher. "Perhaps, for now, Christopher should be a guest at our special place. No harm is to come to him."

"As you wish, Sabine," Charles said.

I turned to walk away, when Christopher said, "What is your special place?"

Charles chuckled. "It is special because the saying 'you will never see the light of day again' is actually truth there."

Christopher started to struggle. "It will do you no good to fight it."

"Do you people do everything she says?"

Charles smirked. "I am bound to Sabine. I am her Guardian. If she asked me cut the head off my own brother, I would do it. It is not my job to question her. It is my job to protect her, and if she feels you need to visit her special place, then that must mean she is worried for the safety of her family. She is not your ordinary woman, Christopher. I thought you were a smart man."

"What does that mean? Are you all so struck by her beauty that you would do anything to win her favor?"

Charles did not answer him. Instead, he dragged him down the many stairs into the labyrinth below Whispering Wind and found a lovely dark corner to put him.

"You will be safe here until Sabine decides if you can be trusted or not. I will make sure you have food and clean clothing, but you will not be released until she believes you will not harm her family."

"What about Julia? She will fight to free me."

"She will not. She loves her aunt, and she will listen to what she tells her to do. You do not know the power this family has within them, and for them to let you in and then you speak to our Queen in the manner in which you did, you are lucky to be alive."

"What could a woman full with a child possibly do to me?"

"She could cut your head off," Charles said as he chuckled and walked away.

I made my way to our room, where I stood outside the door, thinking about what he had said about me. Could it be truth? I went inside, and there was Blake, pouring the last pot into the tub. I sat down by the fire.

"What is wrong, my love?" he asked as he sat next to me.

"Are you afraid of me?"

He laughed. "Why would you ask me such a thing?"

"Are you?"

"Of course not, why would you ask me that?"

"Something Christopher had said to me. He said that I throw fits, and people do what I say because they are afraid of me. Is that truth?"

"You do not throw fits, my love. Never mind what he has to say."

"Oh, I minded so much that I had Charles give him a room in our special place."

"What? What did he say to you?"

"Nothing really. I did not like the way he was watching Westin, or the way he spoke to me. I do not have a good feeling about him anymore, so I thought, if he is good, then he will still be there after we seal the land. If he is not, he will be ash."

"That sounds reasonable, but what about Julia?"

"I will deal with Julia later. Right now, I would like to take a bath with my husband and my child."

"I like the sound of that." He pulled me up and helped me out of my dress, then put his arms around me and held our baby and me. "This is so beautiful, our child growing within you." He helped me into the tub and then climbed in behind me. We lay in the water and enjoyed each other. We got a great deal of water on the floor, but I did not care. I always loved when he made me quiver.

He carried me to bed and took his time loving me. We settled ourselves and fell asleep entwined in one another's arms.

Chapter Eighteen

𝕴 woke before Blake because the baby was rolling around and making me very uncomfortable. I watched him while he slept. He looked tired. I touched his eyes, noticing the dark circles under them. He was worried about what was coming. He was worried about the baby and me. *How did I ever get so lucky to have a man love me like this?* I could not stop myself as I leaned down and kissed him gently, running my tongue along his lip. He slipped his just a little bit out of his mouth to touch mine, and my body exploded. I covered his with mine, and his hands came up to my face, one on either side, then ran down my body. He closed his arms around me and rolled me on top of him. It was difficult to lay flat on him.

"I do not fit any more," I whispered in his mouth.

"You will always fit," he said.

We spent our morning lying in bed, talking about the baby, and discussing what we might want to name it. We giggled at some of the silly names we came up with. Kissing and giggling, we loved one another until the baby wanted food, and it was not quiet about it. I swear, we could see its feet pushing out of the skin on my stomach. We laughed about that as well. We giggled all the way down stairs. Though we had missed the morning meal, Francis had made a feast for us.

I laughed as I sat down. "I think I should blame you, Francis, for this huge belly I have."

She laughed. "Nonsense, you are all baby, and I can guarantee you I had nothing to do with that."

Blake laughed so hard he had milk coming out of his nose, which threw us into another round of giggles. "That is the greatest sound I have ever heard," he said.

"What sound is that," I asked, still giggling.

"That sound, your giggle. It fills my heart with so much love I feel like I am going to burst sometimes."

I smiled at him. "Thank you for loving me enough to make me laugh."

He leaned across the table and kissed me. "You are most welcome, My Lady."

I heard Francis sniffle, so I looked past Blake to see her wiping tears from her face. I got up and went over to hug her, and Blake joined me. We stood there for a few minutes, and then Julia came in.

"Can I speak to you, please?" she said to me.

"Of course you can." I let go of Francis and sat down.

"I mean in private." She was not happy.

"Of course." I got up and walked to my study. "Come on in and have a seat."

"I prefer to stand. Why did you send Christopher away?"

"Who told you I sent him away?"

"Charles did. He said that you sent him away last night. Why did you do that?"

"Julia, Charles has misinformed you. I did not send him away."

She stopped walking and looked at me. "Are you saying that Charles is telling me an untruth, because I find that hard to believe?"

I raised my eyebrows at her. "You would be careful to mind your tone with me."

"Or what, you will run me through?"

I stood up. "Julia, sit down!" I yelled.

She stood there looking at me. "You are not my mother, and I am not one of your precious Guardians. I do not take orders from you."

I turned around and walked out of my study, leaving her standing there. She was far too angry to speak to, and I really was not in the mood to deal with her. I went out into the courtyard and sat by the fountain. She actually had the nerve to follow me.

"Do not think you can walk away from me and ignore me!" she shouted.

I stood and turned to look at her. "Do not believe for one minute that you may speak to me in this manner."

"You do not scare me, Sabine."

"Well, she very well should," Westin said in his not Westin voice.

Julia turned around. "Father," she said in a calmer tone.

"Why are you attacking your aunt in the middle of the courtyard?"

"Because she will not address me in a civilized manner in the house," she snapped at him.

"It is all right, brother. I will handle this." I looked at him, and he nodded and walked away.

She spun around. "My father is even afraid of you, but I am not. Where is Christopher?"

"I would imagine that you need to ask Christopher that." I went to walk past her, seeing Camille standing in the door and Westin a few feet away. What I did not expect was for Julia to grab me, but she did, and whirled me around to face her.

"Do not walk away from me!" she screamed at me.

I looked her right in the face. "I will give you this one, but do not think it is ever acceptable to touch me in anger again." I pulled my arm, but she would not let it go. "Julia, let me go."

"Or what, Sabine, you will run me through with your sword?"

I was finished with this child. She was actually hurting my arm. I grabbed her by the throat and slammed her on her back on the stone. "Do not think you will ever hurt me. Do not touch me again out of anger, Julia, or I might forget you are my niece."

When I turned to walk away, I saw Camille come out of the house, and then I saw her face. I felt Julia coming just as Camille screamed. Being so huge with this baby, spinning was not my best feat, so I just stepped aside and let her blow past me. She spun quickly, and I heard Westin yell.

"Sabine, she is my daughter!"

She lunged at me, and when I caught her in the stomach with my fist, she bent over in pain. I put my hand on her head and slammed her to the ground. "Stay down, Julia," I told her and started to walk away. She grabbed my leg and flipped me backwards.

"I will do no such a thing. You do not scare me."

Westin was on her in an instant. He grabbed her around the waist and walked away. Camille was at my side. Blake came riding up and was off his horse before I knew what was happening.

"Oh, Sabine, I am so sorry," Camille cried. "Are you all right?"

"What the hell is going on here?" Blake was angry.

"Julia attacked her," Camille said through tears.

"I am fine, fat but fine." They helped me up.

"I do not know what has gotten into her," Camille said.

"I do, Camille. It is all right. She is very angry at me."

"She had no right to do this to you."

Blake picked me up and carried me into the castle. He went straight to our room and laid me on the bed. "Are you all right?"

I smiled at him. "Yes, my love, I am fine, a bit embarrassed but fine."

"She bested you." He smiled.

"She did indeed," I giggled.

"So what happened?"

"She was angry. Charles had told her that I sent Christopher away, and I told her that he was wrong, that I did not send him away. I did not." I smiled. "To hear the words coming out of her mouth was like hearing the same words coming out of Christopher's all over again. They have been talking about me. I think he has been poisoning her mind where I am concerned. I should go and speak to her." I stood to leave.

"Please, do not. She slammed you on the ground. You cannot hurt her, Sabine. She is our niece."

"I am not going to hurt her. Westin carried her into the house, so I know he is with her now. Will you come with me?"

He stood up and put out his hand for me to lead the way. We walked to Westin and Camille's room, and I knocked on the door. Camille answered it, but Julia was not there.

"Where is Julia?"

"Westin locked her in the tower until she calms down."

I looked at Westin, who said, "I am so sorry, Sabine. I had no idea she was capable of something like that."

"It is fine. Would the two of you please come with us to the tower? I would like to talk to her, or at least let her get all of her anger out."

Westin nodded, so we made our way to the tower. After Westin unlocked the door, Blake went in first. She hit him with a chair, and I smiled. The girl had a temper. That was for sure. Blake grabbed her around the waist, and we went in.

"Now, hold on there, Julia," he said.

"Let me go, Uncle!" she screamed as she fought him.

"I will let you go when you start acting like a young lady, and not one moment before. You could have hurt Sabine and our baby."

"Oh, are you afraid I will hurt her? LET ME GO!" she screamed.

He laughed so loud it filled the room. "Oh, I am not afraid you will hurt her. It is you I am protecting."

She looked at me. "Why did you make him leave? I love him. He has asked me to be his wife. You cannot control me like this. I will find him."

"I will tell you where he is, but first, you will talk to me in a civilized manner and answer my queries."

She calmed down a bit, but Blake still did not let her go.

"Why did you say that to me?"

347

"Say what?" she snapped.

"Why did you say you were not afraid of me?"

"Because everyone is afraid of you. Even my parents fear you and your little fits of rage you throw."

I looked at Blake. "Why do you think people are afraid of me?"

"Because you think you are some kind of God or something," she said.

"What do you know about who I am?"

"Oh, I know enough."

"Would you enlighten me?" I asked.

"That you are the Bringer of Peace, the chosen one, which is a joke. You are nothing but a witch who casts spells on people to make them believe."

"Who told you these things?"

"Christopher said that is what everyone here thinks of you!" Julia yelled.

"Everyone like whom?"

"The people in the village, people like Clare. Christopher said you sent Charles to drag her back here so she could make your gowns. He said that Boland was forced to return to make you rugs. Then you nearly killed poor Sarah because Blake cannot keep his hands off her."

"So would it be safe for me to say that Christopher has filled your head with these facts?"

"That would be correct. He loves me. He would not tell me untruths."

"You are my brother's daughter and my husband's niece. You are my blood, and I love you very much, but know this, Julia you will never see Christopher again. I did not send him away. I took him away. He threatened me, just as you did. You will remain here until I have my baby. You are a threat to my child

348

and me, and I cannot have you trying to harm me. There is no way out of this tower, and this is where you will remain. If you try to get out, I will shackle you to the floor." I nodded to the binding on the floor. She turned her head and looked at it. "Your food will be delivered at meal times, through that slit in the door. You will not lay eyes on your mother or your father until after this baby is born. Then and only then will you be let out."

"You cannot do this! Mother! Father, you cannot let her do this!"

Camille looked at her. "You could have killed their baby, Julia. You are a danger to that baby. I will abide by her decision, and so will your father. I am sorry, but you attacked our Queen, and that is punishable by death."

Julia looked at me. "Is that what you did to Christopher?"

"Christopher still breathes, but as I have told you, you will never lay eyes on him again." I turned to walk away and looked at Westin. "I am sorry, brother."

He looked at me with his not Westin eyes, and he nodded. Blake waited for me to get clear of the door before he let her go. She was screaming and crying, begging Westin and Camille to let her out. Westin shut the door and locked it, handing me the key.

"I might let her out." He smiled sadly.

I could not stop the tears as we made our way down the stairs. Westin hugged me. "I know you had to do it," he whispered.

"She is so angry," I cried.

"This is not your doing, Sabine. The things she said are not truth," Camille said, hugging me.

"I am so sorry."

"It will be fine, sister. She will survive. I just want to thank you for not dragging her down to the dungeons."

I chuckled. "I could not do that. It is where Christopher is."

He laughed. "Well, that is a good place for him, but why did you have him taken there?"

"He kept commenting on you and the way you are, then he insulted me. He said the same things that Julia was saying."

"Sabine, you know it is not truth what they say."

"I know." Blake pulled me close. "I would like to go see Clare please," I told him.

"Can you walk that far?"

"Yes, please, will you take me?"

"Of course."

We left Camille and Westin at their room and continued to Clare's. I knocked on the door. Looking at Blake, I asked, "Would you mind staying out here?"

He gave me a funny look and kissed me on the forehead. "Of course."

Clare answered the door. "Sabine, come on in." I walked past her, and she looked at Blake. "Are you coming?"

"No, this is Sabine's visit."

She gave him a funny look then closed the door. I did not move into the room. "Clare, I need to ask you something."

"Sabine, what is wrong?"

"When Charles came to find you, did he force you to come back here?"

"Of course not, he told me that you had returned and that you wanted me to come back."

"Did you feel obligated to return because I wanted you to? Or did you come because you wanted to yourself."

"I had a nice life where I was, but I love it here and have grown very fond of you. I came on my own."

I threw my arms around her and hugged her. "Thank you." I turned to leave.

"Hey, what is going on?"

"Just some things that I have heard, I wanted to hear it from you."

"All right," she said, opening the door for me.

"Is everything all right?" Blake asked.

"Yes, it is fine." I smiled at him. We made our way back to the castle. I went to my study, where Charles and Rebecca were. He had picked the Marker he was going to go to. I think they were having a bit of alone time. Reaching out, I touched Rebecca's arm. "Will you stay with me for a bit?"

"Of course." She smiled at Charles as he left. "What is going on?"

I smiled at her. "I thought I would ask you the same thing."

She giggled. "After the night Blake stabbed himself with the dagger, we let it all go. He realized how much he loved me, and I did the same. To see Blake, take his own life to be with you in death changed us. I do love him, and he loves me."

"I am so happy for you."

"When this is over, we are going to be married."

I think my face broke from smiling so big. "Oh, it will be so wonderful. I cannot wait for you to experience all the things there are."

"Well, I was sort of hoping you could fill me in on this union thing." My smile left my face, and I turned away from her. "Sabine, what is wrong?"

"I would love to tell you how wonderful it is, except I do not know."

She giggled. "Oh, I forgot."

"Well, I have a bit of more news. I have locked Christopher up in our special place."

"I know. Charles told me, and what was all that with Julia?"

"Oh, he has poisoned her mind against me. I have locked her in the tower until the baby comes. After I finish this, anyone with a pure heart may enter the Kingdom, while anyone with a dark heart will be turned to ash. The way I look at it is if he is still there when it is over, then I will let him out. I think he is trying to get Julia away from us. I am not sure, but I have other things to do right now, and trying to figure him out is not high on my list."

"All right, that sounds good to me, but what do Westin and Camille say about this?"

"Westin was the one who locked her in there. He gave me the key." I smiled.

"Obviously, I have been too busy with myself to have taken notice of the things going on around here, and I am sorry for that. You are getting so big. I should be helping you with all of this."

"It is all right. Blake has been helping a great deal. He is very protective of us." I put my hand on my stomach.

"Well, I do not blame him. I would have done the same thing if I were him." I looked at her for a long time. "What is it?" she asked.

I whispered, "I am scared of what is to come. I have no idea what is going to happen, Rebecca."

She reached up and held my hand, comforting me. "It will all be all right. Your mother and father have been here with you throughout this whole time. Blake will make sure nothing more happens to you."

"You see, that is what I am afraid of. He will not be able to help me once the Coming starts. No one will. This is all on me."

"I am sorry you are so scared. I will be there to help you."

"You cannot be there, only Spirit and Raiden, remember."

352

"Oh, I forgot about that. Well, I will not be far away, and if anything happens, I will tell Spirit to come right away and get me. I will sit by the fountain and wait for you all to return."

"Thank you. I am glad that you and Charles have found your way back to each other."

"I think I am, as well. When all that happened, I think I healed when he came to me for comfort instead of pushing me away like he did last time. If I go, are you going to be all right?"

"Yes, I will be fine. Tomorrow, we will get the Markers, and we shall see what happens then."

She smiled, hugged me, and then left. I sat there looking at the map. *Did Christopher do the right thing and find the correct boundaries?* I was going to have to trust him, and that was something I was not sure I could do. I went to the secret room and opened the last tome. Still nothing. Then I went to the desk and got Father's drawings out, laid them on the floor, and tried to see if they had some of the same boundaries and markings as Christopher's map. They seemed to match up at all points, so hopefully, they were right. I found the Markers, and they were marked correctly on his map, so it must be right.

I heard a soft knock on the door. "Come in," I said.

It was Westin. "Can we talk?" I nodded. "Is there someplace where we will not be interrupted?" I nodded, and he helped me up. I went and triggered the latch to the secret room, took him by the hand, and led him into it before closing the door.

"Stay here," I told him as I made my way into the room. I found the candle and the striker and lit it. "All right, come on in."

He walked in smiling. "I knew this room was in this castle somewhere. I just did not know where until Camille brought me here."

I giggled. "There are a great many rooms like this."

"Really?" I nodded. "I knew something was going on between Christopher and Julia, and I am so sorry that she attacked you. That, I had no idea she would do. I have been watching him, hiding in places he could not see me." I smiled at him. "He did not start acting differently until after you came back from killing Kelvin. Julia began to watch me very closely, and so did Christopher. I put her in the tower because I think she has figured something out."

"Yes, I think Christopher has as well. That is why I had Charles put him in our special place. He kept giving me his observations concerning you and me. Do you think he knows who you are?"

"I think, with the help of Julia and the knowledge she has of that day I slapped her and you ran me through with your sword, he may have figured out I am not a simple minded man. The rest, I am not so sure he knows. I was going to end his life and make it look like an accident, so she would not think it was me. No one must know until the end."

"I am sorry about Julia. I am the one who encouraged him to pursue her. Boy was I wrong."

"Sabine, you must never forget that things must play out accordingly. You cannot change anything. Each thing that happens is a lesson learned. Do not forget that. This was no more your fault than it was mine. It had to happen. So at the light of the day, we begin raising the Markers?"

"Yes, Westin, do you know how big they are?"

"Truth is, Sabine, I knew nothing about the Markers until you told me. I know just about everything else that is supposed to take place until we seal the land, but that was a secret meant only for you."

"All right then, I am going to have a chat with Raiden, and at first light, this begins."

He hugged me. "Do not worry, little sister, and I am glad she did not hurt you."

I laughed. "She has spirit. That is for sure."

"Yes, just like her aunt."

We left the secret room and walked to the courtyard together. "I think I will sit here for a bit and wait for Blake to return." I sat down by the fountain.

"I am going to find my wife," he whispered and kissed me on the forehead. I watched as his whole body changed back into the simple minded Westin. I smiled and shook my head.

I searched for him in my head.

'Are you here?'

'I am always here.'

'When the light of the day comes, you and Spirit need to take everyone where they need to be and then come back for me.'

'Who is first?'

'Whoever shows up.'

I giggled and shook my head.

"Are you laughing at yourself?" Blake said as he sat down.

"No, at Raiden. When the light of the day comes, it begins."

He nodded. "Everything all right?"

"Yes, I wish this was over. There is just less than three weeks left until the fortnight begins before the harvest, and this baby could come at any time."

He laughed. "If she is anything like her mother, she will be late." We laughed and went in for our evening meal. There was a seat empty around the table, but no one seemed to ask where Julia was. Stephan had fallen in love with the girl from the village, and Westin had approved. He wanted to bring her to dinner to meet us all, so we settled on it in four days' time. I felt a bit sorry for her having to come and meet us. Apparently, the village feared me, so I could just imagine how worried she might be.

Blake and I retired to our room. I was in need of a hot bath. Sitting in the tub with Blake behind me as he rubbed my stomach and hummed a lullaby into my ear was quite calming.

"Did your mother sing that song to you?"

"Yes, she did, and I am looking forward to singing it to our child."

He helped me out of the tub and into the bed. We did not love one another; he just held me as we slept. It had been an exhausting day.

Blake was up before the light of the day came, and had organized everyone. Spirit took Joseph and Aiden, and Raiden took Steven and Edward. When they got back, Westin and Camille went on Spirit, and James and Juliana went on Raiden. By the time they got back, the village was coming to life.

After Blake brought me some food, I put on my large boy clothes and grabbed my sword. While we were walking out the door, he placed my crown on my head. "No matter what happens today, know that I love you in this life and in death."

I kissed him. "There will be no death today."

Once we went down, Spirit took Charles, and Raiden took Blake and me, dropping me off in the middle of the land. I kissed Blake, and they were gone. I waited to hear Raiden in my head.

'We are ready.'

I stood in the center of the land and drew my circle around me. Raising my sword to the sky, I kissed the hilt. I closed my eyes and turned three times, while saying the words from the tome.

"Stones of Time
Black to White
Dark to Light
Come forth to thee
Come forth to life."

Then I knelt, slamming my sword into the ground once, twice, three times. The ground rumbled; it did not stop for some time. When I stood and removed my sword from the ground, light filled me as warmth and love held me in my spot. I heard voices blessing me, blessing our child, holding me. I did not hear Raiden come up with Blake and Steven, or Spirit with Camille and Westin.

They stood there watching the light engulf me. Westin cried because he knew what was happening. I did not, but I just felt so much peace. When the others arrived, they all stood with their Markers in a circle around me. As the light left, I sunk to my knees. Blake started to move toward me, and Westin stopped him.

When I looked up at him, he finally saw it. He saw what they had done to me, what they had put within me. Westin cried, and Blake looked terrified at what he saw. The light came from my eyes, from within me. It had only lasted for a moment, but it had been there.

I closed my eyes, and Westin removed his hand from Blake, who then quickly ran to my side.

"My love," he whispered.

I fell into his arms and held him. He lifted me off the ground and held me close.

No one said a word. I leaned into my husband's chest. He felt the warmth flow from me to him, and it weakened his knees, forcing him to the gound. Charles and Westin came to us. "Blake, are you all right?"

He looked at me and smiled. He knew now what the Coming was. Westin knew what it was. I knew what it was.

"Come on, beautiful girl. Let us get you home," he whispered.

I smiled, holding on to him while he stood. He put me on Raiden and then climbed up. "I will send him back for you," Blake said to everyone. We rode into the courtyard. Rebecca was waiting by the fountain in the courtyard. When she stood, I could see the shock on her face.

"What happened? The whole place shook, and then there was this light that covered everything. Sabine, are you all right?" she asked while she helped me down.

I did not speak to her. I just smiled and nodded.

"You look different. Both of you do. It is like you have this glow surrounding you."

Blake spoke, "Rebecca, we are fine. Sabine needs to lay down for a bit. I will come and get you when she wakes."

I put my hand on her, and she calmed instantly. "All right, are you sure you are all right?"

I nodded, and as Blake picked me up, I put my arms around his neck and let him carry me to our room and lay me on the bed. We did not speak as he wrapped his arms around me and pulled our baby and me into his chest to hold us both. When I slept, I believe it was the most peaceful sleep I have ever had.

I woke to see his beautiful green eyes looking at me. I smiled and kissed him. "I love you," I whispered into his mouth. His love was so beautiful, powerful, and gentle all at the same time. He loved me for a long time, and when we were finished, we lay in one another's arms with tears in our eyes.

"I had no idea, my love, no idea."

I giggled. "Me neither."

He got up and went to get us some food, so I put on a new gown that I had been saving for him the green one that matched his eyes. Clare had made some adjustments for my very ample breasts. When he walked in the room, he stood there looking at me.

"You positively glow. You are so beautiful."

I smiled. "Thank you. I love this color," I told him, running my hands across the front of my dress. He did not move, just stood there staring at me. "What is the matter? Do you not like it?"

"I love it." He smiled and went to set the tray down. "I know I should not ask this, but are we going to talk about what happened yesterday?"

"No, my love, not yet. Are you all right?"

"I am. I feel as if I have been imbued with a piece of what you are going through." He took my hands in his. "Sabine, I never understood what you saw or how you felt about any of this. I just saw you as this incredibly strong woman. I did not truly know how all this has changed you into such an unbelievable woman facing a world that would crush any one of us. You have always squared your shoulders and just did what needed doing. But now, I know. Now, I know what this has all been about. You are a gift from those who have come before us. You were not just born, my love. You were created to achieve this monumental task. As a man, a strong man at that, I do not believe that I would be capable of doing what you have done, or what you are going to do in a few weeks' time."

"You do not understand anything, Blake. You were created for me. Apart, we are just two people, but together, the energy we have is unstoppable. I did not know this until I left you when I discovered I was having a baby. I am not doing this alone. That is why you saw what you did, and that is why you were given what you were yesterday. I need your energy to finish this. I cannot do it alone. Our love is the key. Our child is the key. I know that now, even more so than I did before."

"Well, I cannot say to you enough how honored I am to call myself your husband."

"No other man would have left me pure. Deep down inside, you knew it meant something. Your reward in all of this will be me. It will be our child born of purity. I was so scared, but now I am not. I have you. I will always have you."

"Damn right you will." His hands grabbed my face, and his mouth covered mine. "Come, wife, you must eat and feed our child. I had Charles put all the Markers in your secret room. After we eat, we need to go and check them out."

"Oh, I know. I cannot wait to see them. What do they look like?"

"They are just stones, but each one has a symbol on it."

"Different symbols?"

He nodded. We finished our meal and made our way down to my study, where he bolted the door before we went to the secret room. My lace gown was on the desk, wrapped in a cloth. Charles made sure he did not disturb it, though I am sure that he looked at it. I could not help but smile at what he must have thought.

"Something funny?" Blake asked, his eyes following mine to the cloth. "What is that?" He moved toward the desk.

"Oh, nothing, just never you mind. It is a surprise."

He laughed as he picked up the Markers. "I will carry these. Can you grab those there?"

I picked up the two that were left. They did not look it, but they were very heavy.

We laid them on the floor. Their size was a little bigger than my hand, more like the size of Blake's. Each Marker had a design on it.

"Do we know who brought which Marker?"

"No, but it would not hurt to ask if anyone remembered. Why? Do you think it has some significance?"

I shook my head. "I am not sure. Thank you," I said, turning to him.

"Does this mean you are asking me to leave you?"

I smiled. "I never want you to leave me."

He laughed, saying, "I will go check and see if anyone remembers which Marker they brought." He kissed me and left me in the room alone with the Markers.

I stood there looking at them for a moment, then I walked in a circle around them, picking one up and moving it to another spot. I did this until Blake returned. He did not speak, just watched me. When I placed the last Marker, only then did I stop moving in a circle. I stood there looking at them then stepped in the middle, and one of them began glowing behind me. As I turned to look at it, I noticed it had a symbol that looked like a flame. *This will be the one I face when we go to the center of the land.*

"Well, that was interesting," Blake said.

I did not look up. "Yes, it was, and each one of these symbols on these Markers means something. This one," I pointed to the one that glowed, "is the one I face when I begin."

"What do those symbols mean?"

"I am not sure yet. Did you talk to everyone?"

"I did, and they all remember which one they picked up."

"Good, this is good. I think this is the order in which they are placed around the circle."

"I am going to go jump off the roof of the castle."

"Do not be silly, Blake. You will break your neck. Now, each of you is supposed to bring forth the Marker you carried. The problem is, I do not know which Marker belongs to whom."

"So you are listening to me then?"

I turned and smiled at him. "I always listen to you."

He laughed and grabbed me, pulling me close to him, well as close as my stomach would allow, and kissed me. "I will leave you to figure this out. I have some things to do and a niece to attend to."

"How is Julia?"

"She is still very angry. She needs to bathe, so I have to hang on to her while they bring the tub in and fill it with water. She tried to attack one of the kitchen girls." He chuckled. "That girl has a great deal of spirit."

"Well, it will all be over soon enough, and we will see if Christopher survives."

Just then, Juliana knocked on the door. "Blake said you wanted to know which stone I brought back."

"I do, yes. Thank you."

She walked around the circle. "It was this one," she stated, pointing to the one with the flame that glowed when I faced it.

"Thank you. Do you know which one James brought back?"

"No, but I will have everyone come in. I was going for a walk anyway."

"Thank you, my love."

As she was leaving, Westin and Camille came in.

"I brought this one," Westin said. It was the one with the X on it, and Camille's had an arrow on it.

"This is good. Thank you so much. I think you all need to bring forth the Markers you received. Blake, which one did you bring?"

"This one." He pointed to the one with the sideways square on it. He kissed me then, saying, "I have some things to do. I will be back later." He left with Westin and Camille.

I stood there wondering what it all meant. Then the tome popped into my head. I turned to look at the tapestry and smiled. Popping the latch, I made my way to the tome. When I opened it, the first words were glowing. I smiled then, knowing it was ready to be read. Picking it up, I carried it to my desk and placed it down. I sat and took a deep breath before opening the book.

The Coming

The Markers of Time are the Markers of the Elders

Each with its own sign to be placed in the order

Twelve paces by the Heir from the center to the North

Place the Marker of Kenaz the Vital Fire of Life

Twelve paces to the East

Place the Marker of Algiz the Shield of Protection

Twelve paces continuing the circle

Place the Marker of Wunjo the Joy and Comfort

Twelve paces past

Place the Marker of Ansuz the Harmony Truth and Wisdom

Twelve paces past

Place the Marker of Raidho the Rhythm

Twelve paces past

Place the Marker of Nauthiz the Endurance and Survival

Twelve paces past Twelve paces past to the South

Place the Marker of Ingwaz the Love

Twelve paces past

Place the final Marker of Ehwaz the Harmony trust and Loyalty

Twelve paces past

Place the Marker of Mannz the Skill and Ability

Twelve paces past in the circle West

Place the Marker of Tiwaz the Honor Justice and Victory

Twelve paces past

Place the Marker of Gebo the Sacrifice and Generosity

Twelve paces past

Place the Marker of Eihwaz the Strength Trustworthiness and Protection

I sat back in my chair, absorbing what I had just read. The Markers of Time were the Markers of the Elders. The Coming was just that, the Coming of the Elders, and I was to be the channel. I was the center Marker, so they would come through me to seal the land. I looked at my hands and watched them shaking.

I saw something move and looked up, seeing Westin. He was to me before I had a chance to blink. Westin pulled me into his arms.

"It will be all right, Sabine. I promise."

I cried. I was terrified. "What about our baby?"

"Your baby is the channel, Sabine. You are the magic that brings them all together. Do not be frightened."

I needed to anywhere but where I was. I needed to ride, to be free. Pushing away from Westin, I took off running, which was not an easy feat, being ready to have a baby, but I managed to get to the stables just fine. I led Raiden out to the courtyard and used the steps that Blake had made for me to climb on him. I leaned in as best I could and said, "I need to be free. Do what you can to not hurt the baby."

We were gone. Blake saw me fly out of the village and onto the plain. He tried to catch me, but Raiden was flying. *I cannot handle this. My child is the channel.* It made me wonder if the baby was Blake's after all. *Did they just somehow magically put this child inside of me? We love it. Is my baby the sacrifice the tome spoke of?*

Raiden slowed down once we got to the little river. I could not get down because I would not be able to get back up alone. I leaned my stomach over his side, lay my head on his great neck, and cried. *I cannot do this. I cannot sacrifice our child, my child.* It was asking too much of me.

So much I had given up, so much I had lost already. It was my destiny, so they said, though it had been nothing but a burden, and now, I might very well have to give the life inside of me for my happiness.

I shook my head and screamed, "Nooooo!"

I did not hear Spirit slide to a stop.

Blake pulled me from Raiden, and I collapsed in his arms in a fit of tears, rage, and fear. Beating him in the chest with my fists, I screamed again. "No, I will not do it!" He held me close as we sank to the grass. He rocked me and held me while I shook, while I cried and screamed.

As I started to calm down, his hold on me lessoned. "My love," he whispered.

"I will not do it, Blake. I will not, and no one can make me do this."

"It might help if I knew what the matter was."

I pushed away from him, stood up, and began walking back and forth. "I believe I am expected to sacrifice our child for this Coming. Each Marker is the Marker of an Elder. I am the magic, and our child is the channel. Through our baby and me, this Coming is to happen. I have given my life to this, but I will not give my child."

"Sabine, they would not want you to give your child as a sacrifice. I do not believe it. Why would you think that?"

"Each Marker has a name associated with it, and each name has a meaning. I am to put them in order around the circle. Each time I place one, the magic gets stronger. Once I place the last stone, it begins. I will be in the middle with our child. The energy alone could kill us both. I do not care if my life ends to save everyone, but I will not sacrifice our child."

He sat there looking at me, shaking his head. "How can this be truth? How can it be expected of you to give so much of yourself? And now, the life you carry within you is to be given to whatever this Coming is?"

"Westin said it would be all right, that I had nothing to fear. He was there when I finished reading about the Markers. I put the rest together myself. I will not do this, Blake." I was getting angry now. My fear was being overridden by my anger. "After everything I have lost, everything I have done for this stupid legend, I am now expected to pay the ultimate price." I shook my head. "I will not do it."

He stood and held me. "We will find a way out of this, my love. I will not allow you to put yourself in harm's way. Come, we can think about this all later. Come home with me, and we will have a nice warm bath and talk it over. You can tell me everything you know. We will get through this together."

I nodded into his chest. He lifted me onto Raiden, and we made our way back to the castle. I stopped by my study to put away the Markers and the tome.

Blake went to close the book, and I heard him say, "Uh!"

I turned to look at him. "What?"

He looked up at me. "I can read this."

I dropped the Markers to the floor and went to him. "You can see the words?"

He nodded and started reading aloud. I could not tell you why I was crying, but I was. He read everything I read. I put my hand on his to stop him from turning the next page. "I have not read that yet. Do you think you can read the others?"

We both looked at the tapestry, and the next thing I knew, we were in the secret room. He opened each tome, and each tome allowed him to read it. He was learning all that I had learned. I sat quietly at the desk and watched him walk back and forth reading. As he finished one book, he would look at me then pick up the next.

When he finished them all, he stood in the center of the room, just looking at me. We did not speak. We closed the secret room and went to our room, where we lay in our bed and held one another. *He knows now. He knows all of it, everything I am to do. All that I know, he knows.*

I fell asleep, but Blake did not sleep. He lay in bed holding me, thinking over all that he had read.

When I woke, he was looking at me. He gently moved my hair off my face and smiled at me.

"I do not think we are to sacrifice our child. I have been thinking all night about this. I think the Marker represents the sacrifice we have already made. I do not believe that, with everything you have done, our child would be the price we pay for our happiness. Sabine, when you ended Kelvin, they came to save you and the baby. Your mother promised it would be all right. You... no, we need to trust her. She loves you very much, enough to bring you back from death, not once but twice."

"Yes, but it was only to finish this and seal the land, whatever that means."

"I believe it means that no evil will ever get in, at least not in our lifetime. It said only those with pure hearts would be able to enter, and the dark would turn to ash. You said it yourself concerning Christopher."

I looked at him; he was right. "I think being with child has clouded my mind. I know it has weakened me."

He laughed. "Well, that is to be expected, my love. You are growing another person within you. You should be weaker and more vulnerable. Besides, I like having to take care of you. I enjoy that you need me for things. It is very difficult being your husband." He smiled. "It is a husband's duty to protect and care for his wife, not the other way around."

"I like that you care for me and that you protect me."

He laughed and pulled me close. "It is an illusion. That is for sure. We have a great deal to do. What we need to do is figure out who brought what Marker, so when it is time, everyone can be where they are supposed to be."

"We know which ones Camille, Westin, you, and Juliana brought forth. The time is coming, and fast. Thank you for doing this, for helping me, for making me feel more relaxed about it."

He kissed me. "I would not for one moment allow anything to happen to you or our child. It would make no sense for us to have lived through all that we have and come out of this with nothing."

I leaned forward and kissed him. He gently rolled me over, placing his hands on my stomach and holding our baby.

"I love you," he whispered into my mouth.

"I love you," I whispered back.

We got dressed actually, he dressed me. I was finding it very difficult to do anything with such a huge stomach in front of me. I could no longer put my own shoes on, and bending down was near impossible. Our child would be coming soon. I should talk to Clare about making me some clothes for it. "My love, will you stop by Clare's on your way to do whatever it is you do during the day, and ask her if she could come by today? I am not really up to walking over to her cottage."

"I will indeed. Is this about what is under that cloth?"

I turned to look at him in a panic. "You did not look, did you?"

He smiled. "No, I would not do that. I would not take away your surprise."

"Thank you, and please stay true to your word."

"You can trust me." He chuckled and shook his head.

We made our way down to the kitchen to eat. I missed seeing Julia at the table. I inquired as to how she was doing.

"She is still fighting," Camille said.

Blake laughed. "Yes, she is like her mother." We all laughed then.

Westin did not say much, as he was deep in thought. He looked at me a few times with his not Westin look.

"Well, I have some things to take of and a book to read. I will be in my study if anyone needs me. Blake, please do not forget about Clare."

"I am going there right now," he said then kissed me.

I made my way to the study and sat in the chair by the window. Westin came in.

"How are you doing?" he asked in his not Westin voice.

"I am better now. Blake is able to read the tomes, so he calmed me down. I am sorry about yesterday."

"It is fine. Are you ready for this?"

"I think I am. Are you?"

"I am ready to not be this simple minded man anymore."

"Yes, I like this brother, but I love the other, as well. It will take some getting used to. Will you still play your jokes?"

He laughed. "I will always play my jokes. I am worried about Julia and Christopher. What if he has a pure heart, Sabine? He will want to marry Julia."

"He cannot marry her without my approval, or without yours. I am the Queen. Hey, when this is over, you can be the King again."

He laughed. "I do not want to be King, Sabine. It has always been your crown."

"Well, you can have it if you want it."

"No, thank you. I like being who I am."

"Do not worry, brother. I will not give my consent to allow them to wed. We will figure it all out."

He grabbed my hand, just as there was a knock on the door. It was Clare, so Westin kissed me on the cheek and bid us farewell.

"Oh my goodness, Sabine, you have gotten so big!"

I laughed. "I know, but soon, it will be over. Then I will not feel like a cow."

She smiled. "You do not look like a cow. You are very beautiful, and you are glowing. It is so wonderful for you and Blake. I could not be happier for you."

"Well, thank you, Clare. Listen, I was wondering if you could make some clothes for this little one, and a few blankets, as well. I have nothing. The warm months are coming, but he or she will still be a baby when the cold months come, so I am going to keep you very busy. Oh, and thank you so much for making those gowns for Sarah's daughter. I saw her playing, and she seems to be adjusting well."

"Yes, she is a sweet girl, despite everything that happened to her."

We visited for a while longer, and then she left to get busy on the new baby clothing. Deciding to finish the tome, I went to the secret room and picked up the book. As I was leaving, I caught a glimpse of the cloth. I walked over, sat the book down, and pulled it back to look at the lace sleeping gown wrapped inside. I could not help but wonder if I was ever going to wear it. Would Blake and I ever have a real union between us or would we just continue the way we were? I shook my head and put the cloth back, then picked up the book and turned to leave, when Blake was standing there watching me.

"Hello," I said.

He smiled. "Hello. Are you ever going to tell me what is in the cloth?"

"One day I hope to, yes, but right now, no, it is best left covered. I am going to read the tome. Would you like to read with me?" I started to walk to him.

"You look so sad, my love. Are you sure you are all right?"

"I am sure. Clare is going to start making the baby some clothes."

"Would it not be best to wait and see if it is a boy or a girl?"

I laughed. "It will not matter at first."

We left the secret room, leaving my secret gown inside. One day, I wanted to wear it for him.

I sat the tome on my desk. "You want to read or no?"

"I think you should read it first, and alone. I will wait in the sitting room." He kissed my forehead and left me alone.

I opened the book and turned to the page I had left off at.

The Heir and the Unknown Heir in the center makes the circle complete

Bringing forth the forged to the sky

Drawing the light from the dark of the night

The words said are hidden within

"This must be the scroll that Blake found."

Bringing forth the Elders through the Unknown Heir

The Unknown Heir is the knowledge needed to seal the land

The Keeper welcomes them with his words of old

The Elders bring forth the seal

When the seal is complete, the Unknown Heir will be born from purity

The lineage of the Elders is completed and renewed to begin again

Settling the land, giving happiness to all who dwell

Evil will rest for eternity and Good will reign

Life will span in time

F

T

T

T

T

I sat there looking at the last line, but it made no sense. It was as if some of the words were missing. I turned the page, but there was nothing. Closing the book, I sat back in my chair and stared at the map, shaking my head. I was at a loss for thought. In just days would begin the fortnight of the lights in the sky.

Putting the tome away, I looked at my gown again. Someday, I hoped to wear it. I was coming out of the secret room when Blake came in. I looked at him and smiled.

"Did you finish it?" he asked.

I nodded and walked up to him, wrapping my arms around his waist. "I am tired, husband... scared, tired, hungry, and fat."

He laughed. "You are not fat. You are ripe with our child, my love."

"I know, but I feel so huge. How can one person be so big? This baby is huge," I said, sighing.

"Yes, she is a big girl. That is for sure."

"If this is a girl, she is going to be a beast." I chuckled. "I believe it to be a boy, and a big boy at that, just like his father."

He laughed. "Come, wife, let me feed you and then take you to bed."

"To sleep?"

He laughed again. "Yes, my love, to sleep. We do not have much time left before we will not be sleeping at all."

We left my study and went to our room. Blake went to the kitchen to get us something to eat, while I tried to get out of my gown. It was terrible. I could not even reach behind myself to untie it. Blake came in and laughed while he watched me struggle.

"Let me help you," he finally offered, laughing.

"I cannot wait until I have my body back," I said frustrated.

375

He untied me and then helped me put my sleeping gown on. I climbed on the bed and ate until I could not take another bite. He cleared away the tray, then took off his clothes and climbed into bed with me. I curled up in my favorite spot with my head on his chest, so his heartbeat could lull me to sleep, and sleep we did, for the entire dark of the night and most of the light of the following day. It was just about the evening meal time when I woke to find him looking at me with yet another tray of food.

"Hello, beautiful girl," he greeted me

"Mmmm, is that food I smell?"

"It is, and lots of it. Apparently, we slept the day away. It is in fact time for the evening meal."

"Good, can we eat and go back to sleep? I do not want to get up."

He smiled as he set the tray down and lifted the lid. It smelled wonderful, and I stuffed my face yet again. He curled up with me, and I quickly went back to sleep.

When I woke, it was in fact the light of the day. I was alone in our room, so I sat up and decided I would get dressed to go out for a nice walk for some fresh air. I was putting on my gown when he came in.

"Here let me help you," he said.

He reached down, running his hands down my sides to grab my gown. Slowly, he pulled it down over my stomach, stopping long enough to hug our baby, kissing me on the neck. My hands came around to rest on his thighs. He let go of my gown with one hand and reached for my face, turning it so he could kiss me. I turned in his arms and wrapped my arms around his waist, placing my hands on his bottom, kissing him deeply. We would have ended up back in our bed, but there was a knock on the door. We parted breathlessly.

"Who is it?" Blake asked, trying to catch his breath.

"It is Camille."

"Just a minute, Camille," I said as Blake pulled my gown the rest of the way down. His eyes sparkled, and I could not help but kiss him again. Once we separated, I said, "Come in." Blake turned me to tie my gown.

"Oh, I am sorry," she said as she turned to leave.

"No, it is fine, Camille," Blake told her as he tied the last tie.

"I will be at the barracks. Come find me and we can go for a nice walk," he said as he left.

"Sabine, can we talk?"

"Of course we can. Come sit." We walked to the chairs by the fireplace. "What is the matter?"

"Julia," she said. "She has refused to eat, and she just lies on the bed and does not speak to anyone."

I smiled. "She is trying to make you let her out. She will not starve herself. This is almost over, Camille. I cannot have her running off and looking for Christopher, or trying to hurt me. I do not want to hurt her. I love her, but I am afraid I would be forced to defend myself."

"I know. I am just worried."

"When I was younger, I got in a fight with my father and hid in the tower for three days with no food. The only reason I came down was because I was so hungry. She will eat. Just keep putting the food there."

"That is what Westin told me. I want to let her out, Sabine. She is my only daughter, and I miss her."

"I know, Camille, but right now, none of us need this distraction. Please, be patient with this. I promise, the minute it is over, I will give you the key so you can let her out."

"I know you will. I am sorry. I am just worried."

I squeezed her hand. "She will be fine."

Camille got up, and we walked to the great doors together. She went her way, and I made my way to the barracks. The guards sitting at the door stood when I walked up.

"Your Majesty," one said as he bowed.

I smiled. "Would you be so kind as to go find Blake for me?"

"Your Majesty, he is not here. There was a problem in the village, and they all went to see what was going on."

"Oh, all right. Thank you," I told him as I wandered over to the gates. I could see them all in the center of the lane just past Clare's, though I could not make out what was happening, so I started walking toward them. I was just about to Sarah's shop when I heard yelling. I tried to hear what they were saying, but I was too far away. As I moved to Clare's, I heard someone call me a witch. I tilted my head and took a few steps closer.

"You are breeding witches! How is it possible to allow a witch to have a child?" someone shouted.

"Be very careful how you speak of our Queen," Charles said.

"What are you going to do, put me to death for saying what I believe? Oh, yes..." The person turned to face those behind him. "The witch has cast a spell upon these men, so they defend her." He turned back to Charles. "We are the people, and we demand that she be burned at the stake!"

I raised my eyebrows, and without me telling them, my feet started to move. I was a few steps away from Blake when the man began pointing at me and yelled, "There she is, the witch! Look at how huge she is! There is a demon within her!"

Blake turned and looked at me. "Go back to the castle," he said.

I smiled at him. "And miss all this fun?" I said sarcastically.

The man grabbed Blake's dagger before anyone knew what was happening, and he ran toward me with it raised in the air. He was just two steps from me when Blake's sword appeared through the front of his chest. The man's hand came down and cut my arm, and I stood there, watching the blood pour from the wound. When I looked up, Blake was there. I looked past him to the crowd that had gathered.

"Do you all feel the same as this man?" I demanded.

An uproar of yells proceeded, and then they moved on me. It was a flurry of swords and shouts of anger. Blake shielded me the best that he could. I heard Rebecca scream my name, and I turned just as she shoved my sword in my hand. Spinning around, I began to fight them off. When it was finished, they were all dead in the lane of the village in my peaceful Kingdom.

Blake was not happy at all. "You are to go the castle and remain there until I return."

I looked at him, and I do not know what happened or why, but I giggled.

"Sabine, do not argue with me. Go now." He was so cute when he was angry.

"My love, you should probably calm down before that vein in your neck bursts. I am fine."

"You are bleeding," he said as he grabbed my arm to show me. When I looked down, there was no mark on my arm. We stood there looking at one another, and I shrugged my shoulders as he wiped the blood away and found nothing there. "Please, will you go back to the castle?"

I stood on the tips of my toes and kissed him. "That is much better," I said as I turned to walk away. I looked back at him, and he smiled at me and shook his head. By the time I got comfortable in the big chair in my study, Blake was at the door.

"What were you doing out there?" he asked as he came in, looking at my arm again.

"You told me to come and find you so we could go for a walk."

"How are you not cut?"

"I do not know, but apparently, I heal rather quickly these days. What was that about?"

"Some men were getting everyone riled up in the village, saying you are a witch, that you are possessed by a demon, and that our baby is a demon. They wanted to burn you at the stake after they cut the demon out of you. You know, the usual stuff."

I could not contain my laughter. "Seriously?" I managed to get out.

"We were trying to get them calmed down, and then you showed up, and well, that man wanted to kill you. I thought it best they did not see that you cannot die, so I had to kill him. You know, even with this baby here, I still would not want to go around with you and that sword."

"Scared, are you?" I giggled.

He pulled me to my feet and covered my mouth with his. "Damn right I am," he said into my mouth as he covered it again.

Charles cleared his throat. "Are you all right, Sabine," he asked.

I laughed. "Apparently, I heal miraculously nowadays. Charles, how do people like this get into this Kingdom?"

"Sabine, there are a great many people in the village now, and there are always men who do not believe that a woman should rule them, so they find all sorts of reasons to defy."

I looked at Blake, my mind made up. "All right, that settles it." I got up. "Both of you, stay here." I walked out and went upstairs to my parents' room, where I got my father's crown. Going back into my study, I said, "Blake, would you please kneel before me?" He did. "With this crown, I make you my King." I placed it on his head. "You will now hold the title of King of Whispering Wind, and as the Queen, I give this right to you." I turned and looked at Charles. "Please spread the word that this Kingdom now has a King."

He bowed and said, "Your Majesties." Then he chuckled softly and left.

Blake stood. "You did not need to do that."

"Well, it would seem that all of this fuss is about a woman ruling this Kingdom, so what better way to stop it all then to make you a King? I will be busy with the baby anyway, and I really do not want to be a ruling Queen. I will still be Queen, but you can do the ruling part."

He put his arms around me. "You will never stop being my Queen, or ruling me for that matter. But what if I do not want to be King?"

I looked at him and put my lower lip out. "But I do not want to be the Queen anymore. Please?"

He laughed loudly then. "Do not tease me, woman," he said as he covered my mouth with his.

Westin cleared his throat. "May I come in?"

We both laughed. "Of course," I said.

"I see we have a new King," he said, bowing and laughing. "It is good that you have given him his place in all of this."

I crinkled my eyes. "What does that mean?"

"You read the tomes. He is to be King."

"I did not read that in the tomes. The last pages would not allow me to read them."

"Well, there you go. I guess I told you something you do not know." He smiled. "Blake is to be King of Whispering Wind." He shook Blake's hand. "I am just glad it is not me, brother." We laughed. "I heard of the trouble in the village. Is everything all right? I heard you were stabbed, Sabine."

I looked at my arm. "I was, yes, but it seems to have healed itself."

"That is good. I am here to let you know that this is the last night before the lights of the fortnight begin. Remember what the tome said?"

"Time will stand still just as when time began. The current will light the dark of the night for a fortnight. No sound shall pass through this enchanted time."

"Do you understand what that means?"

I smiled at him. "That time will stand still for a fortnight and there will be no sound. Even our voices will be gone?"

"No sound. I just want you prepared. When the dark of the night comes tomorrow, it will begin. If you need to communicate, we will need to write things down." He smiled. "Now, I am going to go and find my wife. She is having a hard time with Julia being gone."

"I know. I am so sorry, Westin."

"Do not worry, Sabine. She only has a fortnight left." He smiled and left.

I turned to Blake. "So you were supposed to be the King all along?"

He stood up and smiled at me. "This is not necessary. I am honored that you did this, but I am not so sure it should be this way."

I walked into his arms. "I asked you that day in our room to move in with me and to be my King. So now, I have made you King. You are of royal blood, and you should have a Kingdom to go with it."

He laughed. "You do realize that you just gave me a Kingdom. I cannot top that one."

"You gave me something no other man could give me."

"What is that?"

I stepped back, resting my hand on my stomach. "You gave me our child, and you gave me this." I put my hand on his heart. "These are the only things I ever really wanted."

His hands came up to my face, and he kissed me so sweetly. "You are the only thing I ever wanted. The rest is just gravy." We laughed.

Chapter Nineteen

Charles declared throughout the kingdom that Blake was now the King, and he was received well among the people. He would make a wonderful King. Blake was kind like my father, reasonable and good.

The next day went by very slowly. We waited for the dark of the night to come, which seemed to take forever.

But as the light of the day left, an eerie calm fell over the land. I was in my study when the light disappeared. Blake came in, and there was no sound. He motioned with his hand for me to follow him, and he was smiling. We walked into the kitchen, where Francis was standing by the fire, but she was not moving. The flame in the fire was not moving. I looked at Blake, and he was still smiling.

We walked out the back door, where Charles and the brothers were all standing, looking at the sky. Westin, Camille, and Juliana were there. I followed their gaze to the sky. What I saw was unbelievable.

The sky was lit up with an eerie incredible purple color that seemed to dance across it. We stood there for a very long time watching it. I touched Charles on the arm and mouthed 'Rebecca' to him. He shook his head, telling me she would not get to see this.

Blake took my hand and led me to the great gates so I could look out into the village. Everyone seemed frozen in time. The tome said that time would stand still during this time of lights in the dark of the night. We stood there looking into each other's eyes. This was magic, pure and simple magic. Whatever this place was, Whispering Wind was magic.

It was hard to sleep, knowing that all those people, Rebecca included, were frozen in time, even the animals and the horses, but not Raiden or Spirit. We were the only ones who could move through time. Blake held me, but the rhythm of his heart was not soothing like it normally was. I felt a bit strange.

The light of the day came fast for me, even though I did not sleep. I got up and went to the window, where I was shocked to see the people coming back to life. I turned to Blake, finding him looking at me.

"How is this possible?" I said, surprised I could speak.

"I do not know, my love, but what I do know is that you did not sleep."

"How do you know that?"

"Because I did not sleep. I am worried about what is to come."

I smiled at him. "We cannot do anything about what is to come. I am scared, Blake, very scared."

He was next to me before I finished speaking. "I will not let anything happen to you, my love."

"You will not be able to stop it, Blake. No one will." He wrapped his arms around me and held me close. "That was day one. We have thirteen more to go," I told him.

"Then I think we should enjoy these days the best we can." He kissed me. "I think we should make sure that those we love are at least in bed before the dark of the night comes again. I know we cannot tell them what is happening, but it was a bit scary to see Francis just standing by the fire like that. I wonder what she thought when time began again."

We got dressed and went down for the morning meal. I noticed that Francis was out of sorts. "Is everything all right, Francis?" I asked.

"I am not sure. I just feel like I have not slept."

"Well, why not take a rest this afternoon. We can fend for ourselves."

"Perhaps I will, child. Are you sure that would be all right?"

"I am. Go on. We will be fine."

She smiled at me and left. I looked at Blake. "This is going to be hard on all of us."

"I think you are right. Will you promise me something?"

"Anything, my love," I promised, smiling at him.

"If at any time you get tired, will you please sleep?"

"Yes, I promise." We ate our meal then went for a walk around the courtyard.

Each day was the same; everyone was tired, but there was no explaining it. Thirteen days had passed, and it was the last day. We all gathered in my study.

"This is the night. We need to get to the center of the land long before the break of the day. Once the dark of the night comes, I think it would be safe for us to go. Everyone must come and get the stone they brought back. I will have Raiden and Spirit take each of you out there, and then I will be the last to go."

We all agreed, and as everyone was leaving, I asked Westin to stay.

He closed the door and turned to face me. "Tonight, everyone will know about me," he stated.

"I know. Are you all right with that?"

He laughed. "Oh, Sabine, I have waited for this night for longer than you know. I finally get to be myself and have real conversations with people. I think I might open a shop or something. I made the sheath for your sword, and I enjoyed that, so maybe I will go into leather work." He happened to see my face. "Sabine, are you scared?"

"I am terrified, Westin. I am afraid for the baby."

He smiled. "The baby will be fine, Sabine. I promise."

"I know you keep saying that, but what is required of me puts this child in grave danger."

"I know you think that, but that is not the case. You will see, my love." He pulled me into his arms and held me for a moment before he left.

I sat in the chair and found myself crying. This was my last day. I put my hand on the baby in my belly. This was its last day. This night, according to the tomes, my baby would be born into peace.

I did not hear Blake come in, nor did I realize he was there, until he put his hand on my arm. "What is the matter, my love?"

I looked at him, then climbed into his lap and sobbed. He held us and rocked us. "Today is our last day," I cried. "Tonight, our baby will be born. I am so scared, Blake. I do not know if I can do this. What if it dies? What if I die?"

He pulled me close. "You cannot believe for a moment, Sabine, that you will die. Your mother promised you happiness. She has brought you back from death two times."

"Yes, but it was allowed so I could finish this, so the land could be sealed. Once it is done, what is the point to have me here?"

"Oh, my love, no matter what happens, I will be with you. No matter what, I will never leave you."

He held me for a long time. I think I might have even fallen asleep in his arms. When I woke, he was still sitting on the floor with me in his arms.

"I am sorry," I whispered.

He chuckled. "Why would you be sorry?"

"For being a baby and for crying all the time."

"There is no reason to say you are sorry. What is going to happen is huge for all of us. No one knows what will happen. What I do know is that you need to eat. We are going to be out there for a very long time, and the dark of the night will be here soon." I got up and helped him. His legs were wobbly from sitting with my giant self on him.

We went to the kitchen, where we found everyone eating. We sat at the table, and Francis brought us our food. I could not help but notice the light of the day moving across the door. I looked at Westin, and he nodded.

Everyone said good night, and I sent Francis on to bed. Blake and I went to stand in the back courtyard. It was quite spectacular to watch the day turn to night, and then the lights dance across the sky. On this night, they were a beautiful pinkish-red color, and I wondered briefly what color Boland would call it.

As we stood there, one by one, they came Charles, Steven, Aiden, James, Juliana, Joseph, Westin, Camille, Edward, Raiden, and Spirit. We all stood with our heads turned to the sky, none of us knowing if we would be around to see the light of the day come again.

After a while, we all went to my study, where each of them took their Markers. Blake and I then went upstairs so I could change my clothes and get my crown and my sword. I also penned a note to Rebecca, just in case I did not make it back. Sitting in the chair by the fire, I wrote.

My Beautiful Sister Rebecca,

I do not know what the future holds for me. I just know what you mean to me. You have been the greatest friend, my only sister in this mad life we have shared. We have lost one another to death, and we have gained one another in life. I would not be who I am today without you being a part of this life with me. I love you so much. If I do not come back, I want you to take care of my child. Help Blake through this. He says he will not live in this world without me, so if that is the case, I am trusting my child to you and Charles. You are the only one I would. Know that I have always loved you, and even in death, you are in my heart.

Always, Sabine

I folded the note, wrote her name on it, and sat it on the table next to my bed. Blake watched me. "You all right?"

I was shocked to hear his voice, "I thought we couldn't hear any sound."

"Perhaps it is because it is the last night."

I nodded answering his question. "I will be all right. If anything happens to me, I have asked Rebecca to help you with our child. If you choose to end your life to be with me, I have asked her to raise our child with Charles. Is that all right with you?"

"Of course it is, but we will all be coming home when this is over. Come on, my love. Everyone is already on their way."

I took his hand and picked up my sword. At the door, I turned to take one last look at our room, at our life. He smiled at me, and we walked down the hall to the grand staircase. Once out in the courtyard, we waited for Raiden and Spirit. James and Juliana, and Westin and Camille were all who remained. After they were gone, it was just Blake and I left. He held me in his arms while we waited. The horses arrived, and Blake helped me up. Raiden took his time, and when we got to the edge of the village, I turned him so I could have one last look at my home.

Sitting there, I recalled everything that had happened the memories that were made, the lives that were lost, my life, Rebecca's life, Blake's life. My family died there; it was my home. Blake touched my hand. "We will return, my love." I nodded, and we took off.

When we arrived at the center of the land Raiden, walked over and slammed his hoof into the ground a few times, making a mark.

"This is the center?" I asked him, and he nodded his head. "Can you tell me which way is north?" He turned his body so his head was facing north. "Thank you."

I looked at everyone. "You all ready for this?" They nodded.

I turned to face north and took twelve steps. "Juliana, would please bring me your Marker?" She handed it to me, and I placed it on the ground, where it began to glow. "Stand here, facing the center." Looking at her I whispered, "My love, I will always love you." Juliana reached up to touch my hands as I turned to the east and took twelve steps, starting the circle. "Raiden, I need your Marker." He walked over and dropped it out of his mouth into my hand. I placed on the ground it glowed. "Now, you must stand here facing the center." He nodded. Reaching up I touched his neck. "No matter what happens, I love you." He put his head on my shoulder and I hugged him. I turned and took twelve more steps. "Edward." He brought his Marker to me, and I placed it on the ground. He nodded, letting me know that he knew what to do. Twelve more steps around the circle. "Joseph." Twelve more. "Aiden." Twelve more. "James." Twelve more, making half of the circle complete. "Blake, my love." He handed me his Marker, and after I placed his on the ground, it rumbled. I looked up at him. "I love you. No matter what happens, I love you."

"I will love you always," he said and kissed me hard.

I pulled away and put my hand on his face as I turned to take twelve more steps. "Camille." Twelve more. "Steven." Twelve more. "Charles." When I placed his Marker, the ground rumbled again. Twelve more. "Westin." Then I took the last twelve steps to make a complete circle. "Spirit."

I turned in a circle to look at them all. "I love each of you. No matter what happens, I am glad I have had you in my life." I wiped the tear from my cheek and made my way to the center.

Before I stepped on my spot, I looked at Blake. He looked as scared as I felt. "I love you," I said to him.

"I love you, beautiful girl."

I stepped on my mark and turned north to face Juliana. The ground started to rumble. I looked to the east and waited for the sky to start to change as the light of the day began. I was so scared of what was going to happen. I did not want to do this. I did not want to sacrifice my baby, our baby. Blake was so scared. He said that he would be with me even in death, but when I was dead, there was nothing. Maybe that was because I was not really dead but in some kind of place between life and death. I could only remember feeling love and warmth. I wanted to look at him, but I needed to keep my eyes on the sky. I had to finish this, no matter what the price. I was the chosen one, the legend, whatever that meant. I was so tired of living in this fear, living and fighting. There was no happiness here. Even when I was with Blake, it lasted only for the moment we were in. The peace I felt while sitting on that hilltop that is the peace I wanted.

No matter what I had to do to get it, I would. *Mother, if you can hear my thoughts, please let my baby live. Let us all come out of this alive.* I heard him in my head.

'Begin'

I drew my circle in the ground around me, and the ground began rumbling beneath me. As I looked up at Blake, he looked as terrified as I was. When the circle was complete, I heard him again.

'Now'

I stepped forward toward Juliana and began to say the necessary lines as I walked in a circle.

"In this place, this circle round
I consecrate the sacred ground
With golden light this space surround
All power here contained and bound."

The ground shook uncontrollably. Coming full circle, I chanted the next lines.

"From earth, the things that manifest
From air, the things of mind
From fire, the things that motivate
From water, the souls refined."

The sky was lighting up, but it was not from the light of the day. As I started the third circle, continuing with the words I had to speak, I could feel the energy.

"And yet no place or time there be
Between the worlds, my word, and me
Welcome, Ancient Ones and see
This place is sealed."

I stepped on my mark and touched my sword to the ground.

"So Below…"

I raised it to the sky as the energy swirled around me.

"As Above…"

The energy from the night lights swirled to a point and touched my sword. The stones lit up, and I saw them, all twelve of the Elders of this land. They came to me, standing in a circle around me.

I heard Westin's voice.

"Earth by divinity, divinity by earth

The Elders here, the elements here

I call upon the Elders twelve,

I call upon the elements four,

The strength of the elements by my side

The strength of the Elders in our time

Use your power to shield this land,

Protect it from harm and any plight,

Use your strength and all your might

Hide it so none can see

This is my will, so make it be

In no way shall this reverse

In this place, this circle round

I consecrate the sacred ground."

When he finished, I felt the energy flow through me from my feet to the tip of my sword and fly out into the sky. I looked up, seeing the barrier forming from the energy. It spread through the sky as the light of the day turned it the color of my hair, then it began to fall to the ground. Each Elder touched my stomach while I stood there holding my sword in the air as the barrier

394

touched the ground. Then they all moved away, and just as it started, they were gone.

The flash of light knocked me down, slamming me to the ground. The Markers disappeared when I fell, and a gut wrenching pain shot through my stomach all the way down to my private parts. My hand grabbed my stomach as I yelled out. Blake was at my side.

"The baby," I said as another pain wracked through my body. I rolled onto my side. "It hurts. Something is wrong, Blake."

"I am here, my love. Hold on." He looked around for Westin. "What do we do?"

Westin was there, trying to help. "I do not know. Camille was never in this much pain."

Camille came over as I screamed out in pain again. "Sabine, you are having your baby. I need to get your pants off. Everyone, turn around. I need something to cover her with. Blake, help me get her undressed."

Juliana took off her gown. "Here, use this," she said as she handed it to Camille.

They managed to remove my clothing, and I heard Camille say to Blake, "She is still pure. This is not going to be easy on her. You have got to keep her calm." He nodded and moved to lay my head in his lap. "Sabine, I am going to have to check to see where the baby is." I nodded, and she looked under the gown, then I felt her hands on me. She looked at Westin. "How is this going to happen?"

"I do not know. I do not know," he said.

I screamed in pain again. "It hurts," I managed to say. Again, another piercing pain came, and I screamed out.

"Come on, beautiful girl. You can do this. After everything we have been through, you can do this."

I was crying, saying, "I cannot. It hurts," as I continued to scream out in pain. It did not take long before another pain came.

Camille said to Westin, "The baby should be ready, but it is not. What do we do?"

"You have to get it out!" Blake yelled.

I screamed again. The pain was so intense the darkness took over.

"Sabine! Sabine!" Blake was calling my name. "Camille, help her."

"I cannot, Blake. I do not know what is wrong. The baby should be coming, but I do not see it. I cannot feel it."

He looked at Westin then at Charles. "Help her. She is dying."

The soft amber glow filled the circle, and Westin stood to see them. They all took a step back, watching her as she knelt down next to Camille and placed her hands on my stomach. Closing her eyes, she ran her finger down the center of my stomach, not cutting me but opening my stomach. Her warmth I felt in my heart as she reached in and took out not one but two babies, handing one to Camille and one to Juliana. With the same motion, she closed me up. Looking at Blake, she said, "She must remain pure. There is a great evil coming." Then she looked at Westin. "Julia is in grave danger." She reached for my cheek and leaned in, kissing me on the forehead. "Your heirs await you," she whispered, and she was gone.

They all just stood there, looking at one another. Juliana and Camille were holding the babies. Juliana got down on her knees and placed the baby on my chest, and then Camille did the same with the other. Blake held them there. He was crying as I lay in his lap in the darkness with our children with us. When I did not awaken, they took the babies.

"Help me get her on Raiden," Blake said. Charles lifted me off the ground, while Blake climbed on Raiden. Charles and Westin handed me up to him.

Camille and Juliana climbed on Spirit, and James and Joseph handed them the babies. We were back at the castle quickly. Juliana gave the baby she was holding to Camille and helped Blake get me down. Together, we went into the castle and to our room, where he laid me on our bed. Camille and Juliana cleaned the babies and wrapped them in blankets, putting them on the bed next to me. Blake lay on the other side, with our children lying between us.

"You have a son and a daughter, Blake," Camille said.

He laid there with tears in his eyes, touching them.

The light of the day came, and the village came to life. Rebecca came flying into our room to see us in the bed. Charles was right behind her. "What happened?"

With tears running down his cheeks, he waved her over to see the babies. She was crying, as was Charles.

"Why is she sleeping?" Rebecca asked.

"The pain was too much, and she fell into the darkness. It just happened moments ago."

"Are you all right? Do you want me to take them so you can hold her?"

"No, I would just like to be alone with her if you do not mind."

"I will be right outside in the hall. They are beautiful, Blake."

"They look like their mother," he replied.

He laid there while our children slept, while I slept, holding his hand on my heart so he could make sure I was still with him. My heartbeat changed, and he propped himself up on his elbow, looking at me.

My eyes fluttered, and instinctively, my hand moved to my stomach. My bump was gone. "No, not the baby," I whispered. I felt his hand move, and I turned my head to see his beautiful face. He had tears in his eyes. "I am so sorry," I said. He shook his head and looked down. I followed his eyes to see our baby lying between us. My heart started beating faster, and I looked up at him.

"Hello, Momma," he whispered.

"What happened?"

"You went into the darkness, and you were dying. Your mother came when the Elders did, and she took the babies from within you."

"Babies? There are two babies?" I looked again. There were two babies sleeping wrapped in blankets between us. "Two?"

"Yes, my love, a boy and a girl." He smiled.

I giggled. "Two babies?" He nodded. I leaned over and kissed him. "Is it done?"

"It is done. We are safe in Whispering Wind."

I turned on my side to look at my children. They were so beautiful. She had hair the color of mine, and he had the same hair as Blake. "They look like us," I whispered and giggled. As I reached down to touch them, the little girl opened her eyes and grinned at me. Then I touched her brother, and he stretched. Blake and I giggled together. He put his finger on my chin, lifting my face to meet his beautiful green eyes.

"My heart is full of so much love it gives me great pain. You are the most incredible woman I have ever known." He then covered my mouth with his. His kiss was different. I do not remember him ever kissing me with such tenderness. I felt his tears on my cheek as we pulled apart, and he rested his forehead on mine as we looked into each other's eyes. "I love you, Sabine."

I nodded, too full of emotion to speak. One of the babies moved as we separated. I reached down to pick them up, wanting to hold my children. I chose my son, bringing him to the fold in my arm and running my finger along his chin. "I believe your name is Richard," I said, looking at Blake.

"Richard it is," he said as he picked up our daughter. He held her in the fold of his arm and said, "I believe your name is Elizabeth."

"Elizabeth and Richard of Whispering Wind, welcome home," I whispered. Blake moved over so I could lie in his arm and be closer to Elizabeth. "No wonder I was so huge. There were two of them in there." He laughed so loud that they both woke up and looked at us, which caused us to start giggling. I saw the door move. It was Rebecca. "Come in, my love, and meet my children."

She was beaming and crying. "You have children, Sabine, not one but two."

"I know," I said and giggled. "This is Richard," I told her, handing him to her. "And this is Elizabeth." I took her from Blake and placed her in Rebecca's other arm. "This is your aunt, my sister Rebecca," I said to the babies.

"Oh, Sabine, they are beautiful. One looks like you, and the other like Blake." She turned to Charles, handing him Richard. He had tears streaming down his cheeks.

He looked at Blake. "Brother, how wonderful for you."

Blake nodded to him. "I am a very lucky man." I snuggled into his chest, and he kissed my head and wrapped his arms around me.

Camille and Westin came in then. He was the new Westin, which shocked Rebecca and Charles.

"Let me have a look at my niece and nephew," he said. "You did good, Sabine. They are beautiful. When you are feeling up to it, we need to talk."

Charles was looking at him. "So you are the Keeper?"

Westin laughed. "Yes, I am."

Charles shook his head. "I would have never guessed that."

Westin laughed so loud he woke the babies. Elizabeth started to cry, and Rebecca looked so cute trying to comfort her. She turned to me, so I sat up and reached for her. The moment she placed her in my arms, Elizabeth stopped. We all giggled.

Camille said, "She might be hungry. Gentlemen, would you please excuse us? I need to show Sabine how to feed her children." Charles and Westin left, and Camille looked at Blake.

"Oh, no, sister, I am not going anywhere," he stated, and I giggled.

"All right now, you need to expose your breast and then put your nipple by the baby's mouth. She should just latch on, and the milk will come as she suckles you."

I could not get my shirt undone, so Camille untied it for me. Blake watched intently as I removed one of my very ample breasts and placed my nipple by Elizabeth's mouth. I was shaking, for I did not know what to expect. Blake, I think, was just as nervous watching. She did not react to it, so I looked at Camille.

"Rub the nipple on her mouth," she said. When I did, I heard Blake moan ever so lightly. I looked at him and saw he was biting his lip, which caused me to burst into laughter, so I kissed him. The baby grabbed a hold of my nipple, which hurt a little and I flinched.

"What is happening?" Blake asked in a panic.

"It hurts a little."

"It will the first few times. You need to toughen up your nipples, which will happen naturally." I looked at Blake, and he looked sad. Camille leaned in and whispered to him, "Do not worry, brother. It only heightens the feeling for Sabine." I swear he turned bright red, and I laughed again. There was a knock on the door, so Blake covered me with the blanket.

"Come in," he said.

James and Joseph came in, carrying a cot. I looked at Blake.

"Remember when you asked me what I do all day? Well, this is what I have been doing."

It was all hand carved, not too big and not too small. The detail was incredible. The symbols on my sword were at the foot of the cot, and the spindles on the sides were carved in swirls. It was incredible. The tears just fell from my eyes.

"You did this?" I whispered.

He reached up to wipe the tears from my cheek. "Yes, our child needed a bed. I did not know we would have two of them, but it is big enough that they can sleep in it together. I will make another for them."

"It is beautiful. Who made the blanket?"

"Clare, and she made the canopy, as well."

"She is out in the hall with clothes and blankets right now," James said.

I called her, "Clare, come in please."

She came in with her arms full of clothes and blankets. "I am so happy for you, Sabine. I could not believe it when they told me you had two babies. Good thing I made all of these." She held out her arms. We laughed. She laid them on the bed then looked at Richard in Charles' arms.

"This is Richard," he said, beaming.

"I have Elizabeth. She is eating right now, but I would like for you to come back later so we can have a proper visit."

"Oh, I would love it." She smiled at me.

"Bring Charlotte, as well, maybe after the midday meal."

"I sure will, and again, I am so happy for you both."

"Thank you, Clare," Blake said.

Camille made everyone leave again, and Charles gave Richard to Rebecca.

"All right, here you go. You two enjoy yourselves. Sabine, I will see you later today." Clair turned to leave and saw the cot. "Uhh, oh, this is beautiful. Who made this?"

"Blake made it," I said, smiling.

"It is wonderful. I had no idea. You do very good work, Blake. Perhaps you should open a shop." She giggled.

"I think I am going to have my hands full with these three."

She smiled. "Oh, yes, and let us not forget ruling a Kingdom, Your Majesty," she said as she giggled and bowed, pulling the door closed as she left.

I laughed. "See, it is not so funny when it happens all the time, now is it?"

"All right, she should be done," Camille stated.

Blake removed the blanket, and sure enough, Elizabeth was sleeping. I pulled her away a bit, and she latched onto my nipple again, which hurt. It made a pucker sound when I pulled her completely off. Her little eyes opened, and she looked at me as I handed her to Blake.

Camille took Richard and laid him in my other arm. "Now, do the same with him on the other breast." I did and he latched on more quickly than Elizabeth had. "You are going to have to do this at least six to eight times a day. As they get bigger, it will be less often because they will sleep longer. Now, while you are away from them, take some cloth and fold it up and put it over your nipples inside your gowns." I gave her a funny look, and she laughed. "Your breasts will fill with milk continually now. When they get too full, they will leak. That is when you will know it is time to feed them." I looked at Blake, who was listening very attentively. "I will show you how to swaddle their bottoms later. For now, I think we should just leave the two of you alone. I will be back later. Oh, one more thing Sabine, you must eat. Do not miss any meals. Blake, you must make sure she eats so she will continue to produce the milk."

Blake laid Elizabeth in the cot and then took Richard from me and laid him next to her. He stood there looking at them. I got up and went to stand next to him, putting my arm around his waist. "Thank you, Sabine, for completing my life."

"You had a hand in this, as well. I did not do this on my own. So you want to tell me what happened out there?"

He turned to me. "You went into the darkness. You were dying. The Elders and your mother came, and she touched you from here to here." He moved back and lifted my shirt, touching my stomach just below my breast, and ran his finger to the top of my hair down there. "Then she reached in and pulled the babies out. After that, the Elders blessed them, and she ran her finger back up to close you. It was what she said after that scared all of us."

"What do you mean?"

"She looked at me and said that you needed to remain pure, that a great evil was coming. Then she looked at Westin and said that Julia was in grave danger. She then kissed you and told you that your heirs were waiting for you."

"A great evil? That must be Kracken. He cannot get into the Kingdom, but he must be the last one. I thought when we ended Roman that it was over."

Westin came in the room. "Roman was the evil that escaped this land, and Kracken is the evil that Roman made while he

403

was out. Julia is in grave danger, is what Mother said. I checked on Christopher. He is alive, so he is pure of heart. I do not understand what she meant."

"Well, I think, until we all get some rest, we should leave Julia and Christopher where they are for now. Blake is King now, and he will forbid them from marrying. In the light of the day, I will go up and let Julia out, but until we are sure of things, Christopher is to stay where he is," I said to him.

"Agreed," Westin said. "I will leave you two." He hugged us both and left.

Blake walked over and bolted the door. When he turned to look at me, I saw the look in his eyes. I could not help but giggle. I turned to run from, him but he gently caught me by the waist, scooping me into his arms.

"Wife, I would like to spend some time kissing you and holding you in my arms. You gave me yet another scare, and I would like to calm down by holding the most precious thing in my heart."

I could not contain myself and kissed him. We lay in our bed for a very long time, just holding one another and kissing every now and then. My huge stomach was much smaller, but my breasts were huge. I looked at them. "I wonder how long they will stay this big?"

Blake chuckled. "For a very long time, I hope."

I giggled. "You wish."

Francis brought us food. She was so sweet googling at the babies. We ate in our room, and then it was time to feed them again. Richard was very patient, waiting for Elizabeth to finish. Blake held him and then took Elizabeth when it was Richard's turn. They went back to sleep, and I thought it a good idea to put some clothes on. My gowns were too big, but my other ones were too small. "Nothing fits me," I said and giggled.

"Well, I do not mind what you have on now," Blake said with a smile.

"So it would be acceptable for you, then, if I just went around wearing this?" I asked as I put my boy shirt on. "That is fine. I need to go down to my study. Will you keep an eye on the babies for me?" I headed for the door. He nearly broke his neck getting to the door before me.

"I do not believe that is proper attire for anywhere but this room. I would not want one of the Guardsmen to view those incredible legs of yours."

I could not stop the giggles. "But, Sire, I have nothing to wear."

He grabbed me around the waist then stopped. "Did I hurt you?"

"No, I am sore, though, so perhaps we should not be so rough. I have my other boy clothes. I could wear those." I went to my trunk and grabbed a pair, then slipped them on. "I will be back in a bit."

"Really? You are going to leave me here with two babies?"

I laughed. "They are babies, my love. They are not going to hurt you. You will be fine." I walked out and left him in the room.

I went into the secret room and got the last tome. Setting it on my desk, I opened it to the last page, and it allowed me to read. As I turned the page, the words appeared.

For time slows down under the seal for those pure of heart

The Unknown Heir and the Keeper are together within

To be brought forth by the Elders

The Guardian shall become the King so the land will rest

The purity of the Heir must remain for a time

To lay to rest the spawn of evils past

I turned the last page, but that was it. I closed the tome and looked up to see Blake standing in the door. I smiled at him. "You gave up already?"

He chuckled. "No, Camille and Juliana are with them. So what did it say?"

"Our children are the new Heir and Keeper. Life slows down for us, and I need to remain pure for a time to lay to rest the spawn of evils past. Oh, and the Guardian shall become King."

"Are you all right?"

"Yes, but I am worried about Julia. My mother said she was in grave danger. Now I find out that I have to take care of the evil that is coming. Blake, Kracken cannot enter into the Kingdom unless he has a pure heart. What if Christopher is planning on taking Julia out of the Kingdom? That would put her in grave danger."

"Sabine, he is pure at heart. He lives."

"Did the Coming work? I know we all saw what happened. What happened to the Markers? They are not in the secret room."

"They disappeared when it was over."

"I need to speak to Christopher. Will you come with me?"

"Oh, I do not think it is wise for you to go down there, Sabine. You are pretty weak. I will have Charles bring him up to his quarters. Would that be better?"

I smiled at him. "If it makes you feel better, then yes, that is fine. Do you think the babies will be all right?"

"I will run up and see if they can stay with them." He kissed me on the forehead and left. I put the tome back in the secret room and went to wait for him in the great hall.

Together, we walked to the barracks. Charles went down to get Christopher, and we waited in his quarters. I sat at the table, while Blake put a chair in the middle of the room. "Hey, you do not have your crown on," I said to him.

"Neither do you, my love."

I reached up to touch my head. "Where is my crown? I had it on last night."

"On the table next to mine. I still cannot believe you made me King."

"It was written in the tome, so it must be truth."

Just then, Charles threw Christopher in the door. He landed on the floor next to Blake's feet.

"Charles, is it necessary to be so rough? He is, after all, planning on wedding your niece. Is that not correct, Christopher?"

He looked up at me. Charles grabbed him by the arm and sat him in the chair.

"It would seem we need to have ourselves a little chat. Your answers to my queries shall determine whether or not you live another day," I said.

"Where is Julia," he asked.

I smiled. "She is in the house, completely devastated that you left her."

He hung his head. "I love her."

"Well, let us just say for the record that is truth. Shall we see how much? Now, while you were out there mapping my Kingdom, did you run across some not so nice men?"

"I saw no one but you."

I looked at Blake. "Why did you try and poison Julia against me?"

"Because of the control you all have over her."

"Why would you think that a close loving family is control?" I smiled.

He lifted his head, and I did not like his eyes. "What kind of people keep such close watch on someone as you do her."

I tilted my head. "People who do not trust others. Now, you have spent weeks in my special place with no light. Have you been fed properly?"

"Yes, the guards have been very kind."

"Good, because that is where you will be staying for a while longer. When I decide to let you go, you will be escorted to the boundaries of this Kingdom, and you will be banished from here. If I find you on my land again, you will be put back where you are going now. Next time, I will not be so kind. Julia is not an option for you. Blake is the King now, and he will not allow a marriage between the two of you. Julia will abide by the rules of her upbringing."

"You cannot stop the love we have."

I laughed. "I already have. You will not see her again in this lifetime. If you try, I will cut your head off right in front of her." I stood and left the room.

I heard him as I was leaving. "She made you King, so now you are her puppet." I turned around, walked up to him, and shoved him backwards, putting my foot on his throat.

"He is the King of this Kingdom, and you will speak to him with respect." He tried to say something, and I pressed harder. "Do you understand me?" He nodded the best he could. I took my foot off of him. "Take him back." I stood and watched Charles drag him coughing and sputtering out of the room. I turned to Blake. "He cannot be trusted, but I cannot end his life for no reason."

"No, but he can spend his days down there. We must keep her safe."

"Have all of his belongings taken down there, as well. We need to get rid of his horse before we let Julia out of the tower. She must believe that he left her."

"I have an idea. You go back to the babies, and I will be along in a bit." He kissed me on the forehead and left.

I got back to our room to find Juliana and Camille lying on the bed with the babies between them. "Are we having fun?"

"Oh, Sabine, they are so beautiful," Juliana said.

"Thank you. I still cannot get over the fact that there were two of them inside of me."

Camille smiled. "Your body will take time to get back to normal."

"I know. Nothing fits. One gown is too big, the other too small." We all giggled. I climbed on the bed and sat between them, looking at my children. I could not believe that I had children. It was amazing, just sitting there looking at them. "Soon, this place is going to be filled with even more children. I think my father and mother would be happy."

"We sure did bring new life to the place. Mine and Westin's eight, Juliana's one, and now your two." She looked at Juliana. "So could there be another in your future?"

She laughed. "I would hope so, but James and I are still learning to trust again."

I rubbed her arm. "In time, my love, in time. Look at Charles and Rebecca. They are going to be married soon, now that this is all over." They both looked at me. "I know there is a great evil coming, and I know what I must do."

"Sabine, I am proud to call you my sister. You have so much inner strength. I understand why my brother loves you the way he does. He always has, from the moment he laid eyes on you."

"Yes, well it was my father and your father who arranged our marriage long ago. Before we ever met, he knew he had to

410

marry me. Good thing he fell in love with me first." We all laughed, and the babies stirred. "I am going to need help with this, you know."

"You will get the hang of it, but try and stop us from coming in here," Camille said. "I wish I could have had just one more."

"Well, I want lots, lots, and lots of babies," I said.

We chatted for a bit more, and then they left. I laid on the bed next to my children, watching them sleep so peacefully. I must have closed my eyes and fell asleep. I woke when I felt his weight on the bed. "No the…" I started, but he had put them in their cot.

"I have something for you." He smiled and handed me a paper.

"What is this?"

"Read it," he said as he got comfortable. I opened the paper.

My Dearest Julia,

I am sorry to have left you, but I am not one who wants to battle an entire family. I do not love you as I should, and for that I am sorry. Please go on with your life and find someone who is your age. I do not want to be cruel, but you are not worldly enough for me.

Thank you for the time we spent together. It was lovely, as you are a lovely girl. I thought by telling you all the untruths that I did, it would help fight your family, but all it did was cause more problems.

Thank you and goodbye
Christopher

"Do you think it will work?"

"Well, I am going to leave it on his bed in the barracks. I have spoken to a few men, and they told me that she has been there a few times."

"All right, so should we let her out?"

"After you eat, yes, we can go up there. I will take this and put it there now. Francis is on her way up, and then we will get Westin and Camille and go up."

"All right, hurry back so you can eat with me. I do not like eating alone." He kissed me on my forehead and left. I heard him talking in the hallway, and then Francis came in.

"I brought you some fresh fruit, and some stew that I just made, and some pie."

"You are the best. Thank you, Francis," I said as she set the tray down and had a peek at the babies.

"Sabine, they are beautiful."

"Thank you. I think so too."

"If you ever want some time to yourself, you just give me a yell. I will gladly come and have a sit."

"Well, as a matter of fact, we are going up to the tower to let Julia out after this. If you want to, you can come back and sit with them."

"Oh, that would be lovely. I will be back in a little while," she said, smiling as she left.

Blake came back, and we ate. "Do you think this will work?" I asked him.

"Well, I can only hope. She will just have to move on with her life. She has been up there for three weeks now, so hopefully she has gotten over her anger."

I laughed. "She is our niece. Do you think she has?"

"Probably not," he replied, chuckling.

Francis knocked on the door. "Are you ready?" She was eager to sit with the babies.

I giggled. "Yes, come on in." I turned to Blake. "Francis is going to stay with the babies until we finish with Julia."

"Oh, that is great," he said, smiling at her. "We should not be too long, and they just ate a little while ago, so they should be good."

"Do not worry. Would it be all right if I held them?"

"Of course," I said as I got up and reached in the cot to pick up Elizabeth. "This is Elizabeth. Elizabeth, this is Francis. She is sort of your grandmother." I looked at Francis. "Is that all right? You really are the only mother I have known for most of my life."

She was crying. "Oh, child, it is more than all right. I am honored. Blake, is that all right with you?"

"It is more than all right, Francis. You take care of us all as if you are our mother."

She took Elizabeth and snuggled her into her very large bosom.

We went and got Camille and Westin and made our way to the tower. When we walked in, Julia was defiant as usual, so Blake had to restrain her.

Westin spoke first. "As you can see, Sabine and Blake had their children, so we are going to keep true to her word and let you out."

She looked at him with a funny look.

"But there are restrictions to your freedom."

"Well, if there are restrictions, then I am not free, now am I, Father?"

"You will mind your tone with me, or you will stay up here indefinitely," he said.

"What is wrong with your voice?" she asked.

"There is nothing wrong with my voice, but you will abide by your restrictions or Blake will bring you back here, where you will remain until you can learn your new rules. You will not leave the castle grounds for any reason whatsoever. If you want to go into the village, either myself, your mother, Blake, or Sabine will accompany you. You can have access to the library and Sabine's study to choose books to read."

She looked at him. "Who are you? Where is my father, the simple minded man?"

"I am he, and be very careful how you speak to me."

"Julia," I said. She gave me a look that could have shot daggers out of her eyes. "I have given my throne to Blake. He is now the King of Whispering Wind. It seemed the best way to keep the peace."

She turned and smirked a Blake. "A commoner who marries the Queen and becomes King, oh, that is laughable. Are you kidding me? Christopher was right about you."

Blake leaned down and said to her, "I have more royal blood in my little finger than you do in your entire body, niece."

She looked at him and then at Camille. "Why do you people continue to spout untruths?"

I had had enough, and I walked right up to her. "Listen to me," I said. She spit in my face, so I slapped her hard. "You, my dear child, will learn the meaning of the word respect. I will not tolerate you disrespecting your mother or your father. You may think you know what you are talking about, but you do not know a thing. You are blinded by what you perceive as love, which is in fact nothing but a pretty man manipulating you for whatever reasons he had in doing so. You will remain here until you can show some respect to your father and your mother." I turned to walk away. I felt her struggle against Blake's hold.

"You cannot do this to me! You are not Queen anymore!"

I looked at Westin, who nodded. I turned and walked right up to her and stated, "I will always be Queen, little girl, and if you are not careful, you will find yourself in the valley where you grew up, all alone with no way out. Do you hear me now, Julia dear? I will not tolerate this behavior."

"Mother, how could you let her speak to me like this? How can you let her do this to me?"

"It is better you hate me than hate your mother or your father. I am just saying what they are feeling. You are a very selfish young lady. You have no consideration for anyone but yourself. You will respect your parents, or you will grow old in the valley. You decide, Julia."

Tears welled up in her eyes. "Mother, how could you let her do this to me?"

"Julia, you have turned into a child I do not know, and I cannot allow you to go on thinking or believing that we are against you. As your parents, we know what is best for you. You continue to show much anger and rage against us. We love you beyond your knowledge, and you must trust in that and know that we want nothing but the best for you."

"But Christopher is the best for me..." She was crying now.

"At one time, I would have agreed with you, but the minute you attacked Sabine while she was with child and spouted all the untruths you did against her, you proved to me that Christopher was not a good choice for you at all. If he was any kind of honorable man, he would have never said such horrible things about us. You are wrong, and as your Mother, it is my duty to show you that."

"I am going to be an old hag before I am allowed to have a life!" she screamed through her tears.

"Sabine kept us hidden in that valley because there were evil men out there who would have used us to make her do what

415

they wanted. We should have stayed in that valley, and then you would not be locked in a tower because you want to harm your aunt. You have grown up to be a self-centered, privileged young woman, and until you realize that it is a privilege to be who you are and not what you believe you deserve in life, then you will stay here," Westin said to her in a very sad voice.

"You are becoming a disappointment to me and your mother, and that saddens my heart. I raised you to be a kind and caring woman, and you have grown up to be this hateful and spiteful person I do not even know." He reached up and wiped a tear from his cheek. "Julia, we miss you in our life. We want nothing more than for you to find the happiness you deserve, and to give us lots of grandchildren, but it seems that you want nothing more than to blame people for the things you believe you deserve, which is wrong. If you only knew what Sabine and the rest of us have sacrificed to give you this life, you would think differently, but you just want to believe the untruths that one good looking man who paid you a bit of attention has whispered in your ear. I am sorry, daughter, but you will remain here until I decide, not Sabine or Blake or your mother, but me. I will decide when you can be trusted enough to live the life we all worked so hard to give you." He turned and walked out of the room.

I reached up to wipe away my tears. As I looked at Julia, it was evident that what Westin had said to her hit her hard. I left the room, and Camille followed. Julia did not scream, nor did she not yell. Blake let her go, and she slumped to the floor. He left after Camille, and we locked the door on her.

Westin went to their room and cried. I tried to comfort him, but it did not help. He truly had a broken heart. Camille took over, and Blake and I went to our room.

Francis was holding Richard when we walked it.

416

"Thank you, Francis," I said.

"I take it things did not go so well with Miss Julia?"

"No, I am afraid they did not. I think Westin is in worse shape."

She handed me Richard. "Do not worry, child. She will come around. Are you coming down for the evening meal, or would you like me to bring it up?"

I looked at Blake, who told her, "I think it would be best to eat up here for now, and thank you, Francis."

She patted him on the arm and left.

I fed Richard and then Elizabeth, then Blake and I curled up in our bed, and I fell asleep. I suppose he did as well, but when Elizabeth started moving around, he got up with her. He was sitting by the fireplace, talking to her, when I woke up, so I laid there to listen to him.

"Your momma is a great warrior," he said. "She is a very special momma, and she loves you very much."

"As does your father," I whispered. "Is everything all right?"

"Oh, yes, we were just having some Father-Daughter time."

I stretched and sat up. "Blake, I love you."

"I love you, as well."

Chapter Twenty

The hot months and the harvest had come and gone, and the cold season was beginning. Blake had been visiting Julia each day, telling her the story of the legend and bringing her firewood. She was still defiant and unbelieving, though, for Christopher had really gotten inside her head.

The babies were getting bigger by the day. I had a great deal of help with them, but it was still nice to have them all to myself. I had weaned them off of my breast milk, and my body had gotten back to normal. I tried on my lace sleeping gown again with the help of Clare, and it fit perfectly. Now, I just had to get up the nerve to wear it.

I was sitting on the floor in our room, playing with the babies, when there was a knock on the door. "Come in," I said without looking up.

"Sabine." I looked up to find Julia standing in the doorway with Blake behind her.

"Julia," I said.

"Sabine, Blake has told me the legend and everything that has happened to you and to our family, and I understand it all now. I wanted to come see you and to meet my cousins, if it is all right with you. I also wanted to apologize to you and to beg for your forgiveness."

"I appreciate that, Julia, but it is not me who needs that apology. I am afraid that I am not as easy as your uncle." I looked past her at Blake. "You put my children in harm's way when you attacked me. You will need to earn my respect again. I am sure that this is just a ploy to get Blake to agree to let you out. When you show me through your actions that I can trust you and that you are truly remorseful, then and only then will I forgive you. Until that time, I would appreciate it if you did not assume you can come into this room at any time you choose, or that you are free to be near or alone with my children. You were so very careless with them while they were in my stomach. If you were to harm them in any way, Julia, I would not hesitate to end your life, and that would cause me great pain. I do love you. I have always loved you, but I do not trust you."

The tears streamed down her face. "I understand. Is it acceptable to you that I am released from the tower?"

I looked at Blake. "I am not the King, so it is not my call. It is between your father and Blake. If they choose to allow it, there is nothing I can do to change that. Just keep in mind what I said to you. If at any time I feel you can or will cause harm to these children, I will not blink."

She nodded. "I understand. I will prove to you that I have changed and that I am truly sorry for all that I have done and said to you." She turned to walk away. I closed my eyes to see her energy, finding it still held darkness in it. She was just playing along to gain her freedom. This was not going to end well. I looked at Blake, who knew I was not happy, but he was the King and I could not go against what he wished. He left with Julia, to go to Westin and Camille's room, I was sure.

When he returned, he was very cautious coming in our room. "Are you going to yell at me?" he asked.

I giggled. "No, why would you think I would yell at you?"

"Because I brought Julia here, and from the way you looked at me when I did."

"I am not happy about this, but as I told her, you are King and I am not going to go against you. It is your call, but if I believe or feel she is a danger to these children, I will end her."

He looked at me seriously. "Westin said the same thing to her. I have spent an entire season with her, talking to her, explaining things to her. She knows now."

I smiled at him. "Husband, I do not wish to believe I know more than you, but I know more than you. Her energy is still very dark. She is just saying and doing what we want so she can have her freedom."

"Well, she made me believe in her." He smiled.

"Let us hope she does not disappoint."

Julia made every effort to be kind, but it did not feel right to me. She had gone to the barracks and found the note Blake made Christopher write. She was crushed, as we expected, but I did not think for a moment that she believed he wrote it on his own. I had seen her many times talking to the guards, and I was sure she was questioning them as to when he left and where they thought he might have gone.

The cold months were leaving, and it was the season of the blossoms. The babies were nearly finished with their first year. Richard was starting to walk a little. He would hold on to things and move his little legs. Elizabeth, well, she would rather her father carry her around, and Blake was more than accommodating. They still shared our room with us, but Blake made a screen so that they could not see us. He said it would make it easier on them when they transitioned into their own room, which he had decided was right next door to us. He was planning on making a doorway between the two rooms, so we could hear them in the night. He was a very doting father, a very good father. I think sometimes, I enjoyed watching him play with our children more than I did watching them play. Our life was full, and it was happy. I just did not like the feeling of anguish hanging over our heads.

Julia waited to make her move. She went along with every restriction Westin had put upon her. She did not argue, and she did not show any ill feelings. One day, however, she walked out of the castle just as the light of the day was invading the dark of the night, saddled up a horse, and rode out of Whispering Wind without anyone knowing she was gone.

Even when we all had our morning meal, her absence went unnoticed. We were all so involved in the children and ourselves, we had not even taken notice. She had skillfully made us all believe she understood and was happy to be whom she was, and we trusted her again.

The light of the day came and left, the dark of the night came and went, and no one noticed she was gone. As the dark of night came the second time while we were having our evening meal, I noticed she was not at the table.

"Westin, where is Julia tonight?" I asked.

"I have not seen her today. Camille, have you seen her?"

"No, I just thought she was in her room."

Westin got up from the table and walked out of the kitchen. He was gone for quite some time before he returned. "She is not in her room, and it does not look like she has been in there for some time."

Blake stood up and ran out the door, and my heart started racing. "Camille, will you help me with the children?" We took them to my room, and I changed into my boy clothes. "Will you stay with them?"

"Of course," she said.

"I do not know when I will be back." I kissed them both, and then grabbed my sword and my crown, along with Blake's. I ran out the door and yelled for Rebecca, just as her and Charles walked into the hallway. "Change now. Get to the courtyard." Then I ran down the hall to the grand staircase and out into the courtyard. Blake was coming from our special place.

"He is still there," he said.

"She is gone, Blake. We need to find her."

"I will talk to the guards. You gather everyone."

Rebecca had gotten Juliana and James. Aiden was with Blake. We got all the horses ready and met by the fountain in the courtyard.

"A few of the men said she has been asking questions about Christopher. They told her what we told them to say, that he just up and left. She wanted to know which direction he went, and they all told her west." Blake said as he walked up.

"If she makes it to the boundary of the Kingdom, she will not be protected," I said.

"Sabine, you have to find her." Westin sounded panicked.

"We will find her." Looking at Rebecca, I said, "You ready for this?"

She was smiling, and it was never a good thing when she smiled like that. "Oh, you know I am," she said as she climbed on Spirit.

"Sabine, we are right behind you. Please, my love, be careful."

I leaned into him. "I am still pure. I still have my magic." He grabbed me and kissed me hard.

"I do not care. Be careful. We need you. I love you."

"I love you," I said as I got on Raiden. Looking at my husband, I saw fear in his eyes. I saw it in all of their eyes. We all knew what was coming, what was out there just outside the boundaries of Whispering Wind, the spawn of great evil, and Julia was riding right into it.

I kicked Raiden in the sides, and we were gone, flying through time. "Find her," I said to him. Before I knew it, we were sliding to a stop.

'This is the boundary. She is on the other side.'

I looked at Rebecca. "Should we wait for them?"

"Yes, we should at least we have Juliana."

I got off of Raiden. "Go back and get Juliana."

He was gone. "Rebecca, I have a bad feeling about this. When I killed Kelvin, the energy that came from him nearly killed me. What if this is worse? What if we cannot defeat him?"

"Sabine, you took out Roman, and he was the evil that came from here. Kracken is just his spawn. Do not doubt yourself. Remember, you were born with this magic. They were not."

"You are right. I think motherhood has clouded my thinking. My children are safe. No matter what happens, they are safe. No one can touch them."

She nodded just as Raiden skidded to a stop.

"You called," Juliana said.

We laughed. "Yes, My Lady, Julia left the boundaries, and we know what is out there, so we thought it would probably be a good idea if you were with us," I said as I climbed on Raiden.

"Take me to her, Raiden, or as close as we can get." No sooner did I finish, and we were flying through time again. It was not long at all until they stopped. We were in the forest, so we would not be seen. It was nearly the same place that Thomas had Rebecca.

"Why are we stopped?" Juliana asked.

"Because great danger lies ahead. I wish I had the vision of sight right now." I looked at Rebecca. "Blake would not want me to do this. Should we wait for them?"

"We should, only because they are the Guardians. They were a great help when we fought Kelvin."

I searched for him in my head.

'How long until they get here?'

'Not for two days' time.'

I got off of Raiden. "Sabine, what are you doing?"

"We cannot wait two days for them." I drew a circle in the ground with the tip of my sword.

"Round about the hands shall go
Around and around time shall flow
In other's minds will not leave a trace
Fast forward time in this place."

I slammed the hilt of my sword into the ground three times. The wind picked up. I closed my eyes, put my sword in the air, and turned around three times. When I opened my eyes, they were riding up.

"Wow," I heard Juliana and Rebecca say at the same time and then giggle.

I looked up to see Blake looking at me. "You scare me sometimes," he said as he climbed off his horse and kissed me. "How did you do that?"

I giggled. "I do not know. It just comes to me. Their camp is just ahead. I knew you would be angry if we did not wait, and this is going to be bad. We all need to do this together." I looked at Westin. "I do not know what you are capable of, but this is not going to be easy. Raiden and Spirit can get us in un-noticed at least until we stop, but we need to all be together."

"He has my daughter. I am capable of a great deal."

"Then let us go get her back and end this." I leaned into Blake and whispered in his ear. "Do not die, husband. I have something for you when this is over." I turned and got on Raiden, leaving him standing there with his head tilted, smiling.

We rode into camp at full gallop, and Raiden took us right to Julia. We were surrounded. I whispered to Juliana, "Get ready and hold onto me." She wrapped her arms around my waist.

We sat there looking around, and I knew this was not going to be easy. There was a tent of sorts in front of us, with men standing on either side of what looked to be a doorway. All around were tents and fires, with men everywhere. If I had to guess how many, I would say ten times as many as Kelvin's army. *Where do these people come from?* I heard myself say, "Huh."

Blake looked at me. I smiled and shrugged my shoulders.

The flaps of the tent were opened by two men standing on either side and a huge man covered in an animal skin of some kind came walking out. He had something in his hand, but I could not make out what it was, not until he pulled his hand forward. It was a chain. I followed it as he lifted it in the air. Dragging on the ground behind him on the end of the chain was Julia. My heart stopped.

"Westin do not move," I whispered. She had on her under gown and nothing more. She was filthy, her hair was cut off, and she was bleeding from her nose and mouth. I felt Blake's anger as it projected outward. I wanted to reach for him, but I could not move. I felt Raiden twitch, and I rubbed my finger along the saddle to sooth him.

Rebecca was having visions of her time with Thomas. I looked at her hands, which were shaking. Juliana was getting warmer as each moment passed. It seemed to all happen so slowly, almost like it was not happening at all.

The man who walked out of the tent spoke. "I am Kracken."

I had to bite the inside of my mouth to stop myself from giggling. I nodded. "I am Sabine," I said.

"I am the son of Roman."

I could not stop myself. "I am the daughter of Stephan."

I heard Rebecca giggle to herself. I wanted to laugh, but I sat there not moving, with one hand on my saddle and the other on my sword, as we all were.

"Do you mock me, child?"

"Not at all, I just thought you would like to know who I am."

"I know who you are, and I know what you have done."

I was about to say something when Charles spoke. "We are here to take the girl."

"This thing?" He pulled hard on the chain, and she went flying out in front of him. "She is worthless, spewing her tales of how the great Sabine is going to kill me for touching her. You want her? Come and take her. I am done with her." He kicked her in the side, and she slammed on the ground when the chain caught her. She laid there, not moving. I hoped she was in the darkness.

Westin moved, but I reached out to stop him, whispering, "You will only die here today."

"You should listen to the mighty Sabine. You will all die here today, and the wealth of Whispering Wind will at last be ours."

I felt Juliana getting hotter, and then I felt the heat burst forth from within her. The flames formed a circle around the camp so no one could get out. "You will never have my land, and you will not live to see the light of the day. Your father tried, your son tried, and his daughter tried. They did not succeed, nor shall you."

"Do you think your trickery is not something I already know? I will take what I want."

I felt him throw something at us, and then I saw his face when he realized it did not work. "You cannot touch me, Kracken. You will not be taking anything here today."

He looked at Blake. "You wear the crown, Guardian. Why would you let this child speak for you?"

"I have learned that my wife speaks for herself."

"Your wife?" he laughed. "Well then, if what they say is truth, you are not pure anymore and your magic does not work."

"I would not believe everything that you hear," I stated.

"Your magic cannot defeat me. These men are mere mortals. I have lived many lifetimes."

Juliana got hotter, and the fire surrounding us roared. I could feel the heat from the flames.

"So the child who sits behind you is my granddaughter's child. She will be staying with me in exchange for the girl. An act of good faith on your part, guaranteeing you will leave here alive."

"We will be leaving here, and we will be alive, but she is not going anywhere with you."

"Do not threaten me!" he yelled.

I moved Raiden in front of Blake. "Sabine, what are you doing?" he whispered.

I did not answer him. "I am tired of this game you want to play. I am taking my niece, and you will not stop me."

He pulled on the chain. "I will exchange her for my granddaughter."

"Well, you see, she is not your granddaughter, and she never will be."

His eyes started to glow. "She will stay!" he screamed, and then I felt the fire blow from within him.

I put up my sword to deflect it, but it knocked me off my horse, slamming me to the ground. I slammed my sword into the ground and said, *"In this time, in this place, seek the refuge that brings you peace."*

He became cold, trying again to throw his fire at me. "What have you done?" he shouted.

I stood and looked at him. "You will give me my niece."

"Sabine, get back on Raiden," Blake said.

I did not listen to him. I walked up to Julia and put my hand on her chest. "If she dies here today, I will make sure your death is painful."

He laughed. "You will all die here today."

The flames from Juliana were very close. She had managed to destroy almost all of his men. It was getting closer, and his men started to panic, charging us. I did not have enough time to get on Raiden. Blake and Charles were off their horses and standing next to me as they moved in. The battle was long. Juliana burned them, and we killed them. When it was finished, blood mixed with the ground. It smelled of death and fire. Kracken started walking toward me.

Blake stood in front of me. "Guardian, you will not save her today," Kracken spouted, drawing his sword, then he ran it through his chest before Blake had a chance to defend.

I did not move. I knew what needed to be done and could only hope I survived this battle.

He stepped over Blake, raising his sword and swinging at me. I caught his blow and felt his power. This man was huge. Again and again, he swung at me. Charles, James, and Aiden came at him to slow him down, but they did not touch him. Rebecca and Steven got Julia and put her on James' horse. I heard Rebecca scream, "Take her back to Whispering Wind!" She slapped the horse on his hind legs.

It was the eleven of us against him. Four were down, and he swung again and again at me. "Juliana, leave!" I shouted. He put his hand up, and she flew off of Raiden, hitting her head and falling into the darkness.

"She will stay with me," he said. I raised my sword in the air, letting the energy of the Elders fill me from within. I swung at him, and when our swords clashed, the flame was blue. I held it as his energy flowed from him to me. I never looked away. His eyes began to show fear as he weakened. Joseph slammed his sword into his back, but he did not flinch. Westin rushed up behind me and put his hands on my shoulders. I felt a surge of energy fill me, making me stronger. I pushed Kracken backwards, causing him to stumble, and our swords lost contact.

Blake was moving, as was Charles. Kracken pushed the sword through him, and it landed on the ground behind him. He smiled and came at me again, swing after swing, pushing me and Westin back. I needed to find a break in his stance. I saw Charles coming at his back. He hit him in the back of the legs, and Kracken wobbled, then Blake slammed his sword into him. I saw the pause in his eyes, and I swung with all that I had and all that Westin had given me. I felt it as his knees gave way, and he struggled to hold his balance. I swung again and again. He was weakening, so again I swung, never losing eye contact. I saw his eyes glow, and I knew that it was now or never. One more swing and he was down. I raised my sword and brought it down, and he put his sword up to protect himself, but when mine hit, it shattered his. The shards flew into his face. He screamed out as pieces slammed into his eyes.

His energy blew out of him, slamming me backwards into Westin. The man was beaten, but he was not going to go down easily. I gained my footing and walked up to him. "It would seem that you have no sword. Somehow, I find that unfair." I picked up a sword that was lying on the ground and handed it to him. "Get up and let us finish this."

He laughed. "You are a foolish child if you think you will win."

I giggled and swung my sword. He had put his up with both hands to protect his head. My sword was flaming, and I watched as he pushed against mine, trying to gain his footing. I felt his energy leaving him. His sword started to glow. I could smell his flesh burning; the pain on his face was obvious.

"How is this possible?" he asked as he struggled. His hands were turning red, but he would not yield. His knees gave way, and he went down hard. I wanted to release and swing, but I just held my sword against his. His hands burst into flames, and he yelled out. I saw Blake stand behind him then Charles. Rebecca had gotten Juliana up, so we were all there standing in a circle around him. His arms were on fire now. He was yelling and screaming. Finally, he let go of the sword, and it fell to the ground in flames, starting the ground in front of him on fire. He opened his mouth to say something, and I swung my sword one final time, taking his head off. The energy and power that flew from him blew us all to the ground, sending us into the darkness.

When I woke, I was in Blake's arms with Rebecca holding my hand. "My love," she said and then hugged me.

I looked at Raiden. "Take Westin to get Julia, and then back to Whispering Wind. Hurry." Westin squeezed my shoulder and was gone. "What happened?"

Blake pulled me to him. "You ended him." He was holding me close, and I felt his tears on my cheek.

"What is wrong?" I whispered in his ear. I tried to pull away, but he would not let me go. I heard James crying, so I pushed on Blake's chest. "Let me go," I said as I started to panic. "Blake, let go of me."

"I cannot," he said as he sobbed.

I pushed really hard, which was not hard at all. He was so strong, and he would not release me. I tried to turn my head, but he held it with his hand. "Please, let go of me," I begged him. He would not let go, so I sunk my teeth into his shoulder. He screamed out in pain, and his arms waivered, allowing me to move. I caught a glimpse of James kneeling on the ground, and then I saw her.

"Nooooo!" I screamed as I fought Blake to release me. "LET ME GO!" I yelled. He finally released me. I crawled as quickly as I could to her. "No, no, no, no, no, no," I said all the way to her. I pushed James out of the way so I could see her. "No, my love, no, no, no, no," I grabbed her hand and laid my head on her chest. "My love, do not leave me."

"She is gone, Sabine," Charles said as he put his hands on my shoulders.

431

"No, no, she is not. She cannot be." I searched for my sword. It was lying next to Blake. I got up and ran to it. Coming back, I drew a circle around her and slammed my sword into the ground. There were no words that magically came from my mind. There was nothing. I slammed it again and again. "Nooooo, you cannot have her." I fell to my knees and grabbed her up in my arms. "Oh, my love, please do not leave me." Blake came over to me. I pushed his hands away. "Do not touch me." He backed away. I sat on the blood soaked ground and rocked her in my arms.

I recalled the first time we saw one another that day at the water's edge, her mangled hair, her dirty little face, her frightened eyes. I closed my eyes so I could see her better, then started to hum the lullaby. In my mind, I could see her eyes change. I could see her light up. I felt her as she ran into my arms, knocking us to the ground. Crying, I said, "My beautiful girl, my love." I swayed as I felt the warmth and the love engulf me. I opened my eyes as she embraced me.

"Take care of her for me," she whispered. "I love you."

I screamed out, "Noooo! Do not leave me!" Then I felt the warmth leaving me, and I turned to see her go to Jenna and Ardes, so I screamed out again. She smiled at me one last time, and then they were gone. Rebecca was at my side, holding me while I cried. Blake and Charles brought James, and we stood there together and cried for the loss of Juliana. Our lives would never be the same. I would never see her beautiful face again. I could not stand the searing pain in my heart. My knees gave out, and I fell to the ground crying. Blake held me, but I pushed him away. I did not want his comfort. I did not deserve anything. I failed her. I failed Jenna and Ardes, and I failed Isabel, who would never know her mother.

Rebecca lifted me to help me stand, but I could not do this. Charles picked me up, and Rebecca helped me get onto Spirit. "I have her. Bring Juliana home." Charles nodded.

I do not remember leaving her, and I do not remember going home. When we got there, the village was quiet, no one was around. Rebecca helped me down, but I just stood there, unable to move. I heard her say to Spirit, "Go back and get Blake. Have Raiden bring Charles and Juliana." She guided me to Westin and Camille's room.

We walked in, and Camille was crying while Charlotte was putting her herbs on Julia's wounds. Westin looked at me and Rebecca. "What has happened?"

I could not say the words. Rebecca had a hard time talking, but between her sobs, she managed to get it out. "Juliana is gone."

Camille looked at her. "What do you mean, gone?" she asked rather loudly.

"She is gone. She did not make it."

Camille screamed as Westin drew her into his arms. She screamed again and beat him on the chest. Westin cried, I cried, and Rebecca cried.

I could not be in here near Julia. It was her fault Juliana was gone. I found my words, looking at Julia who lay in the darkness. "You foolish girl, this is all your fault." My legs started to give out, and Rebecca took me to my room. Francis was with the babies. I shook my head when I realized where we were going. "No, no…" I pulled away from Rebecca and ran. I did not want to see them. I did not want to see anyone, so I ran.

I found my way to the tower and shut the door. Sliding down it, I lay on the cold stone and cried until I had nothing left, and then I slept.

Blake and Charles had returned with Juliana. Charles had put her in Jenna and Ardes' room. Blake came looking for me, but he could not find me. Rebecca told him what happened.

"I had Raiden, so she could not have gotten far. Why would she run?"

"Blake, you need to leave her. She will find her way back," Rebecca said through her tears.

"I will not leave her. She needs to know I am here."

"She knows that, Blake, but she is devastated."

"No more than any of us," he snapped at her.

"You know nothing of the bond they had, of the love they had," she snapped back at him and then left.

Blake made his way to our room. "Francis, there has been a horrible outcome. Juliana did not make it back alive. She is gone. Sabine is shattered, and I need to find her. Could you please stay with the children?"

"Oh, Blake, I am so sorry. Of course I will. You go and find her. I will keep these little ones safe."

"Thank you," he said sadly and left to find me.

Chapter Twenty-One

Blake searched everywhere for me as I lay sleeping on the cold stone floor of the tower. He went to the stables to ask Raiden to find me. I did not hear him in my mind when he called for me. Raiden shook his head. He gathered his brothers, all except for James who would not leave Juliana. They got on their horses and started a search on the plains. Blake went to the secret room, but I was not there. He went through every room in the castle, and he could not find me. Rebecca had no idea where I had gone. She just kept telling him that I would come back when I was ready. He was not going to settle for that.

He did not give up. The light of the day left, and he sat in the hallway of our room through the dark of the night. He did not go in to see the babies. When the light of the day came, he began searching for me.

Rebecca told him which direction I ran off in. He found the second set of stairs that no one used anymore that led to the hallway where the tower was. He climbed them, and when he came out, he was at the end of the hallway to the tower.

"The tower," he said, and took off running, taking the many stairs two at a time. He reached the door and pushed it open, finding me lying on the floor face down. He stopped breathing. "No, no, no, my love, please," he was crying. Slowly and carefully, he got down on the floor and lay next to me. He reached out with a shaking hand and moved my hair from my face. "My love," he whispered. I did not move, for I did not hear him.

He rolled on his back and cried. He did not know if I was alive or dead. Gently, he put his head on my back to listen for my heart. There was nothing, so he wrapped his arms around me as he sobbed and held me while I slept. He believed I was gone. He sat up, lifting me into his lap to hold me, leaning against the door. He cried silently for his loss, his tears falling from his cheeks onto my face. Looking at me, he wiped them with his thumb. My head fell backwards. He put his hand on my chest and whispered, "I love you so much. Why would you do this?" His sobs prevented him from feeling my heart beating. He sat there with me in his lap, holding me and sobbing. He cried so much he fell asleep, and when the light of the day came again, he woke and carried me down to my parents' room and laid me in the bed. He climbed in with me and held me. Wrapping his arms around me and placing his hand on my heart, he vowed to join me in death.

He laid there holding me. When his sobs subsided, he shifted to pull his dagger from its sheath, and his hand that was on my heart moved. That is when he felt the th-thump, th-thump. He rolled me over to face him. Touching my face, he said, "My love." I did not move. "Sabine," he said and then kissed me. "Come on, my love. Wake up." He kissed me again.

He pulled me from my slumber. I opened my eyes to see his red, wet eyes looking at me. "Hello," he said. I did not speak, just closed my eyes again. "Sabine, wake up." I opened my eyes and looked at him. I had nothing to say. I felt nothing but pain and emptiness. I wanted nothing more than to sleep. I did not deserve to feel anything but this pain and emptiness because I let them down. I let them all down. I had to face Isabel and tell her that I let her momma die. The tears just came. He pulled me close and kissed my head. He held me while I cried again. Nothing would ever be right again, nothing.

I must have fallen asleep because when I woke, Rebecca was sitting on the bed crying. I reached for her and pulled her to me, and we held one another and cried for our loss. She was who I wanted, not Blake, not my children, but my sister in this life. We cried for a very long time. Blake came in and brought food. I did not look at him. I had nothing for him. Rebecca tried to get me to eat, but everything tasted like blood and dirt. I smelled it. I tasted it. It was charred skin. I could not eat it. I did not want to eat. I just wanted to sleep. When I was sleeping, I felt nothing, and that is what I wanted to feel, nothing. I lay on the bed, pulling my knees up to my chest, and cried myself to sleep.

"Why will she not talk to me or let me hold her?" Blake asked Rebecca.

"I am not sure. She just sits and stares when she is awake, then she cries and goes back to sleep.

"It has been six days, Rebecca. We need to bury Juliana."

"I know. Will you get someone to fill the tub? I will at least get her washed up and some clean clothes on. I will talk to her about it."

He nodded. When the tub was full, Rebecca talked me through a bath. While she dressed me, she said, "Sabine, we are going to bury Juliana tomorrow. Is there anything you would like to say?"

I looked at her and then past her to the wall. She tied my gown and walked me to the chair, where she sat me down then left. In the hallway, she was talking to Blake.

"I told her, but she did not respond. We need to just go forward with it. I will make sure she is there."

"I need to be the one to help her through this."

"Then you can bring her." She put her hand on his arm.

"She will not let me touch her." He whispered.

Rebecca came back in the room to find me in the bed crying again. She climbed in and held me.

Standing there watching them put Juliana in the ground was the single most horrific thing I had ever experienced. Isabel was crying. James was crying. Blake stood next to me, but every time he put his arm around me, I turned away from him. I did not deserve to be happy. Rebecca led me back into the house after it was over and sat me down in the sitting room. Blake came in and kneeled on the floor in front of me.

"My love, please let me help you," he said with tears in his eyes. I just stared through him. I did not want to see him or be near him. I had nothing left. Rebecca came back and took me to my parents' room, where I sat in the chair all day crying. Francis brought me food, but I could not eat it. The taste of blood and the smell of charred flesh was still in my body. I felt weak and sick all the time.

"Sabine, it has been seven days, my love. You have got to eat something." Blake was holding food in front of me. He took a spoonful of eggs and put it to my mouth, but I turned my head. He put his head down, so I got up and walked out of the room.

I made my way to the stables, telling the guard in there, "Would you please saddle my horse?"

"Yes, Your Majesty," he said and bowed.

I took Raiden to the courtyard and climbed on top of him. I leaned in and said, "Please take me to the secret valley." I needed to heal, and I could not do it here. When I sat up, I saw Blake watching me. I looked at him and left. I did not want to feel. I did not want to do anything but die. There was no happiness for me in this life, not now, not without her. I leaned into Raiden and held him. When he stopped moving, I got down, walked to the tree, and sat under it. Once there, I cried and cried until sleep came.

I do not know how long I had been there in the valley. I ate the fruit from the tree only because Raiden threatened to get Blake. I bathed in the lake, and I slept. No one bothered me. No one came for me. I was completely alone. Day after day, I sat under the canopy.

*****

Blake was frantic with worry. I had been gone for weeks. Rebecca tried her best to calm him. My children were forgetting me. He was having a difficult time being the father he wanted to be because he was scared. He knew he should be with me to help me, but I had shut him out. I had shut everyone out.

"I need my wife," he said to Rebecca. "The children need their mother. How are you sure she is not dead?"

"Her sword is still here. She would not end her life, Blake. She is mourning Juliana now, but she will return."

"Please, Rebecca, ask Spirit to find her. Go to her. Make her come home."

"Blake, I know where she is. She is in the secret valley, where she is healing. You cannot be this man. You have known her most of her life. When she hurts, she runs. I will not go and ask her to come back when she is not ready. You need to trust in her."

*****

I spent nearly the entire season in the valley. I just could not bring myself to return. I did not feel that I deserved any kind of happiness, for I was a failure. As I was sleeping one night, I felt the warmth embrace me. The love and the healing I needed enveloped me, and I knew she was with me. I knew she was letting me know she was happy. When I woke, it was the dark of the night. Raiden was standing above me, looking at me.

"I need to go home," I said to him.

He skidded to a stop in the courtyard just short of Blake. He turned to look at me. I could see in his eyes that fear had worn him down. The light was gone, but that did not stop him from pulling me off Raiden and into his arms. He cried while he held me in the courtyard. He did not let me go for a long time. We cried together.

"I love you," he whispered.

"I love you," I whispered back.

He was crying so hard he was shaking us both. I held my husband as he held me. Together, we went into the house and walked up the grand staircase to our room. He shut and bolted the door then took me to the bed, where he sat me down and knelt in front of me.

Taking my hands in his, he said, "My heart is broken that you could not let me in to help you heal. I know how hard this is for

440

you. It is the same for all of us. We all went and rescued her. We all loved her. But you are my wife, and I vowed to love you no matter what was to come. You pushed me away again, and you broke me. You ran from me." The tears just flowed from my eyes. "I have had time to forgive you for that, but I need for you to understand what you did to me by leaving. I wanted to come to you, but I knew you would just run again. I knew you had to do this on your own, though I do not know why. I am asking you to promise me that you will never do this again, that you will never shut me out, and that you will never leave again like this."

"I promise," I whispered.

"You are my wife, and I am your husband. It means something more than just being bonded to one another. We are living this life together not you alone, not me alone, but together. You not only left me, you left our children. You have been gone so long, Sabine, that they stopped asking for you." He was crying. "I did not know what to tell them. Elizabeth is walking now. She is running, and you missed it all."

I did not know what to say to him. Everything he was saying was truth. I did do everything he said. I had left him and our children, because I did not find peace with them. "You are my happiness. They are our happiness. I am so sorry that I put that in jeopardy. I am home now, and I promise you that I will not be leaving ever again. It is done. That was it, the end. I want to be your wife, and I want to be a mother to our children."

"Then we will not speak of this again. I have forgiven you, and I need for you to forgive yourself. What happened to Juliana was not your fault Sabine. If she was to survive that fight, they would have given her back to us. It was her destiny. It is over now, so we must start living our lives and having the happiness you were promised."

I nodded at him, and he pushed himself up so he was on his knees, then reached up and took my face in his hands to kiss me. His kiss was gentle, tender, and loving. My hands came to his face then moved into his hair. Our kiss deepened, his hand moving to my head, his fingers in my hair. He slid me off the bed and onto his lap. I put my arms around his neck, pulling myself closer to him.

He pulled away from me slightly. "I love you, wife," he said then covered my mouth with his again. We kissed like this for a long time. Breathless, he finally told me, "We need to see the children. They need to know you are home." I nodded and rested my forehead on his. We caught our breath, and he helped me stand. My hand in his, he opened their door to find them sitting on the floor, playing with Isabel and Camille.

I kneeled down, and Camille looked up and smiled at me. "Welcome home, Sabine."

Elizabeth turned and looked at me. "Momma?" she said. I nodded to her.

"Hello, my love," I said as the tears fell from my eyes. Richard got up and stood there, just looking at me. I could see in his eyes that he was trying to remember me. I smiled at him, and he smiled back then ran to me, throwing himself in my arms. Elizabeth was right behind him. It felt good to hold them, to smell them, to feel them.

Blake wrapped his arms around us, and we giggled and played for a long time. I tucked them into their beds when it was time for sleep.

Richard hugged me a little longer. I kissed him on the cheek. "I love you," I said to him, and then he smiled and closed his eyes. Blake and I went into our room and closed the door on our sleeping children.

"I will be right back," he said before he left. A few moments later, the girls from the kitchen were hauling buckets of hot water to fill the tub. Francis came in and grabbed me, hugging me tight.

"I am so glad you are home, but do not ever leave like that again."

I chuckled. "I promise."

"I made you some food. Now, you eat and bring some life back into that man. He has been in the foulest mood for some time now."

I felt my face get warm. "I will do my best, My Lady."

She laughed and shooed the girls out. Shortly after, Blake returned with a tray full of food and some wine.

I tilted my head and looked at him. "Wine?"

"Yes, it is a special occasion."

"And what would that be?"

"My wife has come home. Her tasks in life are complete, and there is nothing more to worry about. We do not have to fear evil coming here, and we can now have our happiness." He set the tray down, bolted the door, and walked over to me and kissed me. "Turn around please." I did so smiling, and he slowly untied my gown, making sure his fingers touched every part of my skin that was exposed. He gently slipped it off my shoulders, his fingers moving all the way down my arms to my hands. His fingers entwined in mine as he lifted our hands and crossed our arms across my chest, then he pulled me to him and lifted me off the floor so my gown would fall, and I lifted my feet out of it. He set me back down. "You are so beautiful. I have missed you, wife." I turned in his arms and kissed him. He undressed then we took a bath and ate our food. When we finished, he lifted me out of the tub, wrapped me in a blanket, and took me to bed.

We loved each other most of the night. When the light of the day came, we were still giggling and holding one another. It was good to be home.

"The children will be up soon," he said. "We should get dressed. They are going to want to spend some time with their mother."

"I would love nothing more." I kissed him then climbed out of bed and got dressed. "I would like for you to come with me to the place where time stands still. I believe now that you will be able to enter the cave with me. I need to return the tomes to their resting place."

He smiled. "Rebecca has already taken care of that. I thought it best they go back. Is that all right?"

"It is perfect. Now, we do not have to be away from the children." I hugged him. "I am sorry, Blake."

"I know, my love. Let us just put it away and live our lives. I think, after everything we have been through, we at least deserve that."

I laughed. "We do indeed." I went to gently open the door to their room, but they were both fast asleep still. "They are still sleeping."

"We had them up pretty late. We could go back to bed." He raised his eyebrows, which made me giggle.

"You are so bad."

He pulled me into his arms. "No, I have missed my wife," he said and kissed me.

Chapter Twenty-Two

$\mathcal{W}$e spent the next week alone with our children. Rebecca came by, as did Camille and Clare. Everyone except Westin visited. I did not want these moments we were having to end. We laughed, we played, and we slept. I was Momma, and Blake was Dadda. I was happy, feeling the weight that I had been carrying around on my shoulders slowly lift and disappear. I was no longer worried or scared.

Our children got back into their routine. Blake went back to ruling our Kingdom, and I really had nothing to do. It felt wonderful.

The children were taking their nap, and Rachael was sitting with them, so I thought I would go in search of my brother. I went to their room, but he was not there. I found Camille. "Where would I find Westin?" "

"He is with Juliana. He goes there every day." I saw the sadness in her eyes, so I squeezed her hand then went to find Blake to let him know where I was going.

"He will be glad to see you."

I walked to her burial plot, where I saw Westin sitting with his knees pulled up to his chest. Sitting down next to him, I said, "Hello."

He looked at me with tears streaming down his cheeks. "Camille told me you had returned."

"Westin, Camille is worried about you."

"Sabine, I raised her. She was like my child. I do not know how to mourn the loss of one child caused by my other child. I cannot find it in my heart to forgive Julia."

"I know. I do not know if I will be able to, either. Westin, if you want, I can have Raiden take you to the secret valley. It is where I went. Julia came to me there. She held me and let me know that she is happy and with Jenna and Ardes. Perhaps if you go, you can heal as well. We have so much life to live yet. We finally have our freedom. You can finally be yourself."

"I do not know who that is without her in our lives."

"I felt the same way, so much so that I left my babies and my husband. It was too much to face them. I felt like I did not deserve this happiness because I failed her, because I could not save her."

"That is how I feel. She died saving Julia. Julia should have never left here. She has no remorse for what she has done," Westin said.

"Perhaps we should take her to the valley and leave her there."

"Believe me, I have thought about it, but I do not think I could bear losing another daughter."

"Why not take her with you, let her find her way back to you. It is a magical place. She grew up there, so perhaps you both can find peace with this, and besides, we all have Isabel to raise."

"This is true, but I am not sure Julia would go with me."

"I am sure that Blake would take her for you. Once Raiden starts moving, she will not be able to get away. Come on. Camille is worried about you. Come for a walk with me. I would like to get to know my new brother."

He laughed. "I am the same brother you knew before. Have you seen Julia since you have been back?"

"No, I have not. Has she healed?"

"Her body has, yes, but her mind is still shattered. She will not talk about what he did to her. Rebecca has been spending time with her, but she said she is not talking about it."

We got up and started walking back. "If you take her, then I can let Christopher out and he can leave here."

"This is true. Perhaps it is a good idea. I will talk to Camille about it and see what she has to say. The children are old enough for me to leave for a bit."

"I will have Raiden come back every now and then to see if you are ready to return. If you are not, then send him home."

He looked at me and smiled. "It is our time now, sister. It is time for our happiness. I think I need to get whole again, like you, and I believe that Julia needs it, as well."

"I believe, Westin, that you are right. Just let me know what you decide. I will miss you, but I want you to enjoy what time we have left."

He put his arm around my shoulders. "We have more time than most, Sabine. Time has slowed for us now so we can enjoy this life. We will be here for a long time to come."

I leaned into him. "I know, because I want lots of babies. I finally get to have a real union with my husband."

He laughed, and he laughed loud. Camille was walking up with a smile on her face. I hugged her, and she whispered in my ear, "Thank you."

Leaving them, I went to find my husband. He was walking up from the barracks when I saw him. My heart was full, knowing it was time for us.

"Mmmmm," he said as he put his arms around me. "You look beautiful."

"So do you. I need for you to do something for me."

"I would do anything you ask, my love."

As we walked, I told him our plan. "Westin is going to the valley, and he is going to take Julia with him. I would like it if you took her on Raiden. She will not fight you. She needs to heal, and so does Westin. He said she has no remorse for what she did and for the loss of Juliana."

"No, she does not. She is even angrier, if that is possible. I will do as you ask. When would I be leaving?"

"I am not sure. But remember when we left to get Julia back?"

"Yes," he said.

"Do you remember what I said to you?"

He smiled. "You said, 'Do not die husband. I have something for you when this is over'."

"And I do. I have been saving it for you, and when you return, I will have it all wrapped up so you can unwrap it."

"Oh, Sabine, you know I do not like surprises."

I laughed. "You will like this one. I have been waiting for a special time, and I think now that all of this is behind us, this would be a good time. Like the wine."

He hugged me. "All right, I will wait."

Westin and Camille walked up. "Sabine, we have talked, and Camille thinks it would be a great idea to go to the valley. I think, if we leave the day after this one, it will be good. Blake, would you go with us?"

"You do not have to ask, brother. I would be more than happy to help you, to help Julia. That place seems to help Sabine, so hopefully it will help you and Julia heal, as well."

"I am sure she is going to put up a fight," Westin said.

Blake laughed. "Well, she would not be our niece if she did not. This might be a good thing for her. Sabine seems to find herself when she goes there. As much as I do not like it, I know, in the end, she comes back to me whole." He hugged me.

"I can tell you, Sire that I will have no need to go again, unless of course you would like to go with me." I smiled at him. "The children should be waking up, so I am going to go up and get them."

"I will go with you," Blake said, and we walked away, leaving Camille and Westin standing in the courtyard.

We spent the afternoon playing, and then we had our evening meal in our room. I was not ready to see Julia just yet. We put the children to bed and got comfortable in our bed, then fell asleep in each other's arms. I woke to his hands trailing along my cheek. I opened my eyes to see him smiling at me.

"You are so beautiful. I will miss you while I am gone."

"Mmmmm," I murmured, kissing him. "Yes, but you will have a wonderful surprise to unwrap when you return."

"I have a surprise for you, as well."

I sat up. "You do? What is it?"

He laughed. "You will just have to wait and see."

We loved one another after we giggled. Then we got up and dressed the children. Rebecca and Isabel had come to play while we set off with Julia. I was in the kitchen with Francis, while Blake dragged Julia down the stairs and out into the courtyard. Finally, I made my way there.

She was screaming. "You cannot make me do this, Father!"

"I can, and we are."

"I will not stay there."

"There is no way out. You and I are going back to heal. I will not be fooled again. And if you are not careful, I will leave you there alone."

She was crying now as she saw me walking up. "This is your doing. Everything was fine until you came back. Why do you hate me so much that you would banish me like this?"

"Because of you, Juliana is dead. Because you believe you are privileged, you caused her death. You have no remorse for what you did. Because of you, Isabel will grow up without her mother. This is not my doing. This is your mother and father's doing. But I will say this to you, niece you will not return here until you are healed, and this time, we will not be so quick to believe your untruths."

"Go to hell, you bitch!" she screamed.

Westin slapped her across the face. "This is why you are leaving here. You are a vile and inconsiderate child. I am banishing you from your home, not Sabine."

"I hate you all," she said through sobs.

"That is fine. You hate us all you want. Our love for you will never falter," I said as I walked away.

Blake got on Raiden, and Westin held onto Julia. With one arm, Blake reached down and grabbed Julia, pulling her up. She was kicking and screaming the whole time.

"You should hang on, niece. Do not fight, for you will end your own life if you fall off." He kicked Raiden in the sides, and they were gone.

Westin smiled at me. "I love you," he said.

"I love you."

I searched for him in my mind.

'Let me know when you are close to home. I have a surprise for my husband.'

I went to find Rebecca and Camille to see if they could keep Richard and Elizabeth for me the next day and night when Blake returns. I found them in the sitting room with Isabel and the babies.

"Hello," I said as I sat down on the floor to join in the play time. "I was wondering if you two would help me with something."

"Of course we will. What is going on?" Rebecca asked.

"Well, I have a surprise for Blake, and I do not know when he will be returning, so I was hoping that between the two of you, maybe you could keep Richard and Elizabeth for me when he returns."

Rebecca looked at me, and Camille smiled. "Can I ask what the surprise is?"

"Of course you can," I said and giggled.

They both sat there looking at me, and I felt my face get warm. Rebecca said, "Really, you are going to finally have your union with your husband?"

"Well, that is my intention. Now, whether or not it happens, we shall see, but yes, that is what I have planned."

"Oh, Sabine, I am so happy for you," Camille said. "Just do not be so afraid. Put your mind in the most wonderful place you know and let it happen. He will take much care. He loves you very much."

"I know, and it is time. He has waited a very long time for me, and he has been very patient. Besides, I want more of these beautiful little faces." I squeezed Richard's cheeks.

Rebecca was still smiling. "Yes, yes, yes, and yes! You take all the time you need. When you want them back, you come and get them. We will not bother you."

I just laughed. We continued to play, and when it was time for their nap, Camille took them upstairs, and I went to my study to get my lace sleeping gown out of the secret room. I walked up to the desk and picked up the cloth it was wrapped in, then carried it out into the sunlight. I unwrapped it and was holding it up in the light when Rebecca came in.

"Oh, Sabine, it is beautiful," she gasped. I turned to look at her, feeling my face get warm, and covered it back up. "Why are you covering it up?"

"It is so revealing," I sputtered.

She giggled. "He has seen you in less, you know."

"I think I am going to need some help. Do you think you and Camille can help me? I mean, I want to look really good, but I do not know how to do that."

She walked over and hugged me and very sweetly, she said, "Of course we will help you. We do not have much time, so come on." She took my hand.

"Let me put this away."

"Oh, no, bring that with you."

I wrapped it back in the cloth, and we went up to our room. Rebecca went and asked Francis and Rachael to sit with the kids, and then got Camille.

They washed my hair, and then Camille rolled it in cloth and tied the ends. "This will put some curls in your long hair. Do

452

not take them out until tomorrow. So I have an idea." And she launched into this elaborate plan for me to seduce my husband. I was so shocked to hear her talk like this, because she has always been such a lady. She even giggled a few times when she would see me make a face. "You know, Sabine, what happens behind closed doors between a husband and wife is very private." She winked at me. "I know many things you would not think I knew."

So the plan was in motion. Now, it was just a matter of waiting for Blake to return.

It was strange to sleep in our bed without him, so I went and snuggled with Elizabeth in her bed that Blake had made. When the light of the day came, I searched for him in my mind.

'Did you make it?'

'Yes, we will be back when the dark of the night comes.'

'Do not forget to let me know when you are close.'

'I will not forget.'

So tonight was the night. I felt sick. I got up, trying not to disturb Elizabeth, and went into our room. Camille knocked on the door, and when I opened it, she was smiling.

"I brought the cape for you to wear." I think she sensed my fear because she reached out and touched my hand. "Sabine, it will be all right. He is your husband, and he loves you very much."

"I know, but I am terrified."

"I know." She leaned in. "But you will see how wonderful it feels."

I think I turned as scarlet as the blanket on the bed. "I will not think about it, otherwise I will run." I giggled.

We made our preparations for the night. Francis was cooking, the fireplaces in three rooms were hot, and the water was ready to fill the tub. The children were tucked into bed in Camille's room, and I had written all the notes. I sat on the bed while Camille took my hair out of the wraps.

"Now, bend over and shake your head, then flip your hair back."

I did but did not understand why until I touched my hair. "Wow, do you think he will like it?"

She laughed. "You really do not know how beautiful you are, do you?"

I smiled at her. "I do not."

"All right, the dark of the night is nearly upon us. I will go and get the water ready."

I nodded to her. Sitting on the bed, trying not to run, I heard him in my head.

'We are nearly there.'

'Slow down. I am not ready.'

'All right.'

I ran to the door and yelled for Camille, "He is nearly here! I asked Raiden to slow down!"

"We should be on time!" she shouted back.

They started to fill the tub, and Francis brought up the food and set it by the tub. When everyone left, I hung a note on the door and then set the other ones around the room for him to find. I took my gown and went into the children's room to change.

'I am ready now.'

I put on the gown, then bent over and shook my head again and put on the cape. When I heard Raiden skid to a stop in the courtyard, I peeked out the window and watched Blake walk up to the door.

This is it. I closed my eyes and took a deep breath, then listened by the door as he walked down the hallway to our room. On the door was a note that read:

Trust

He pulled it off and opened the door. When he walked in, there was a flower petal path to the tub. He stood there and looked down. I had left a note on the floor, so he picked it up and opened it.

My Love,
Your bath awaits you, along with your meal.

He looked at the bath and smiled. He got in and washed his journey away, then ate his meal. Under his plate, I had placed another note. He smiled when he noticed it and picked it up.

My Love,
Dry yourself and follow the path.

He chuckled and looked around the room, noticing the path that led to our bed. He got out and dried himself off, and followed the path. The bed was covered with petals, as well, with a note in the center. Climbing on the bed wrapped in his blanket, he picked up the note.

My Love,

I have trusted you with my life, with my children, and with my love. I need for you to trust me now. Close your eyes and keep them closed. Say the words 'I love you' when you are ready, and no peeking.

He looked around the room and smiled. Closing his eyes, he said, "I love you."

I walked out of the children's room and stood with my back to him in the center of the room. I took a deep breath and said, "I love you." He opened his eyes to see me standing there. Though he did not speak, I felt him move as he slowly walked up behind me.

I whispered, "It is time to unwrap your gift." Then I turned to face him with my head down and the hood of the cape covering me.

I watched his hands come up slowly, and felt his fingers slide across my cheeks, pushing the hood off my head. I did not lift my head. He untied the cape and walked behind me to take it off my shoulders. I felt his heart jump as he slowly pulled it away and saw me covered in nothing but lace. My hair covered my back to my waist, full and wavy, not its usual straight. He took a step back, and I heard the gentle swoosh as the cape dropped to the floor. He stood there looking at me, then moved around me to face me. I was shaking, not sure what he was thinking. I picked my head up to look at him. He had tears on his cheeks, so I smiled at him.

I could hardly hear him when he said, "You are so beautiful." He stepped closer to me, his hands moving to my face, and he kissed me so sweetly and gentle. I did not move. I could not move because I was so scared. He pulled away. "I am honored to have you love me."

"It is I who am honored."

He stepped back. "May I look at you?"

I nodded. He sat on the bed and gazed at me for a moment, then put his hand out for me to take. I forced myself to move; I wanted this. We touched hands, and it was like fire running through me. He pulled me close and pressed his head into my chest, holding me there.

He stood and lifted me into his arms and laid me on the bed. When he lay down next to me, he kissed me for a long time, only he still had not removed my gown. He was lying on top of me, and he scooted to the end of the bed to sit back on his knees.

"What is the matter?" I asked.

"I can feel you shaking, and I cannot help but wonder why."

I smiled and sat up, then got on my knees, placing my arms on his shoulders. I swallowed and took a deep breath then kissed him. He moved his hands to my hips and pulled me closer to him, kissing me back. Bringing my hands around to hold his face, I pulled away and looked into his eyes. "I want you," I whispered and kissed him again.

His fingers started to bunch up my gown, pulling it slowly up my legs, to my hips, to my waist, and over my chest. My hands went in the air so he could pull it over my head, and he dropped it on the floor. He gave me a little push as his hand came to my back, to help me lay down, but I resisted and shook my head.

Placing my forehead on his, I reached down to undo his blanket. He watched my hands shake as I pushed it aside. I brought my leg around him, and his hands instinctively came to my thighs to hold me up while I brought the other leg around him. I was now sitting on his thighs. I kissed him again, and then used my arms on his shoulders to lift myself higher.

He stopped. "Sabine," he whispered.

I smiled. "My gift to you, with my permission... I would like to love my husband."

He sat there looking at me. I saw the tear and kissed it away. As I lowered myself onto him, he held me close. He pushed up and tore through my virtue, while I screamed from the pain and bit his shoulder. He stopped and held me, but I did not want to stop. I wanted to love my husband the way he deserved to be loved. I picked up my head and looked at him; we were both crying.

"I love you husband."

He did not speak, just covered my mouth with his and loved me. He loved me for a long time. I had never felt so much passion from him than I did in that moment. When our bodies shook, we tried to muffle our cries with our kisses, but it was not possible. If I could have been inside him, I would have been he held me that close.

We lay wrapped around each other for a very long time without speaking.

"Are you all right?" he finally asked.

"Yes," I whispered, trailing my fingers down his chest.

"Thank you for the precious gift, my love. I will cherish it for the rest of my days, but you did not have to do this."

"Yes, I did. It was time for us to become one, to be husband and wife. I love you with all that I am. You are my happiness, our children are my happiness, and I am so ready to be happy."

He put his finger on my chin and tilted my head up to kiss me. We loved one another many times throughout the night and day.

"I have a gift for you, as well, but we need to get dressed and go for a ride."

I smiled. "Really?"

He laughed. "Really, do you want to go?"

I nodded and got up. "Gown or boy clothes?"

"Speaking of gowns…" He picked up my lace sleeping gown. "Is this what was under the cloth?" I smiled and nodded. "It has been in there for a very long time?" I nodded.

"Clare finished it when I found out I was having the babies. She was the one who pointed out that I was with child. I asked her after we got married. Remember the lace on the green gown, the one that matches your eyes?" He nodded. "Well, you said that you liked it, so that day, I went to ask Clare if she could make that for me. I planned on wearing it a very long time ago, but well, I had things to do."

"You did this for me?"

"Yes, is that all right?"

I was in his arms, and his mouth was covering mine before I could take a breath. We did not make it out of our room that day, either. He asked me to wear it for him again, so he could really appreciate it. I danced around the room, twirling and giggling. He took it off of me, and we did not come out of our room for two days and two nights. On the third day, we emerged, had some food, and then jumped on Raiden to go for a ride.

"Now, you have to let me put this on your eyes." He produced his sash. I giggled as he tied it on my eyes. "All right, buddy, will you take us there now? Hold on, my love. I would not want you to fall off." His statement threw me into another fit of giggles.

"This is so not fair, you know," I told him.

Laughing, he said, "Oh, I know, my love, but secrets must be kept for your safety."

Raiden came to a stop, and Blake got down then helped me down. He carried me to the spot he wanted me at. "You ready?" Smiling, I nodded. He kissed me while he removed the sash. When he pulled away, he stood directly in front of me so I could see nothing but his chest. Then he stepped aside, his eyes never leaving me.

We were standing on the hill top, where I had felt peace for the first time, looking over the beautiful green valley. Only there was a cottage in the valley. I looked at him and crinkled my eyebrows.

"I built it for us," he said hesitantly.

I did not know what to say, so I just stood there looking at the cottage and then at him. "When did you have time to do this?"

"While you were gone." He smiled.

"You built us a cottage?"

"Yes, come. Let me show it to you." We got on Raiden and rode to the cottage. He took my hand, and we walked through it. It was bigger than the cottage in the valley; it certainly had many more bedrooms. "For all of our babies," he assured me.

I was amazed at the detail in the wood and stone. "You did this?"

"Yes, not alone, but yes."

"All right, do not take this the wrong way, but why? We live in the castle with our family, and besides, you are the King."

He took my hand and led me outside to sit on the fountain, which I realized was just like the one out side of the castle. "There is no rule that says because I am King that I have to live in the castle. Yes, our family lives there, but it is not ours. It was your families, not mine. This is ours, for our family, Sabine, me, you, and our children. Do you not like it?"

I panicked. *He thinks I do not like it.* "Oh, no, my love, I love it! I love that you did this for us, and yes, I want to live here with you, a thousand times yes. I just did not understand why you would not want to stay at the castle."

"The castle is only my home because you are there. My family comes from a cottage like this, not a castle. I want our children to feel the warmth of a cottage, not the cold stone of a castle. We are safe now, my love. No one can hurt us. We have a long life ahead of us, and I want to spend it here with our family."

I threw my arms around him and kissed him. "I cannot believe you built me a cottage. My gift is nothing compared to this." I turned to look at the cottage again.

"Hey," he said, so I turned back to him. "The gift you gave me, Sabine, there is nothing that even comes close to how wonderful that was. Nothing."

"When do you want to move in?"

He laughed. "I was thinking, after Charles and Rebecca get married. He can move into the castle, and then there will be three men who live there, well, four if you count Stephan."

I nodded. "I would love nothing more, but we have a problem."

He crinkled his eyebrows and tilted his head. "What problem?"

I giggled and kissed him. "You forgot one thing. I do not know how to cook."

He laughed so hard. "I have already thought of that. Come on." He took my hand and led me to the back of the cottage. There were more rooms back here. "I asked Francis if she would come with us, and she agreed, as did the two kitchen girls, so I made them rooms here."

"Well, who will cook for everyone at the castle?"

"Francis has a cousin who is coming to take her place."

I giggled. "Leave it to you to think of everything." He picked me up and twirled me around, making me giggle more.

We went back to the castle to get our children we have not seen for days, and they were so happy to see us. We played and played, until we were all tired.

After we had our evening meal in the kitchen, Charles and Rebecca told us they had decided to marry in ten days' time. They wanted to marry just like Blake and I had in the back courtyard. Everyone was finally getting what we had wanted all along. Peace and happiness.

We put the children to bed and made our way to our room. It was wonderful knowing that we did not have to be afraid anymore. I did not have my magic anymore, and I was finally all right with that. I did not need it. We were finally safe.

We lay in our bed asleep and content from our love, when I heard Westin in my head. I thought I was having some kind of vision, so I woke up. I just laid there, listening to Blake's heart beating, as he was still asleep. I closed my eyes and was nearly asleep, when I heard him scream my name. I sat up, startling Blake.

"What is it, Sabine?"

I pushed the covers off of me and got out of bed to get dressed. "It is Westin. Something is wrong. Something is very wrong." I threw on my boy clothes, put on my boots, and grabbed my sword all before he had a chance to get out of bed. "I will get Camille. We need to go now. Hurry up." I ran out the door and down to Camille and Westin's room. I knocked on the door, but it took her a minute to answer.

"Sabine, what is wrong?" she asked.

"Please stay with the children. Something is wrong with Westin and Julia. We are leaving now."

Blake ran up. "I will saddle the horses. Let Rebecca know I took Spirit," he said to Camille.

"How do you know?"

"I heard him in my mind, screaming my name. I have to go. Please keep my children safe." I hugged her and took off running down the hall. By the time I got to the stables, Blake had both of them saddled. I jumped on Raiden. "Take me to Westin, and hurry."

We were off flying through time in the dark of the night. I think he actually travelled through time, because we arrived at the entrance to the valley just as the light of the day cracked the horizon. Once we were down in the valley, Raiden took off. He skidded to a stop right in front of the tree.

I jumped down, searching for Westin, but he was nowhere to be seen. I looked at Raiden. "Where is he? Where is Julia?" Raiden nodded his head toward the lake. I turned and started to run, and Blake was right behind me. I was searching the ground for him, but I could not find him. "WESTIN!" I screamed. "WESTIN!" I heard nothing.

I stopped and spun around in a circle. "Do you see him?" I asked Blake.

"No." He turned to Raiden. "Show us!" he yelled to him. Raiden came running up and blew past us to the lake's edge. My heart stopped as I looked at Blake. We moved together as we ran to the edge. Blake went in the water, and I searched the water's edge. I was nearly half way around the lake when I saw him.

"BLAKE!" I screamed as I bolted toward Westin's feet. I froze when I saw him lying on the ground with blood pouring out of his head. I saw a rock next to his head. I fell to the ground and screamed. Blake came running up and dropped to the ground next to him. He put his hand on his chest then laid his head down to hear his heart.

"He is alive." My heart started to beat again. I looked around for Julia, but she was nowhere to be found.

"Julia is gone." I stood and searched the valley and then scanned the mountains. I could not see anything. I turned to Raiden.

'Did someone take her?'

He shook his head.

"She is here somewhere. She did this Blake. She did this to him, to her own father."

"Sabine..."

I turned and could see Westin's eyes start to flutter. I ran to him. "Westin, can you hear me?"

"I really am sorry for hitting you in the head with that rock," he said and smiled.

"What happened?"

"My daughter happened," he said as Blake helped him to sit up.

"Where is she?"

He looked at me and chuckled. "Hit in the head with a rock, lying in the darkness. I do not know."

"Well, she cannot get out of the valley," I said and turned to Raiden. "Can you find her?" He nodded. "Blake, would you go get her?"

"Oh, you can count on it. My niece and I are going to have some words." He got up and got on Raiden. I helped Westin up, and we made our way back to the tree.

"Sabine, something is very wrong with that girl. She is acting very strange. She mumbles to herself, and she will not talk to me. I was down by the lake getting water, and she slammed me in the head with that rock. How did you know to come?"

"I heard you scream my name."

He chuckled. "I did not think it would work now that you do not have your magic."

I saw Blake coming, and he had a good hold on Julia though she was fighting him. They stopped just shy of the canopy, where he dropped her to the ground. She got up and started to run. I ran after her, and she fought with me, but I managed to pin her on the ground.

"What are you doing? You could have killed your father!"

"Get off me! It was my intention to kill him!"

I slapped her across the face. "You forget, little girl, he is my brother."

She struggled to get away from me. Blake walked up and grabbed her arms, pulling her up, and then wrapped his arm around her waist. "You will not be going anywhere, niece."

"Let me go you barbarian. You have no say over me."

Blake walked over to the lake and threw her in. I giggled just as Westin laughed. She came up out of the water screaming at him. He waded in and grabbed her by the waist, shouting, "You will be respectful or you will go in again!" She did not fight him. He carried her back and stood her up. She was soaked, her gown clinging to her body. "So why did you hit your father with a rock?" Blake asked.

"Because he will not let me leave. I do not want to stay here."

"Do you know why you are here?" he asked.

She turned to look at me. "Because she is back now, and she is throwing her fits to get her way."

"This was your father's doing, not Sabine's."

"My father cannot make a decision such as this. All he does is cry over Juliana. He is just a simple minded man who cannot think for himself."

I had started walking back and forth with my head down. I looked up at her and noticed her figure. I stopped then and looked at Westin, and our eyes locked. I looked at Julia again.

Westin was on his feet and had her stomach in his hand. She fought him, but he was stronger than she was. As she clawed at his face, Blake grabbed her hands. Westin looked at me and then at Blake.

"Do not touch me!" Julia screamed.

I put my hands on her stomach. "Did he dishonor you?" I asked her.

"I am pure. I will die pure because my father is obsessed with me and will not let me marry."

I looked at Blake. "Could he?"

"Sabine, we have seen a great many things. It is possible."

"What are you talking about?" Julia screamed.

I looked her right in the face. "You are with child, Julia. Did he dishonor you?"

She stopped moving, just stood there and stared at me. I saw her fear and felt her pain. "It cannot be so," she said in a voice so small.

I looked at Westin. "Mother said she was in grave danger. She will die, Westin, if we do not do something."

"What can we do, Sabine?" He had tears in his eyes, looking at Julia his only daughter, his pride and joy.

I looked at Blake. "What do we do?"

He shook his head. I looked at the tree, then at Blake and Westin. "The tree is magic. Do you think?"

"Julia, if we put you under the tree, will you stay there?" Westin reached out to touch her hand. Her head was down, but

466

when he connected with her, she threw her head back and started screaming at him, kicking at him. Blake tightened his grip.

"I guess that would be a no, but I have an idea." He picked her up and took her to the base of the tree. "Sabine, help me here." I ran up to him. "Take my sash off." I did as he asked. "Westin, take this and tie her hands around the tree." Julia continued to fight Blake, but he held her arm out so Westin could tie the sash around it. Blake pushed her forward into the tree, so she was hugging it, and then held her other arm while Westin tied it. Then Blake let her go, and we walked out from under the canopy.

I think I was hoping something magical would happen, but it did not. We waited and waited. I walked down to the lake and sat on the edge. I searched for him in my mind.

'Can you help her?'

'Things will be what they are to be.'

'You helped me.'

'You were not meant to die, Sabine.'

'And bringing this evil into the world is meant to be?' I asked.

'As long as she is within the boundaries, it will not survive.'

'Will she?'

'I do not have an answer for you.'

'You cannot take her where you took me?'

'She is not dead, Sabine. The child within her grows fast. Take her back to the boundaries where evil cannot pass.'

Blake came up and sat down. "You all right?"

"I was talking to Raiden. He said we need to take her back within the boundaries of Whispering Wind, that the child will not survive there. He said it grows fast within her. It could be why she tried to get away from Westin."

"Will Julia?"

"He does not know, but if it is born outside of the boundaries, it will live. Then everything we have done will be for nothing. I do not think we were ever meant to have any kind of happiness."

"We have our happiness, my love, and we will continue to have it. If that is the case, then let us take her back to the boundaries."

I got up and hugged him, and we walked back to Westin. "Can we talk?" I asked him. We walked away from Julia. "We cannot stop this here. Raiden said the child is growing fast, and that is why she tried to leave. It is controlling her. We need to get her back within the boundaries of Whispering Wind. If that child comes while we are outside, it will live and all that we have done will be for nothing. I do not have my magic, Westin. If the child is in the boundaries, it will burn. Can you do this?"

"We have no choice, Sabine."

"Westin, either way, she may not survive this. Can you do this?"

"I do not want to lose my daughter, but we cannot allow this evil to live. So I am going to have to do this. It is the right thing to do."

I hugged him. "Oh, my love, I am so sorry."

"This is not your fault, just like Juliana was not your fault. She was with us for a reason, and she left us Isabel. If the same fate comes to Julia, then we will all have to accept it."

We went back to the tree then. Westin untied her, and Blake grabbed her up. We worked our way out of the valley with Julia fighting all the way. When we hit the ground running, she stopped. She knew if she fell off Raiden, she would perish. It did not take long before we reached the boundary. Raiden stopped short and was in my head.

'You must walk her through. I do not know what will happen. The child is growing quickly.'

"Westin, you must walk her through the boundary."

He climbed off Spirit, and Blake handed her down. She fought with him, but Westin dragged her across the boundary into Whispering Wind. She stopped moving and started screaming. He dragged her farther and farther so she would have a hard time leaving again. The entire time, she screamed in pain. Blake and I crossed over and climbed off the horses.

Julia was lying on the ground, holding her stomach and screaming. Westin knelt down next to her to brush her hair from her face. "Sabine, she is so hot to touch."

I looked at Blake. I did not even think about it as I pulled my sword from its sheath and slammed in on the ground, saying the calming spell. Again and again, I did it. I did it three times, but it did not work. She lay in the grass, burning from the inside out.

"I cannot help her!" I screamed.

Blake put his arm around me. Westin was by her side, holding her hand. "I am so sorry, my love," he said to her.

She was crying. "I am sorry, Father," were the last words she said before the darkness took her.

"What do we do, Sabine?'

"I do not know. She is in the darkness now, so there is no pain for her." I knelt down beside my brother and put my hand on her stomach. "She is so hot. The child must be burning inside of her." I tired the calming spell again, this time saying it only in my head, but it did not work.

We knelt there looking at her, watching her face and her arms get redder and redder. I think we expected her to start to glow and then burst into flames. She was getting too hot to touch, so we moved away from her and sat on the ground. The dark of the night was coming.

"Should we take her home?" Westin asked.

"Do you want Camille to see this? What if she does burn? Then the castle will burn. I think we should just stay here until it is over," Blake said as gently as he could.

We sat there all night, falling asleep just before the light of the day came.

I felt warmth and love. Jumping up, I thought Julia was on fire, so I woke Blake and Westin, but she was not. The warm glow had surrounded her, and there were many hands on her. We could not see who it was. We could just see the hands. It lasted until the light of the day burst forth, and then it was over.

Westin crawled over to her and touched her. "She is cool now," he said as he put his hand on her stomach and turned to look at me. "The bump is gone."

"They came and took the baby. They healed her," I whispered.

Westin picked her up. "I want to take her home to her mother." Blake nodded and climbed on Raiden, and Westin handed Julia to him. Westin and I got on Spirit, and we were off and flying through time. We skidded into the courtyard, and Westin carried Julia up the stairs to her mother. He explained everything that happened.

"What do you mean she was with child? Did he do to her what Thomas did to Rebecca?" Camille asked through tears.

"She said he did not hurt her like that. He must have planted the child in her somehow. He was a great sorcerer," Blake said to help reassure her.

"Why will she not wake up?"

I reached for her. "Camille, when we brought her through the boundaries, the evil inside of her started to burn. I am so sorry, my love. We tried to help her. I tried my magic, but it is gone from me. She fell into the darkness from the pain. She was so hot we thought she was going to burst into flames, but then the Elders came and took the baby and we brought her home."

Camille hugged me. "Thank for trying to save her. Thank you for getting to them in time."

I held her for a while, and then we left them to hold their child. Blake and I walked into our room and fell into bed. We were both so tired.

Half way through the day, our door opened and two beautiful little children came running into our room, climbing up on our bed and giggling. This was the best way to wake up. We snuggled them, tickled them, and played in our bed. Then we all went down stairs to eat our evening meal.

"Francis, would you please make up a tray for Westin and Camille? I would like to take it up to them."

"Of course, child."

While we waited, Rebecca and Charles talked about getting married. Now that Blake was the King, he could marry them, so it was all planned out. Then we were going to move to our cottage and have our happiness with our little family.

Time moved on, and Julia stayed in the darkness. I did not think it was right that we leave the castle after Rebecca and Charles married, but Camille and Westin assured us that there really was nothing we could do.

We started to move our belongings to the cottage. Blake had the guards filling wagon after wagon of our things. The last wagon took our bed and the children's beds, and we rode our horses with the children. I had Richard, and Blake had Elizabeth. We stopped by Clare's to tell her and Charlotte goodbye, and to make sure they knew to come and visit us anytime. Then we stopped by Boland's to let him know the same thing. After that, we took our journey.

It was a long day indeed. Francis and the kitchen girls followed in a wagon full of their belongings. When we arrived at the cottage, the children were tired, so they rested on some blankets in the sitting room while we unpacked and carried things in. While I was walking around, I realized that Blake did not put a room in this cottage to eat our meals, like the castle had. He had made the kitchen huge, and in it was a giant round table for all of us to sit at, Francis and the girls included.

After many days of putting things away and setting up our cottage, we settled in. The children's room was right next to ours, with a doorway between them so we could hear them and they could come to us whenever they wanted.

It was the dark of the night, and Rachael and Sophie had filled our giant tub. We climbed in to take a well-needed bath.

"I have missed these things with you," Blake whispered in my ear.

"Mmmmmm, I have missed you."

We had not been together since we left to rescue Westin. So much had happened, and we just fell into bed each night exhausted.

He washed me and then washed my hair. I returned the favor, and then we got out and wrapped ourselves in blankets. He carried me to our bed, laying me down gently. As he dropped his blanket on the floor, he climbed into bed and sat on his knees at my feet. His hands gently opened my blanket, and he sat there looking at me.

"You are so beautiful," he whispered as he crawled up my body to kiss me. His hand slid behind me, and he lifted me off the bed while he moved back to sitting on his knees. I came to rest on his thighs. "I want to relive our first union with you in our new home," he whispered into my mouth. My body started to shake. His kiss was so tender. I put my arms around his shoulders and pulled myself up his body. He pulled back from me, looking into my eyes as I lowered myself. I heard him take in a deep breath as I did, then our kisses exploded while I loved my husband. We lay trembling in one another's arms, kissing. I put my hands on his face when I realized he was crying, and pulled away from him. "I love you so much, Sabine." He kissed me.

We fell asleep together loving one another. This was my life. This was my happiness. This man, these children, this life, it was everything my parents wanted for me, and even in death, they managed to give it to me. My happiness was my husband's love.

Epilogue

It took a long time for Julia to come out of the darkness. Three seasons had passed. When she woke, she had no memory of what had taken place. Charles decided to let Christopher out, and once he was released, he left Whispering Wind.

Stephan had married the girl from the village, and they were living in her cottage. James was raising Isabel, who looked just like her mother, and Rebecca and Charles were going to have a child of their own.

Blake and I had three more children, and I was ripe with another one. We had three more sons and had just celebrated the youngest one's first year. Richard and Elizabeth were in their sixth year. Blake was teaching them how to ride. He was a wonderful father. He never betrayed me again. Our life was full.

We were sitting by the fountain, watching Richard ride the horse Blake had gotten for him. "I wish you would let them ride Raiden," I said to him.

"Once they learn how to handle a horse, perhaps, but they need to learn to do this. It will be all right, my love." He put his hand on my stomach. "How is our baby today?"

"He is huge, just like his brothers." I laughed.

"This will be child number six," he said.

"Yes, it will be, and to keep with the traditions of your family, we will need to have two more sons. Seven sons and one daughter."

He laughed. "I do not have a problem with that." He leaned in close to my ear. "Making them with you is so much fun."

I giggled and turned to kiss him. He pulled me close and kissed me hard.

Just then, I heard Elizabeth scream. I jerked my head to her voice. She was running toward Richard. Blake was already moving. I followed her path to see Richard lying on the ground. He had fallen off the horse and was not moving. I got up and ran as best I could, screaming at Blake not to move him.

Elizabeth made it to Richard before Blake. She was screaming and crying. Blake put his hand on his little chest, and my heart stopped. I stopped when he looked up at me. I saw it in his eyes; I saw it on his face. I shook my head, and then I saw the tears falling onto his cheeks.

He screamed, "NOOOOOO!"

I fell to my knees, my heart broken. Blake reached for Elizabeth, but she pushed his hands away. She knelt down next to her brother, and I watched as she put her hands in the air. Then I heard her say,

"Elders of the old send him home."

I looked at Blake, who looked horrified. She lowered her hands to place them on his chest, and I saw the soft glow surround the three of them. I tried to move, but I could not, so I lay on the ground and closed my eyes.

My son was dead. I had nothing left. I felt the warmth embrace me then. I felt the love surround me, but I could not open my eyes. To see him lying on the ground was not something I could bear. My little love was gone. The warmth was gone as quickly as it came.

I continued to cry. They came to get him just like they had come for Juliana. Sobbing, I felt his hand on my face.

"Mother," I heard. I shook my head. "Mother, do not cry."

I opened my eyes to say goodbye to him, to tell him I love him. He was sitting in front of me, so I pushed myself up and grabbed him, pulling him to me.

"Oh my baby," I said sobbing.

"Mother, I am not a baby," he said.

I laughed. "Of course you are not." I looked up at Blake, who was now holding Elizabeth. As I looked at her, she smiled at me. I looked back at Blake and saw it in his eyes. He knew what I knew.

She was indeed the new Heir, and Richard was now the Keeper.